CHRONONAUTS

VOLUME TWO

Created by **Mark Millar**
and **Sean Murphy**

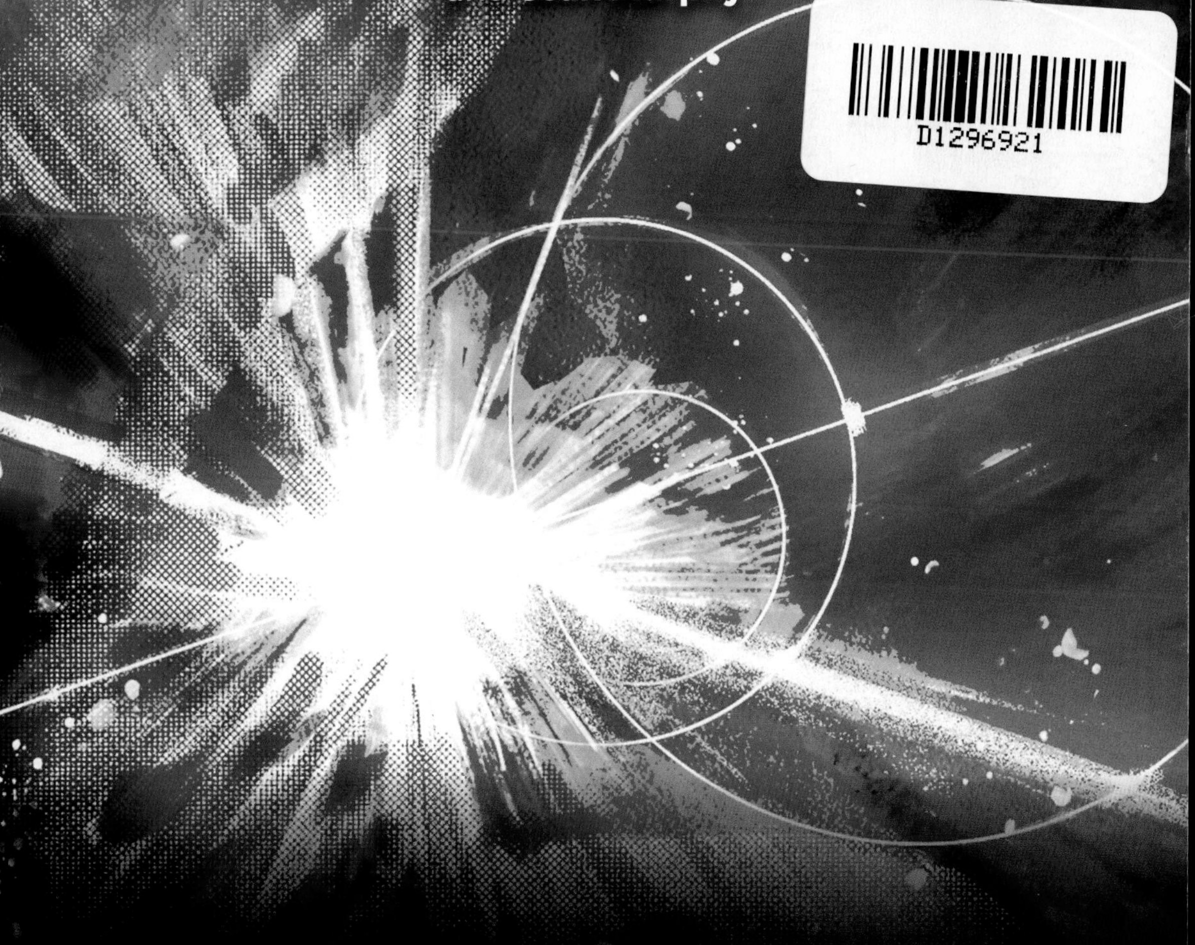

IMAGE COMICS, INC.
Robert Kirkman: Chief Operating Officer • **Erik Larsen:** Chief Financial Officer •
Todd McFarlane: President • **Marc Silvestri:** Chief Executive Officer •
Jim Valentino: Vice President • **Eric Stephenson:** Publisher / Chief Creative Officer •
Jeff Boison: Director of Publishing Planning & Book Trade Sales • **Chris Ross:** Director of Digital Services •
Jeff Stang: Director of Direct Market Sales • **Kat Salazar:** Director of PR & Marketing • **Drew Gill:** Cover Editor •
Heather Doornink: Production Director • **Nicole Lapalme:** Controller • **IMAGECOMICS.COM**

CHRONONAUTS, VOL. 2. First printing. March 2020. Published by Image Comics, Inc.
Office of publication: 2701 NW Vaughn St., Suite 780, Portland, OR 97210.
For international rights, contact: lucy@netflixmw.com ISBN: 978-1-5343-1508-2.

MARK MILLAR WRITER

ERIC CANETE ARTIST

GIOVANNA NIRO COLORIST

PETER DOHERTY LETTERER

OFFICINE BOLZONI DESIGN
AND PRODUCTION

RACHAEL FULTON EDITOR

LUCY MILLAR CEO

MELINA MIKULIC
COLLECTION COVER DESIGN

SERIES
MAIN COVERS

PASQUAL FERRY

ONE

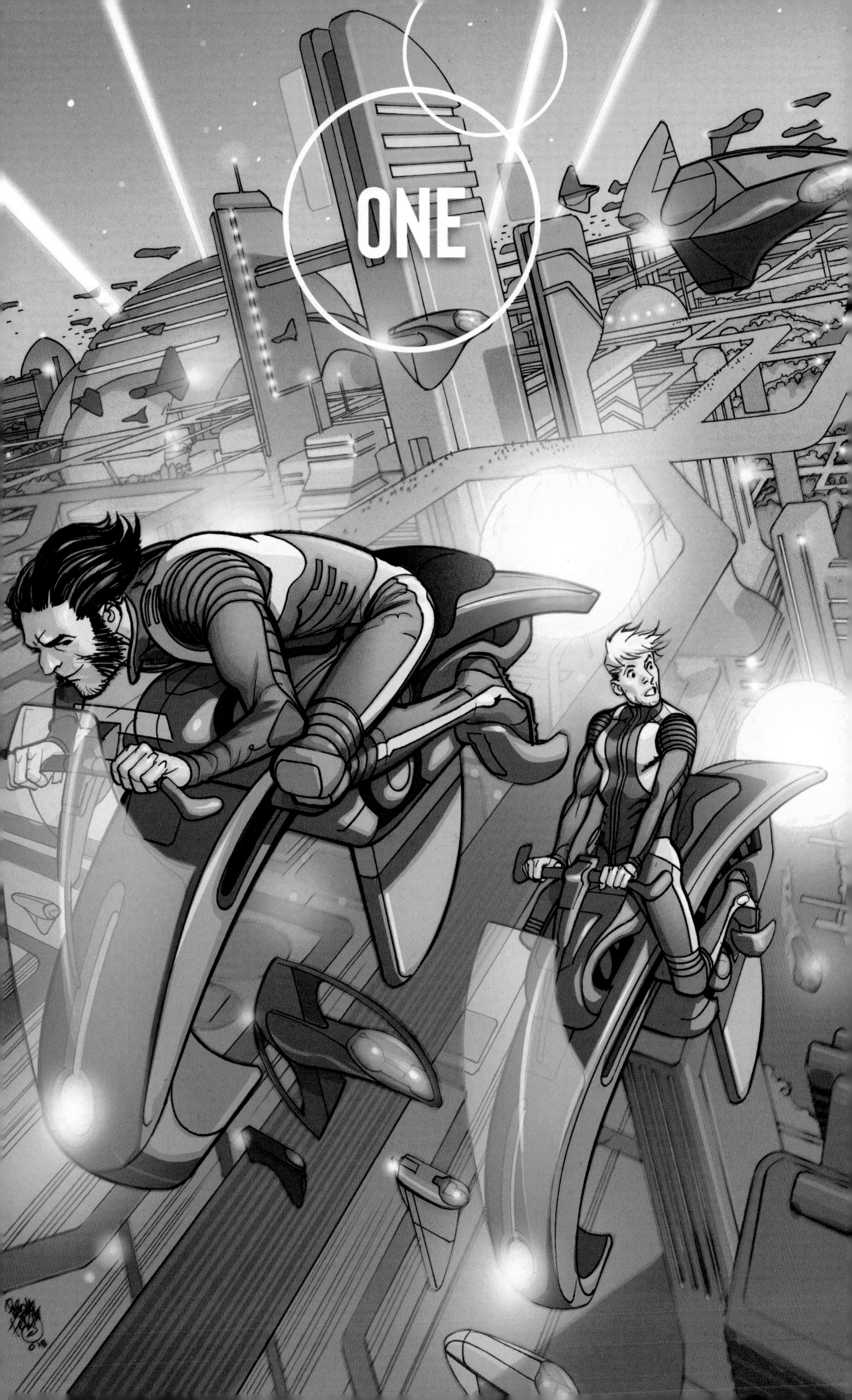

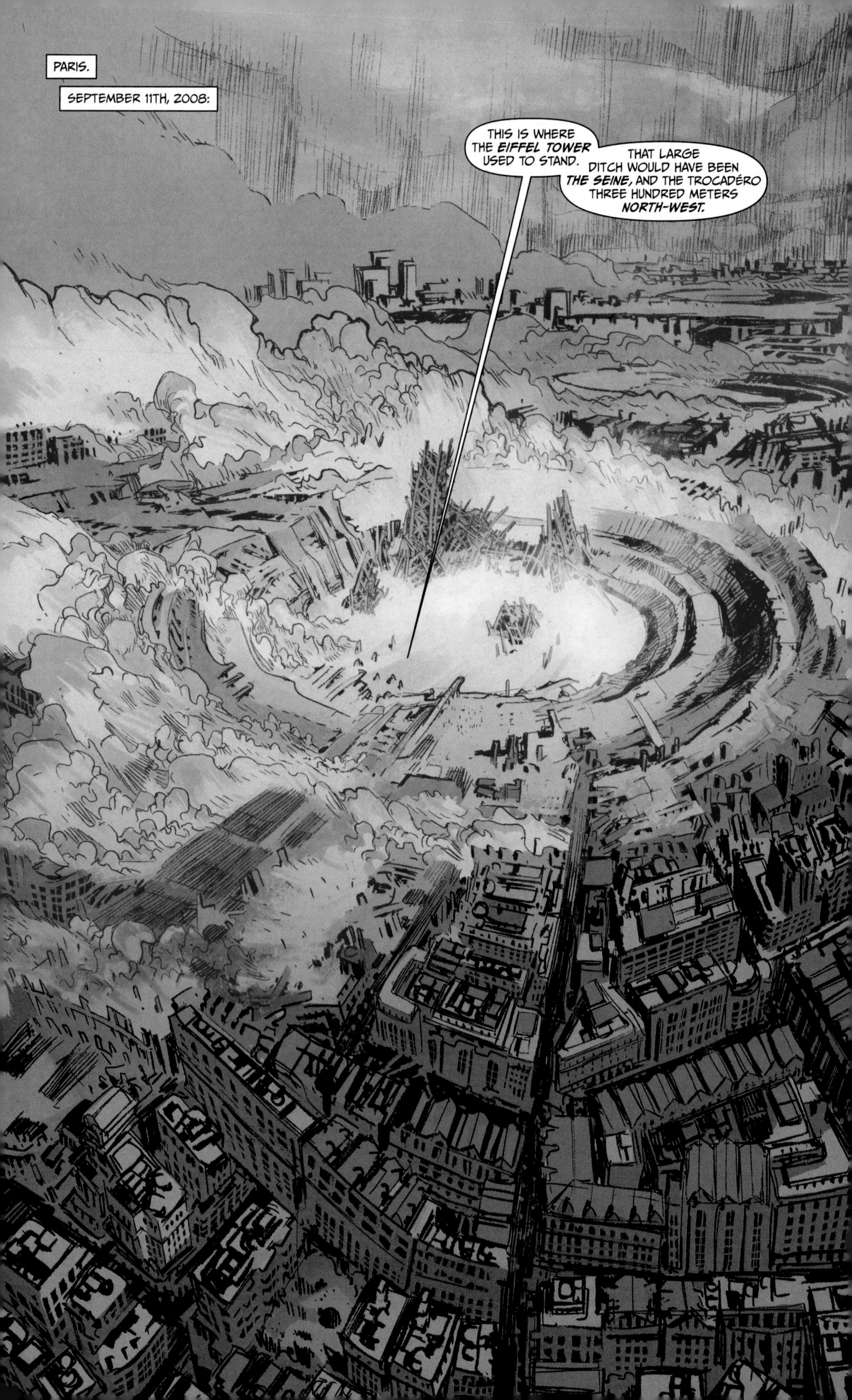
PARIS.
SEPTEMBER 11TH, 2008:
THIS IS WHERE THE EIFFEL TOWER USED TO STAND.
THAT LARGE DITCH WOULD HAVE BEEN THE SEINE, AND THE TROCADÉRO THREE HUNDRED METERS NORTH-WEST.

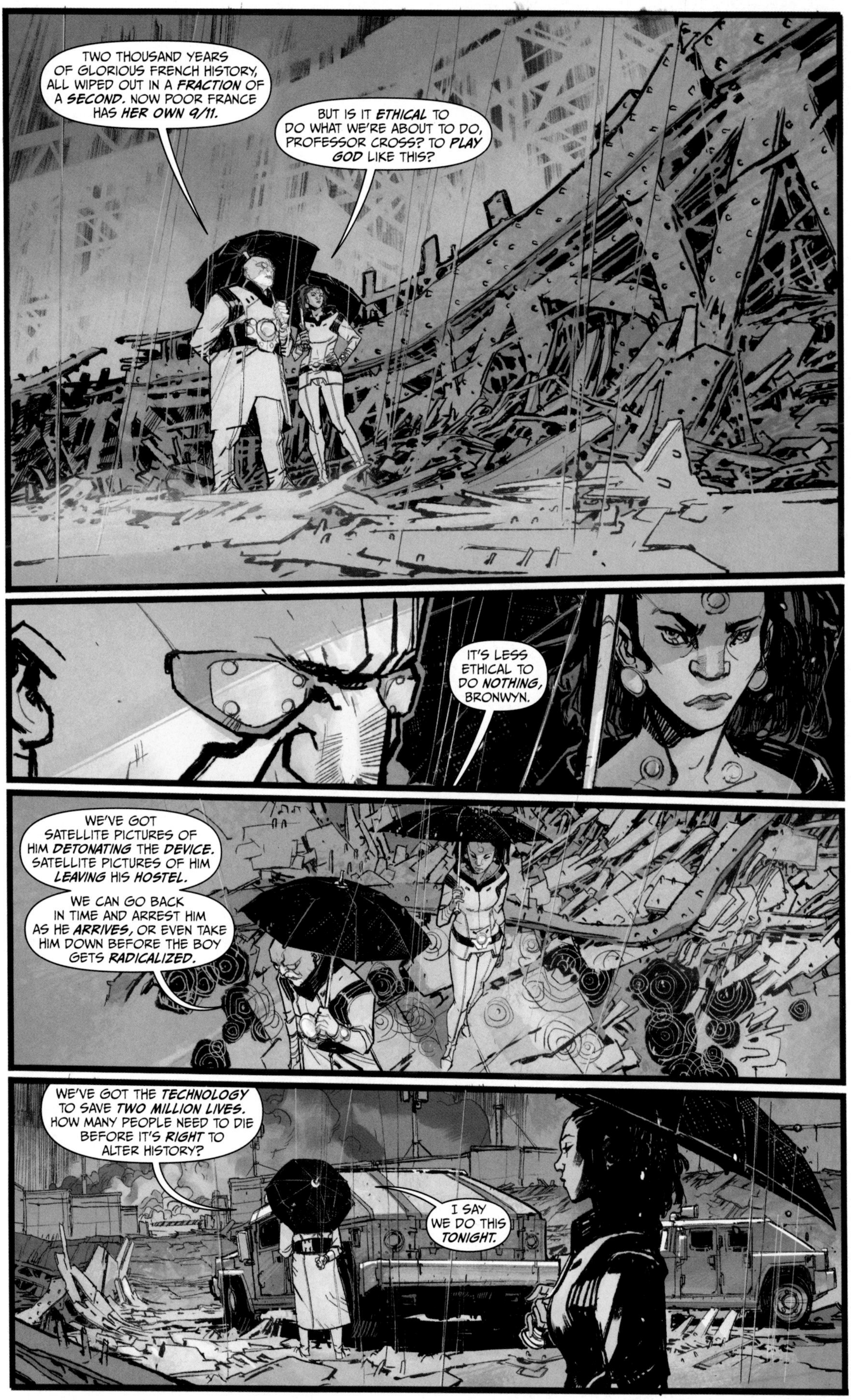

TWO THOUSAND YEARS OF GLORIOUS FRENCH HISTORY, ALL WIPED OUT IN A FRACTION OF A SECOND. NOW POOR FRANCE HAS HER OWN 9/11.
BUT IS IT ETHICAL TO DO WHAT WE'RE ABOUT TO DO, PROFESSOR CROSS? TO PLAY GOD LIKE THIS?
IT'S LESS ETHICAL TO DO NOTHING, BRONWYN.
WE'VE GOT SATELLITE PICTURES OF HIM DETONATING THE DEVICE. SATELLITE PICTURES OF HIM LEAVING HIS HOSTEL.
WE CAN GO BACK IN TIME AND ARREST HIM AS HE ARRIVES, OR EVEN TAKE HIM DOWN BEFORE THE BOY GETS RADICALIZED.
WE'VE GOT THE TECHNOLOGY TO SAVE TWO MILLION LIVES. HOW MANY PEOPLE NEED TO DIE BEFORE IT'S RIGHT TO ALTER HISTORY?
I SAY WE DO THIS TONIGHT.

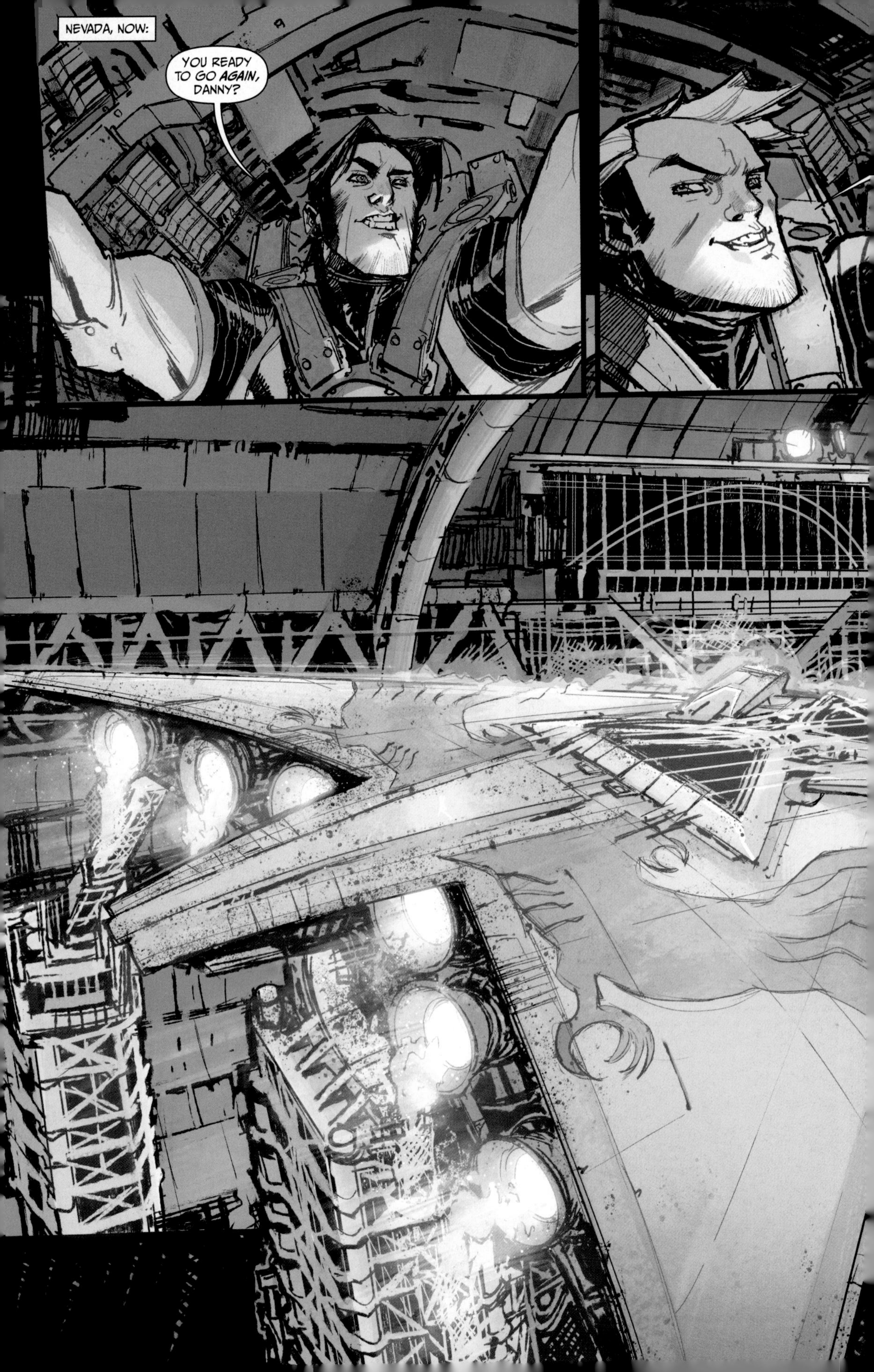
NEVADA, NOW:
YOU READY TO GO AGAIN, DANNY?

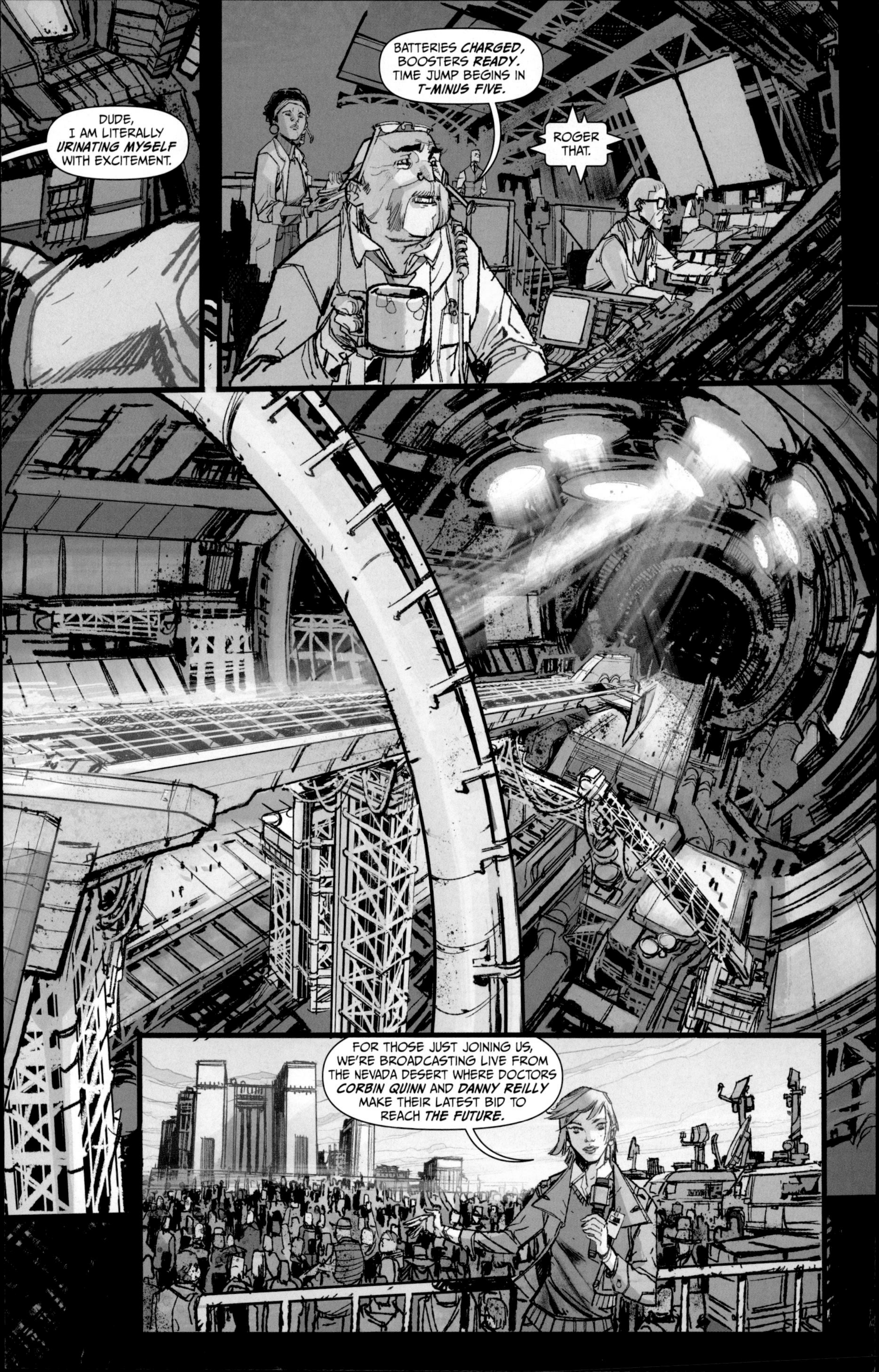
DUDE, I AM LITERALLY URINATING MYSELF WITH EXCITEMENT.
BATTERIES CHARGED, BOOSTERS READY. TIME JUMP BEGINS IN T-MINUS FIVE.
ROGER THAT.
FOR THOSE JUST JOINING US, WE'RE BROADCASTING LIVE FROM THE NEVADA DESERT WHERE DOCTORS CORBIN QUINN AND DANNY REILLY MAKE THEIR LATEST BID TO REACH THE FUTURE.

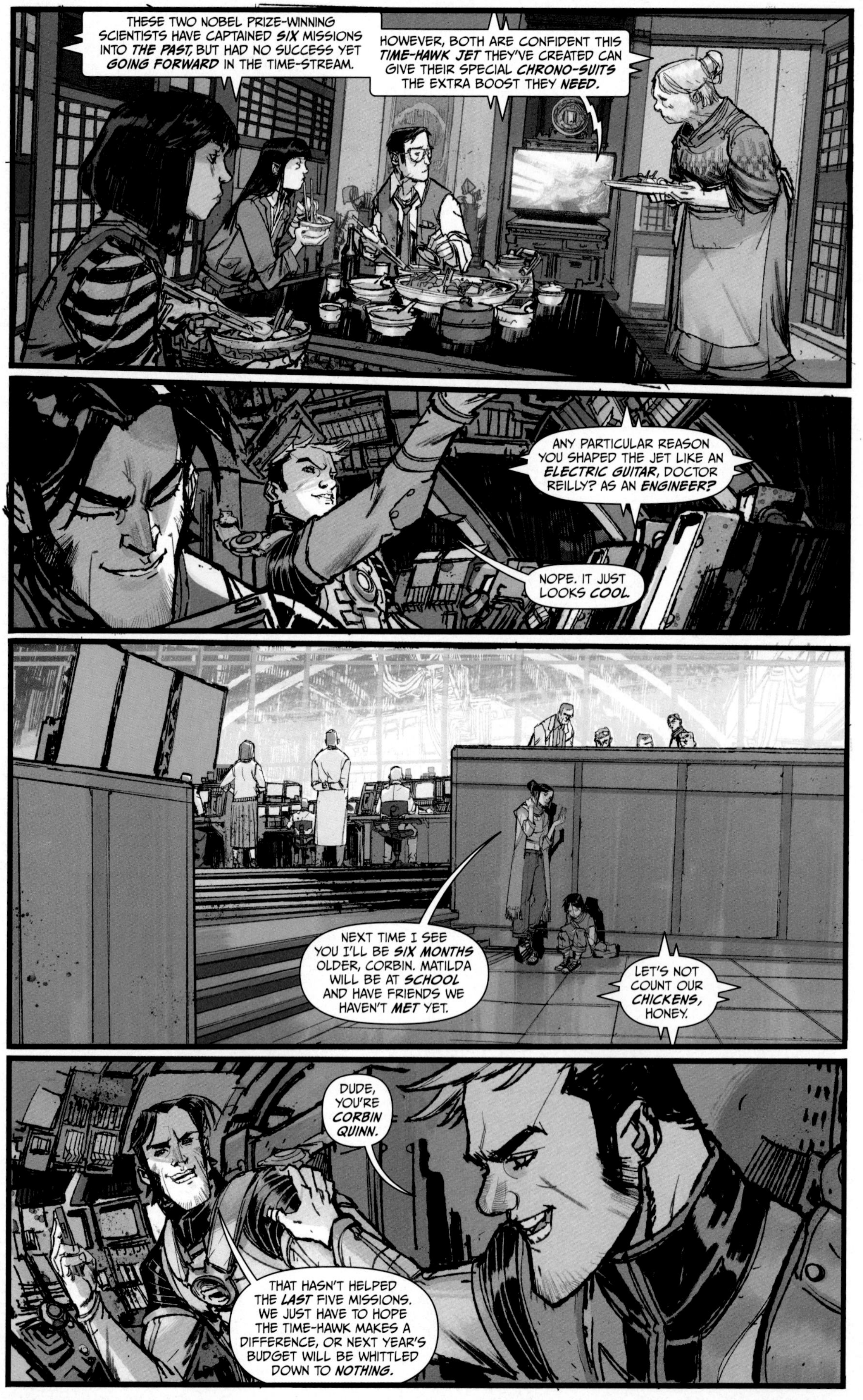
THESE TWO NOBEL PRIZE-WINNING SCIENTISTS HAVE CAPTAINED SIX MISSIONS INTO THE PAST, BUT HAD NO SUCCESS YET GOING FORWARD IN THE TIME-STREAM.
HOWEVER, BOTH ARE CONFIDENT THIS TIME-HAWK JET THEY'VE CREATED CAN GIVE THEIR SPECIAL CHRONO-SUITS THE EXTRA BOOST THEY NEED.
ANY PARTICULAR REASON YOU SHAPED THE JET LIKE AN ELECTRIC GUITAR, DOCTOR REILLY? AS AN ENGINEER?
NOPE. IT JUST LOOKS COOL.
NEXT TIME I SEE YOU I'LL BE SIX MONTHS OLDER, CORBIN. MATILDA WILL BE AT SCHOOL AND HAVE FRIENDS WE HAVEN'T MET YET.
LET'S NOT COUNT OUR CHICKENS, HONEY.
DUDE, YOU'RE CORBIN QUINN.
THAT HASN'T HELPED THE LAST FIVE MISSIONS. WE JUST HAVE TO HOPE THE TIME-HAWK MAKES A DIFFERENCE, OR NEXT YEAR'S BUDGET WILL BE WHITTLED DOWN TO NOTHING.

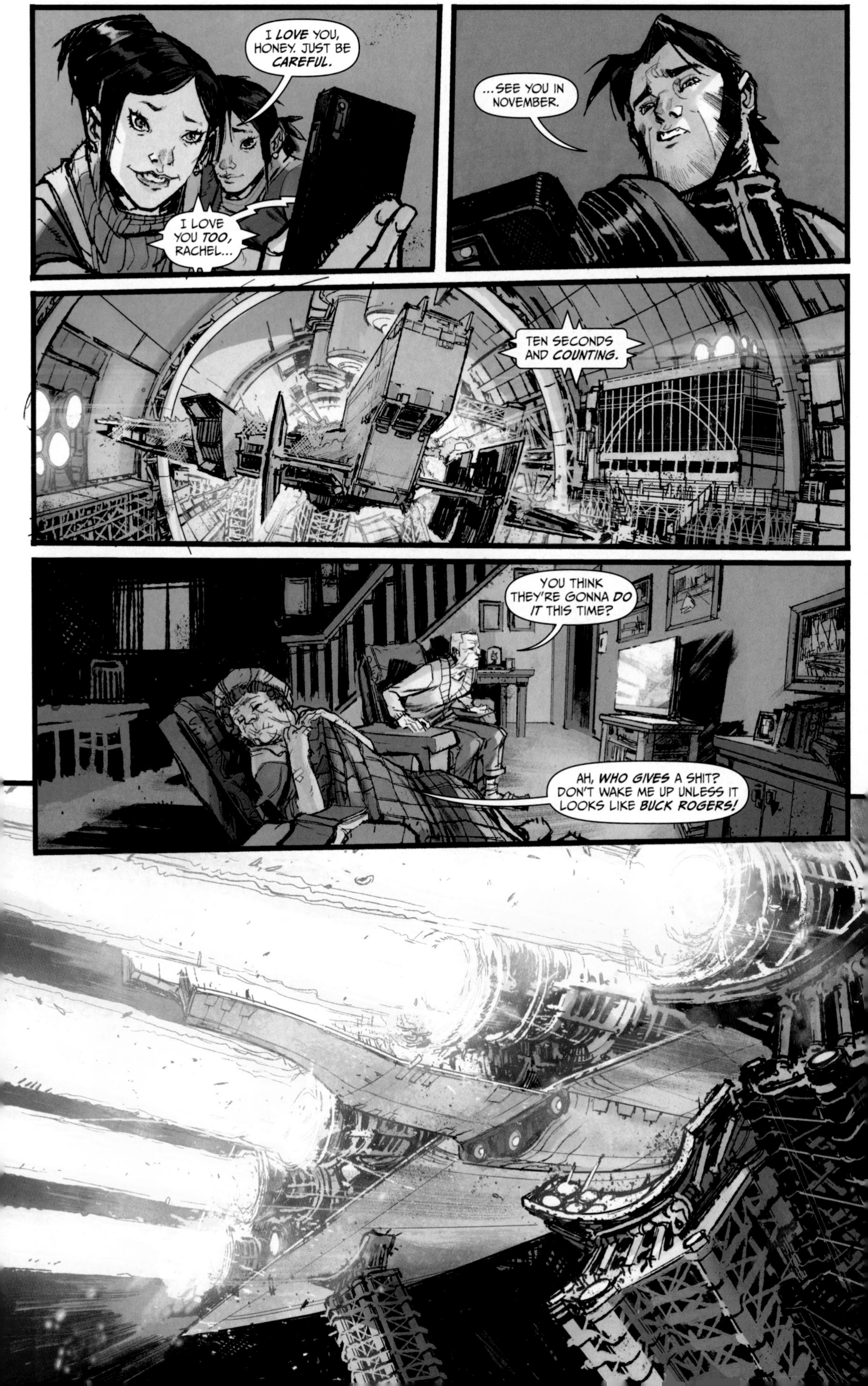
I LOVE YOU, HONEY. JUST BE CAREFUL.
I LOVE YOU TOO, RACHEL...
...SEE YOU IN NOVEMBER.
TEN SECONDS AND COUNTING.
YOU THINK THEY'RE GONNA DO IT THIS TIME?
AH, WHO GIVES A SHIT? DON'T WAKE ME UP UNLESS IT LOOKS LIKE BUCK ROGERS!

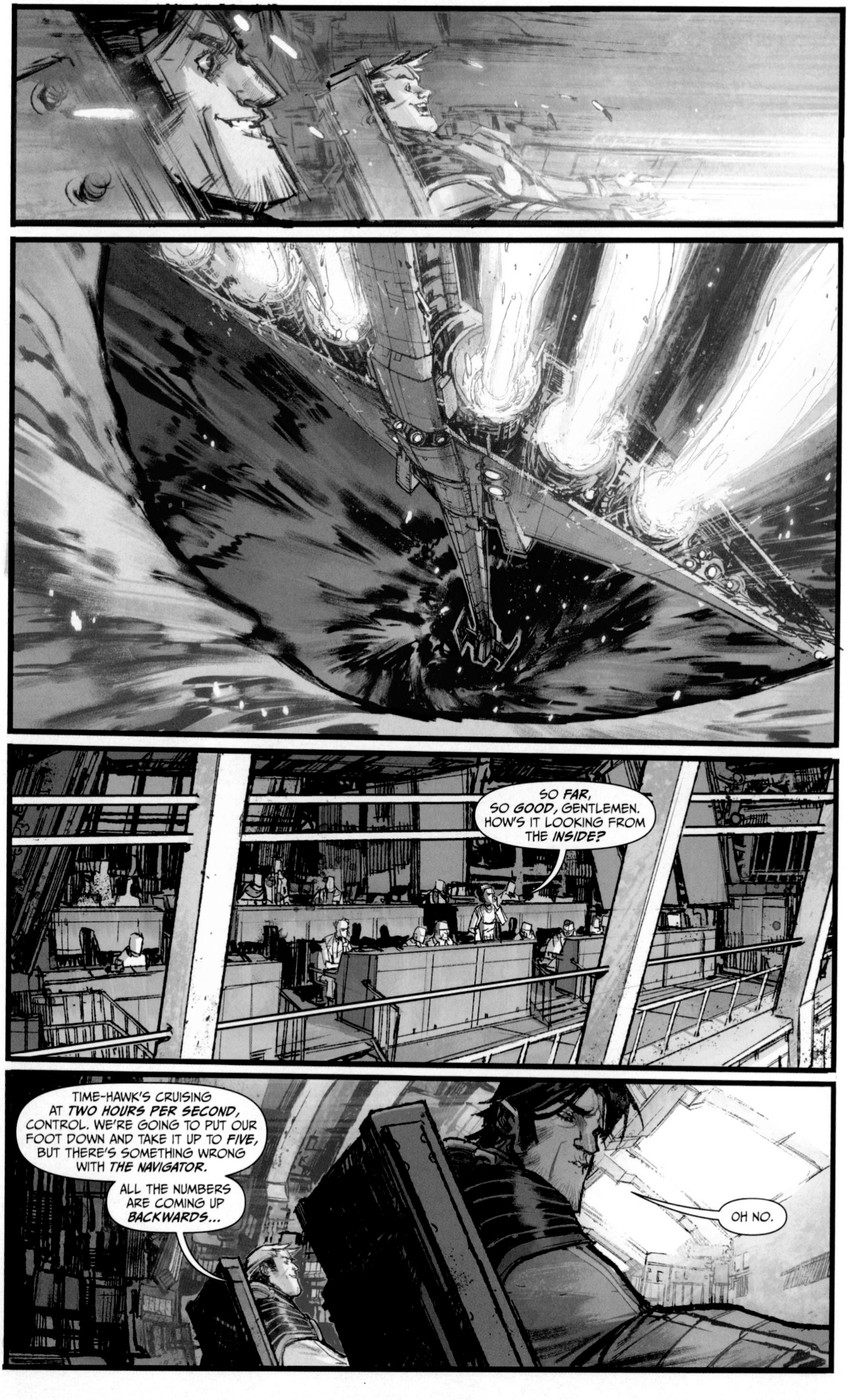
SO *FAR*, SO *GOOD*, GENTLEMEN. HOW'S IT LOOKING FROM THE *INSIDE?*
TIME-HAWK'S CRUISING AT *TWO HOURS PER SECOND*, CONTROL. WE'RE GOING TO PUT OUR FOOT DOWN AND TAKE IT UP TO *FIVE*, BUT THERE'S SOMETHING WRONG WITH *THE NAVIGATOR*.
ALL THE NUMBERS ARE COMING UP *BACKWARDS...*
OH NO.

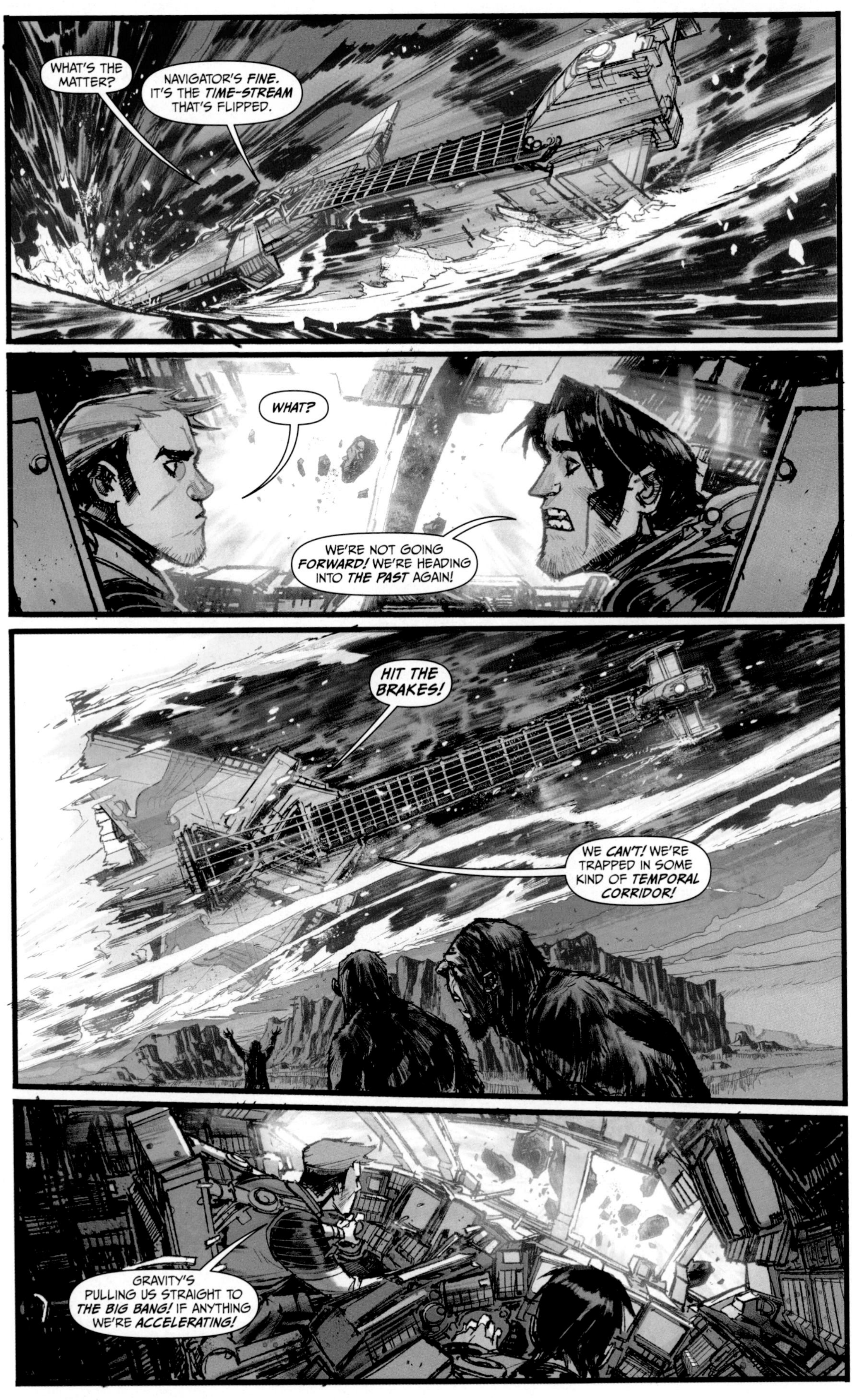
WHAT'S THE MATTER?
NAVIGATOR'S *FINE.* IT'S THE *TIME-STREAM* THAT'S FLIPPED.
WHAT?
WE'RE NOT GOING *FORWARD!* WE'RE HEADING INTO *THE PAST* AGAIN!
HIT THE BRAKES!
WE *CAN'T!* WE'RE TRAPPED IN SOME KIND OF *TEMPORAL CORRIDOR!*
GRAVITY'S PULLING US STRAIGHT TO *THE BIG BANG!* IF ANYTHING WE'RE *ACCELERATING!*

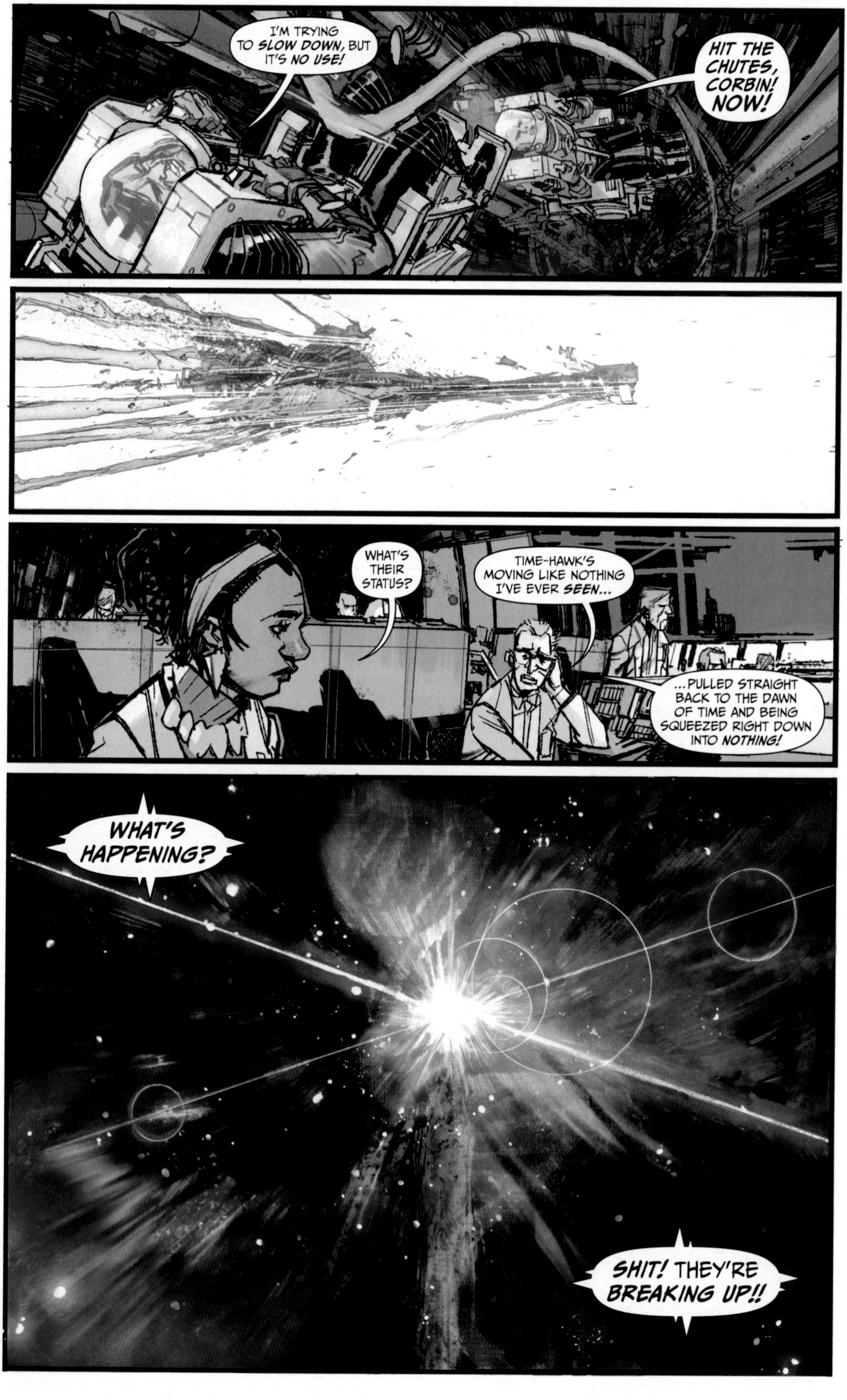
I'M TRYING TO SLOW DOWN, BUT IT'S NO USE!
HIT THE CHUTES, CORBIN! NOW!
WHAT'S THEIR STATUS?
TIME-HAWK'S MOVING LIKE NOTHING I'VE EVER SEEN...
...PULLED STRAIGHT BACK TO THE DAWN OF TIME AND BEING SQUEEZED RIGHT DOWN INTO NOTHING!
WHAT'S HAPPENING?
SHIT! THEY'RE BREAKING UP!!

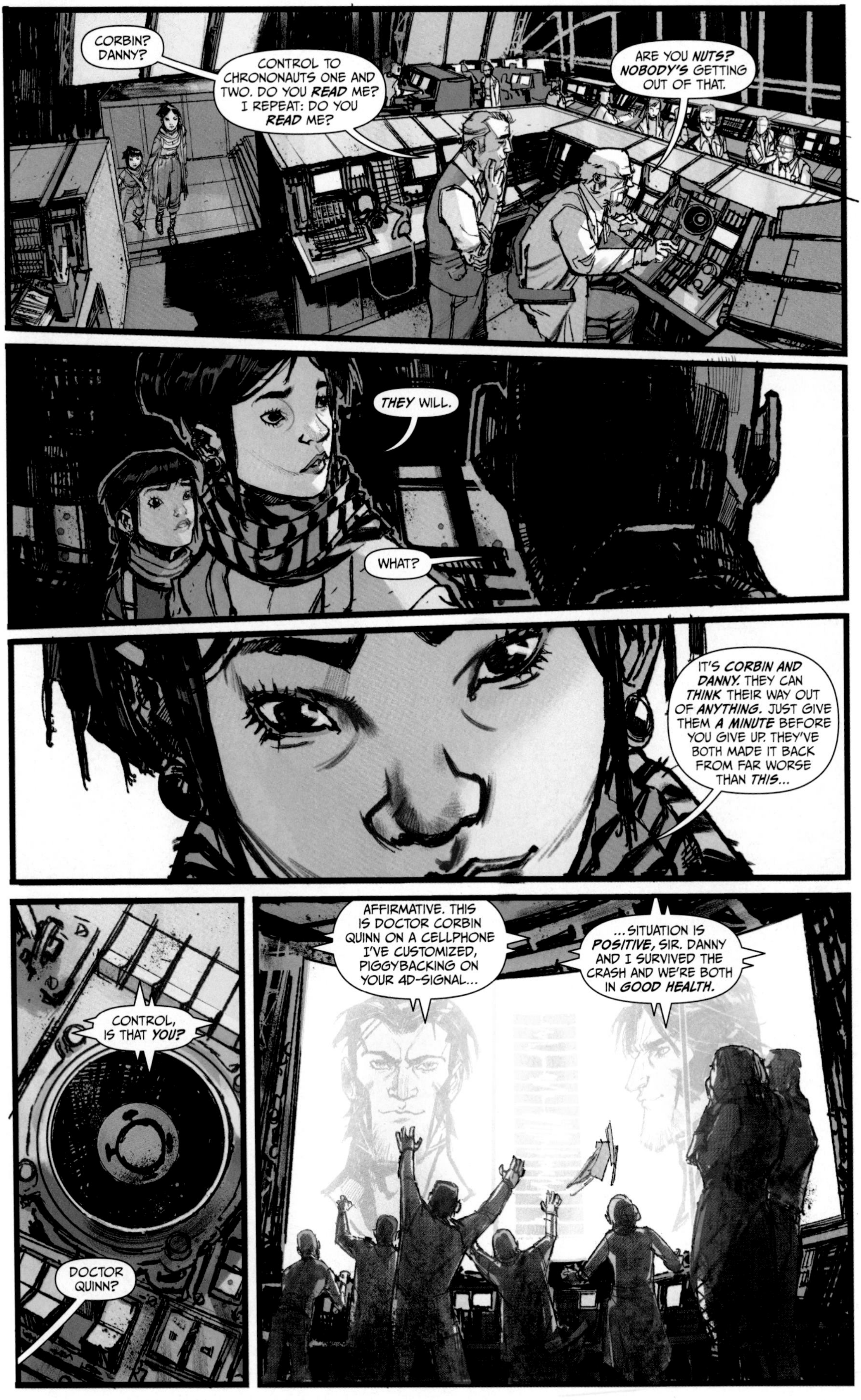
CORBIN? DANNY?
CONTROL TO CHRONONAUTS ONE AND TWO. DO YOU READ ME? I REPEAT: DO YOU READ ME?
ARE YOU NUTS? NOBODY'S GETTING OUT OF THAT.
THEY WILL.
WHAT?
IT'S CORBIN AND DANNY. THEY CAN THINK THEIR WAY OUT OF ANYTHING. JUST GIVE THEM A MINUTE BEFORE YOU GIVE UP. THEY'VE BOTH MADE IT BACK FROM FAR WORSE THAN THIS...
CONTROL, IS THAT YOU?
DOCTOR QUINN?
AFFIRMATIVE. THIS IS DOCTOR CORBIN QUINN ON A CELLPHONE I'VE CUSTOMIZED, PIGGYBACKING ON YOUR 4D-SIGNAL...
...SITUATION IS POSITIVE, SIR. DANNY AND I SURVIVED THE CRASH AND WE'RE BOTH IN GOOD HEALTH.

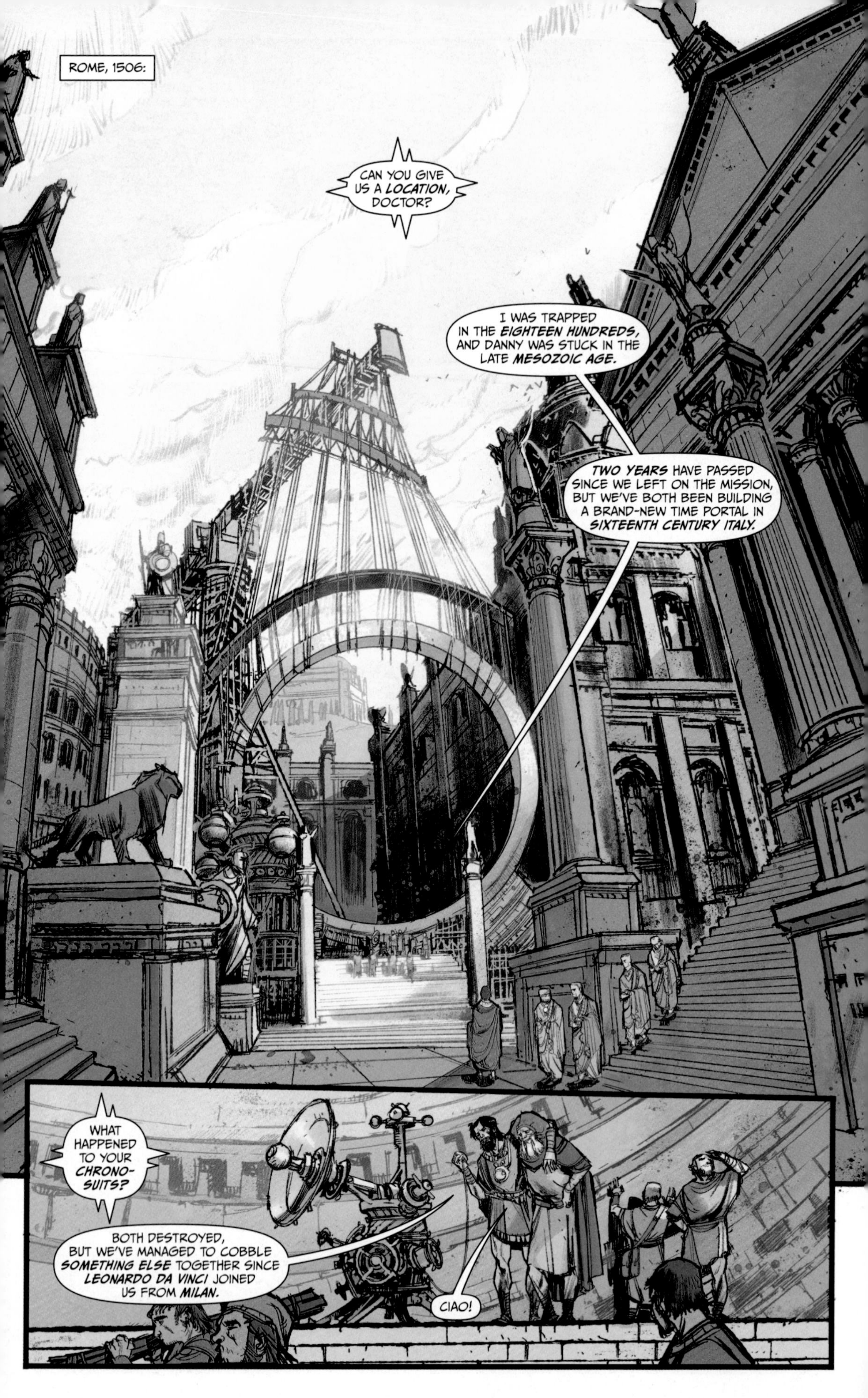
ROME, 1506:
CAN YOU GIVE US A *LOCATION,* DOCTOR?
I WAS TRAPPED IN THE *EIGHTEEN HUNDREDS,* AND DANNY WAS STUCK IN THE LATE *MESOZOIC AGE.*
TWO YEARS HAVE PASSED SINCE WE LEFT ON THE MISSION, BUT WE'VE BOTH BEEN BUILDING A BRAND-NEW TIME PORTAL IN *SIXTEENTH CENTURY ITALY.*
WHAT HAPPENED TO YOUR *CHRONO-SUITS?*
BOTH DESTROYED, BUT WE'VE MANAGED TO COBBLE *SOMETHING ELSE* TOGETHER SINCE *LEONARDO DA VINCI* JOINED US FROM *MILAN.*
CIAO!

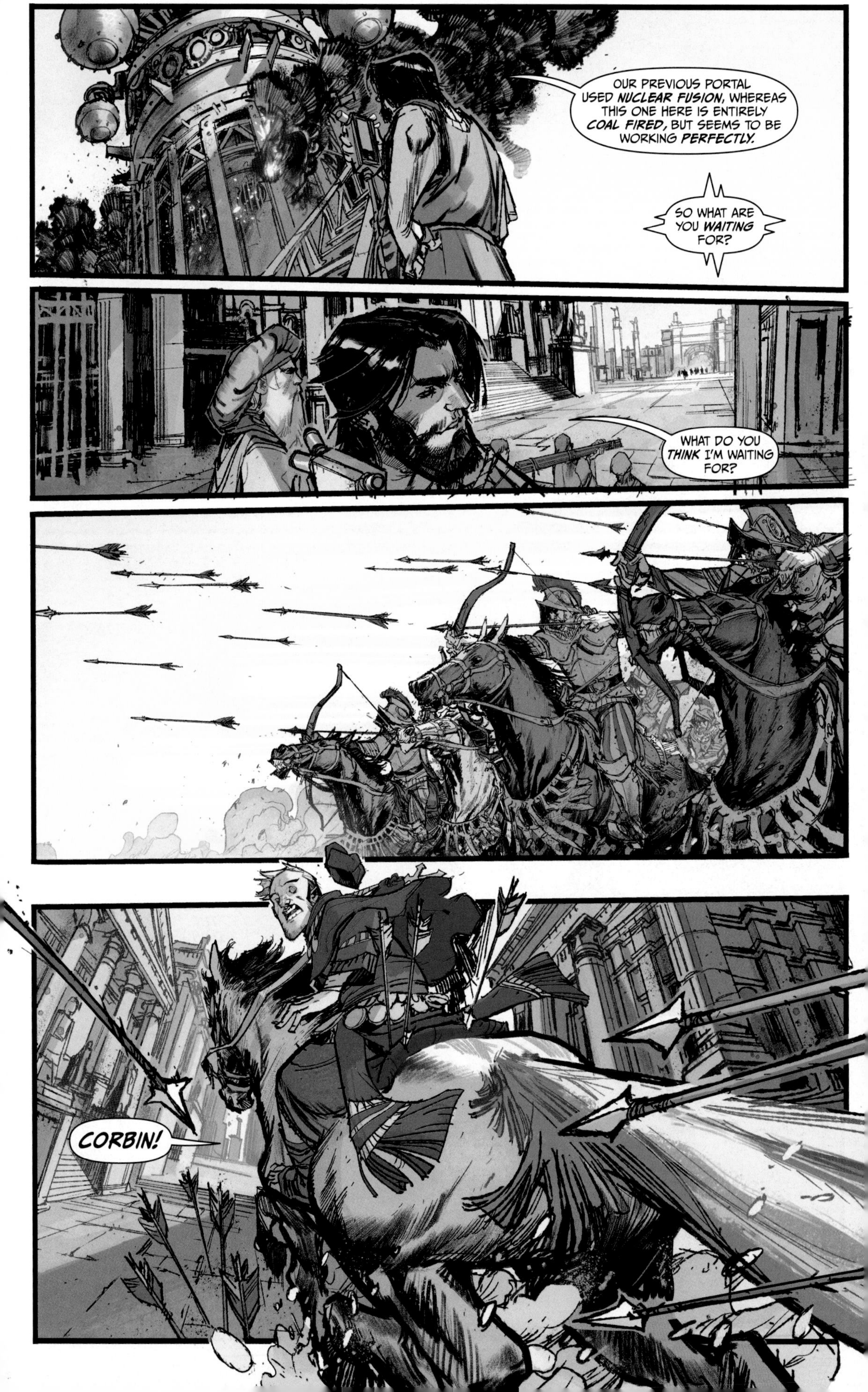
OUR PREVIOUS PORTAL USED NUCLEAR FUSION, WHEREAS THIS ONE HERE IS ENTIRELY COAL FIRED, BUT SEEMS TO BE WORKING PERFECTLY.
SO WHAT ARE YOU WAITING FOR?
WHAT DO YOU THINK I'M WAITING FOR?
CORBIN!

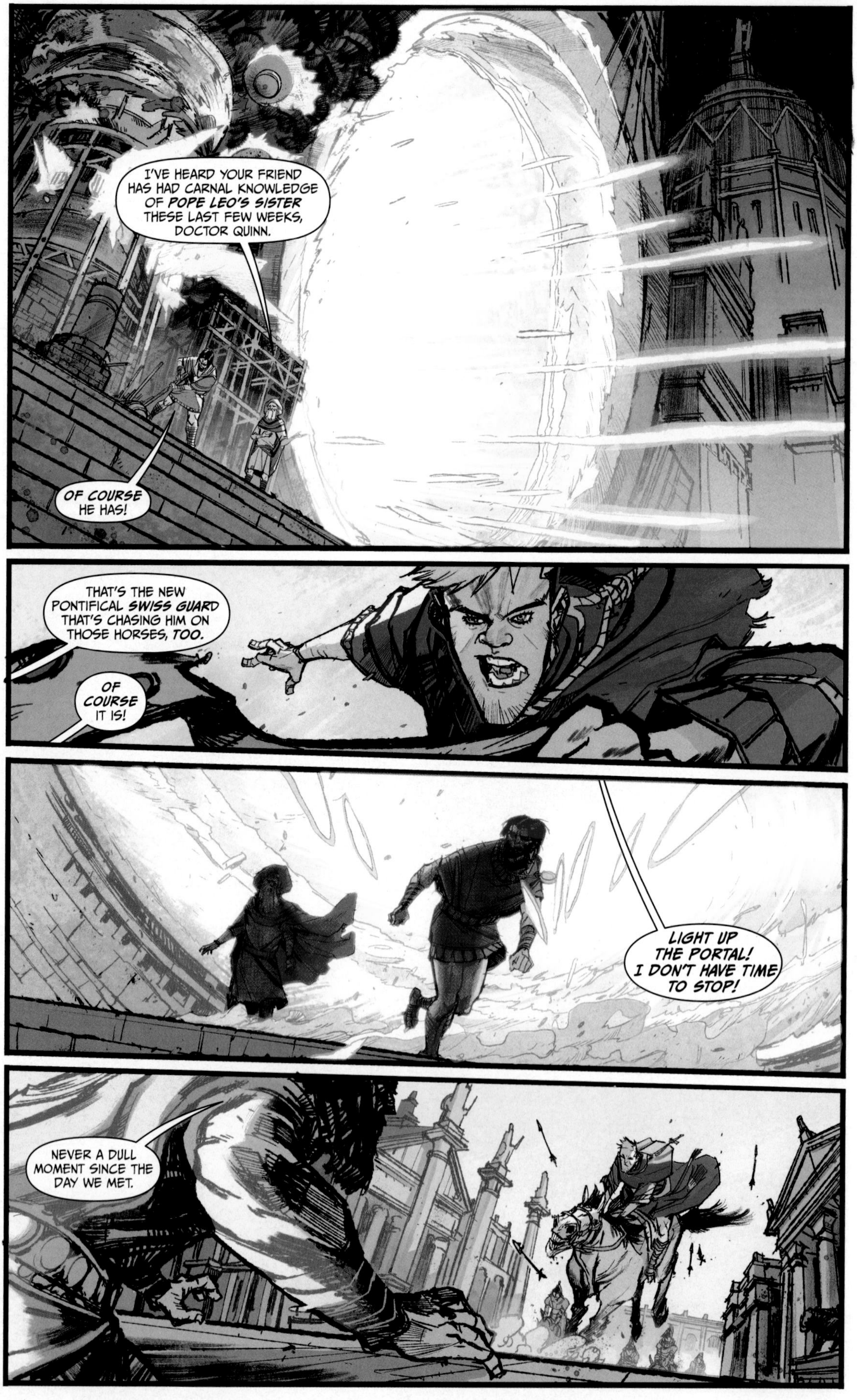
I'VE HEARD YOUR FRIEND HAS HAD CARNAL KNOWLEDGE OF POPE LEO'S SISTER THESE LAST FEW WEEKS, DOCTOR QUINN.
OF COURSE HE HAS!
THAT'S THE NEW PONTIFICAL SWISS GUARD THAT'S CHASING HIM ON THOSE HORSES, TOO.
OF COURSE IT IS!
LIGHT UP THE PORTAL! I DON'T HAVE TIME TO STOP!
NEVER A DULL MOMENT SINCE THE DAY WE MET.

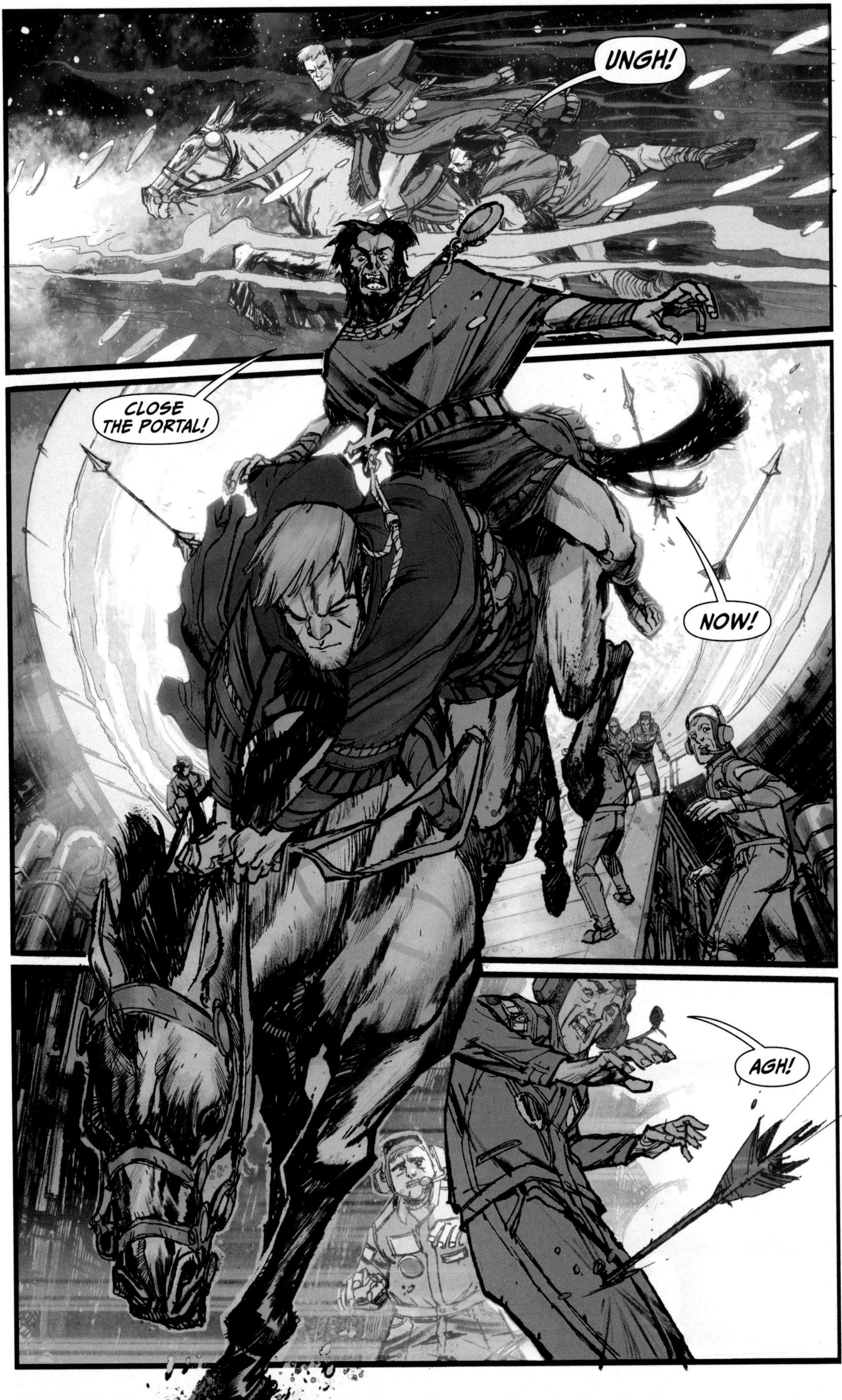
UNGH!
CLOSE THE PORTAL!
NOW!
AGH!

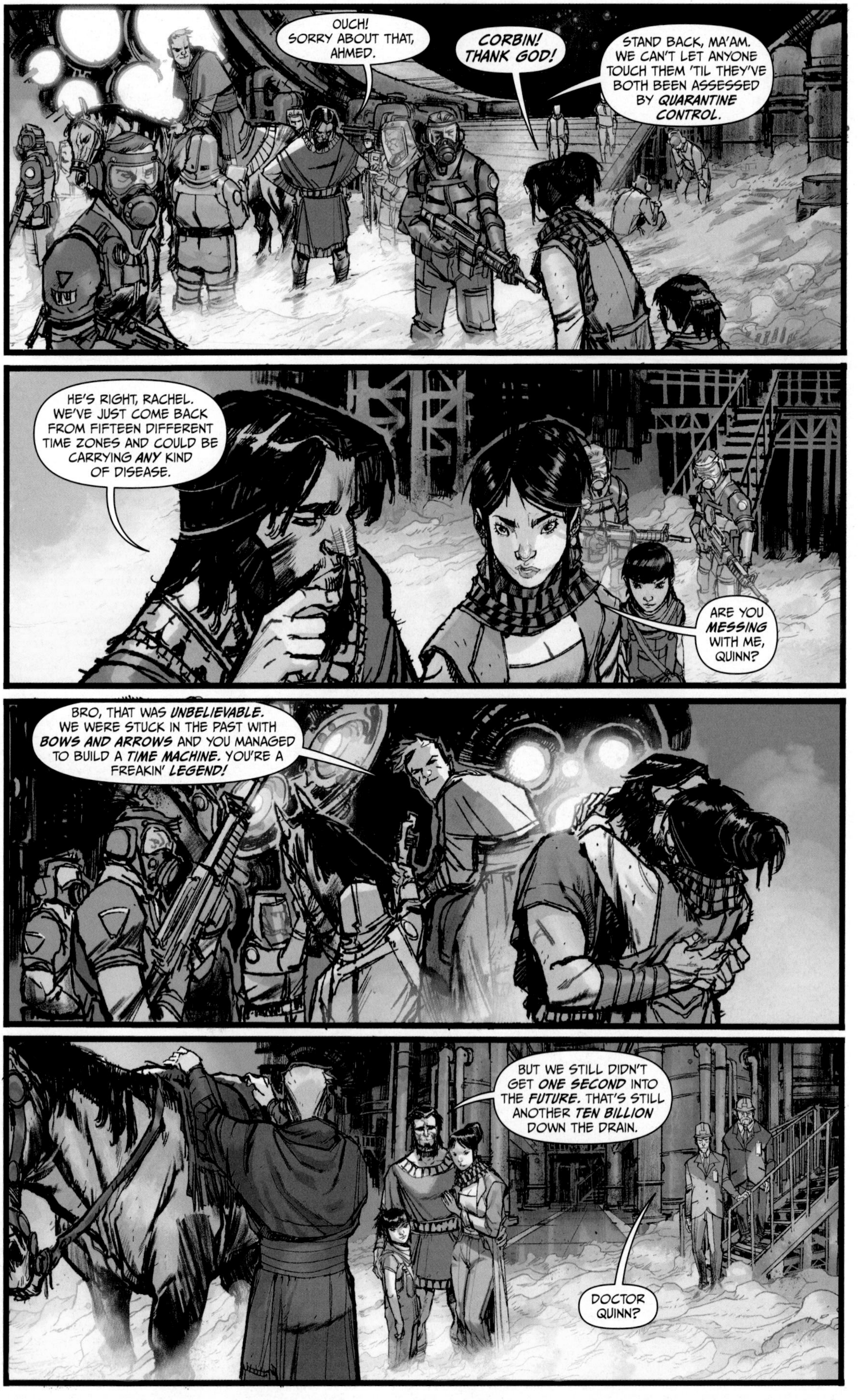

OUCH! SORRY ABOUT THAT, AHMED.
CORBIN! THANK GOD!
STAND BACK, MA'AM. WE CAN'T LET ANYONE TOUCH THEM 'TIL THEY'VE BOTH BEEN ASSESSED BY QUARANTINE CONTROL.
HE'S RIGHT, RACHEL. WE'VE JUST COME BACK FROM FIFTEEN DIFFERENT TIME ZONES AND COULD BE CARRYING ANY KIND OF DISEASE.
ARE YOU MESSING WITH ME, QUINN?
BRO, THAT WAS UNBELIEVABLE. WE WERE STUCK IN THE PAST WITH BOWS AND ARROWS AND YOU MANAGED TO BUILD A TIME MACHINE. YOU'RE A FREAKIN' LEGEND!
BUT WE STILL DIDN'T GET ONE SECOND INTO THE FUTURE. THAT'S STILL ANOTHER TEN BILLION DOWN THE DRAIN.
DOCTOR QUINN?

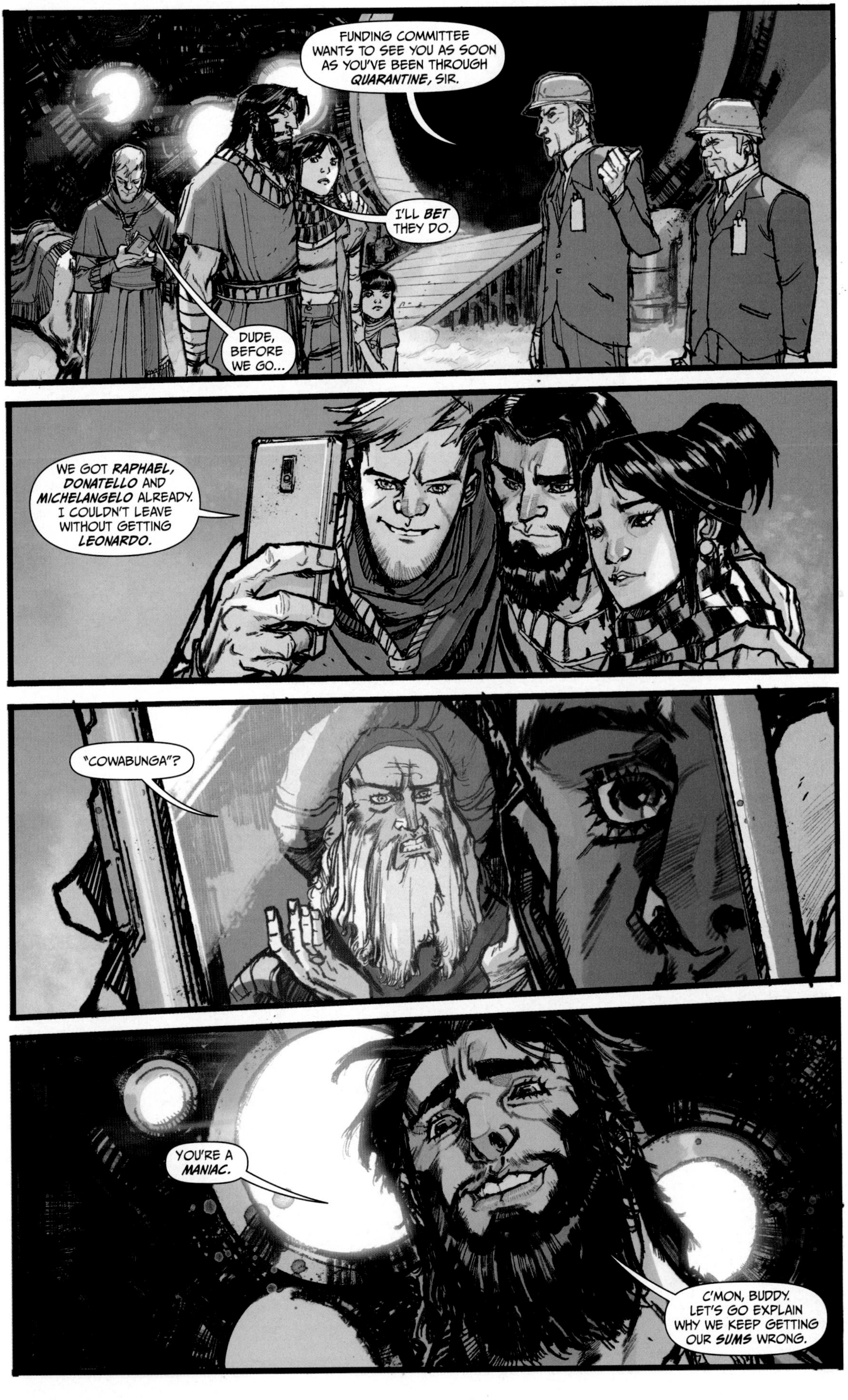
FUNDING COMMITTEE WANTS TO SEE YOU AS SOON AS YOU'VE BEEN THROUGH *QUARANTINE*, SIR.
I'LL *BET* THEY DO.
DUDE, BEFORE WE GO...
WE GOT *RAPHAEL, DONATELLO* AND *MICHELANGELO* ALREADY. I COULDN'T LEAVE WITHOUT GETTING *LEONARDO.*
"COWABUNGA"?
YOU'RE A *MANIAC.*
C'MON, BUDDY. LET'S GO EXPLAIN WHY WE KEEP GETTING OUR *SUMS* WRONG.

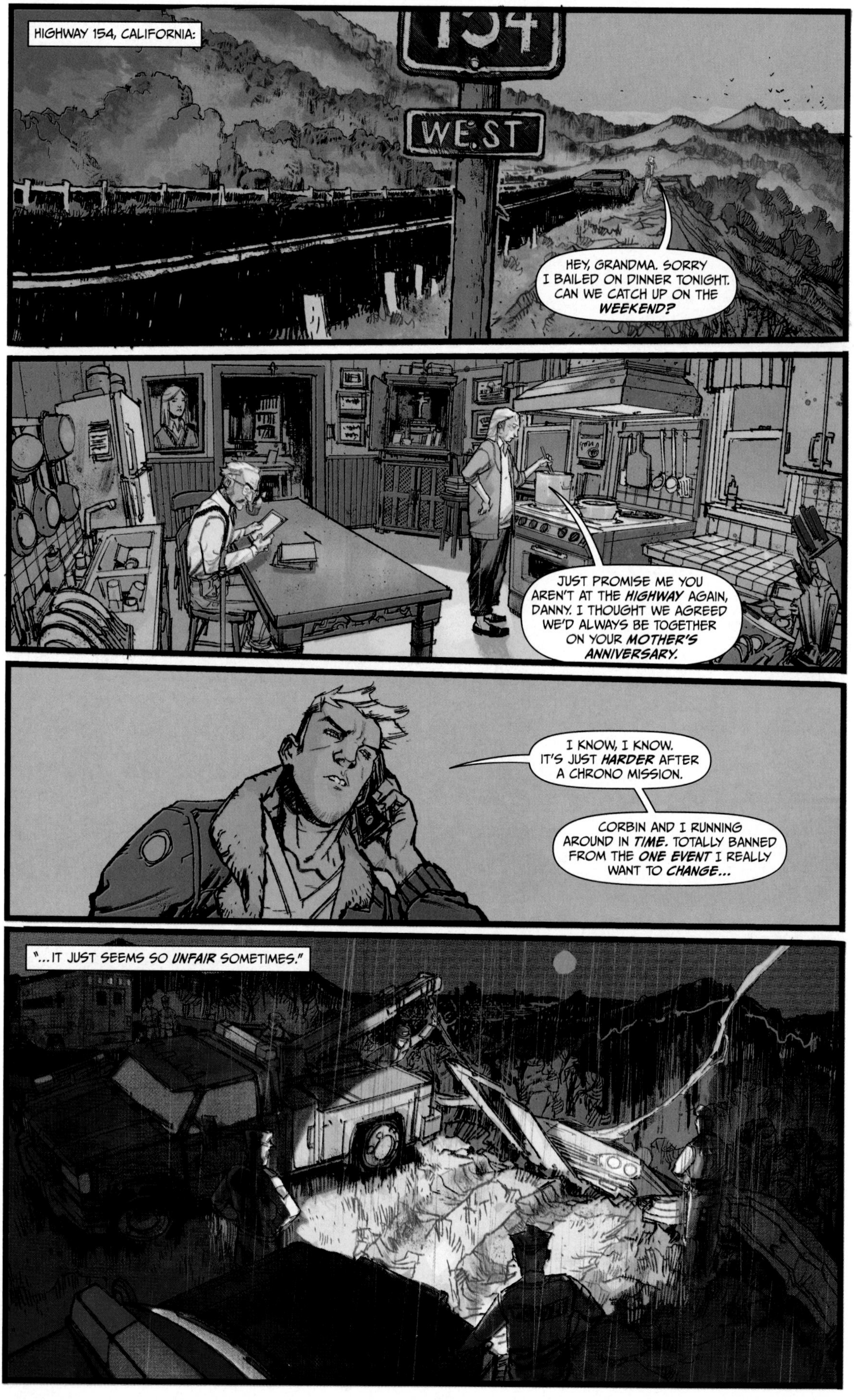
HIGHWAY 154, CALIFORNIA:
154
WEST
HEY, GRANDMA. SORRY I BAILED ON DINNER TONIGHT. CAN WE CATCH UP ON THE WEEKEND?
JUST PROMISE ME YOU AREN'T AT THE HIGHWAY AGAIN, DANNY. I THOUGHT WE AGREED WE'D ALWAYS BE TOGETHER ON YOUR MOTHER'S ANNIVERSARY.
I KNOW, I KNOW. IT'S JUST HARDER AFTER A CHRONO MISSION.
CORBIN AND I RUNNING AROUND IN TIME. TOTALLY BANNED FROM THE ONE EVENT I REALLY WANT TO CHANGE...
"...IT JUST SEEMS SO UNFAIR SOMETIMES."

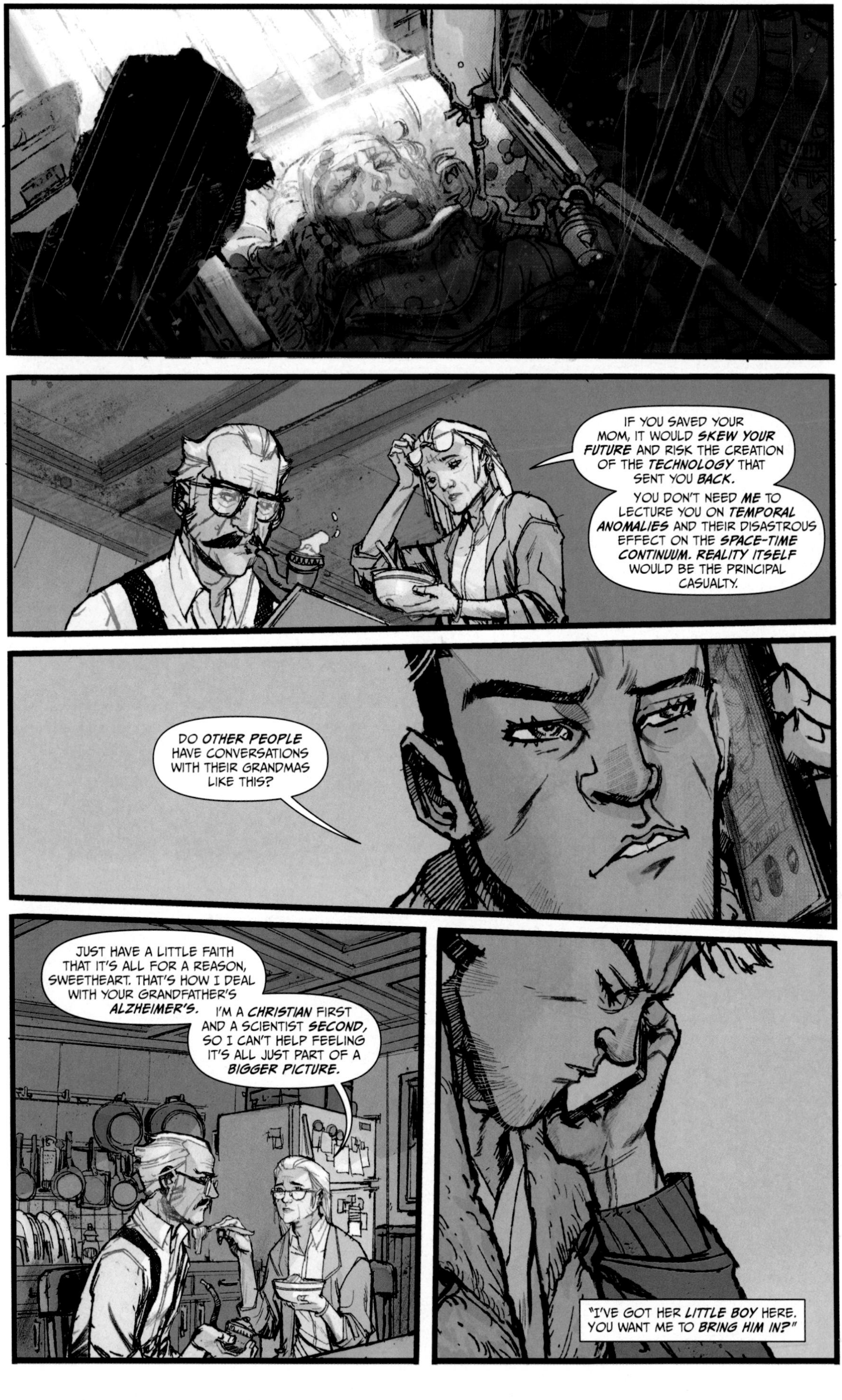
IF YOU SAVED YOUR MOM, IT WOULD SKEW YOUR FUTURE AND RISK THE CREATION OF THE TECHNOLOGY THAT SENT YOU BACK.
YOU DON'T NEED ME TO LECTURE YOU ON TEMPORAL ANOMALIES AND THEIR DISASTROUS EFFECT ON THE SPACE-TIME CONTINUUM. REALITY ITSELF WOULD BE THE PRINCIPAL CASUALTY.
DO OTHER PEOPLE HAVE CONVERSATIONS WITH THEIR GRANDMAS LIKE THIS?
JUST HAVE A LITTLE FAITH THAT IT'S ALL FOR A REASON, SWEETHEART. THAT'S HOW I DEAL WITH YOUR GRANDFATHER'S ALZHEIMER'S.
I'M A CHRISTIAN FIRST AND A SCIENTIST SECOND, SO I CAN'T HELP FEELING IT'S ALL JUST PART OF A BIGGER PICTURE.
"I'VE GOT HER LITTLE BOY HERE. YOU WANT ME TO BRING HIM IN?"

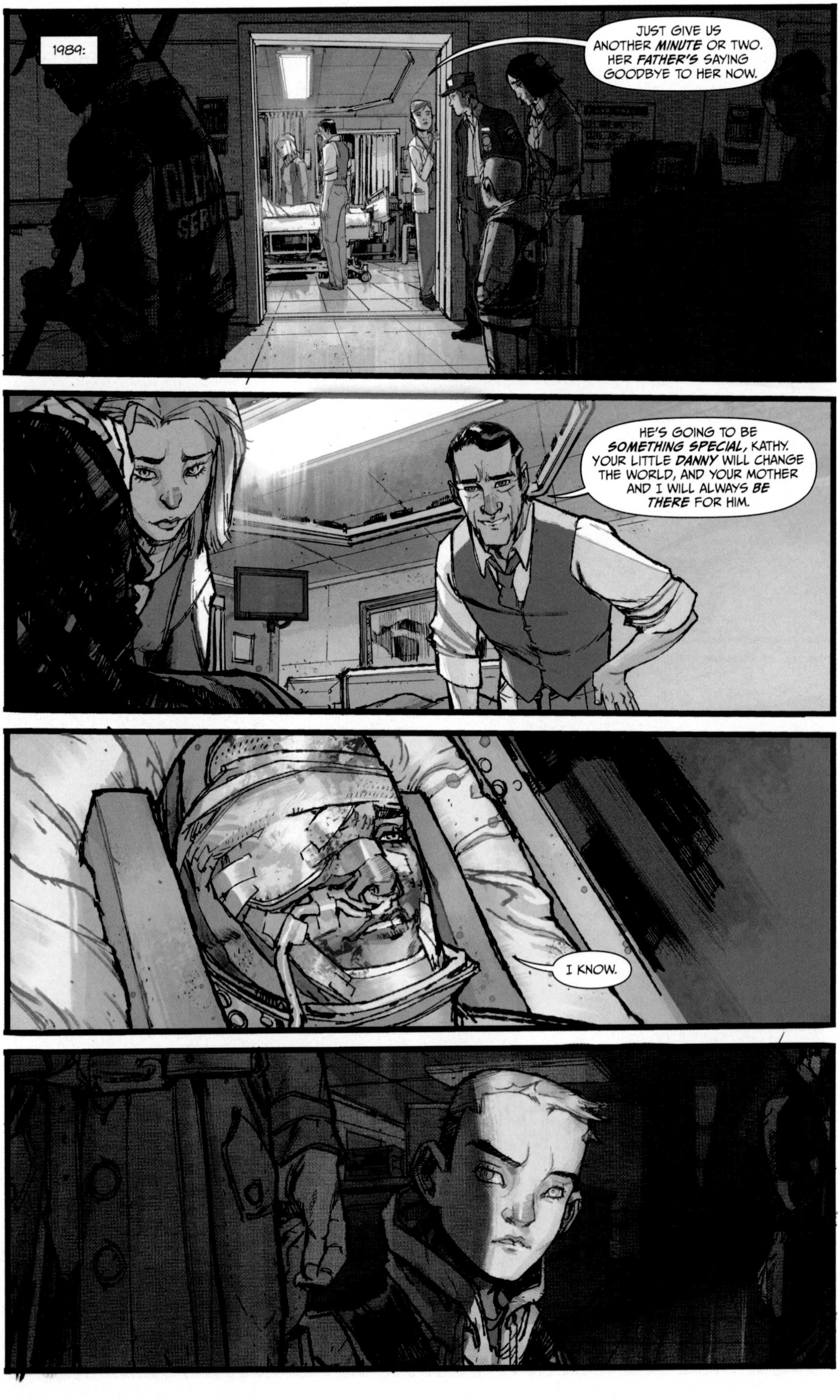
1989:
JUST GIVE US ANOTHER MINUTE OR TWO. HER FATHER'S SAYING GOODBYE TO HER NOW.
HE'S GOING TO BE SOMETHING SPECIAL, KATHY. YOUR LITTLE DANNY WILL CHANGE THE WORLD, AND YOUR MOTHER AND I WILL ALWAYS BE THERE FOR HIM.
I KNOW.

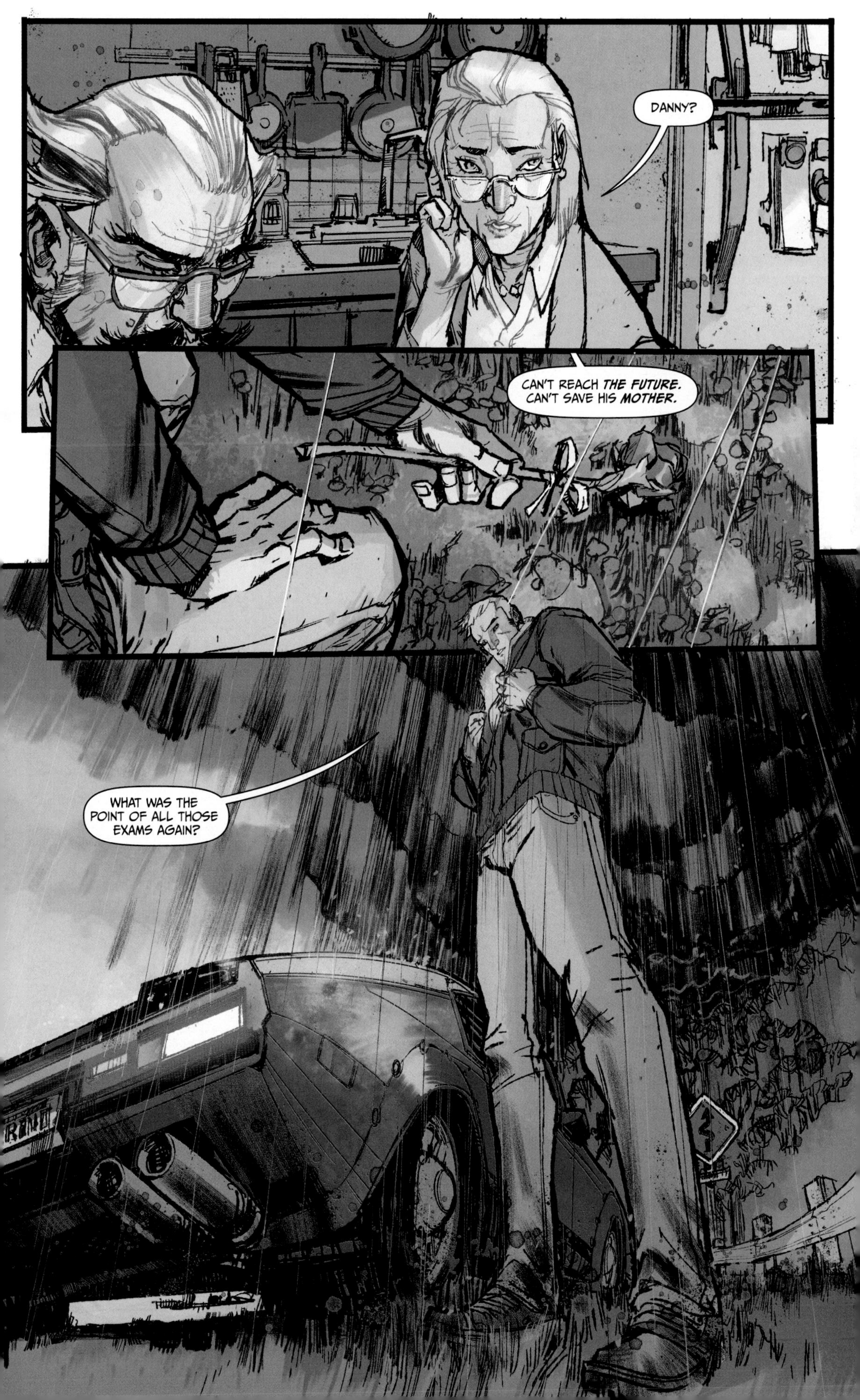
DANNY?
CAN'T REACH THE FUTURE. CAN'T SAVE HIS MOTHER.
WHAT WAS THE POINT OF ALL THOSE EXAMS AGAIN?

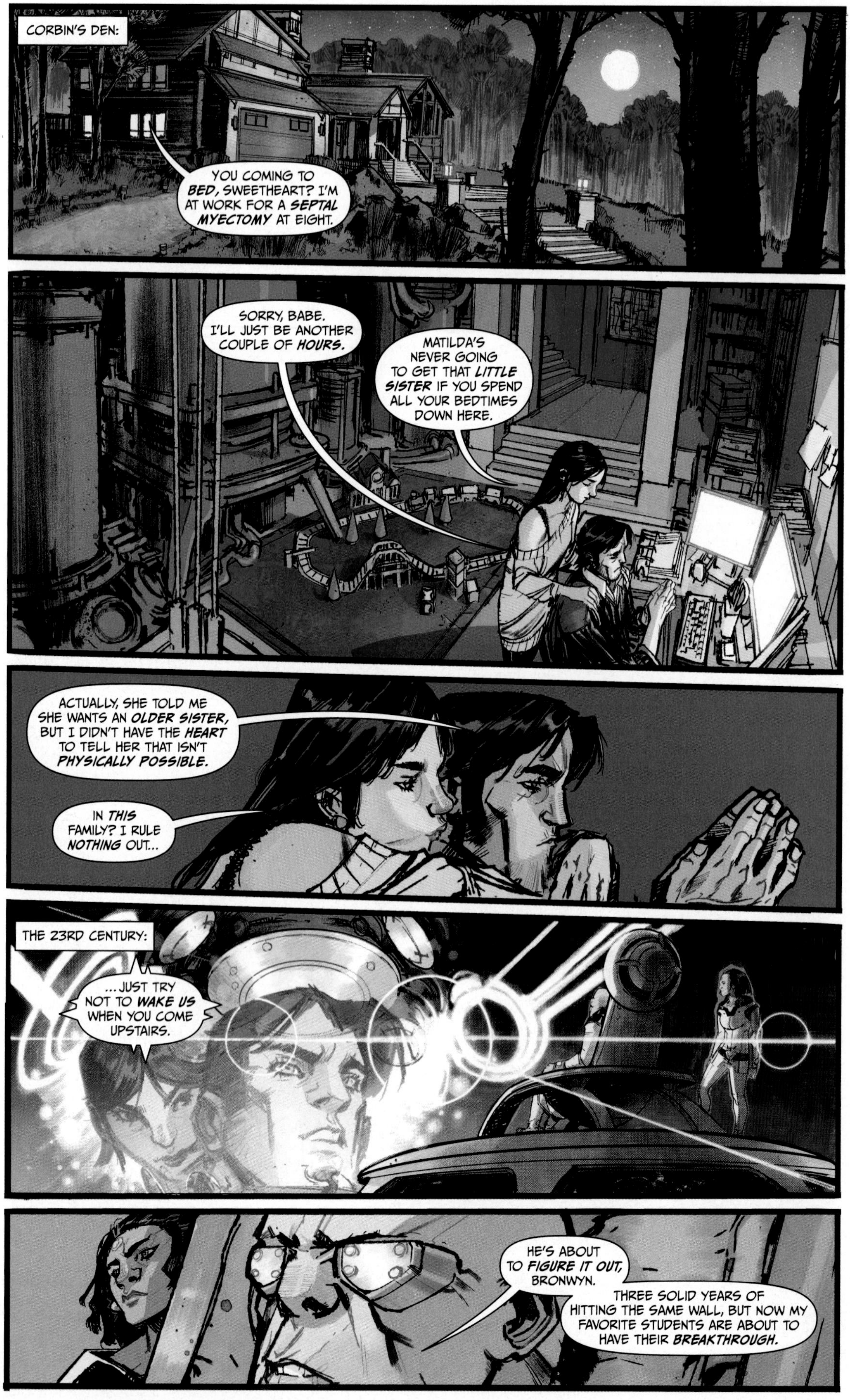
CORBIN'S DEN:
YOU COMING TO BED, SWEETHEART? I'M AT WORK FOR A SEPTAL MYECTOMY AT EIGHT.
SORRY, BABE. I'LL JUST BE ANOTHER COUPLE OF HOURS.
MATILDA'S NEVER GOING TO GET THAT LITTLE SISTER IF YOU SPEND ALL YOUR BEDTIMES DOWN HERE.
ACTUALLY, SHE TOLD ME SHE WANTS AN OLDER SISTER, BUT I DIDN'T HAVE THE HEART TO TELL HER THAT ISN'T PHYSICALLY POSSIBLE.
IN THIS FAMILY? I RULE NOTHING OUT...
THE 23RD CENTURY:
...JUST TRY NOT TO WAKE US WHEN YOU COME UPSTAIRS.
HE'S ABOUT TO FIGURE IT OUT, BRONWYN.
THREE SOLID YEARS OF HITTING THE SAME WALL, BUT NOW MY FAVORITE STUDENTS ARE ABOUT TO HAVE THEIR BREAKTHROUGH.

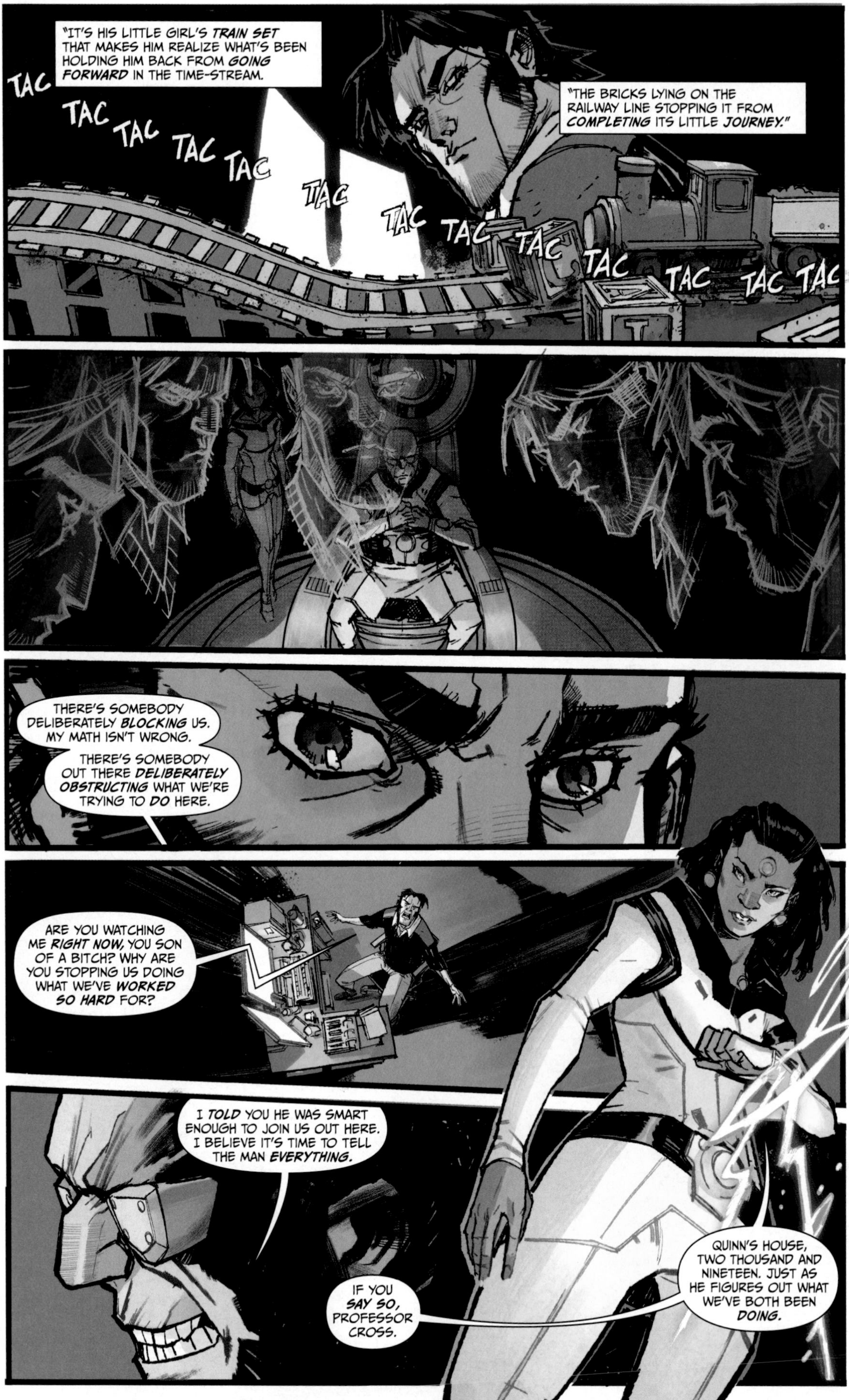
"IT'S HIS LITTLE GIRL'S TRAIN SET THAT MAKES HIM REALIZE WHAT'S BEEN HOLDING HIM BACK FROM GOING FORWARD IN THE TIME-STREAM.
TAC TAC TAC TAC TAC TAC TAC TAC TAC TAC TAC TAC TAC
"THE BRICKS LYING ON THE RAILWAY LINE STOPPING IT FROM COMPLETING ITS LITTLE JOURNEY."
THERE'S SOMEBODY DELIBERATELY BLOCKING US. MY MATH ISN'T WRONG.
THERE'S SOMEBODY OUT THERE DELIBERATELY OBSTRUCTING WHAT WE'RE TRYING TO DO HERE.
ARE YOU WATCHING ME RIGHT NOW, YOU SON OF A BITCH? WHY ARE YOU STOPPING US DOING WHAT WE'VE WORKED SO HARD FOR?
I TOLD YOU HE WAS SMART ENOUGH TO JOIN US OUT HERE. I BELIEVE IT'S TIME TO TELL THE MAN EVERYTHING.
IF YOU SAY SO, PROFESSOR CROSS.
QUINN'S HOUSE, TWO THOUSAND AND NINETEEN. JUST AS HE FIGURES OUT WHAT WE'VE BOTH BEEN DOING.

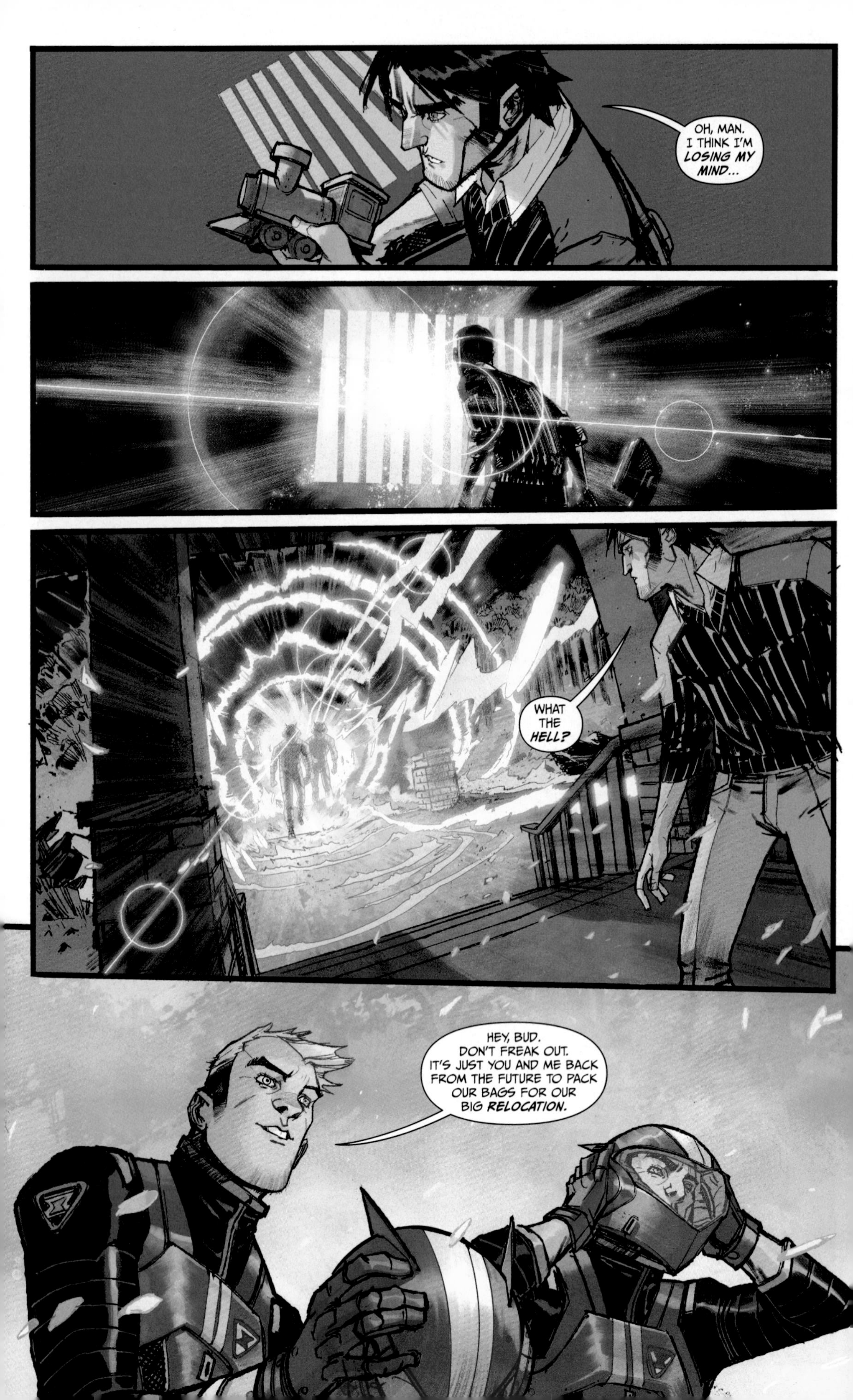
OH, MAN. I THINK I'M *LOSING MY MIND...*
WHAT THE *HELL?*
HEY, BUD. DON'T FREAK OUT. IT'S JUST YOU AND ME BACK FROM THE FUTURE TO PACK OUR BAGS FOR OUR BIG *RELOCATION.*

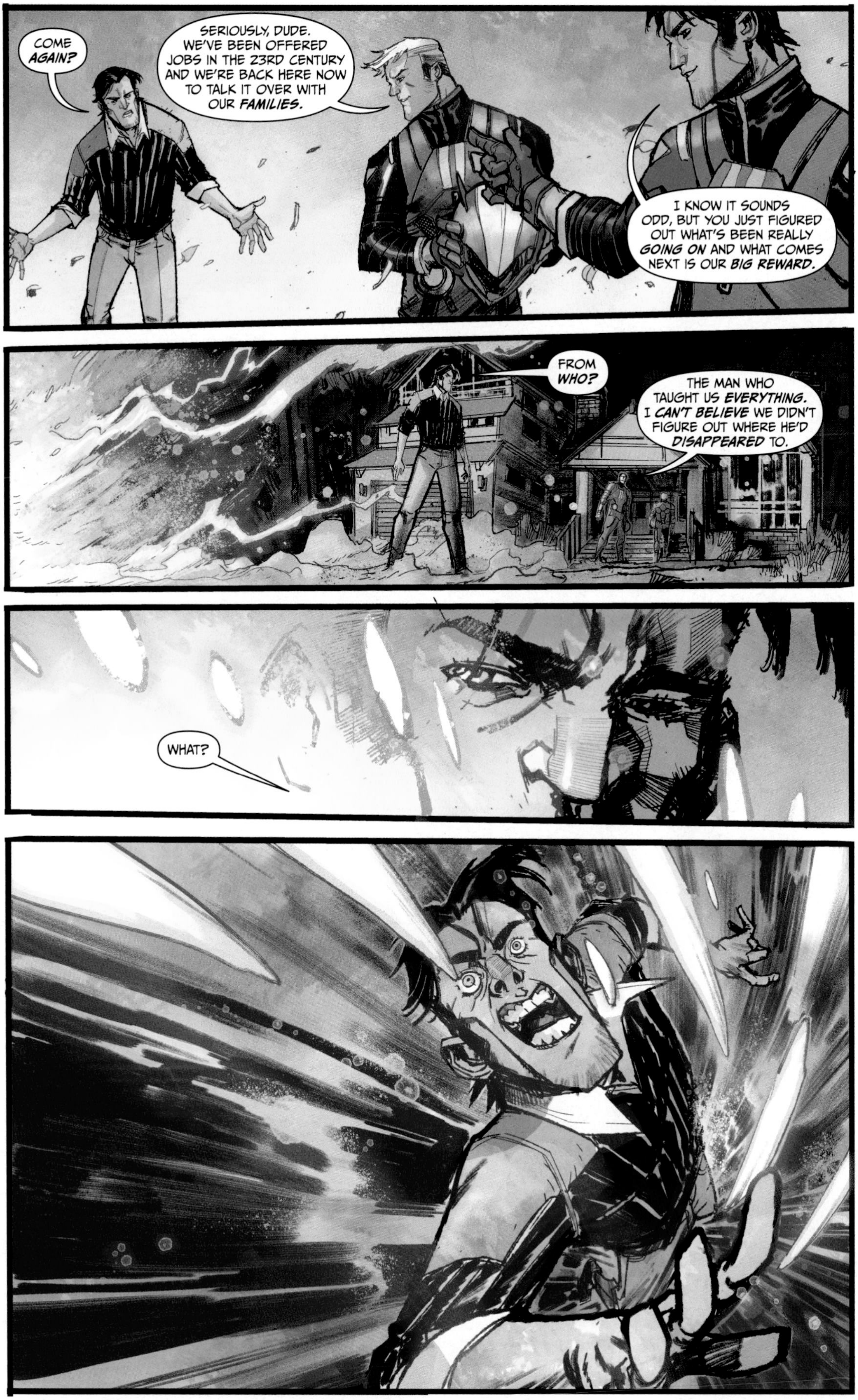
COME AGAIN?
SERIOUSLY, DUDE. WE'VE BEEN OFFERED JOBS IN THE 23RD CENTURY AND WE'RE BACK HERE NOW TO TALK IT OVER WITH OUR FAMILIES.
I KNOW IT SOUNDS ODD, BUT YOU JUST FIGURED OUT WHAT'S BEEN REALLY GOING ON AND WHAT COMES NEXT IS OUR BIG REWARD.
FROM WHO?
THE MAN WHO TAUGHT US EVERYTHING. I CAN'T BELIEVE WE DIDN'T FIGURE OUT WHERE HE'D DISAPPEARED TO.
WHAT?

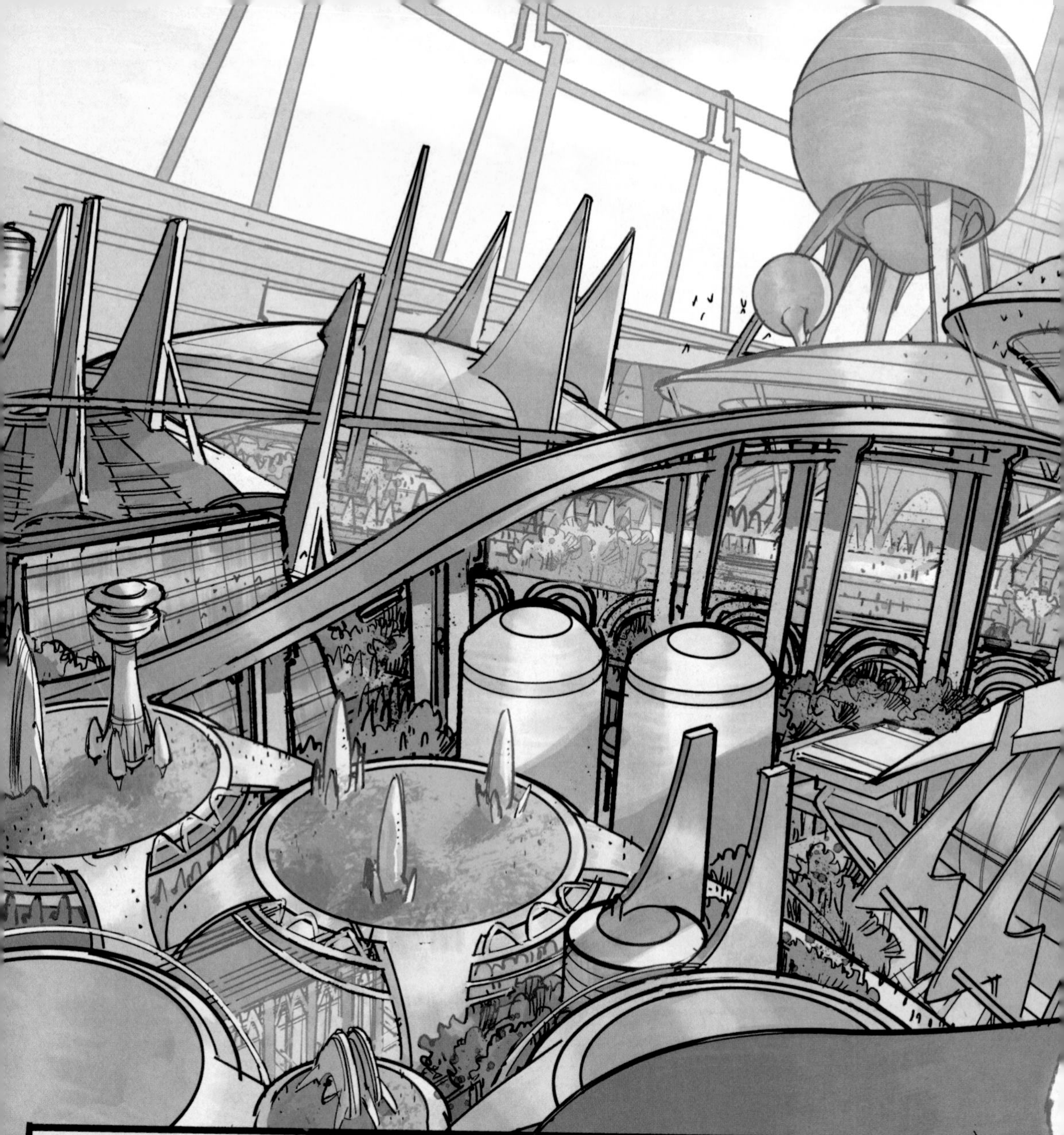

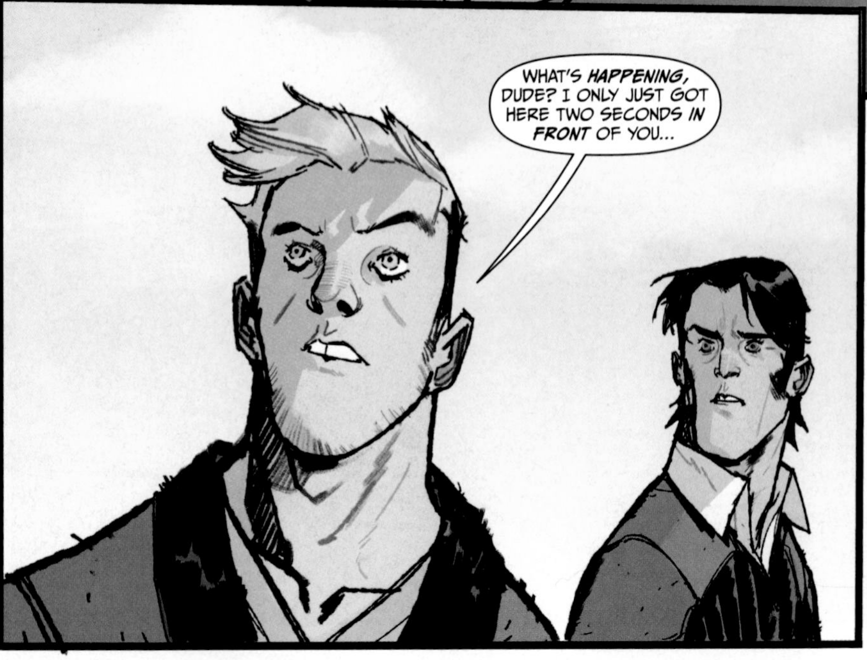
WHAT'S **HAPPENING**, DUDE? I ONLY JUST GOT HERE TWO SECONDS **IN FRONT** OF YOU...

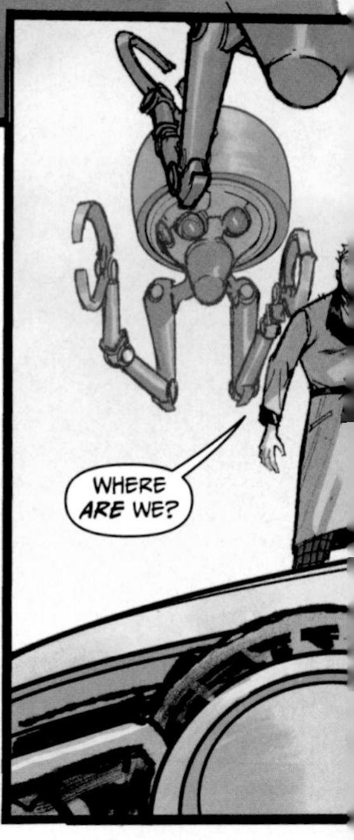
WHERE **ARE** WE?

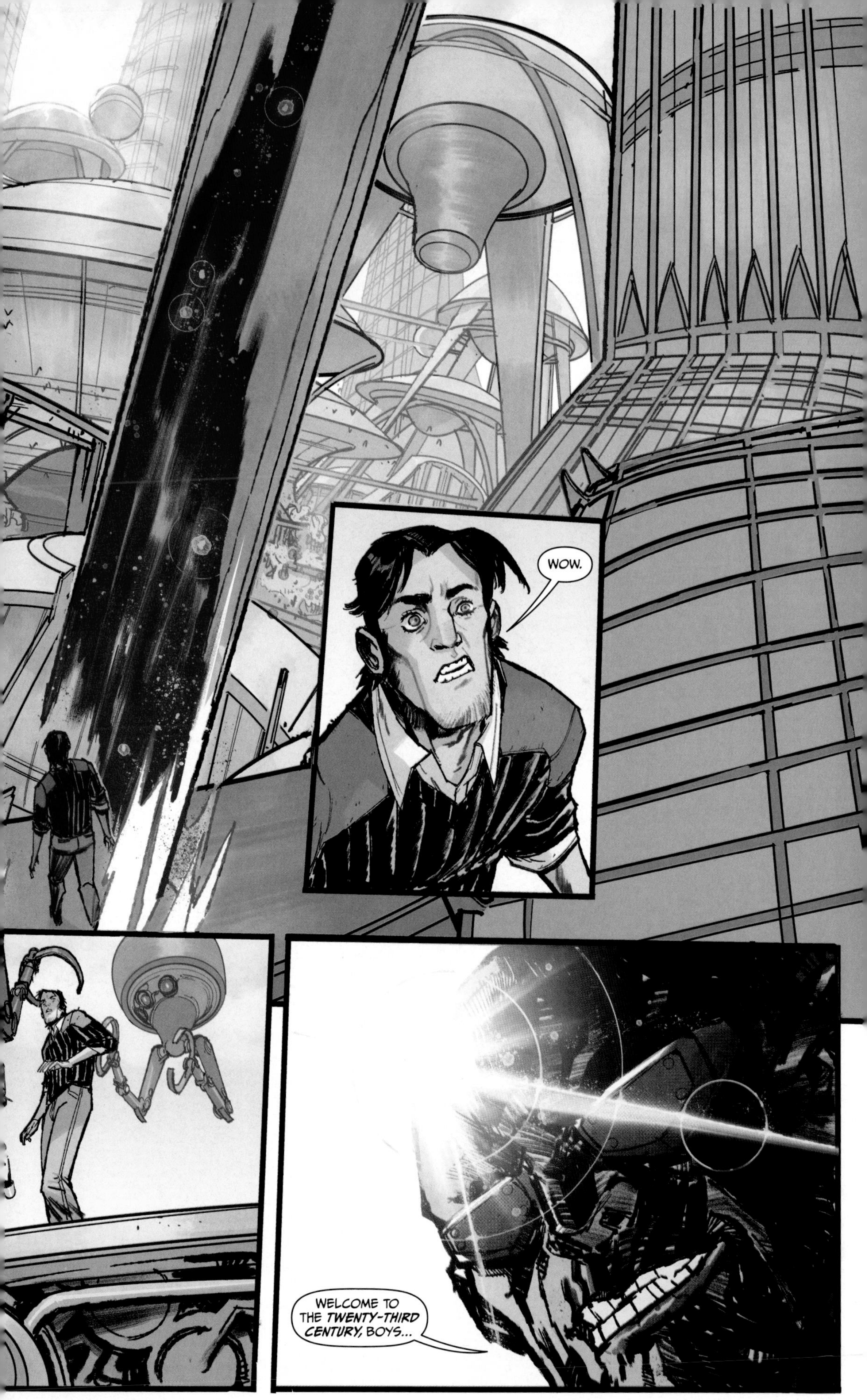
WOW.
WELCOME TO THE TWENTY-THIRD CENTURY, BOYS...

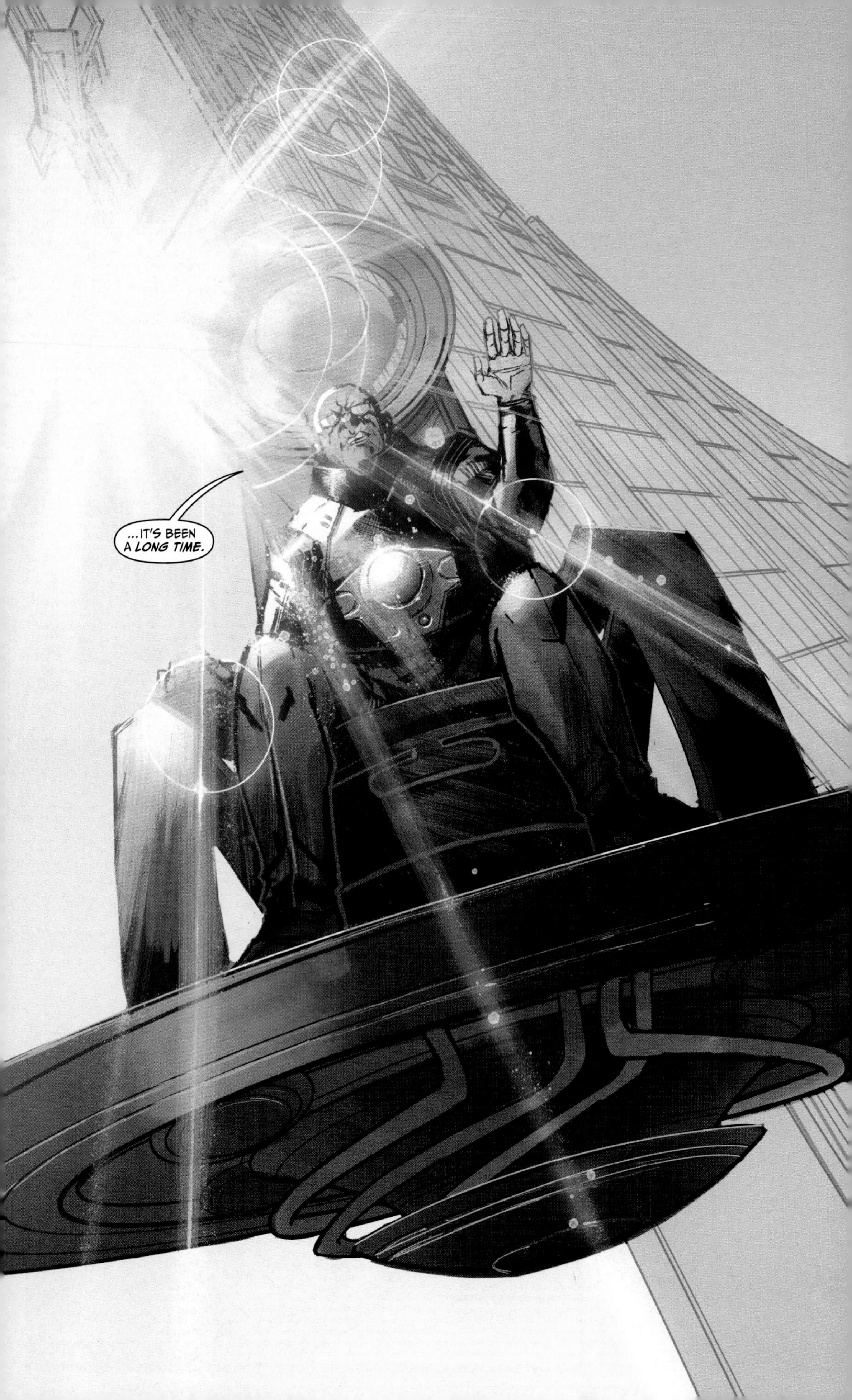
...IT'S BEEN A LONG TIME.

TWO

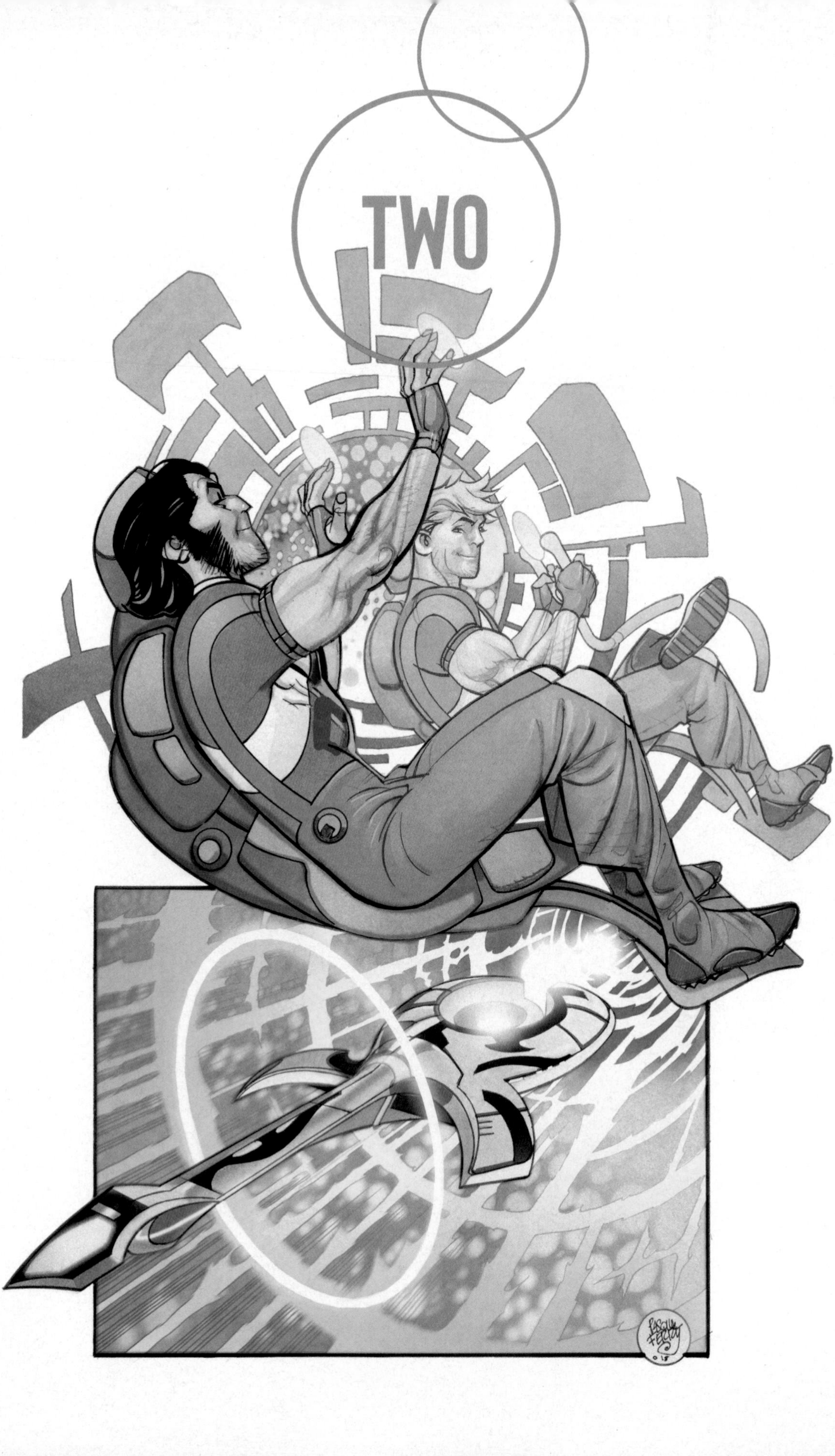

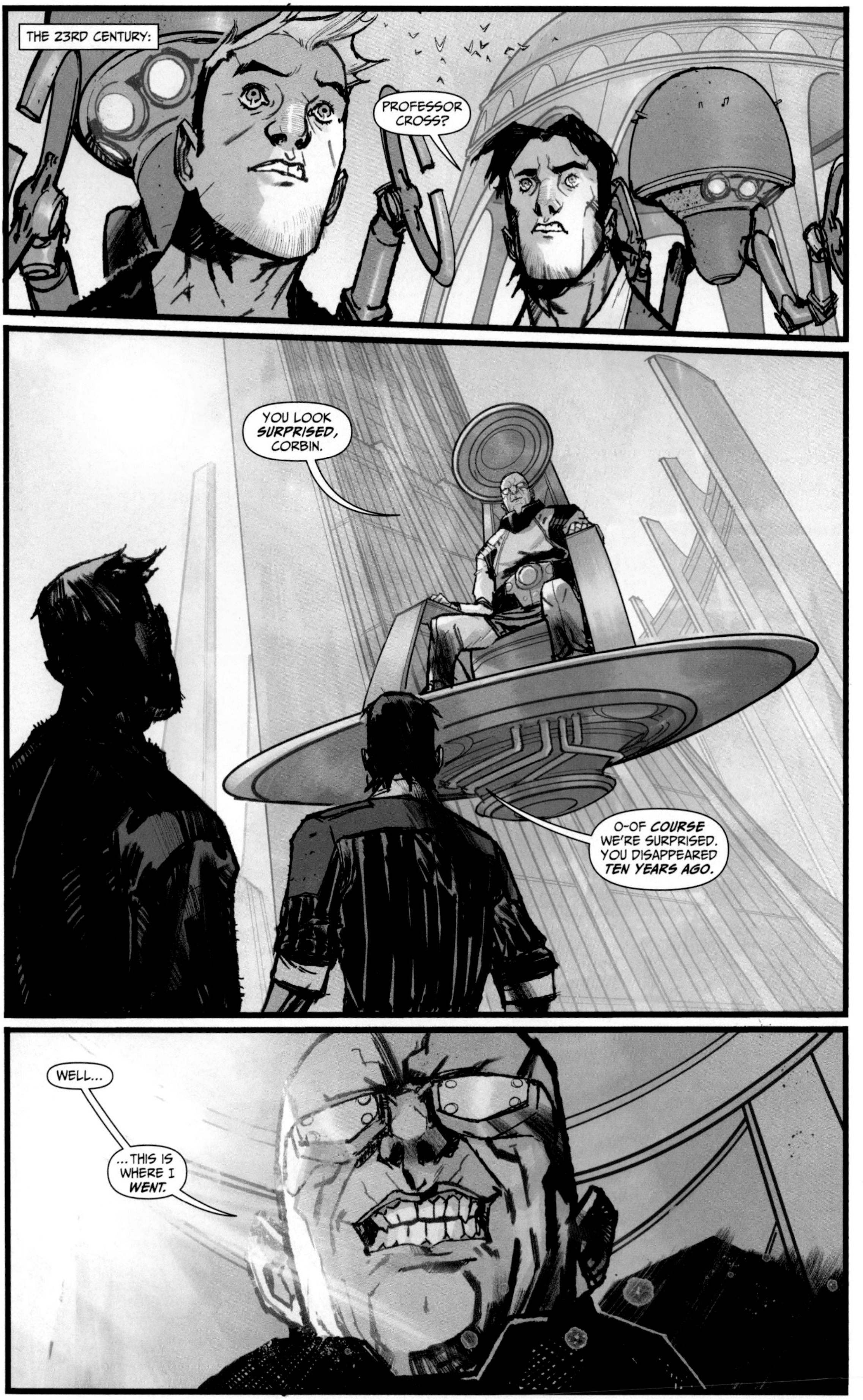
THE 23RD CENTURY:
PROFESSOR CROSS?
YOU LOOK SURPRISED, CORBIN.
O-OF COURSE WE'RE SURPRISED. YOU DISAPPEARED TEN YEARS AGO.
WELL...
...THIS IS WHERE I WENT.

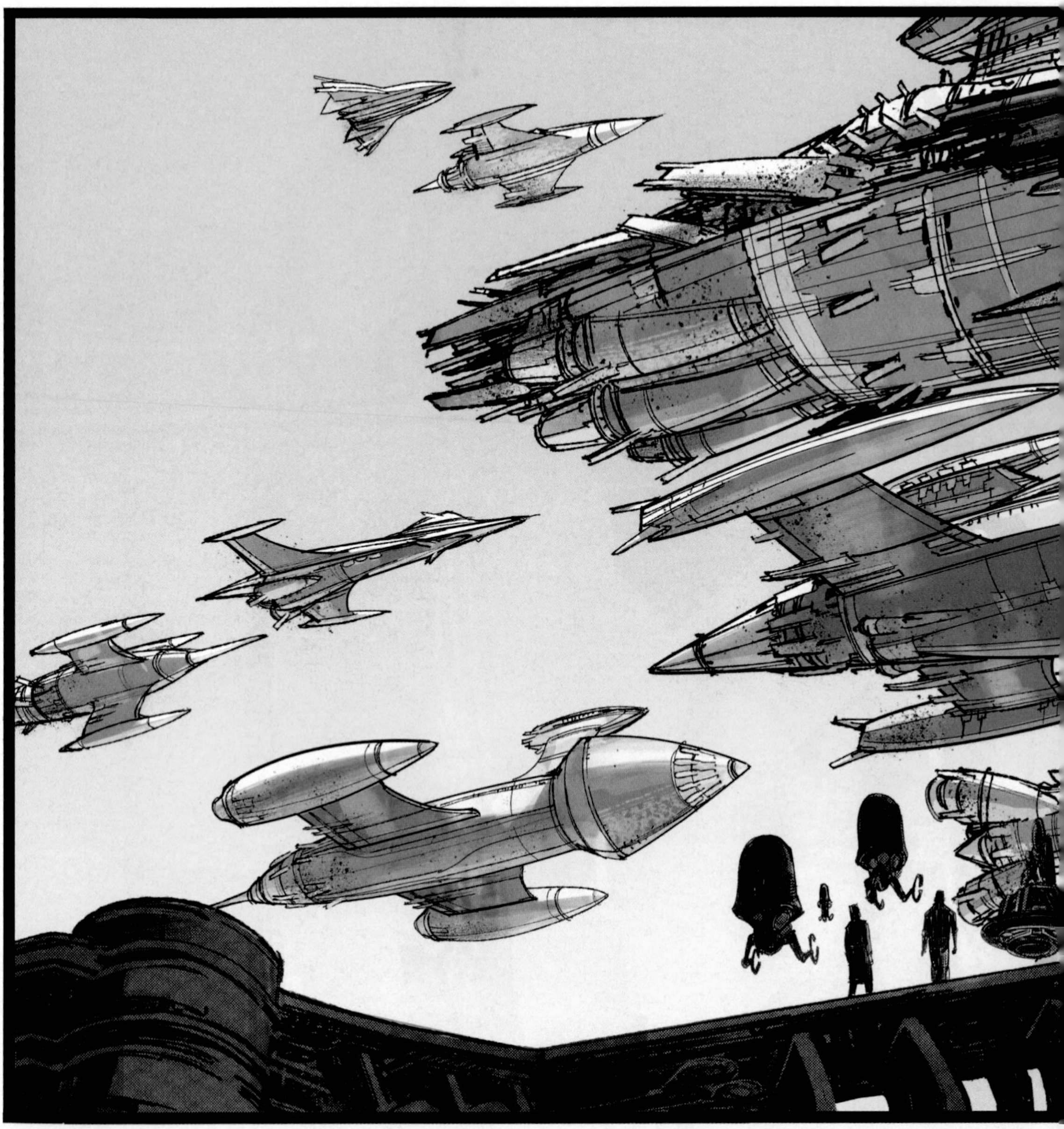

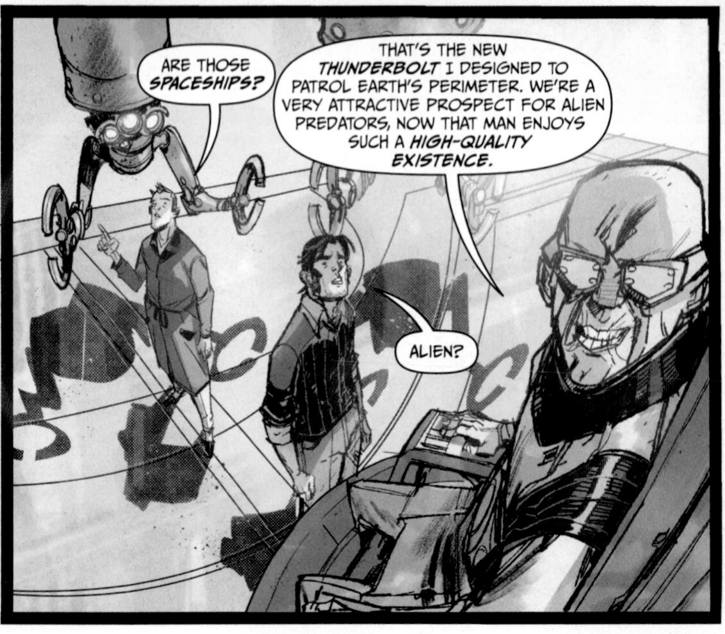
ARE THOSE *SPACESHIPS?*
THAT'S THE NEW *THUNDERBOLT* I DESIGNED TO PATROL EARTH'S PERIMETER. WE'RE A VERY ATTRACTIVE PROSPECT FOR ALIEN PREDATORS, NOW THAT MAN ENJOYS SUCH A *HIGH-QUALITY EXISTENCE.*
ALIEN?

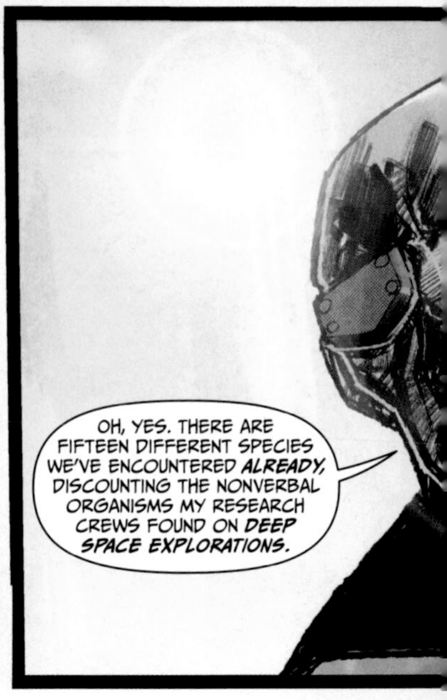
OH, YES. THERE ARE FIFTEEN DIFFERENT SPECIES WE'VE ENCOUNTERED *ALREADY,* DISCOUNTING THE NONVERBAL ORGANISMS MY RESEARCH CREWS FOUND ON *DEEP SPACE EXPLORATIONS.*

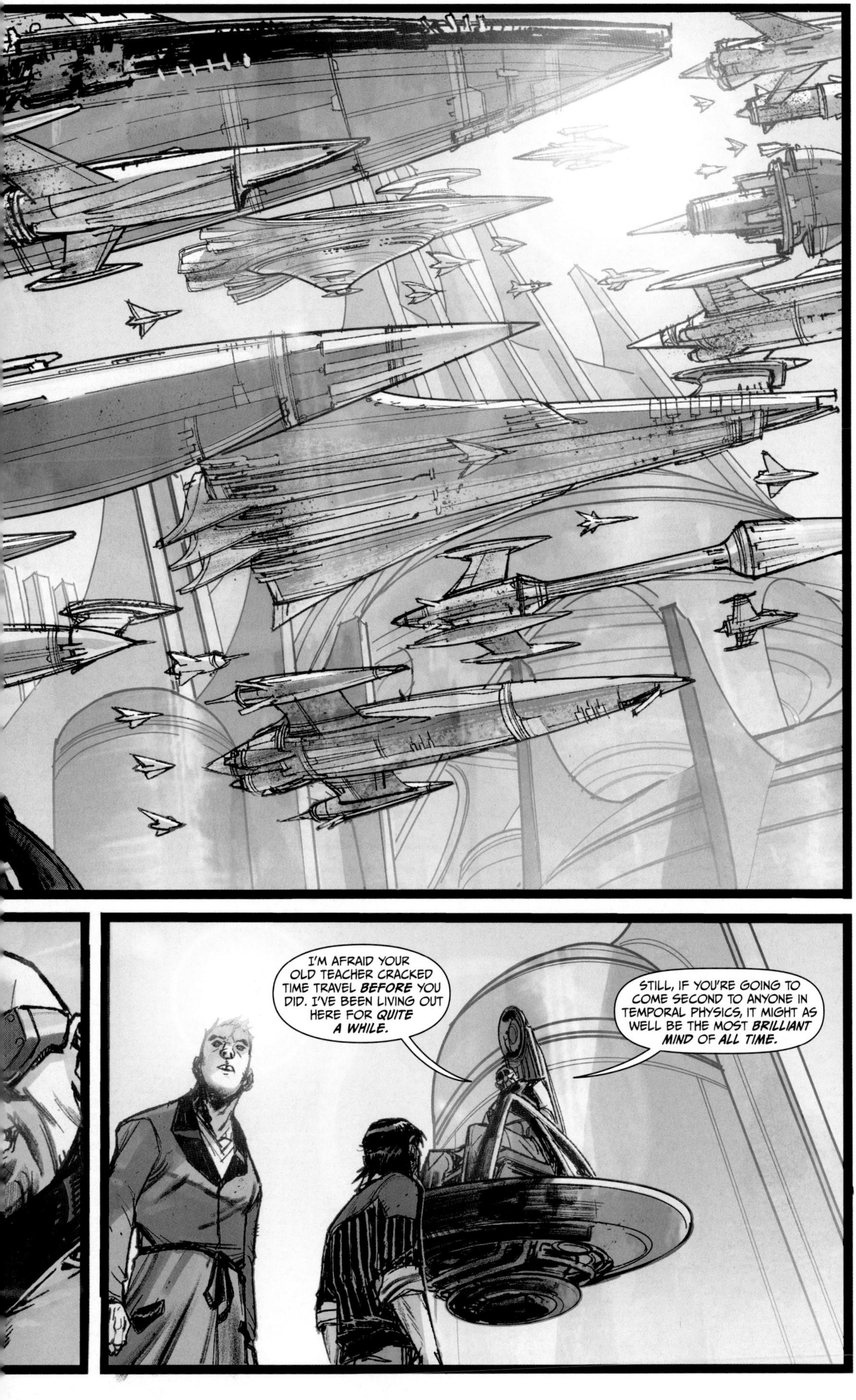
I'M AFRAID YOUR OLD TEACHER CRACKED TIME TRAVEL BEFORE YOU DID. I'VE BEEN LIVING OUT HERE FOR QUITE A WHILE.
STILL, IF YOU'RE GOING TO COME SECOND TO ANYONE IN TEMPORAL PHYSICS, IT MIGHT AS WELL BE THE MOST BRILLIANT MIND OF ALL TIME.

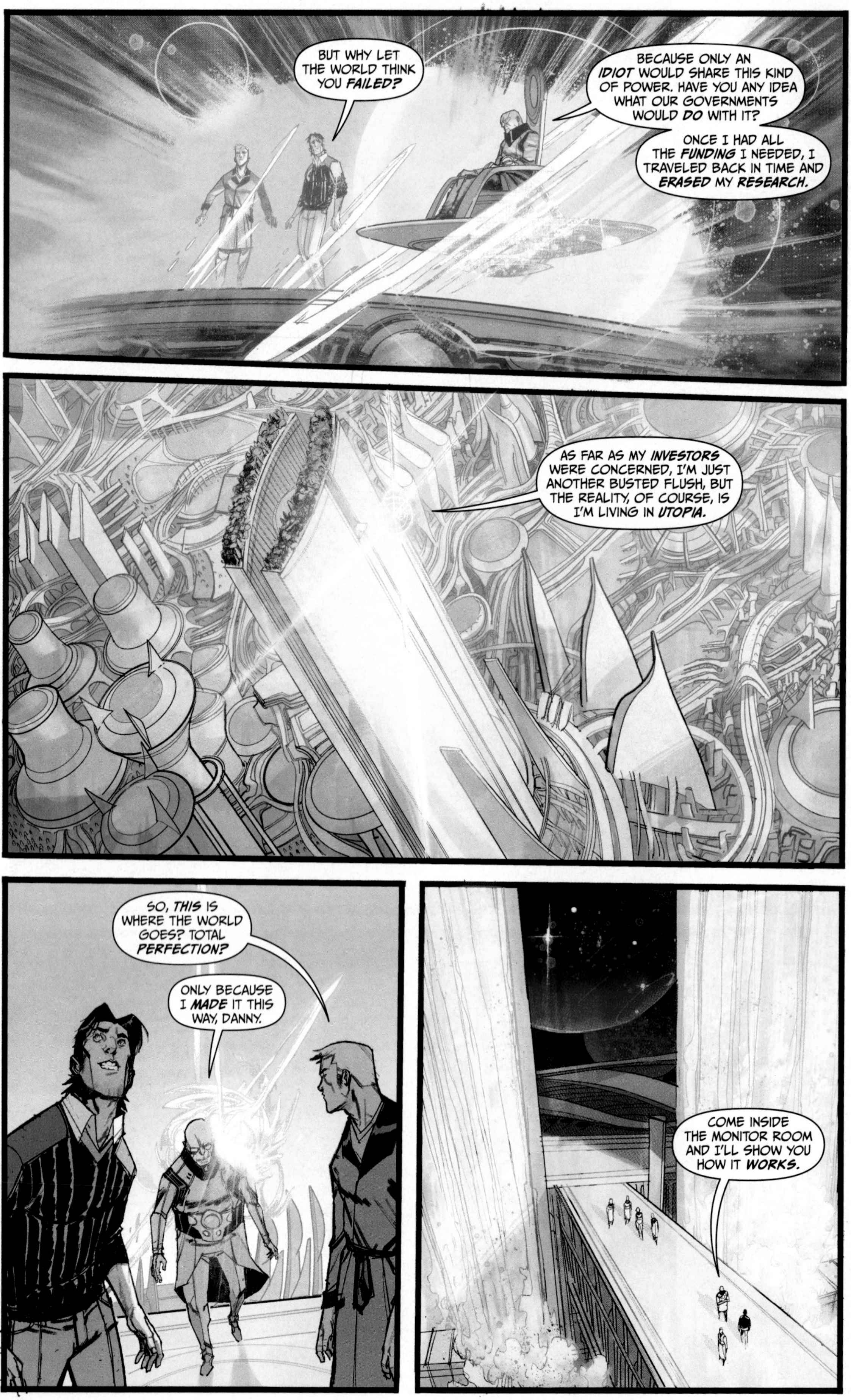

BUT WHY LET THE WORLD THINK YOU FAILED?
BECAUSE ONLY AN IDIOT WOULD SHARE THIS KIND OF POWER. HAVE YOU ANY IDEA WHAT OUR GOVERNMENTS WOULD DO WITH IT?
ONCE I HAD ALL THE FUNDING I NEEDED, I TRAVELED BACK IN TIME AND ERASED MY RESEARCH.
AS FAR AS MY INVESTORS WERE CONCERNED, I'M JUST ANOTHER BUSTED FLUSH, BUT THE REALITY, OF COURSE, IS I'M LIVING IN UTOPIA.
SO, THIS IS WHERE THE WORLD GOES? TOTAL PERFECTION?
ONLY BECAUSE I MADE IT THIS WAY, DANNY.
COME INSIDE THE MONITOR ROOM AND I'LL SHOW YOU HOW IT WORKS.

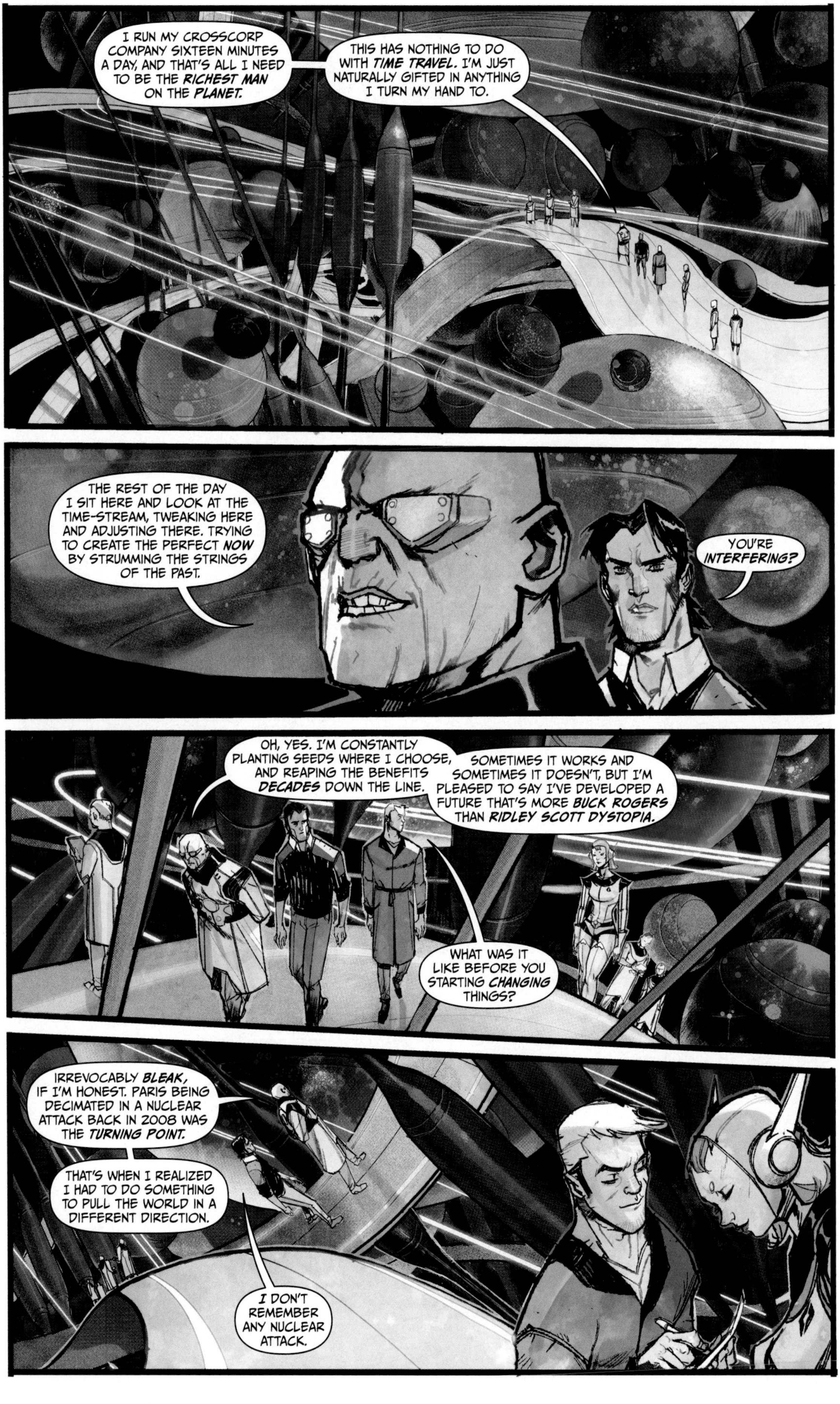
I RUN MY CROSSCORP COMPANY SIXTEEN MINUTES A DAY, AND THAT'S ALL I NEED TO BE THE ***RICHEST MAN*** ON THE ***PLANET.***
THIS HAS NOTHING TO DO WITH ***TIME TRAVEL.*** I'M JUST NATURALLY GIFTED IN ANYTHING I TURN MY HAND TO.
THE REST OF THE DAY I SIT HERE AND LOOK AT THE TIME-STREAM, TWEAKING HERE AND ADJUSTING THERE. TRYING TO CREATE THE PERFECT ***NOW*** BY STRUMMING THE STRINGS OF THE PAST.
YOU'RE ***INTERFERING?***
OH, YES. I'M CONSTANTLY PLANTING SEEDS WHERE I CHOOSE, AND REAPING THE BENEFITS ***DECADES*** DOWN THE LINE.
SOMETIMES IT WORKS AND SOMETIMES IT DOESN'T, BUT I'M PLEASED TO SAY I'VE DEVELOPED A FUTURE THAT'S MORE ***BUCK ROGERS*** THAN ***RIDLEY SCOTT DYSTOPIA.***
WHAT WAS IT LIKE BEFORE YOU STARTING ***CHANGING*** THINGS?
IRREVOCABLY ***BLEAK,*** IF I'M HONEST. PARIS BEING DECIMATED IN A NUCLEAR ATTACK BACK IN 2008 WAS THE ***TURNING POINT.***
THAT'S WHEN I REALIZED I HAD TO DO SOMETHING TO PULL THE WORLD IN A DIFFERENT DIRECTION.
I DON'T REMEMBER ANY NUCLEAR ATTACK.

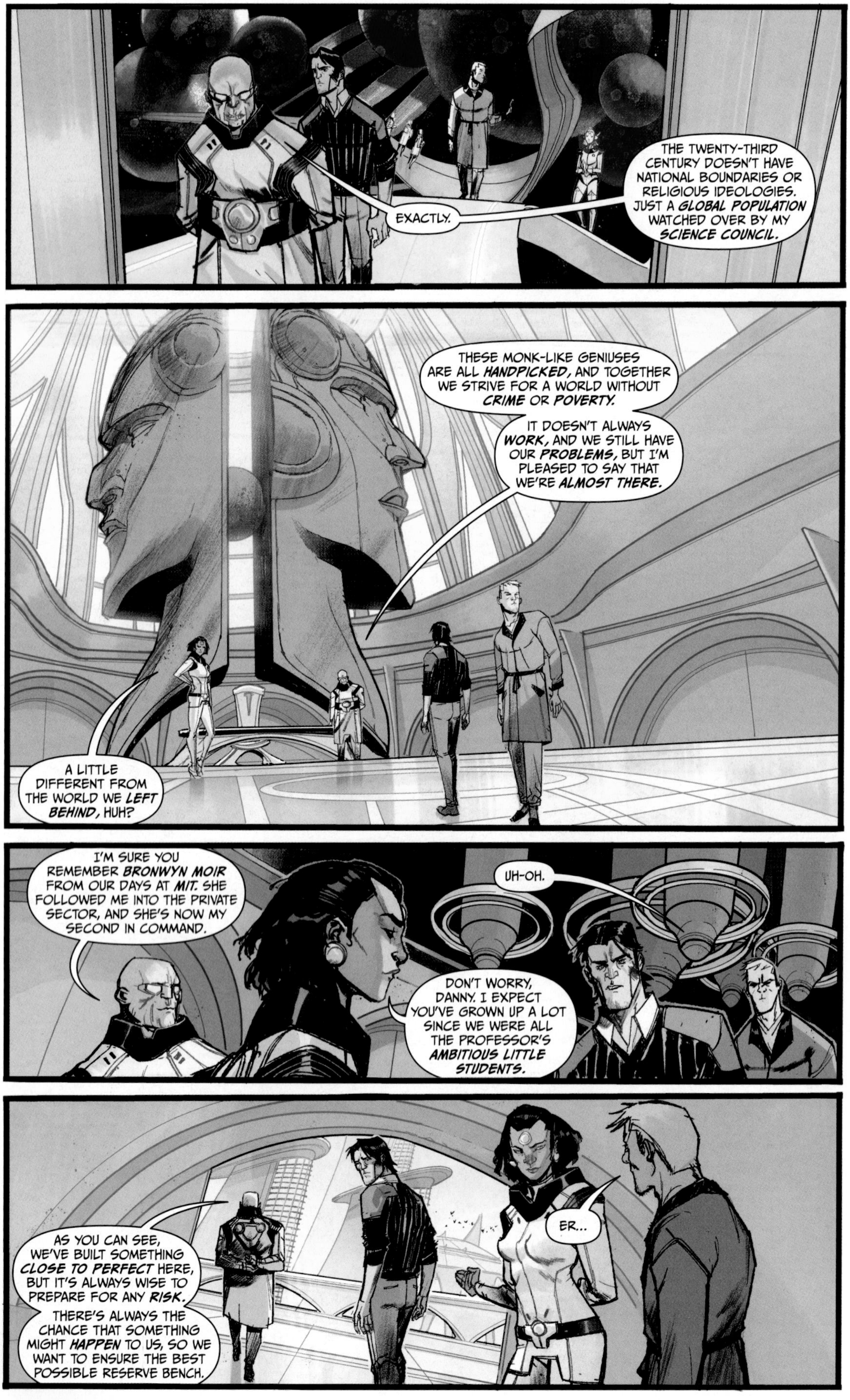
THE TWENTY-THIRD CENTURY DOESN'T HAVE NATIONAL BOUNDARIES OR RELIGIOUS IDEOLOGIES. JUST A GLOBAL POPULATION WATCHED OVER BY MY SCIENCE COUNCIL.
EXACTLY.
THESE MONK-LIKE GENIUSES ARE ALL HANDPICKED, AND TOGETHER WE STRIVE FOR A WORLD WITHOUT CRIME OR POVERTY.
IT DOESN'T ALWAYS WORK, AND WE STILL HAVE OUR PROBLEMS, BUT I'M PLEASED TO SAY THAT WE'RE ALMOST THERE.
A LITTLE DIFFERENT FROM THE WORLD WE LEFT BEHIND, HUH?
I'M SURE YOU REMEMBER BRONWYN MOIR FROM OUR DAYS AT MIT. SHE FOLLOWED ME INTO THE PRIVATE SECTOR, AND SHE'S NOW MY SECOND IN COMMAND.
UH-OH.
DON'T WORRY, DANNY. I EXPECT YOU'VE GROWN UP A LOT SINCE WE WERE ALL THE PROFESSOR'S AMBITIOUS LITTLE STUDENTS.
ER...
AS YOU CAN SEE, WE'VE BUILT SOMETHING CLOSE TO PERFECT HERE, BUT IT'S ALWAYS WISE TO PREPARE FOR ANY RISK.
THERE'S ALWAYS THE CHANCE THAT SOMETHING MIGHT HAPPEN TO US, SO WE WANT TO ENSURE THE BEST POSSIBLE RESERVE BENCH.

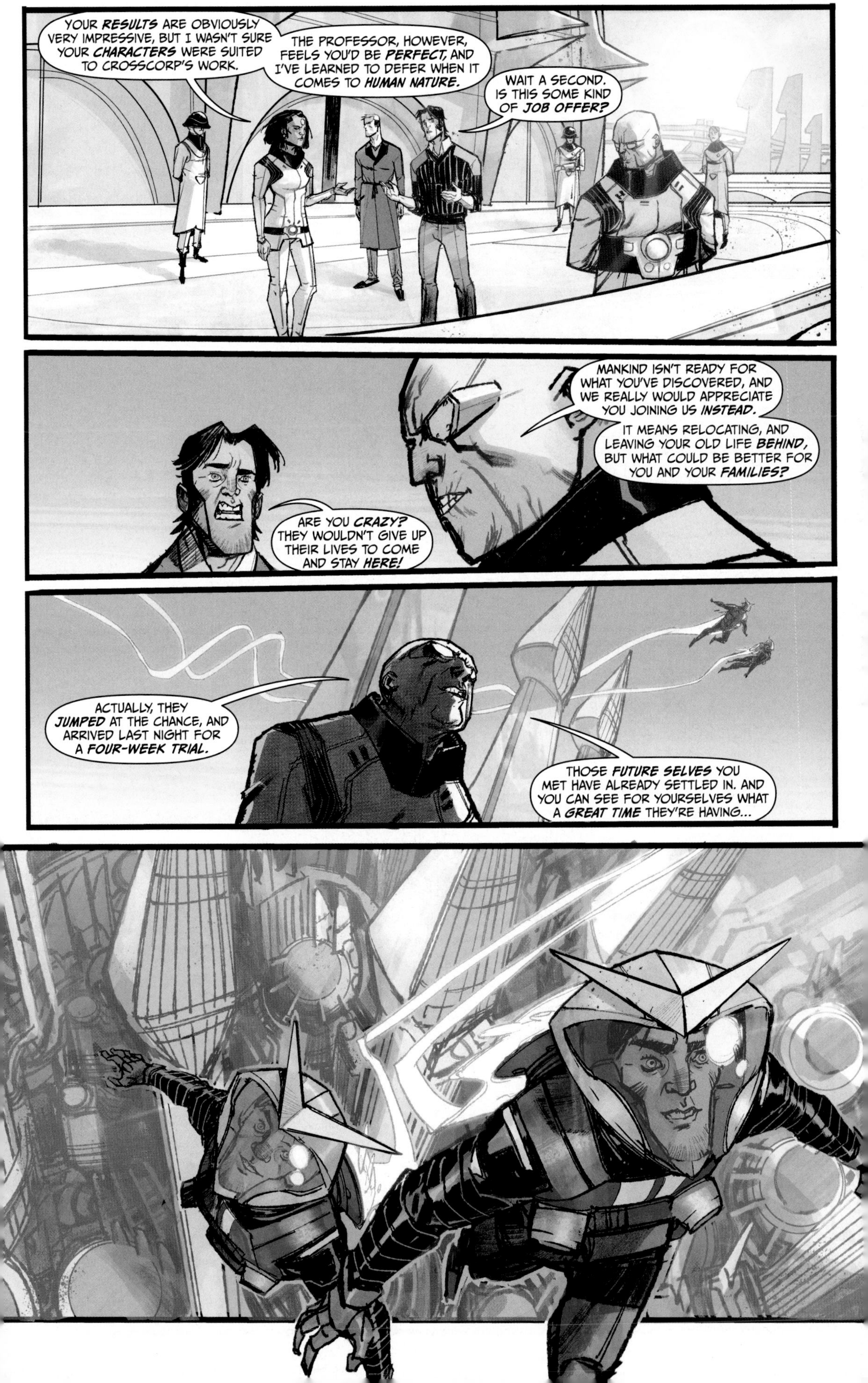
YOUR RESULTS ARE OBVIOUSLY VERY IMPRESSIVE, BUT I WASN'T SURE YOUR CHARACTERS WERE SUITED TO CROSSCORP'S WORK.
THE PROFESSOR, HOWEVER, FEELS YOU'D BE PERFECT, AND I'VE LEARNED TO DEFER WHEN IT COMES TO HUMAN NATURE.
WAIT A SECOND. IS THIS SOME KIND OF JOB OFFER?
MANKIND ISN'T READY FOR WHAT YOU'VE DISCOVERED, AND WE REALLY WOULD APPRECIATE YOU JOINING US INSTEAD.
IT MEANS RELOCATING, AND LEAVING YOUR OLD LIFE BEHIND, BUT WHAT COULD BE BETTER FOR YOU AND YOUR FAMILIES?
ARE YOU CRAZY? THEY WOULDN'T GIVE UP THEIR LIVES TO COME AND STAY HERE!
ACTUALLY, THEY JUMPED AT THE CHANCE, AND ARRIVED LAST NIGHT FOR A FOUR-WEEK TRIAL.
THOSE FUTURE SELVES YOU MET HAVE ALREADY SETTLED IN. AND YOU CAN SEE FOR YOURSELVES WHAT A GREAT TIME THEY'RE HAVING...

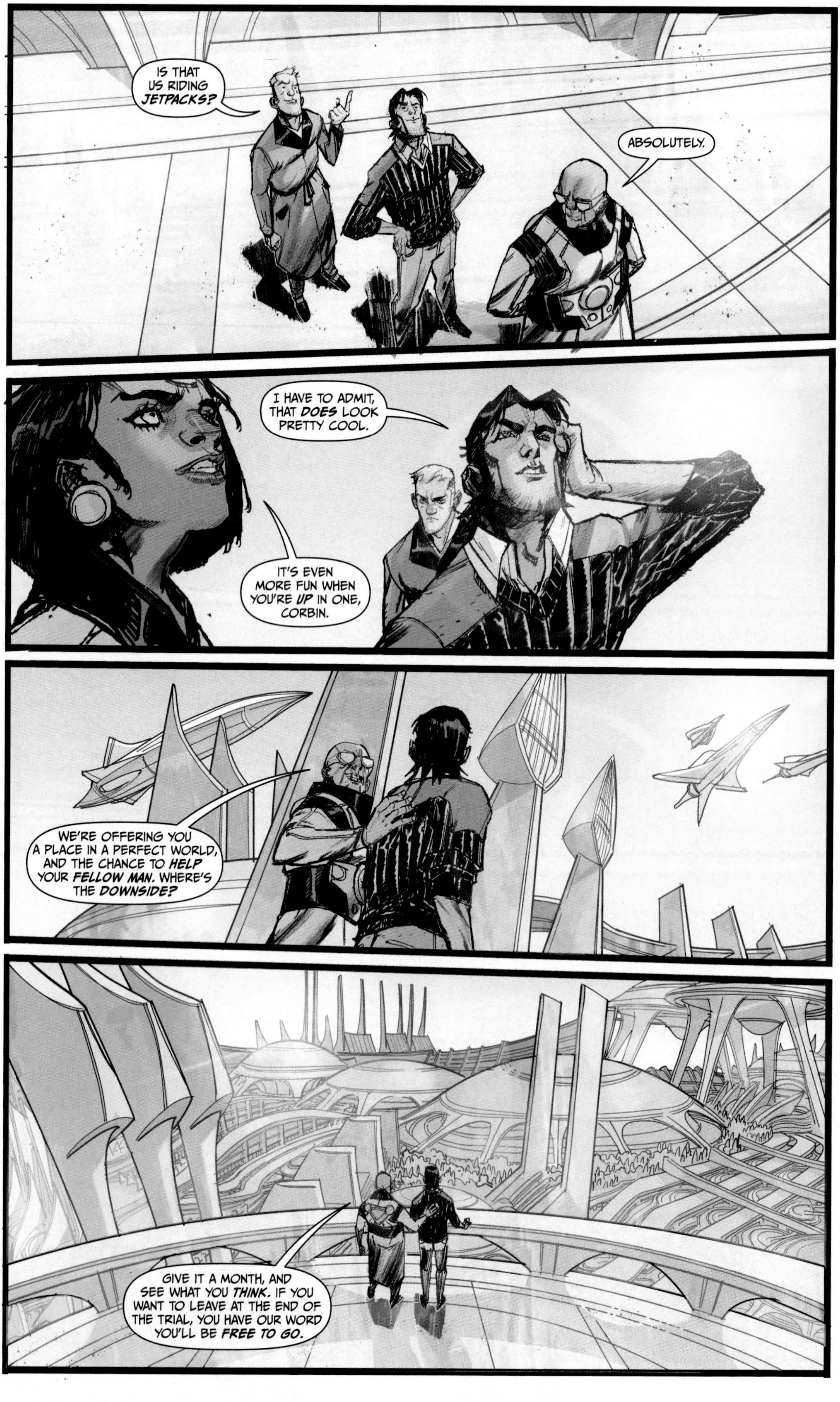
IS THAT US RIDING JETPACKS?
ABSOLUTELY.
I HAVE TO ADMIT, THAT DOES LOOK PRETTY COOL.
IT'S EVEN MORE FUN WHEN YOU'RE UP IN ONE, CORBIN.
WE'RE OFFERING YOU A PLACE IN A PERFECT WORLD, AND THE CHANCE TO HELP YOUR FELLOW MAN. WHERE'S THE DOWNSIDE?
GIVE IT A MONTH, AND SEE WHAT YOU THINK. IF YOU WANT TO LEAVE AT THE END OF THE TRIAL, YOU HAVE OUR WORD YOU'LL BE FREE TO GO.

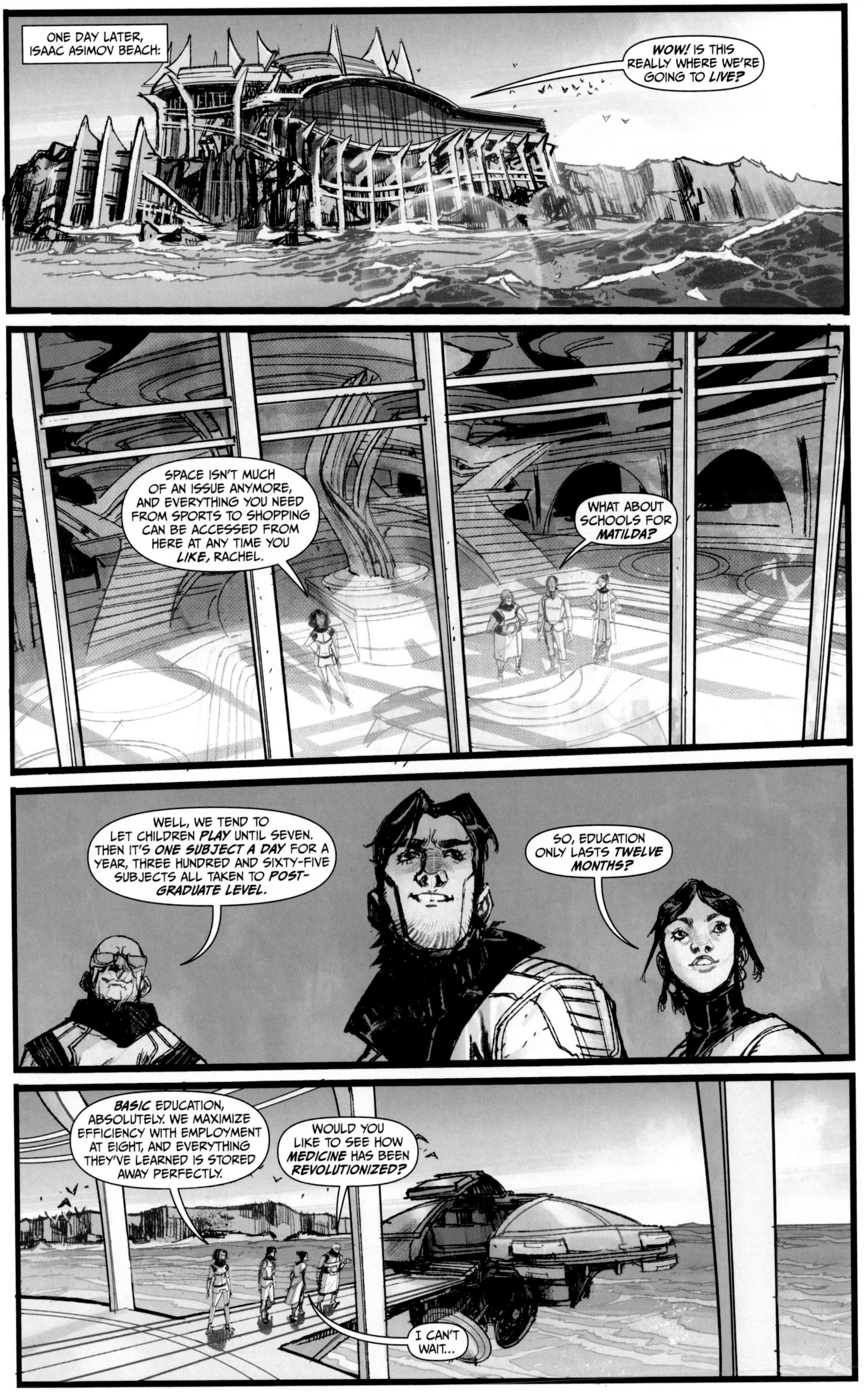
ONE DAY LATER, ISAAC ASIMOV BEACH:
WOW! IS THIS REALLY WHERE WE'RE GOING TO LIVE?
SPACE ISN'T MUCH OF AN ISSUE ANYMORE, AND EVERYTHING YOU NEED FROM SPORTS TO SHOPPING CAN BE ACCESSED FROM HERE AT ANY TIME YOU LIKE, RACHEL.
WHAT ABOUT SCHOOLS FOR MATILDA?
WELL, WE TEND TO LET CHILDREN PLAY UNTIL SEVEN. THEN IT'S ONE SUBJECT A DAY FOR A YEAR, THREE HUNDRED AND SIXTY-FIVE SUBJECTS ALL TAKEN TO POST-GRADUATE LEVEL.
SO, EDUCATION ONLY LASTS TWELVE MONTHS?
BASIC EDUCATION, ABSOLUTELY. WE MAXIMIZE EFFICIENCY WITH EMPLOYMENT AT EIGHT, AND EVERYTHING THEY'VE LEARNED IS STORED AWAY PERFECTLY.
WOULD YOU LIKE TO SEE HOW MEDICINE HAS BEEN REVOLUTIONIZED?
I CAN'T WAIT...

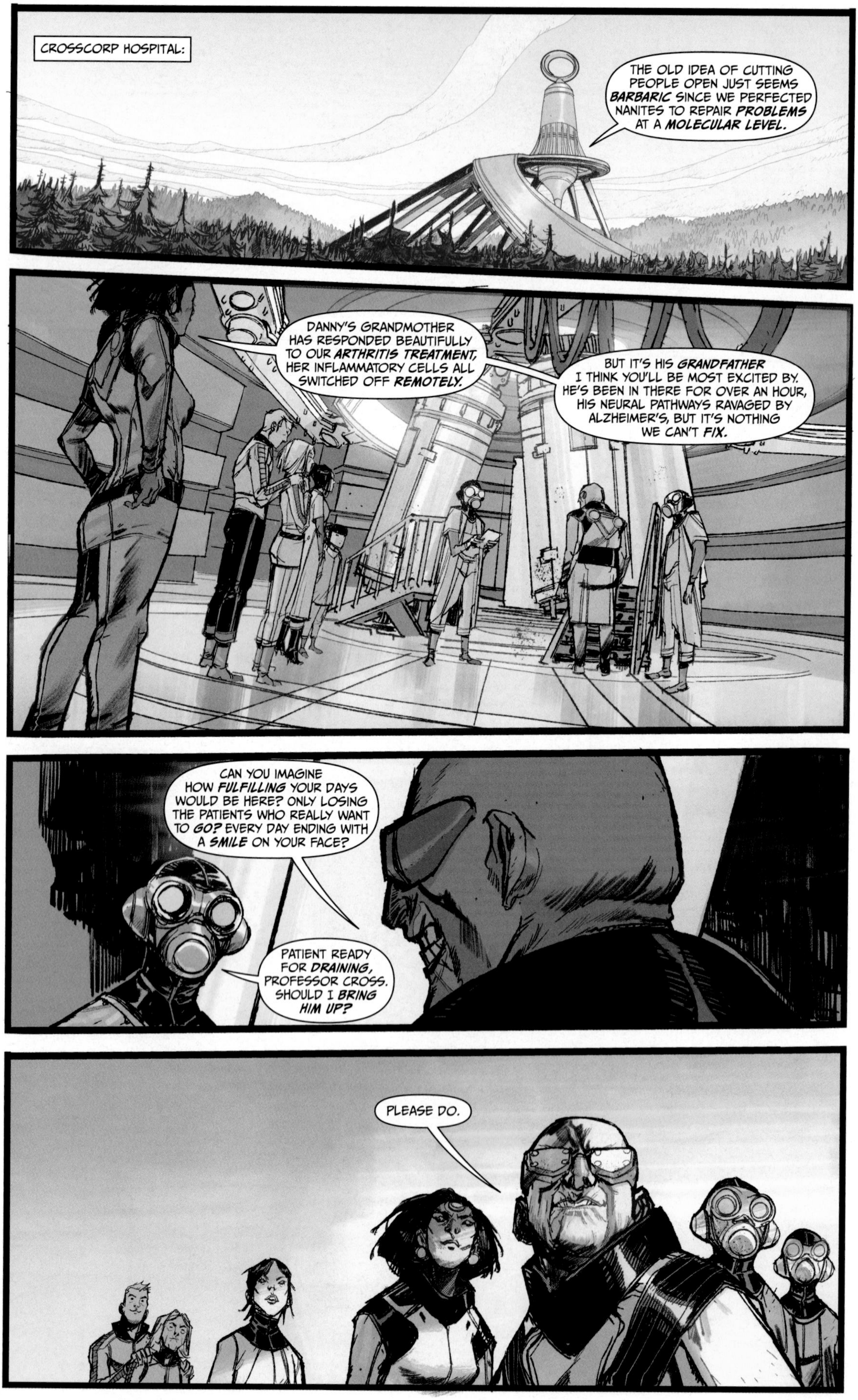
CROSSCORP HOSPITAL:
THE OLD IDEA OF CUTTING PEOPLE OPEN JUST SEEMS BARBARIC SINCE WE PERFECTED NANITES TO REPAIR PROBLEMS AT A MOLECULAR LEVEL.
DANNY'S GRANDMOTHER HAS RESPONDED BEAUTIFULLY TO OUR ARTHRITIS TREATMENT, HER INFLAMMATORY CELLS ALL SWITCHED OFF REMOTELY.
BUT IT'S HIS GRANDFATHER I THINK YOU'LL BE MOST EXCITED BY. HE'S BEEN IN THERE FOR OVER AN HOUR, HIS NEURAL PATHWAYS RAVAGED BY ALZHEIMER'S, BUT IT'S NOTHING WE CAN'T FIX.
CAN YOU IMAGINE HOW FULFILLING YOUR DAYS WOULD BE HERE? ONLY LOSING THE PATIENTS WHO REALLY WANT TO GO? EVERY DAY ENDING WITH A SMILE ON YOUR FACE?
PATIENT READY FOR DRAINING, PROFESSOR CROSS. SHOULD I BRING HIM UP?
PLEASE DO.

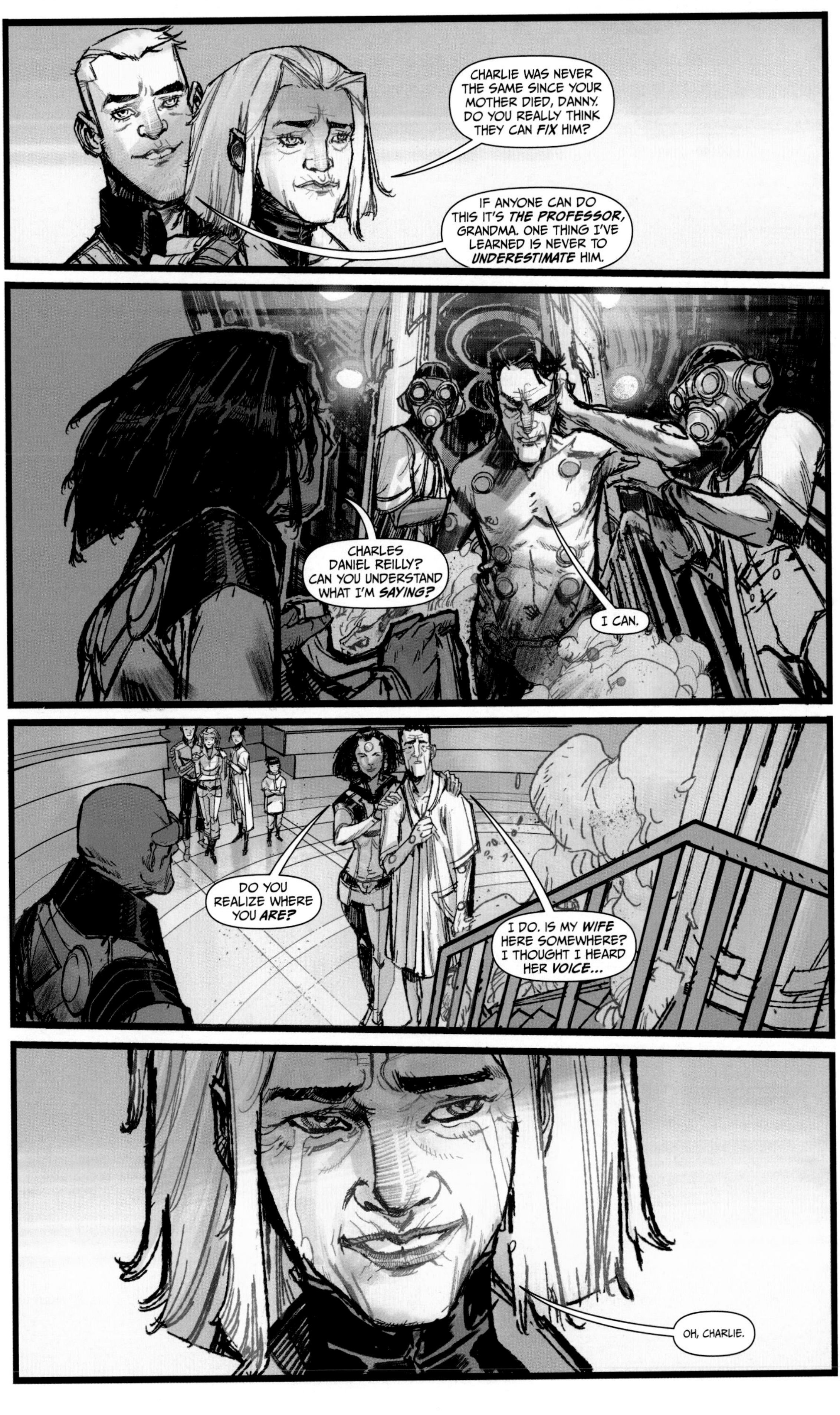
CHARLIE WAS NEVER THE SAME SINCE YOUR MOTHER DIED, DANNY. DO YOU REALLY THINK THEY CAN FIX HIM?
IF ANYONE CAN DO THIS IT'S THE PROFESSOR, GRANDMA. ONE THING I'VE LEARNED IS NEVER TO UNDERESTIMATE HIM.
CHARLES DANIEL REILLY? CAN YOU UNDERSTAND WHAT I'M SAYING?
I CAN.
DO YOU REALIZE WHERE YOU ARE?
I DO. IS MY WIFE HERE SOMEWHERE? I THOUGHT I HEARD HER VOICE...
OH, CHARLIE.

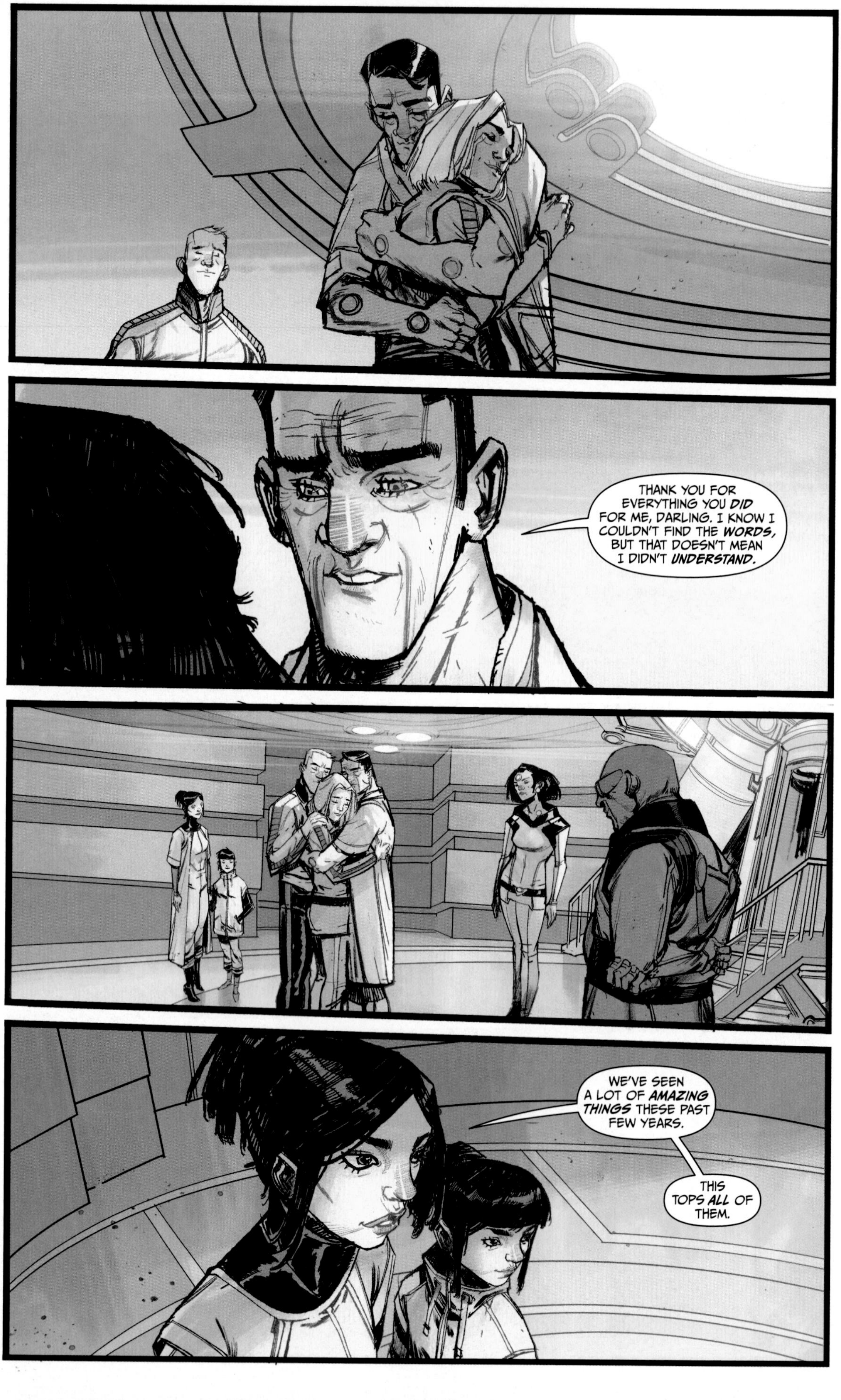
THANK YOU FOR EVERYTHING YOU *DID* FOR ME, DARLING. I KNOW I COULDN'T FIND THE *WORDS*, BUT THAT DOESN'T MEAN I DIDN'T *UNDERSTAND.*
WE'VE SEEN A LOT OF *AMAZING THINGS* THESE PAST FEW YEARS.
THIS TOPS *ALL* OF THEM.

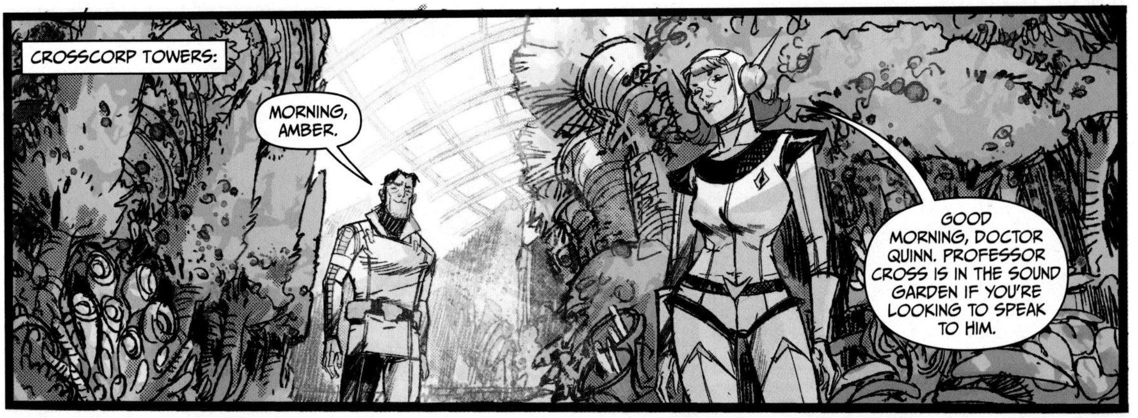
CROSSCORP TOWERS:
MORNING, AMBER.
GOOD MORNING, DOCTOR QUINN. PROFESSOR CROSS IS IN THE SOUND GARDEN IF YOU'RE LOOKING TO SPEAK TO HIM.

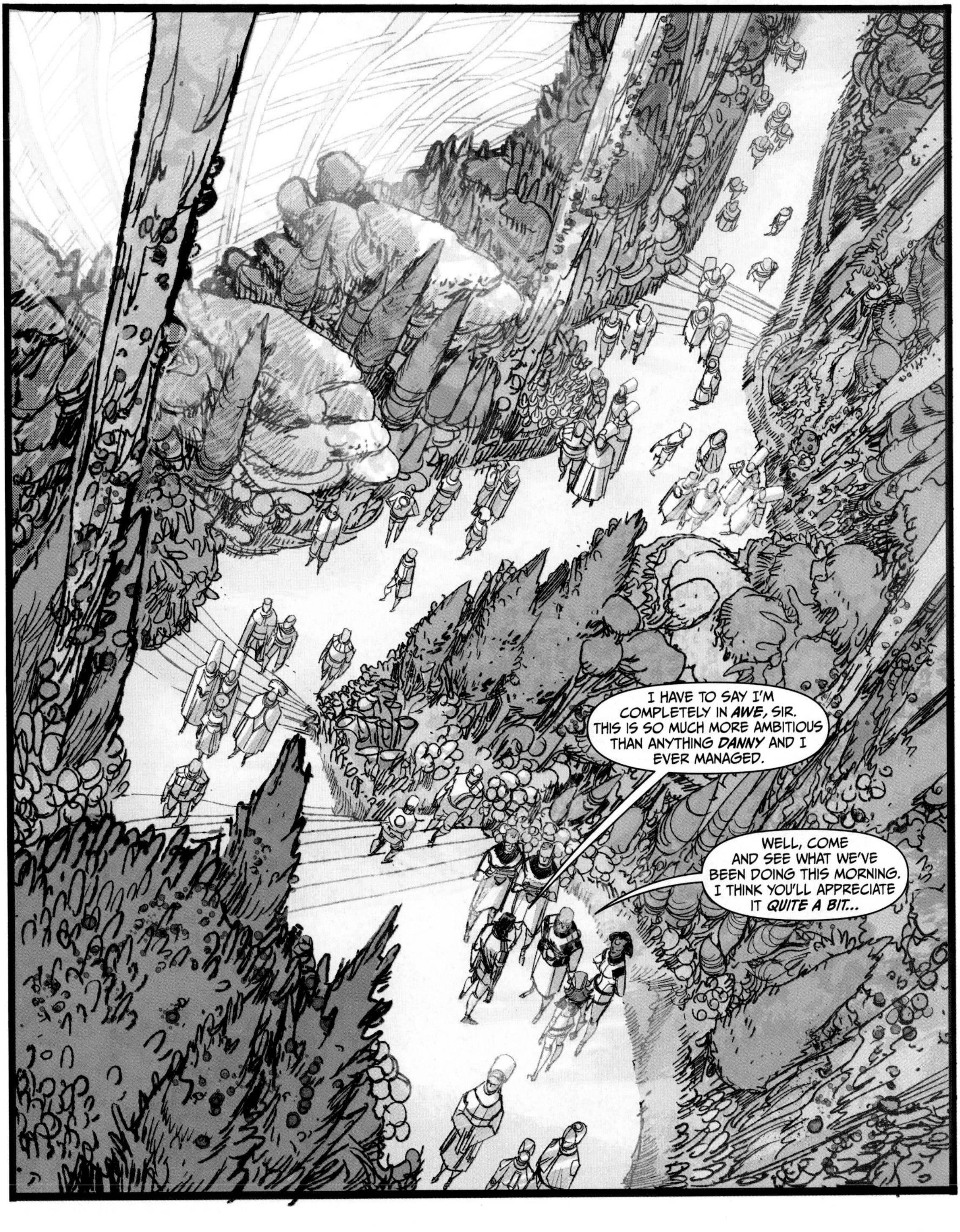
I HAVE TO SAY I'M COMPLETELY IN AWE, SIR. THIS IS SO MUCH MORE AMBITIOUS THAN ANYTHING DANNY AND I EVER MANAGED.
WELL, COME AND SEE WHAT WE'VE BEEN DOING THIS MORNING. I THINK YOU'LL APPRECIATE IT QUITE A BIT...

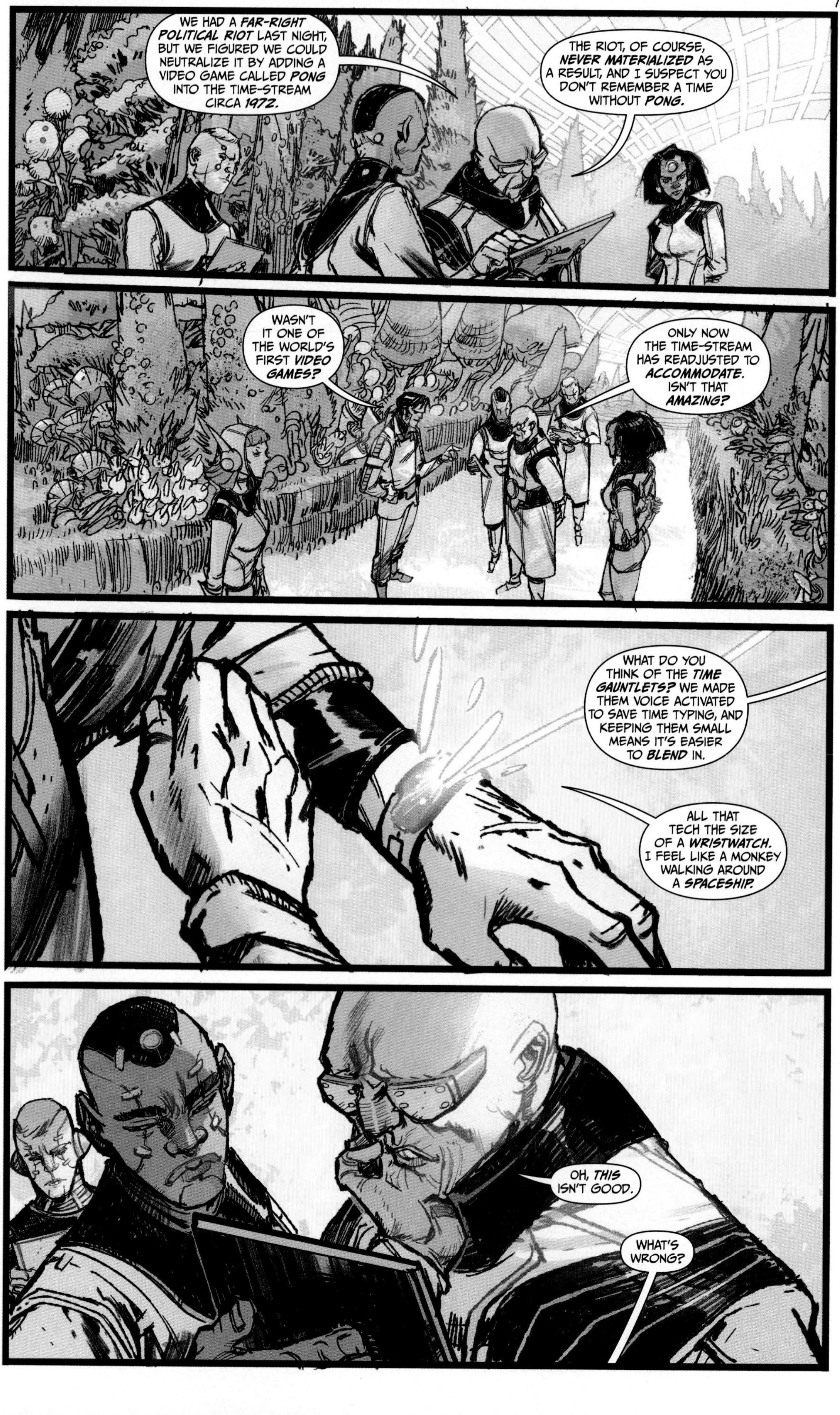

WE HAD A FAR-RIGHT POLITICAL RIOT LAST NIGHT, BUT WE FIGURED WE COULD NEUTRALIZE IT BY ADDING A VIDEO GAME CALLED PONG INTO THE TIME-STREAM CIRCA 1972.
THE RIOT, OF COURSE, NEVER MATERIALIZED AS A RESULT, AND I SUSPECT YOU DON'T REMEMBER A TIME WITHOUT PONG.
WASN'T IT ONE OF THE WORLD'S FIRST VIDEO GAMES?
ONLY NOW THE TIME-STREAM HAS READJUSTED TO ACCOMMODATE. ISN'T THAT AMAZING?
WHAT DO YOU THINK OF THE TIME GAUNTLETS? WE MADE THEM VOICE ACTIVATED TO SAVE TIME TYPING, AND KEEPING THEM SMALL MEANS IT'S EASIER TO BLEND IN.
ALL THAT TECH THE SIZE OF A WRISTWATCH. I FEEL LIKE A MONKEY WALKING AROUND A SPACESHIP.
OH, THIS ISN'T GOOD.
WHAT'S WRONG?

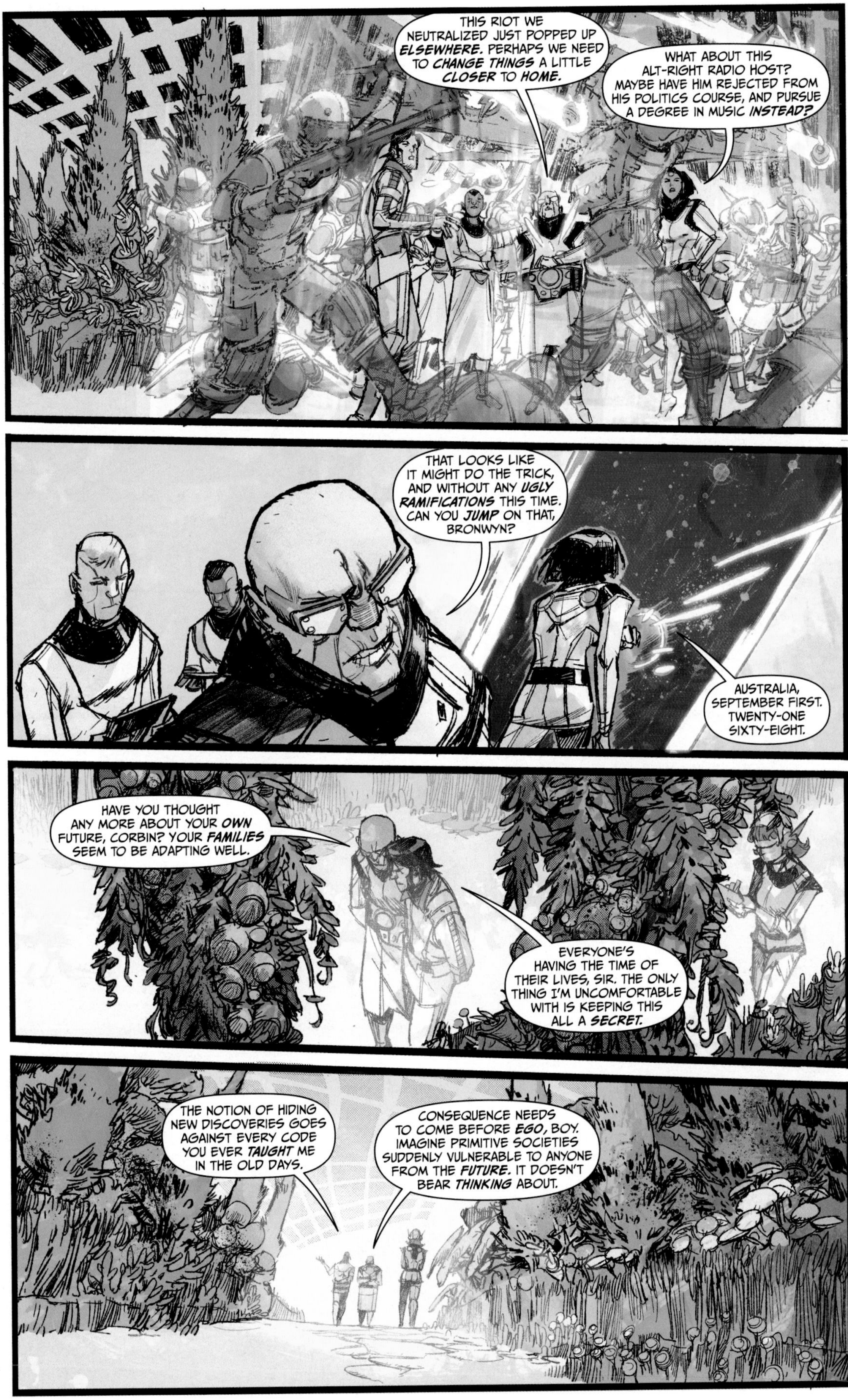
THIS RIOT WE NEUTRALIZED JUST POPPED UP ELSEWHERE. PERHAPS WE NEED TO CHANGE THINGS A LITTLE CLOSER TO HOME.
WHAT ABOUT THIS ALT-RIGHT RADIO HOST? MAYBE HAVE HIM REJECTED FROM HIS POLITICS COURSE, AND PURSUE A DEGREE IN MUSIC INSTEAD?
THAT LOOKS LIKE IT MIGHT DO THE TRICK, AND WITHOUT ANY UGLY RAMIFICATIONS THIS TIME. CAN YOU JUMP ON THAT, BRONWYN?
AUSTRALIA, SEPTEMBER FIRST. TWENTY-ONE SIXTY-EIGHT.
HAVE YOU THOUGHT ANY MORE ABOUT YOUR OWN FUTURE, CORBIN? YOUR FAMILIES SEEM TO BE ADAPTING WELL.
EVERYONE'S HAVING THE TIME OF THEIR LIVES, SIR. THE ONLY THING I'M UNCOMFORTABLE WITH IS KEEPING THIS ALL A SECRET.
THE NOTION OF HIDING NEW DISCOVERIES GOES AGAINST EVERY CODE YOU EVER TAUGHT ME IN THE OLD DAYS.
CONSEQUENCE NEEDS TO COME BEFORE EGO, BOY. IMAGINE PRIMITIVE SOCIETIES SUDDENLY VULNERABLE TO ANYONE FROM THE FUTURE. IT DOESN'T BEAR THINKING ABOUT.

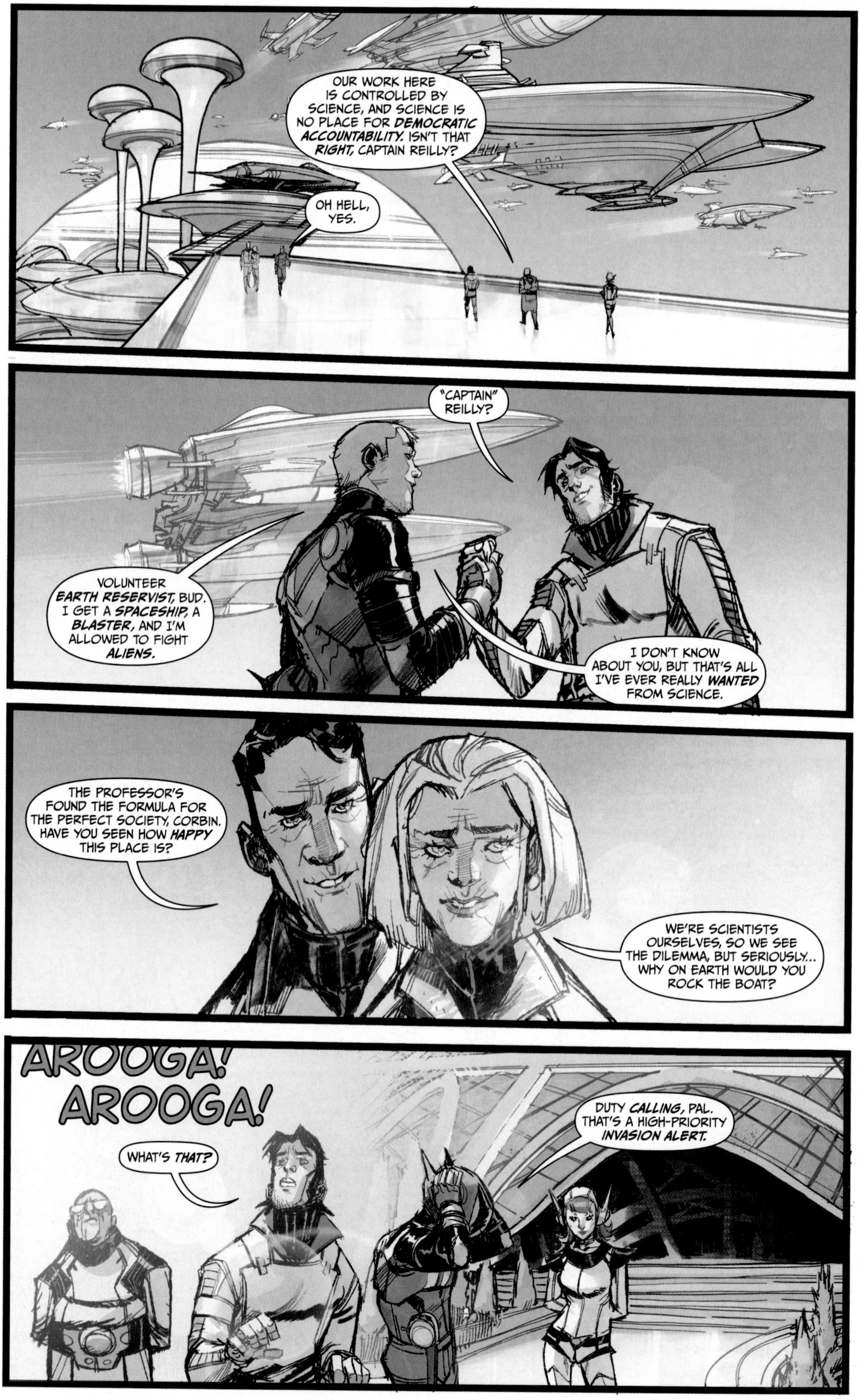
OUR WORK HERE IS CONTROLLED BY SCIENCE, AND SCIENCE IS NO PLACE FOR DEMOCRATIC ACCOUNTABILITY. ISN'T THAT RIGHT, CAPTAIN REILLY?
OH HELL, YES.
"CAPTAIN" REILLY?
VOLUNTEER EARTH RESERVIST, BUD. I GET A SPACESHIP, A BLASTER, AND I'M ALLOWED TO FIGHT ALIENS.
I DON'T KNOW ABOUT YOU, BUT THAT'S ALL I'VE EVER REALLY WANTED FROM SCIENCE.
THE PROFESSOR'S FOUND THE FORMULA FOR THE PERFECT SOCIETY, CORBIN. HAVE YOU SEEN HOW HAPPY THIS PLACE IS?
WE'RE SCIENTISTS OURSELVES, SO WE SEE THE DILEMMA, BUT SERIOUSLY... WHY ON EARTH WOULD YOU ROCK THE BOAT?
AROOGA! AROOGA!
WHAT'S THAT?
DUTY CALLING, PAL. THAT'S A HIGH-PRIORITY INVASION ALERT.

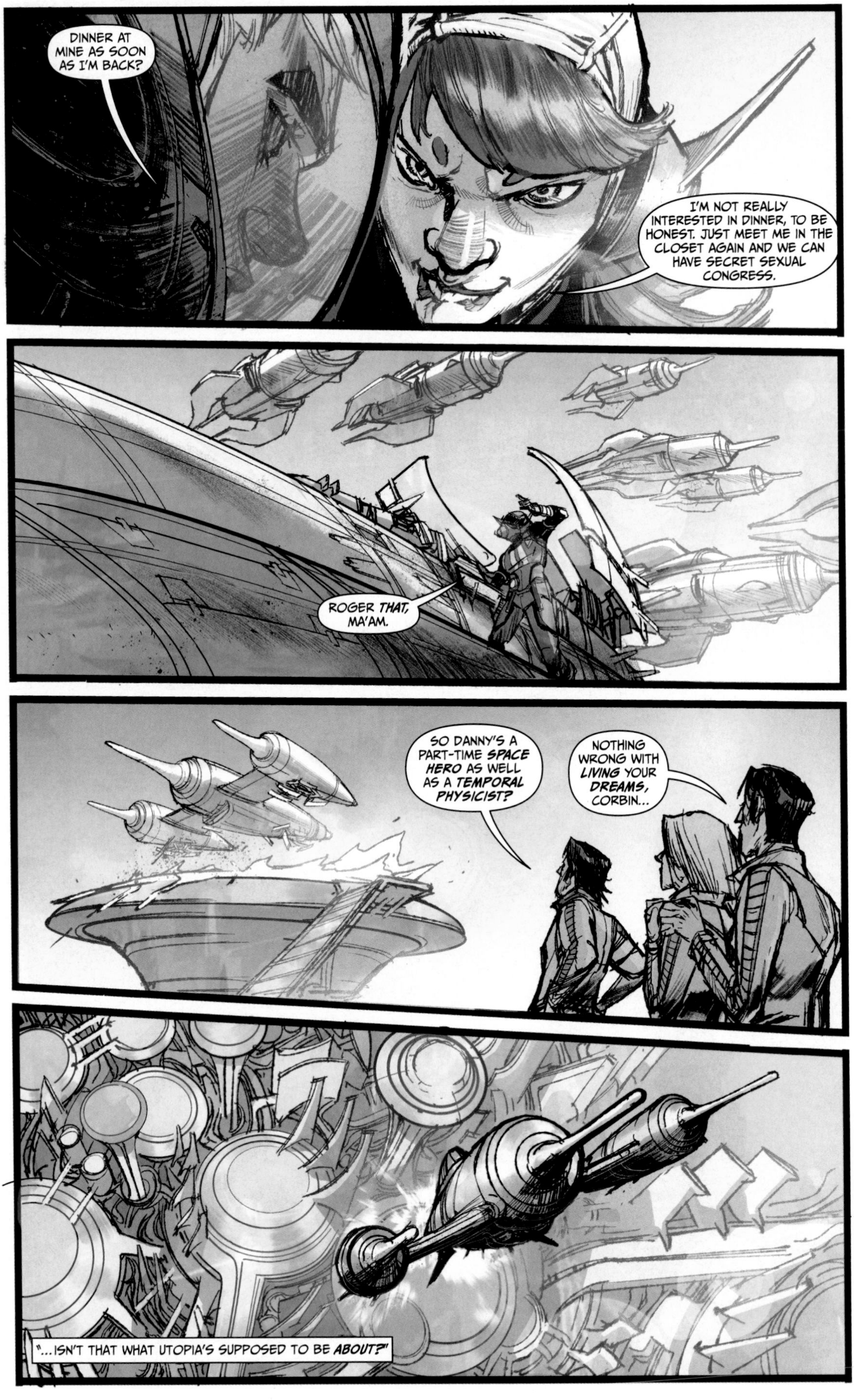
DINNER AT MINE AS SOON AS I'M BACK?
I'M NOT REALLY INTERESTED IN DINNER, TO BE HONEST. JUST MEET ME IN THE CLOSET AGAIN AND WE CAN HAVE SECRET SEXUAL CONGRESS.
ROGER THAT, MA'AM.
SO DANNY'S A PART-TIME SPACE HERO AS WELL AS A TEMPORAL PHYSICIST?
NOTHING WRONG WITH LIVING YOUR DREAMS, CORBIN...
"...ISN'T THAT WHAT UTOPIA'S SUPPOSED TO BE ABOUT?"

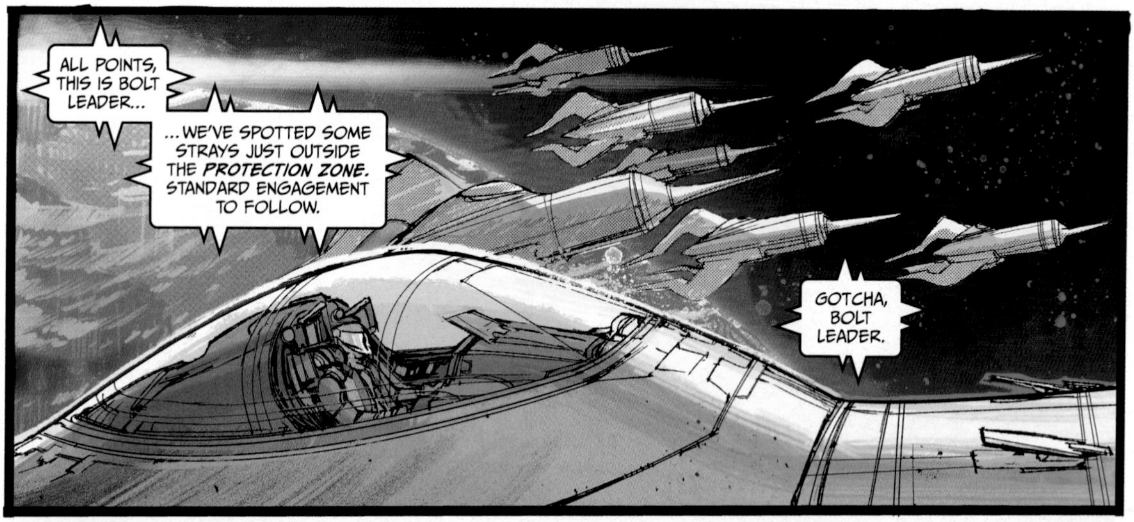
ALL POINTS, THIS IS BOLT LEADER...
...WE'VE SPOTTED SOME STRAYS JUST OUTSIDE THE PROTECTION ZONE. STANDARD ENGAGEMENT TO FOLLOW.
GOTCHA, BOLT LEADER.

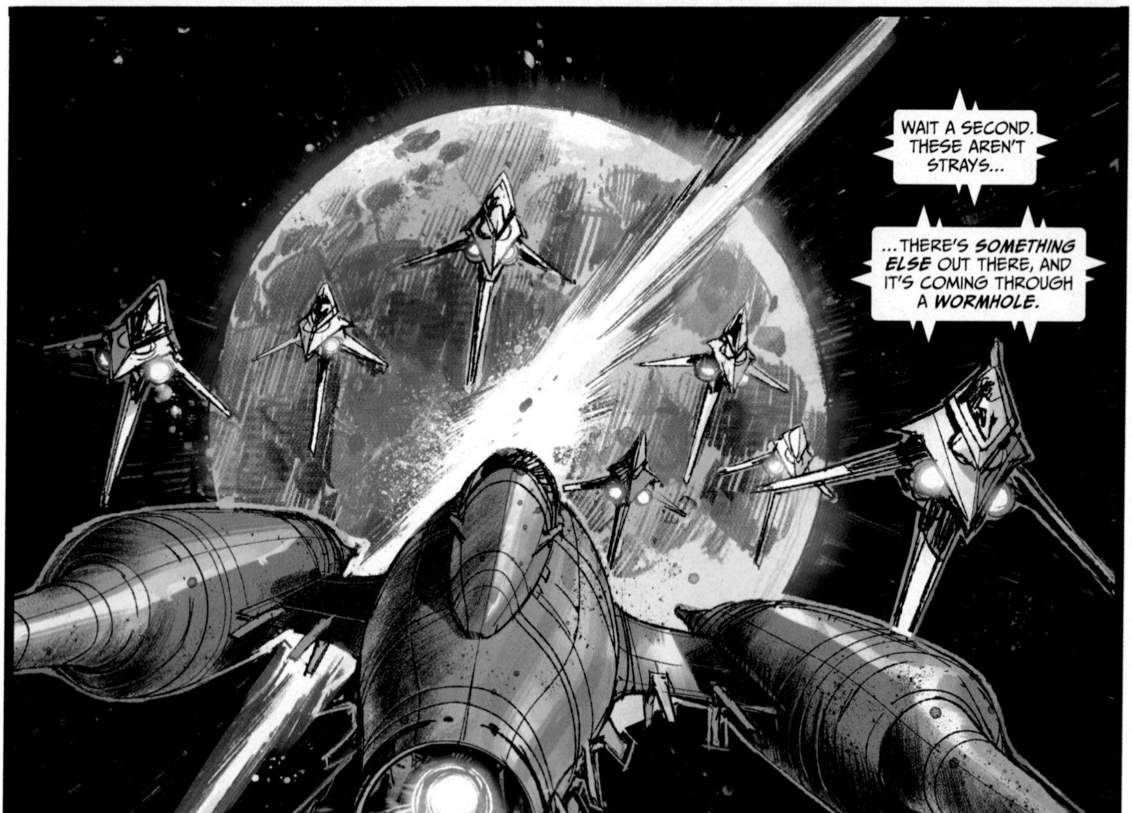
WAIT A SECOND. THESE AREN'T STRAYS...
...THERE'S SOMETHING ELSE OUT THERE, AND IT'S COMING THROUGH A WORMHOLE.

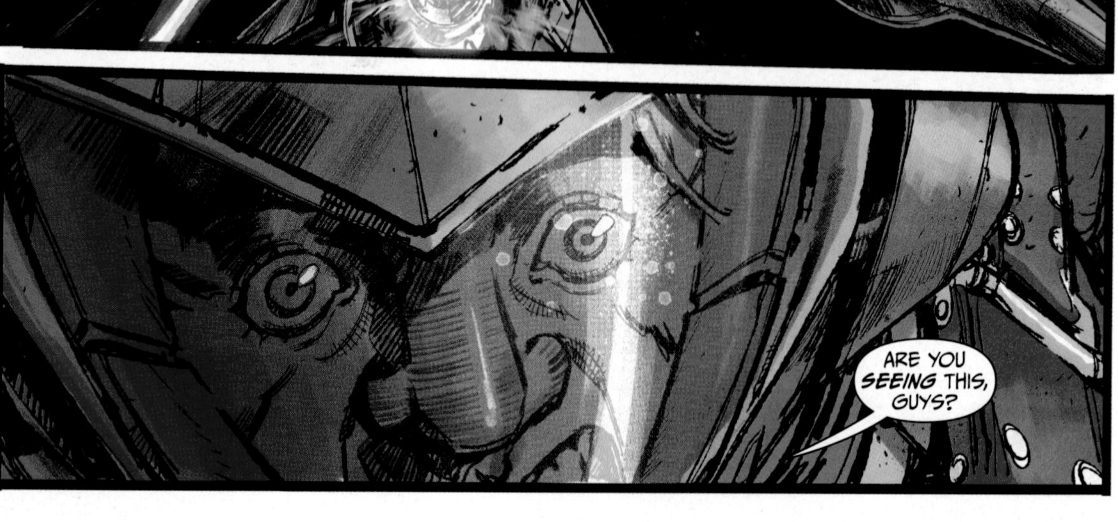
ARE YOU SEEING THIS, GUYS?

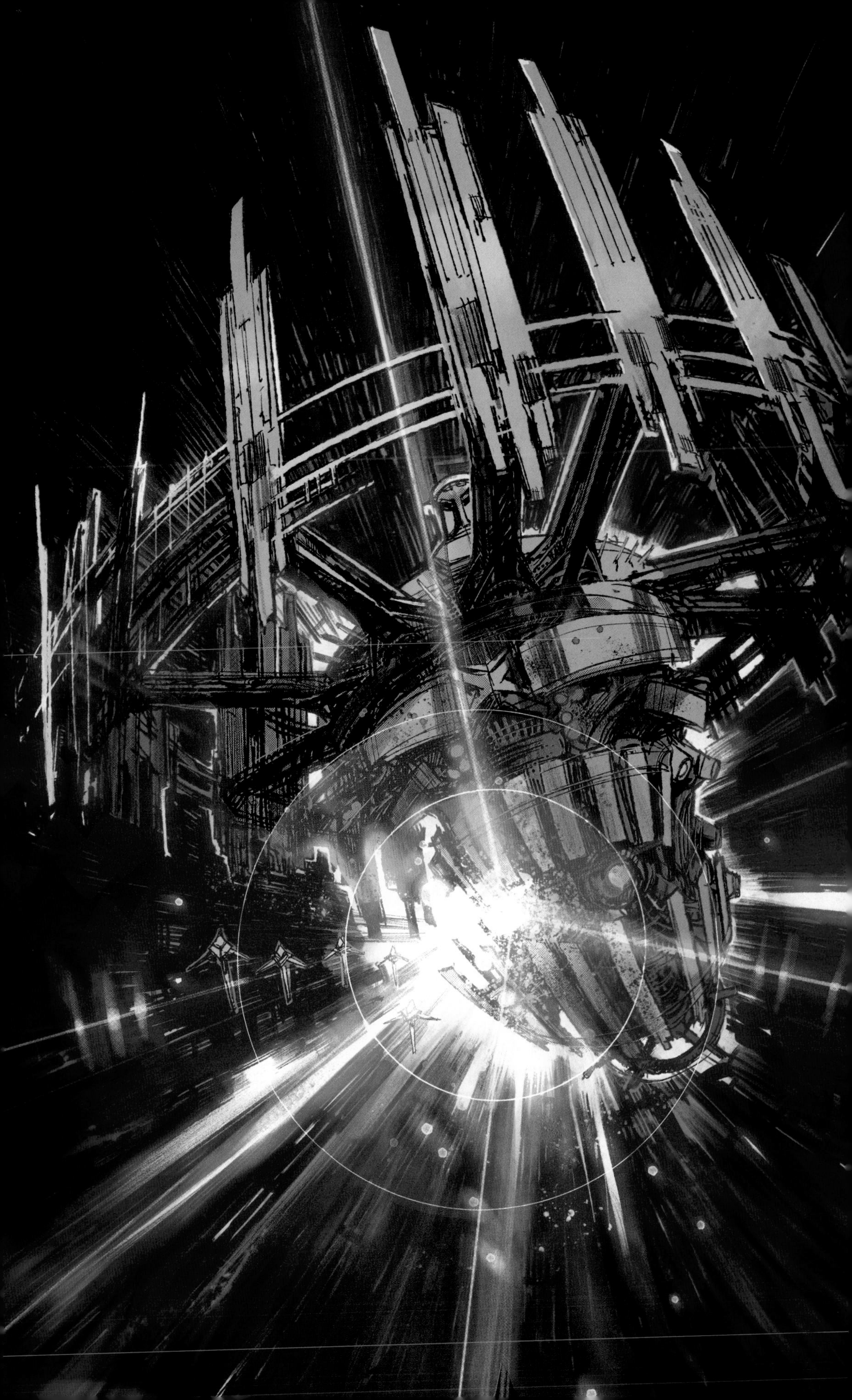

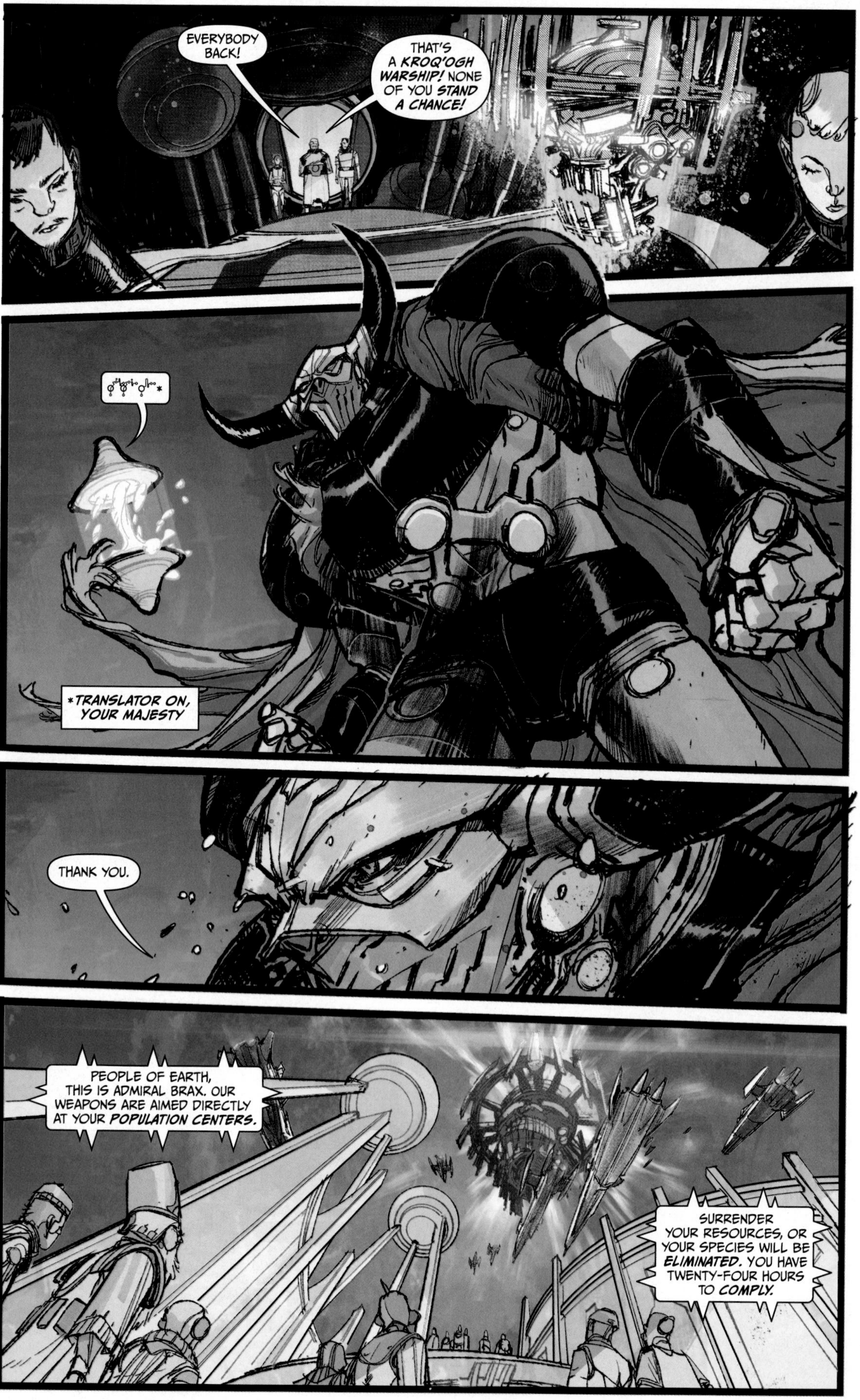
EVERYBODY BACK!
THAT'S A KROQ'OGH WARSHIP! NONE OF YOU STAND A CHANCE!
*TRANSLATOR ON, YOUR MAJESTY
THANK YOU.
PEOPLE OF EARTH, THIS IS ADMIRAL BRAX. OUR WEAPONS ARE AIMED DIRECTLY AT YOUR POPULATION CENTERS.
SURRENDER YOUR RESOURCES, OR YOUR SPECIES WILL BE ELIMINATED. YOU HAVE TWENTY-FOUR HOURS TO COMPLY.

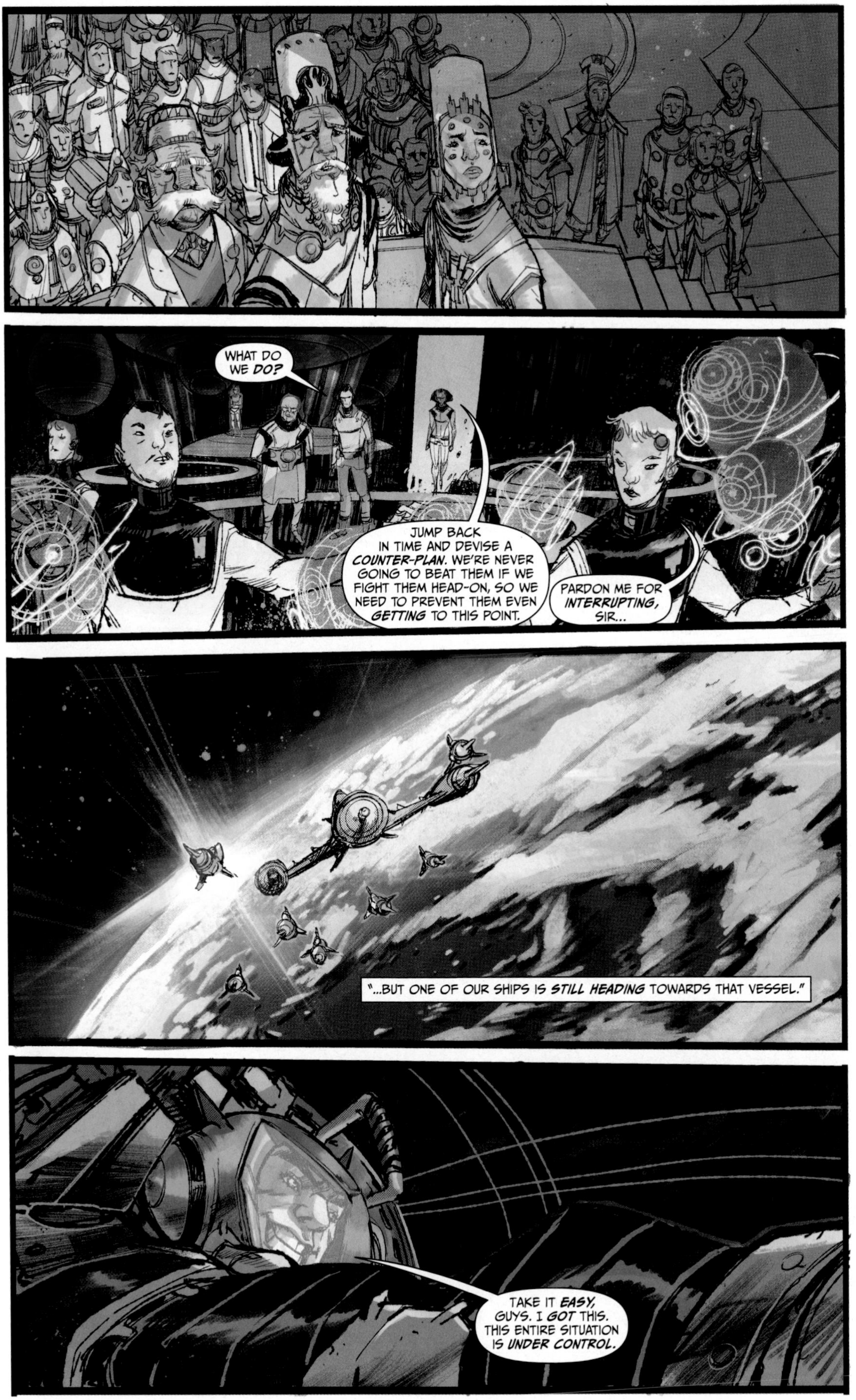

WHAT DO WE DO?
JUMP BACK IN TIME AND DEVISE A COUNTER-PLAN. WE'RE NEVER GOING TO BEAT THEM IF WE FIGHT THEM HEAD-ON, SO WE NEED TO PREVENT THEM EVEN GETTING TO THIS POINT.
PARDON ME FOR INTERRUPTING, SIR...
"...BUT ONE OF OUR SHIPS IS STILL HEADING TOWARDS THAT VESSEL."
TAKE IT EASY, GUYS. I GOT THIS. THIS ENTIRE SITUATION IS UNDER CONTROL.

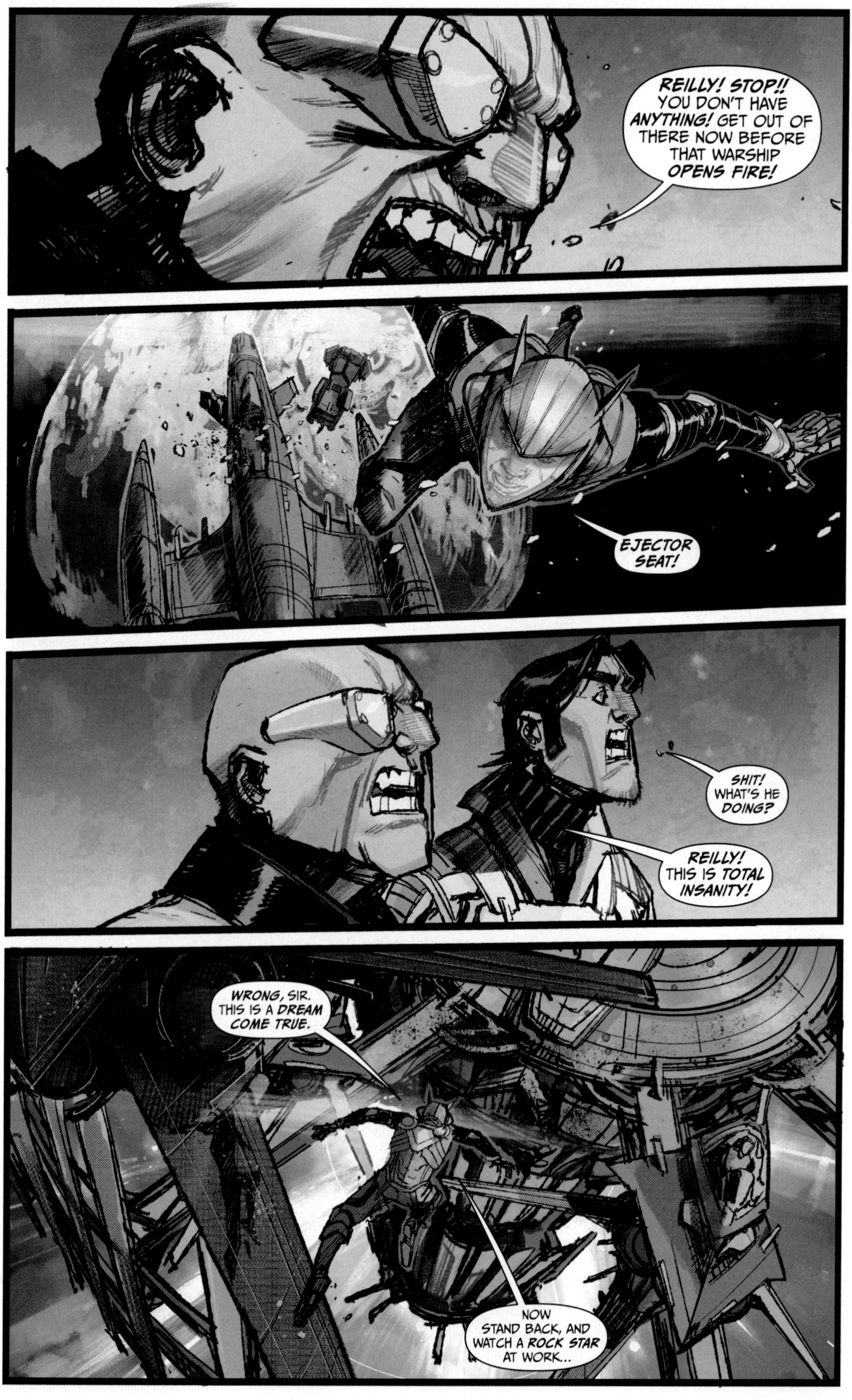
REILLY! STOP!! YOU DON'T HAVE ANYTHING! GET OUT OF THERE NOW BEFORE THAT WARSHIP OPENS FIRE!
EJECTOR SEAT!
SHIT! WHAT'S HE DOING?
REILLY! THIS IS TOTAL INSANITY!
WRONG, SIR. THIS IS A DREAM COME TRUE.
NOW STAND BACK, AND WATCH A ROCK STAR AT WORK...

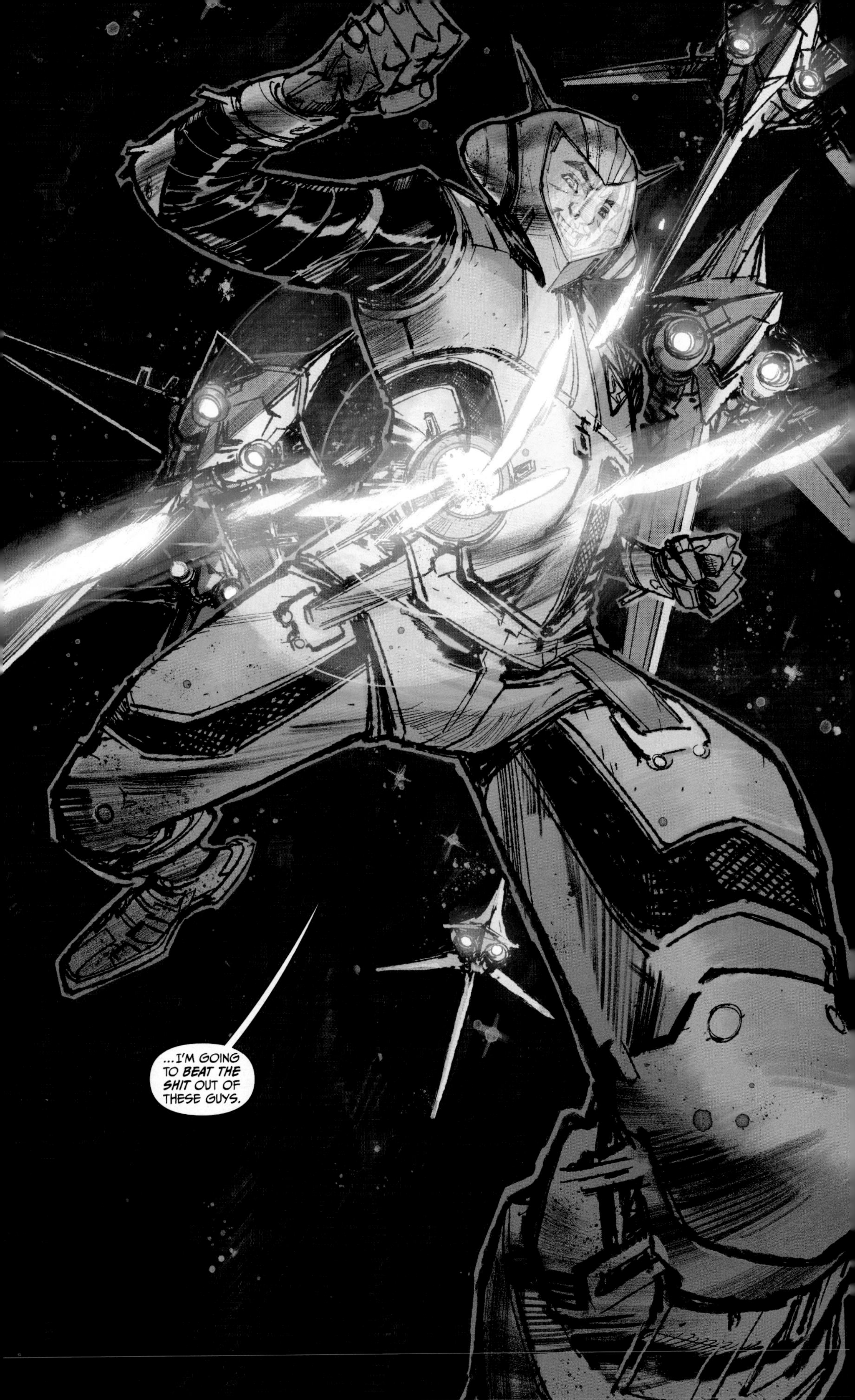
...I'M GOING TO *BEAT THE SHIT* OUT OF THESE GUYS.

THREE

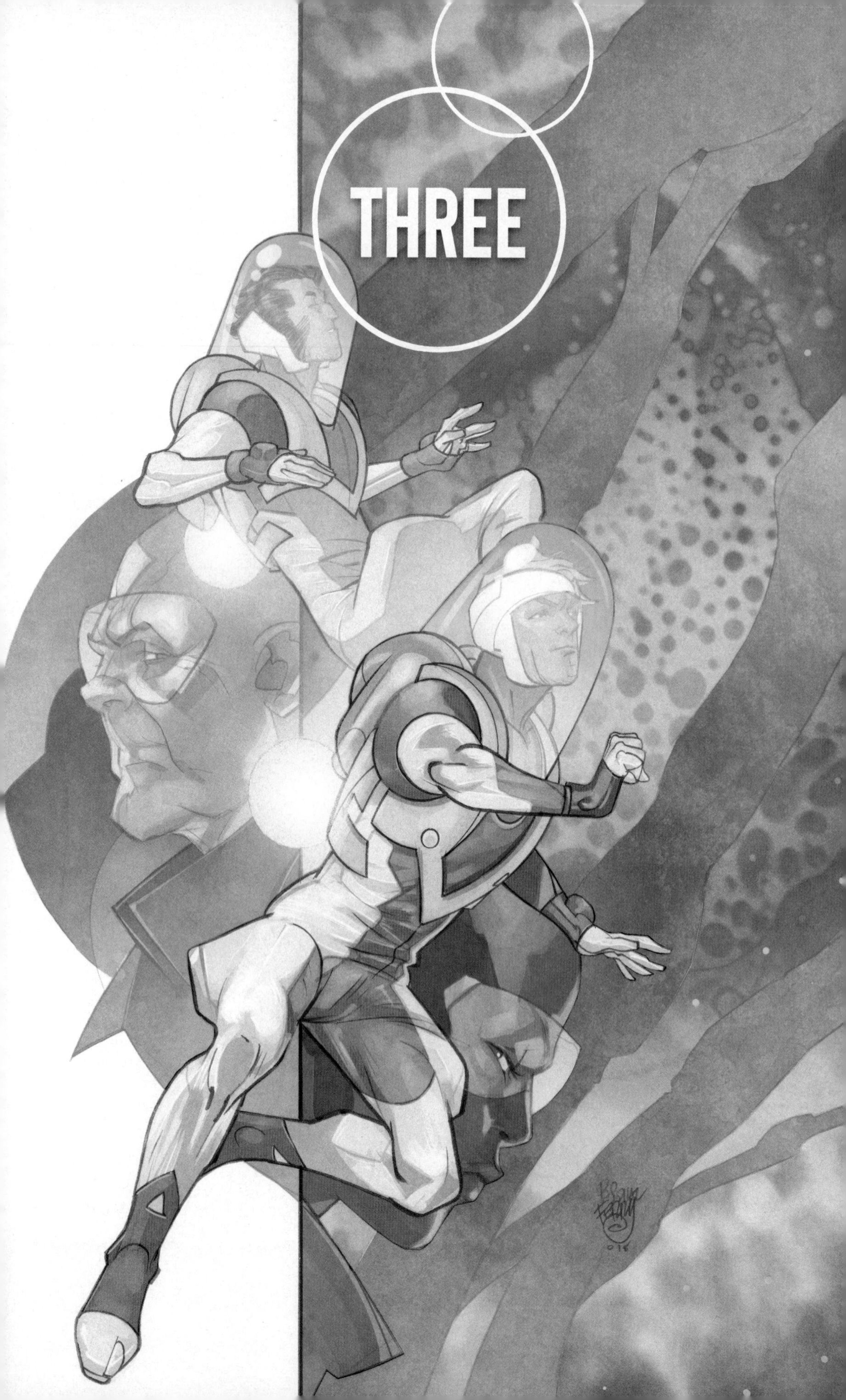

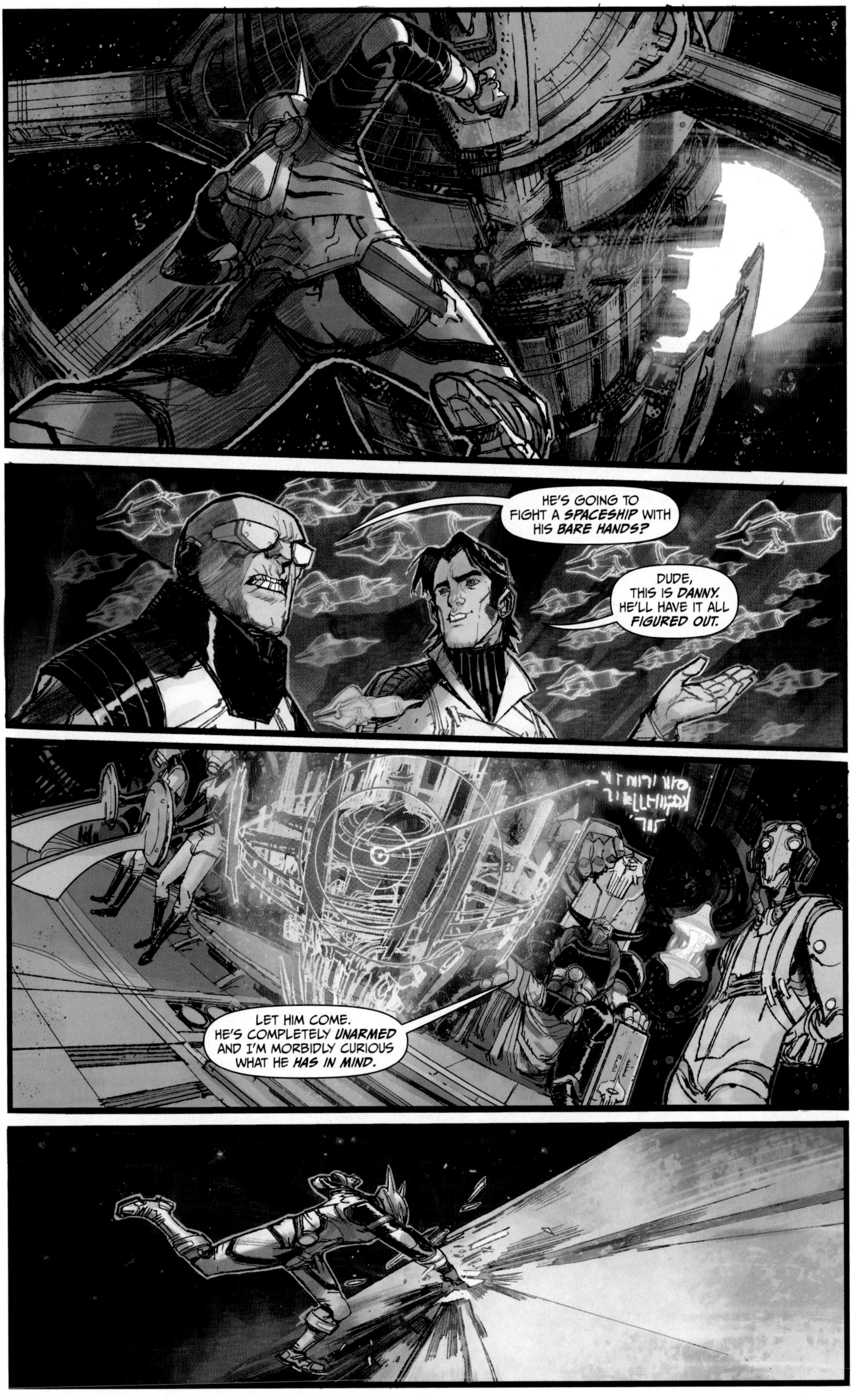
HE'S GOING TO FIGHT A *SPACESHIP* WITH HIS *BARE HANDS?*
DUDE, THIS IS *DANNY.* HE'LL HAVE IT ALL *FIGURED OUT.*
LET HIM COME. HE'S COMPLETELY *UNARMED* AND I'M MORBIDLY CURIOUS WHAT HE *HAS IN MIND.*

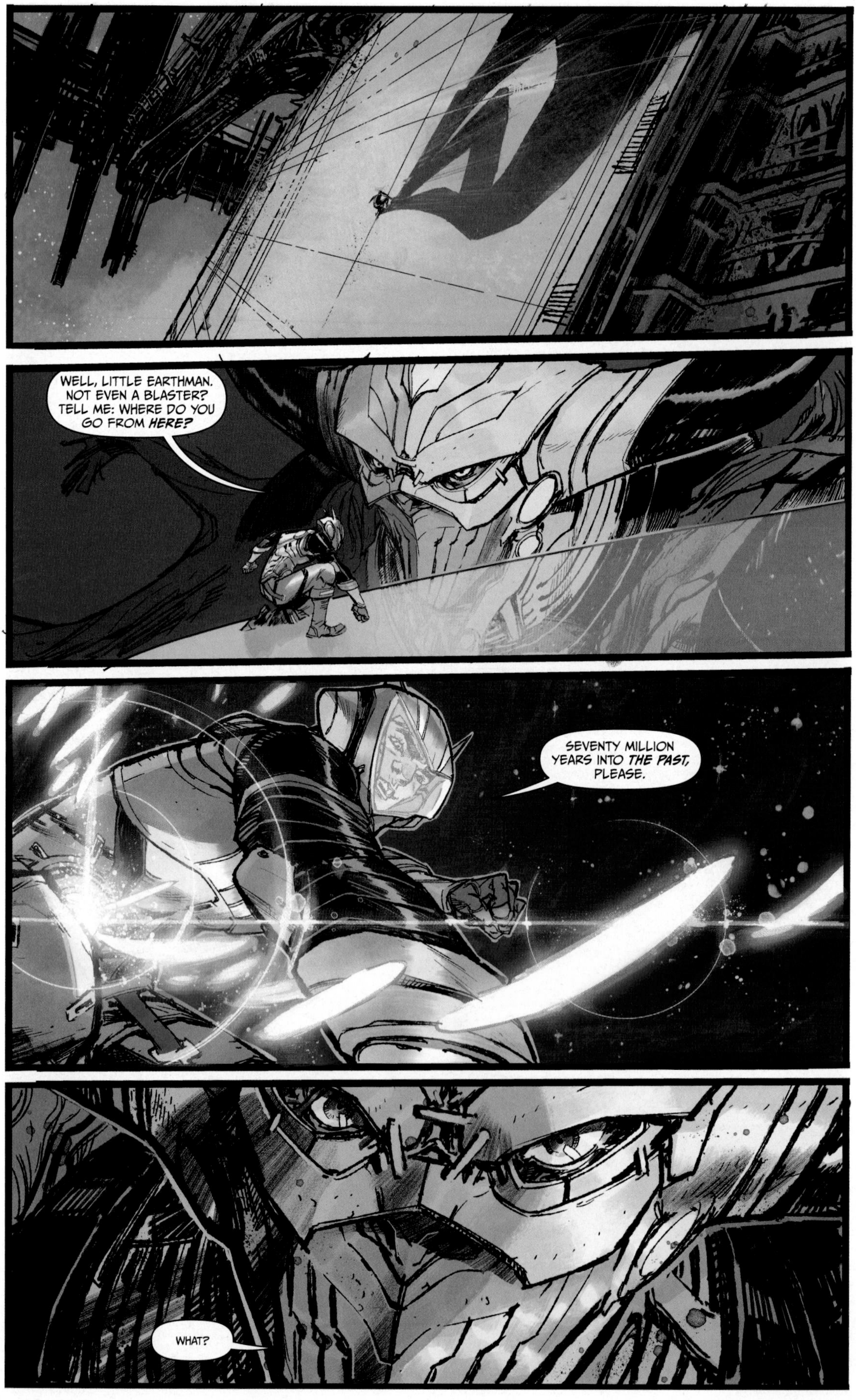
WELL, LITTLE EARTHMAN. NOT EVEN A BLASTER? TELL ME: WHERE DO YOU GO FROM *HERE?*
SEVENTY MILLION YEARS INTO *THE PAST,* PLEASE.
WHAT?

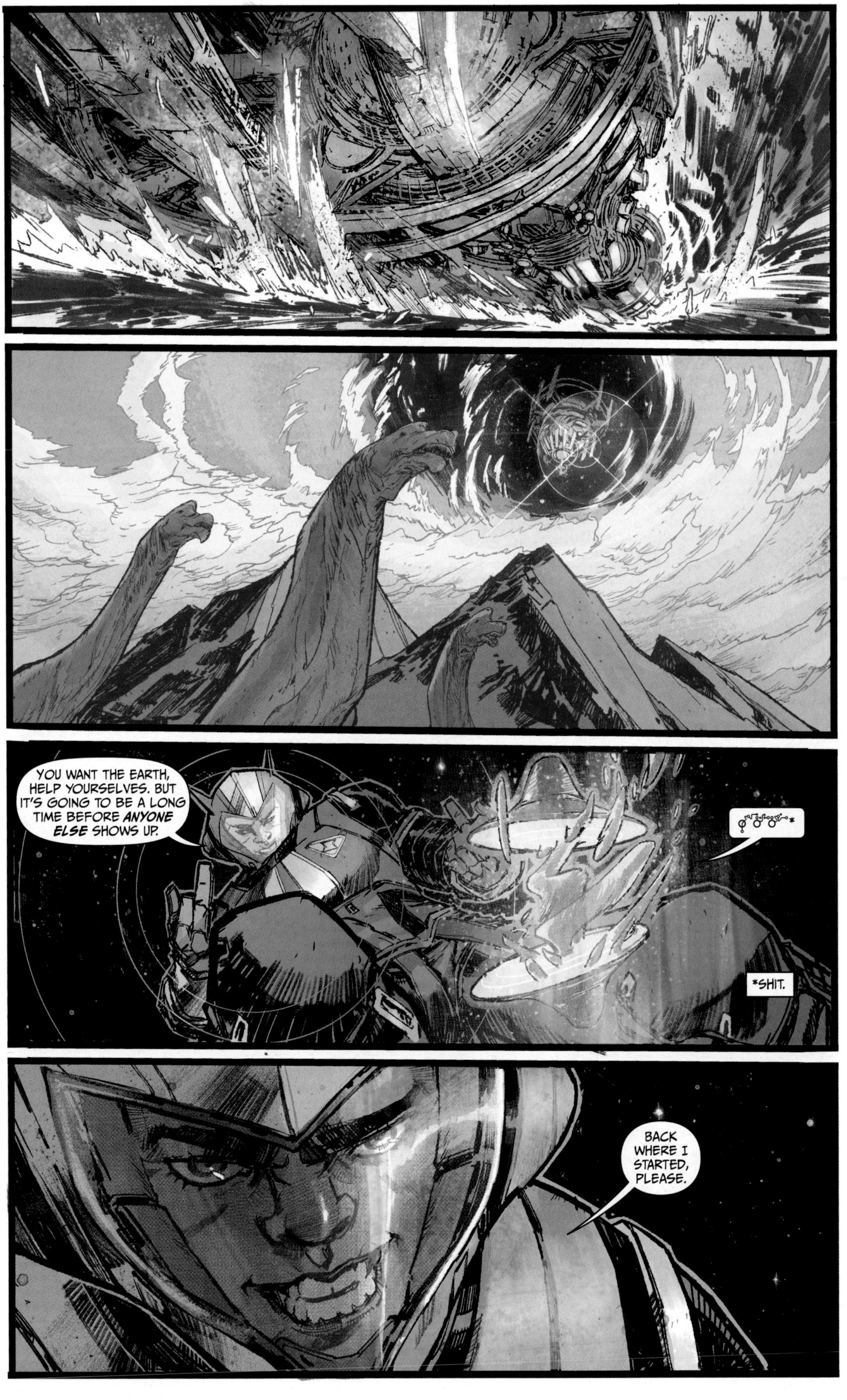
YOU WANT THE EARTH, HELP YOURSELVES. BUT IT'S GOING TO BE A LONG TIME BEFORE ANYONE ELSE SHOWS UP.
*SHIT.
BACK WHERE I STARTED, PLEASE.

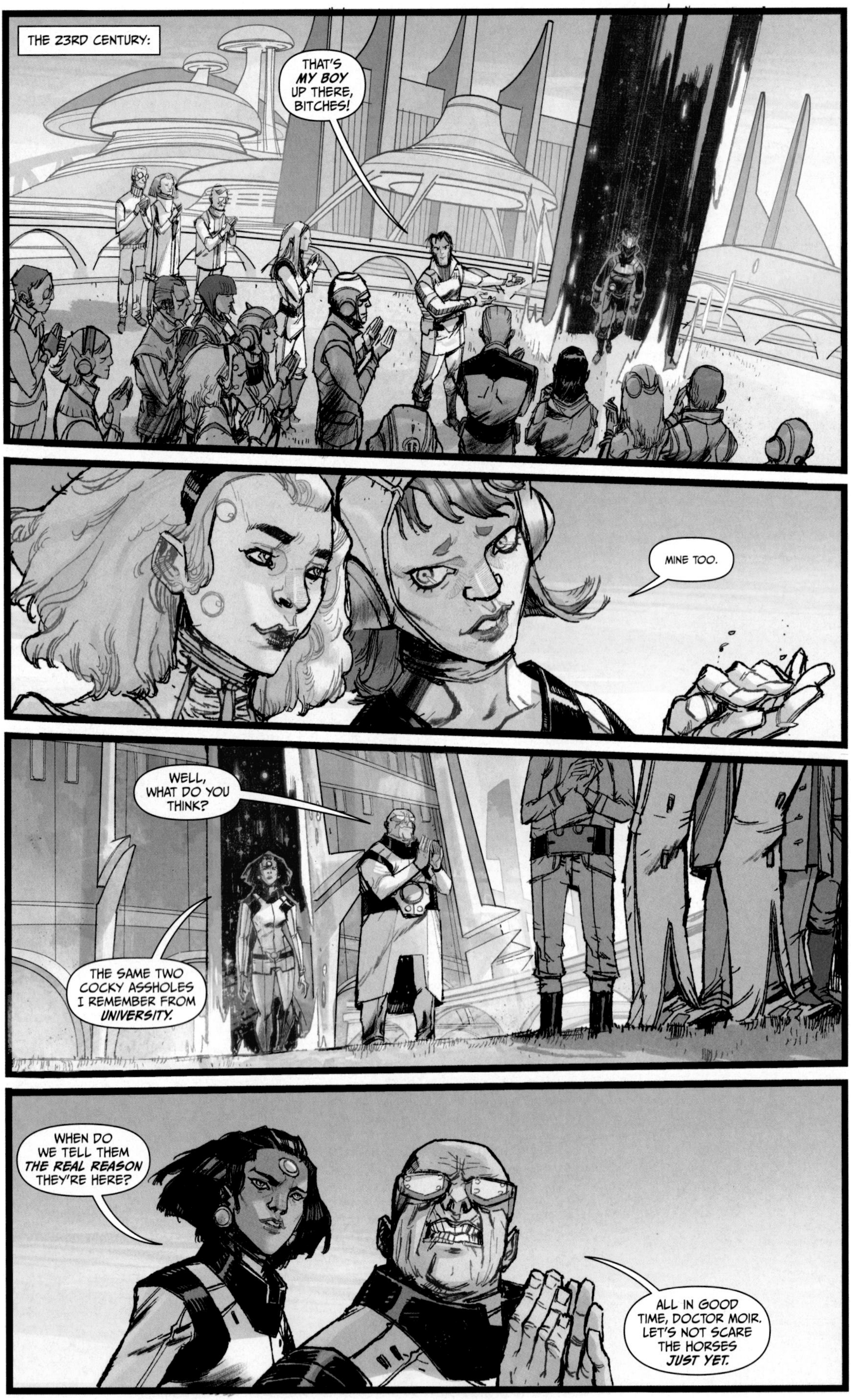
THE 23RD CENTURY:
THAT'S *MY BOY* UP THERE, BITCHES!
MINE TOO.
WELL, WHAT DO YOU THINK?
THE SAME TWO COCKY ASSHOLES I REMEMBER FROM *UNIVERSITY.*
WHEN DO WE TELL THEM *THE REAL REASON* THEY'RE HERE?
ALL IN GOOD TIME, DOCTOR MOIR. LET'S NOT SCARE THE HORSES *JUST YET.*

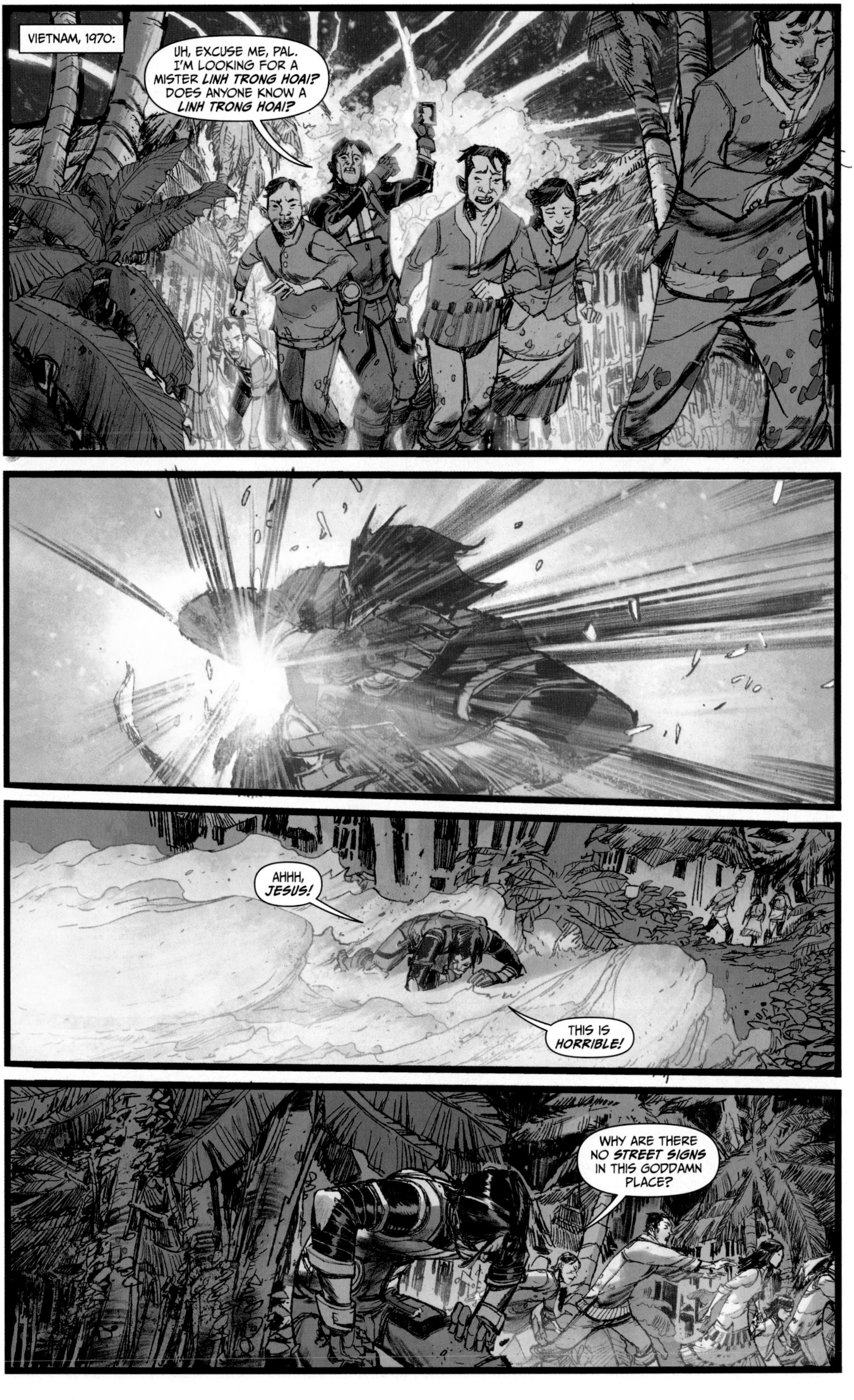
VIETNAM, 1970:
UH, EXCUSE ME, PAL. I'M LOOKING FOR A MISTER LINH TRONG HOAI? DOES ANYONE KNOW A LINH TRONG HOAI?
AHHH, JESUS!
THIS IS HORRIBLE!
WHY ARE THERE NO STREET SIGNS IN THIS GODDAMN PLACE?

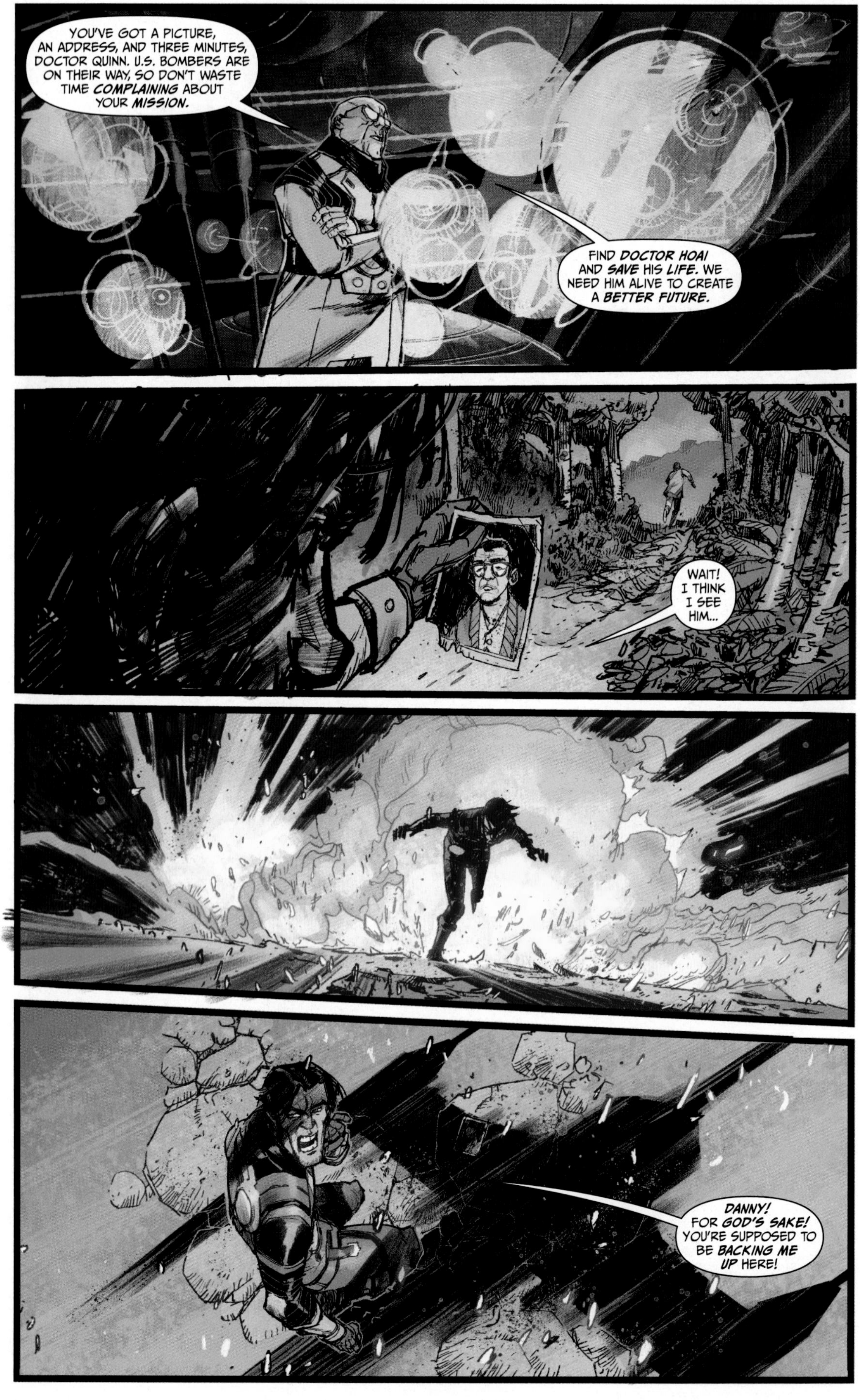
YOU'VE GOT A PICTURE, AN ADDRESS, AND THREE MINUTES, DOCTOR QUINN. U.S. BOMBERS ARE ON THEIR WAY, SO DON'T WASTE TIME COMPLAINING ABOUT YOUR MISSION.
FIND DOCTOR HOAI AND SAVE HIS LIFE. WE NEED HIM ALIVE TO CREATE A BETTER FUTURE.
WAIT! I THINK I SEE HIM...
DANNY! FOR GOD'S SAKE! YOU'RE SUPPOSED TO BE BACKING ME UP HERE!

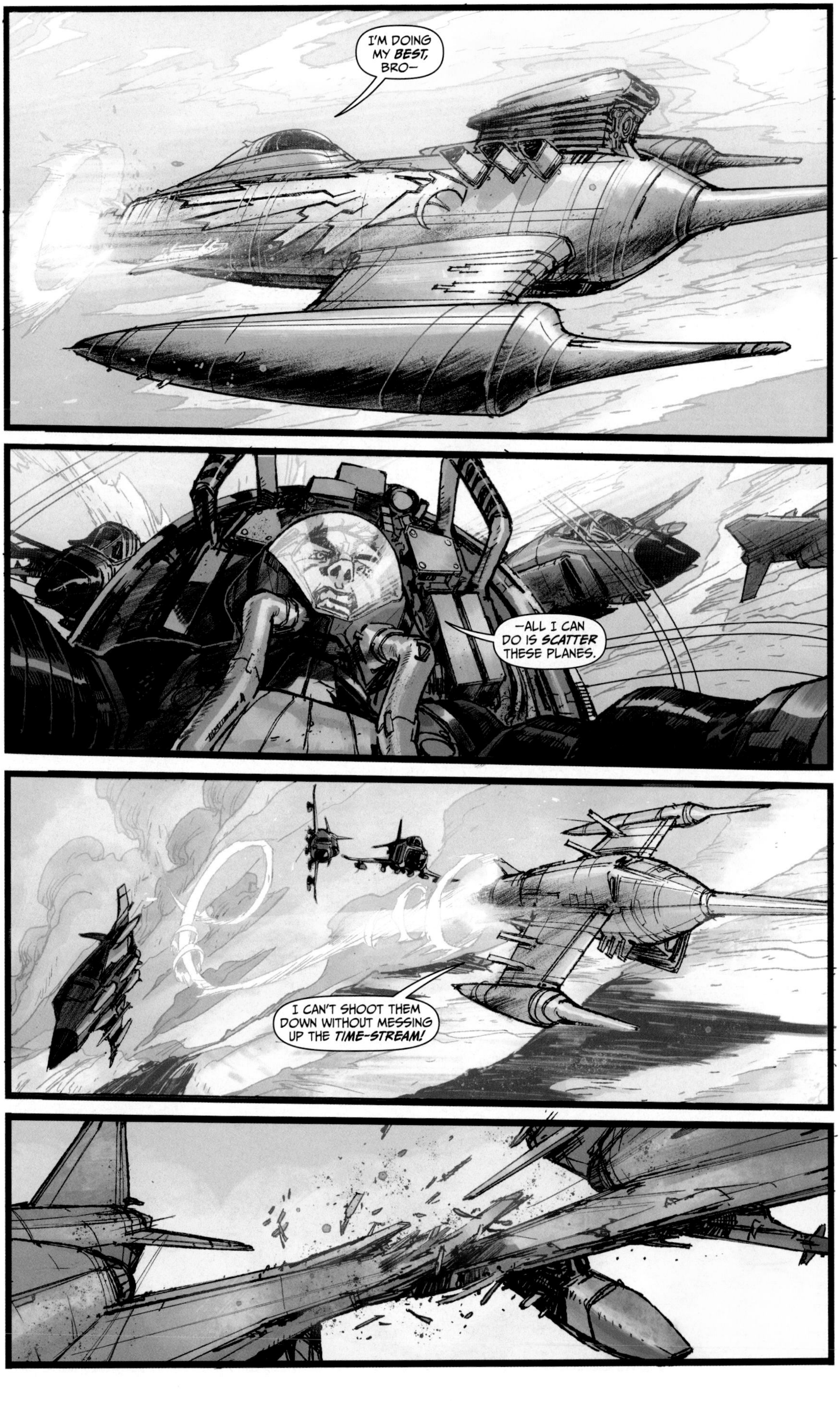
I'M DOING MY BEST, BRO—
—ALL I CAN DO IS SCATTER THESE PLANES.
I CAN'T SHOOT THEM DOWN WITHOUT MESSING UP THE TIME-STREAM!

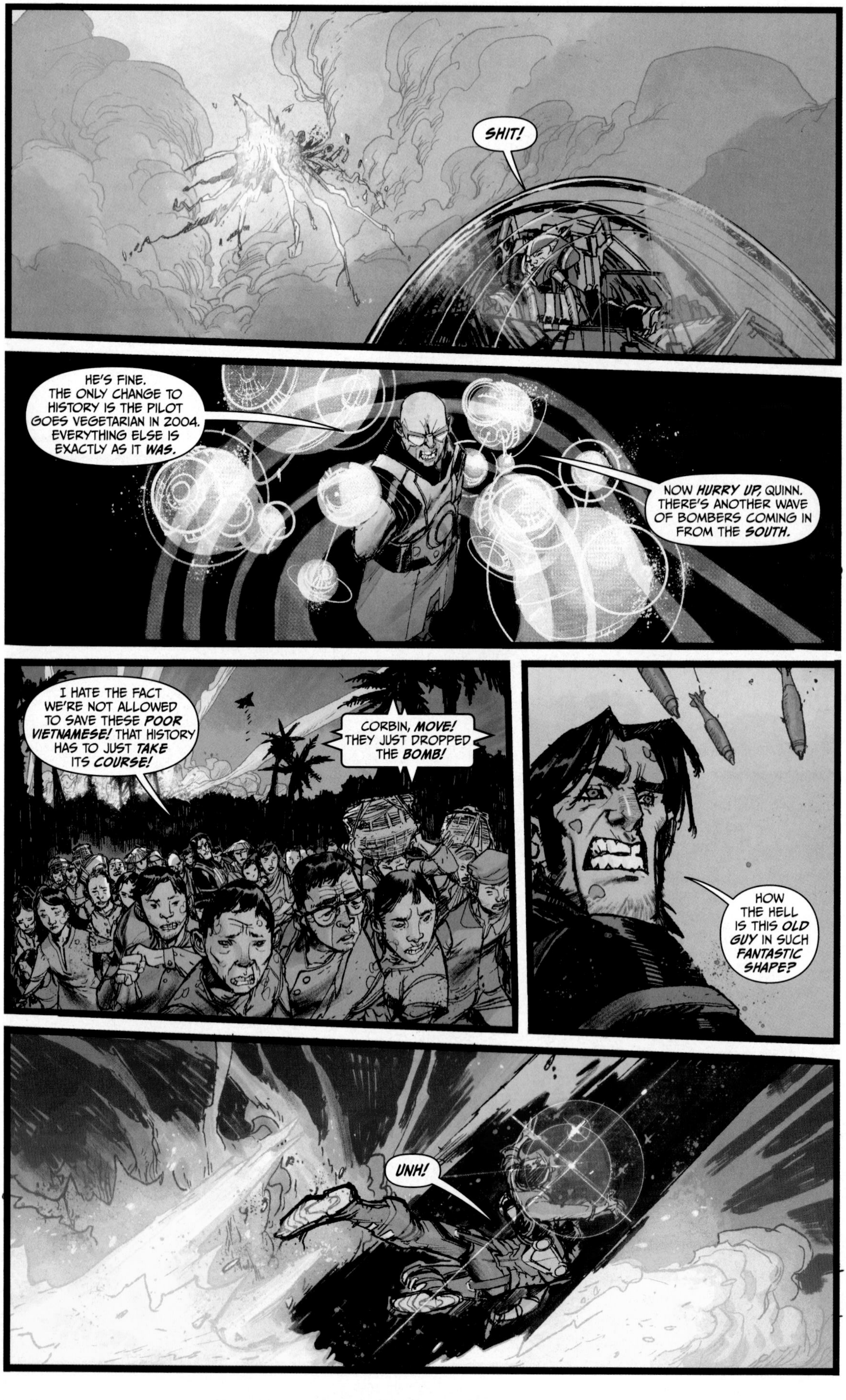
SHIT!
HE'S FINE. THE ONLY CHANGE TO HISTORY IS THE PILOT GOES VEGETARIAN IN 2004. EVERYTHING ELSE IS EXACTLY AS IT WAS.
NOW HURRY UP, QUINN. THERE'S ANOTHER WAVE OF BOMBERS COMING IN FROM THE SOUTH.
I HATE THE FACT WE'RE NOT ALLOWED TO SAVE THESE POOR VIETNAMESE! THAT HISTORY HAS TO JUST TAKE ITS COURSE!
CORBIN, MOVE! THEY JUST DROPPED THE BOMB!
HOW THE HELL IS THIS OLD GUY IN SUCH FANTASTIC SHAPE?
UNH!

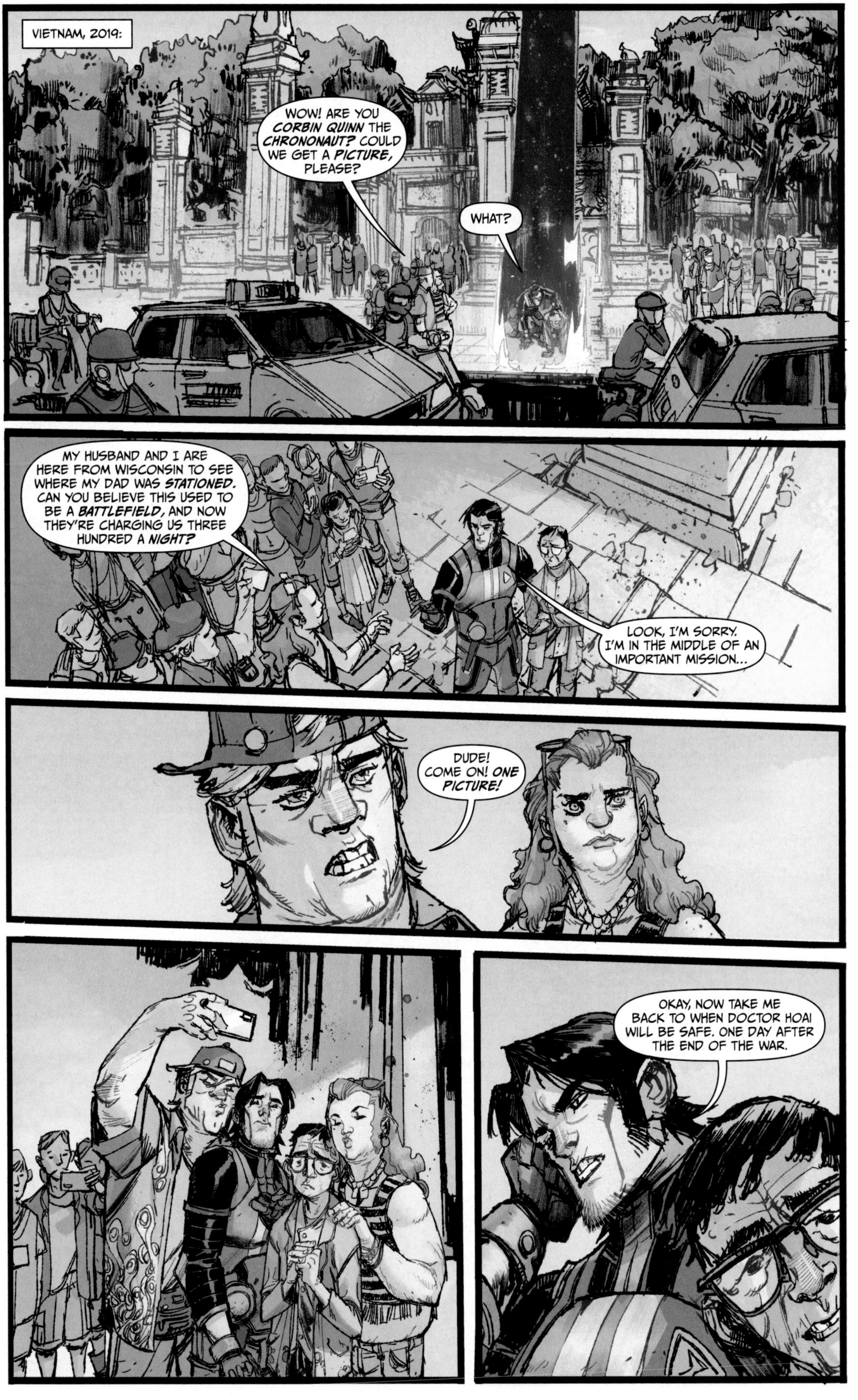
VIETNAM, 2019:
WOW! ARE YOU CORBIN QUINN THE CHRONONAUT? COULD WE GET A PICTURE, PLEASE?
WHAT?
MY HUSBAND AND I ARE HERE FROM WISCONSIN TO SEE WHERE MY DAD WAS STATIONED. CAN YOU BELIEVE THIS USED TO BE A BATTLEFIELD, AND NOW THEY'RE CHARGING US THREE HUNDRED A NIGHT?
LOOK, I'M SORRY. I'M IN THE MIDDLE OF AN IMPORTANT MISSION...
DUDE! COME ON! ONE PICTURE!
OKAY, NOW TAKE ME BACK TO WHEN DOCTOR HOAI WILL BE SAFE. ONE DAY AFTER THE END OF THE WAR.

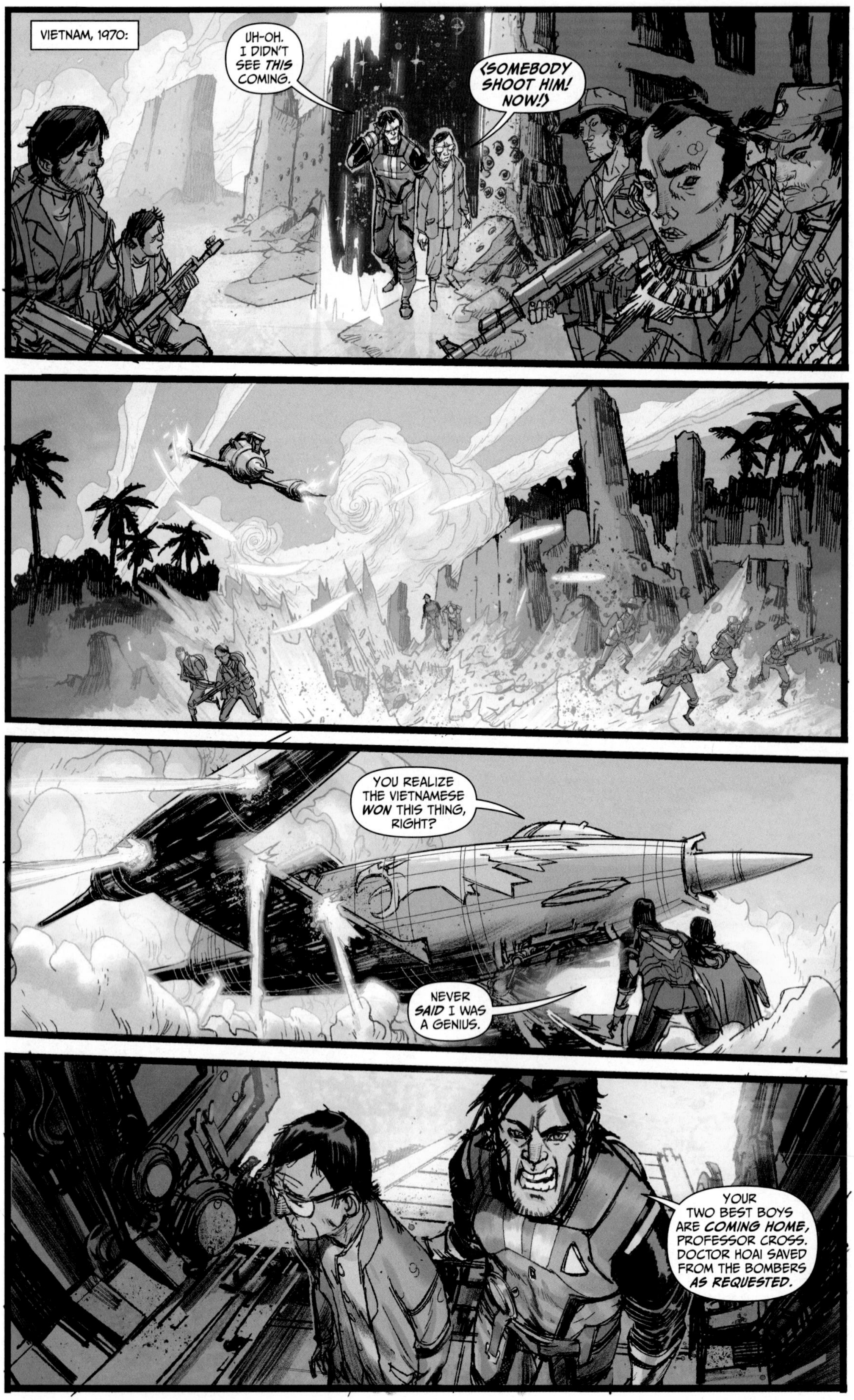
VIETNAM, 1970:
UH-OH. I DIDN'T SEE THIS COMING.
‹SOMEBODY SHOOT HIM! NOW!›
YOU REALIZE THE VIETNAMESE WON THIS THING, RIGHT?
NEVER SAID I WAS A GENIUS.
YOUR TWO BEST BOYS ARE COMING HOME, PROFESSOR CROSS. DOCTOR HOAI SAVED FROM THE BOMBERS AS REQUESTED.

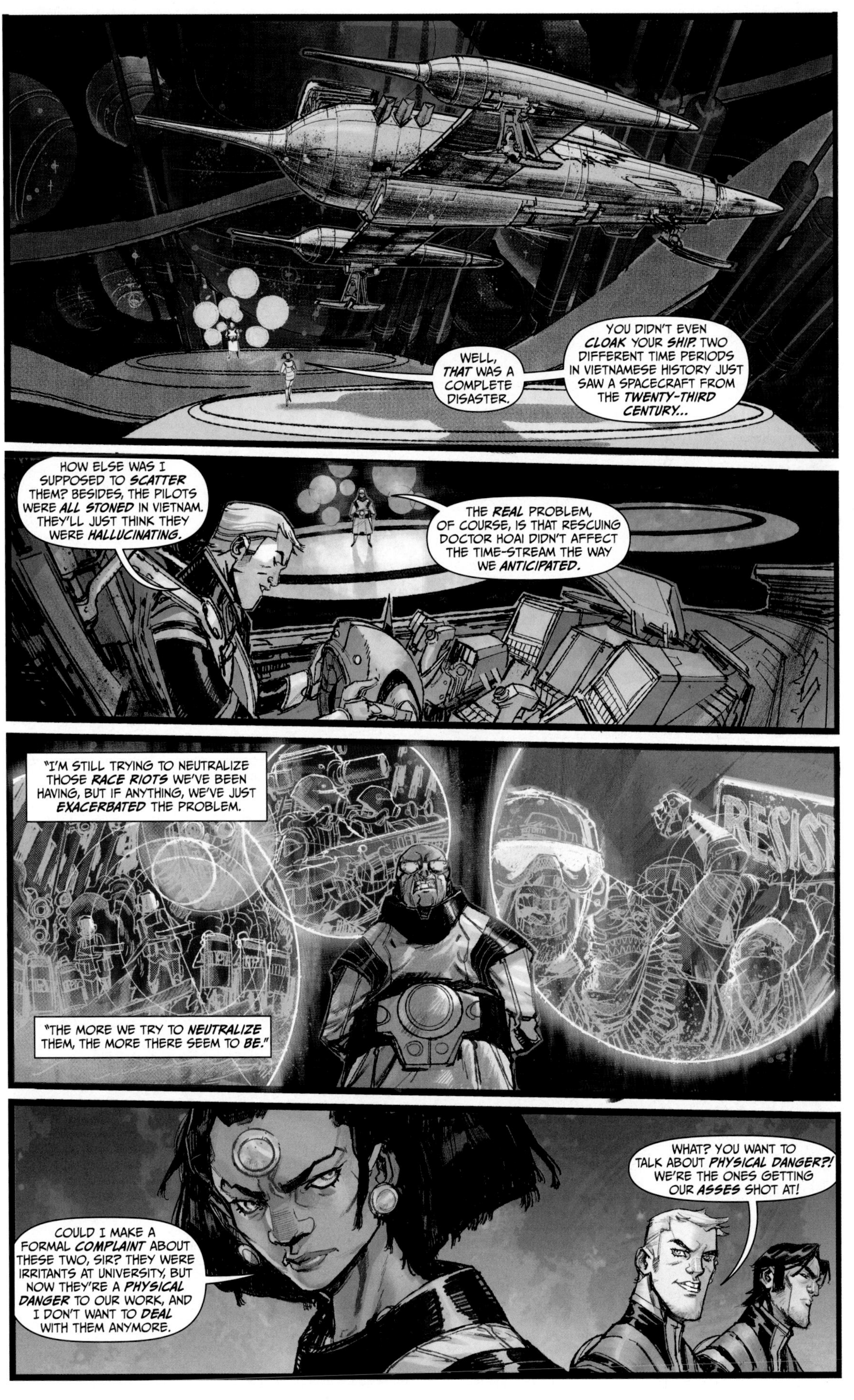
WELL, THAT WAS A COMPLETE DISASTER.
YOU DIDN'T EVEN CLOAK YOUR SHIP. TWO DIFFERENT TIME PERIODS IN VIETNAMESE HISTORY JUST SAW A SPACECRAFT FROM THE TWENTY-THIRD CENTURY...
HOW ELSE WAS I SUPPOSED TO SCATTER THEM? BESIDES, THE PILOTS WERE ALL STONED IN VIETNAM. THEY'LL JUST THINK THEY WERE HALLUCINATING.
THE REAL PROBLEM, OF COURSE, IS THAT RESCUING DOCTOR HOAI DIDN'T AFFECT THE TIME-STREAM THE WAY WE ANTICIPATED.
"I'M STILL TRYING TO NEUTRALIZE THOSE RACE RIOTS WE'VE BEEN HAVING, BUT IF ANYTHING, WE'VE JUST EXACERBATED THE PROBLEM.
RESIST
"THE MORE WE TRY TO NEUTRALIZE THEM, THE MORE THERE SEEM TO BE."
COULD I MAKE A FORMAL COMPLAINT ABOUT THESE TWO, SIR? THEY WERE IRRITANTS AT UNIVERSITY, BUT NOW THEY'RE A PHYSICAL DANGER TO OUR WORK, AND I DON'T WANT TO DEAL WITH THEM ANYMORE.
WHAT? YOU WANT TO TALK ABOUT PHYSICAL DANGER?! WE'RE THE ONES GETTING OUR ASSES SHOT AT!

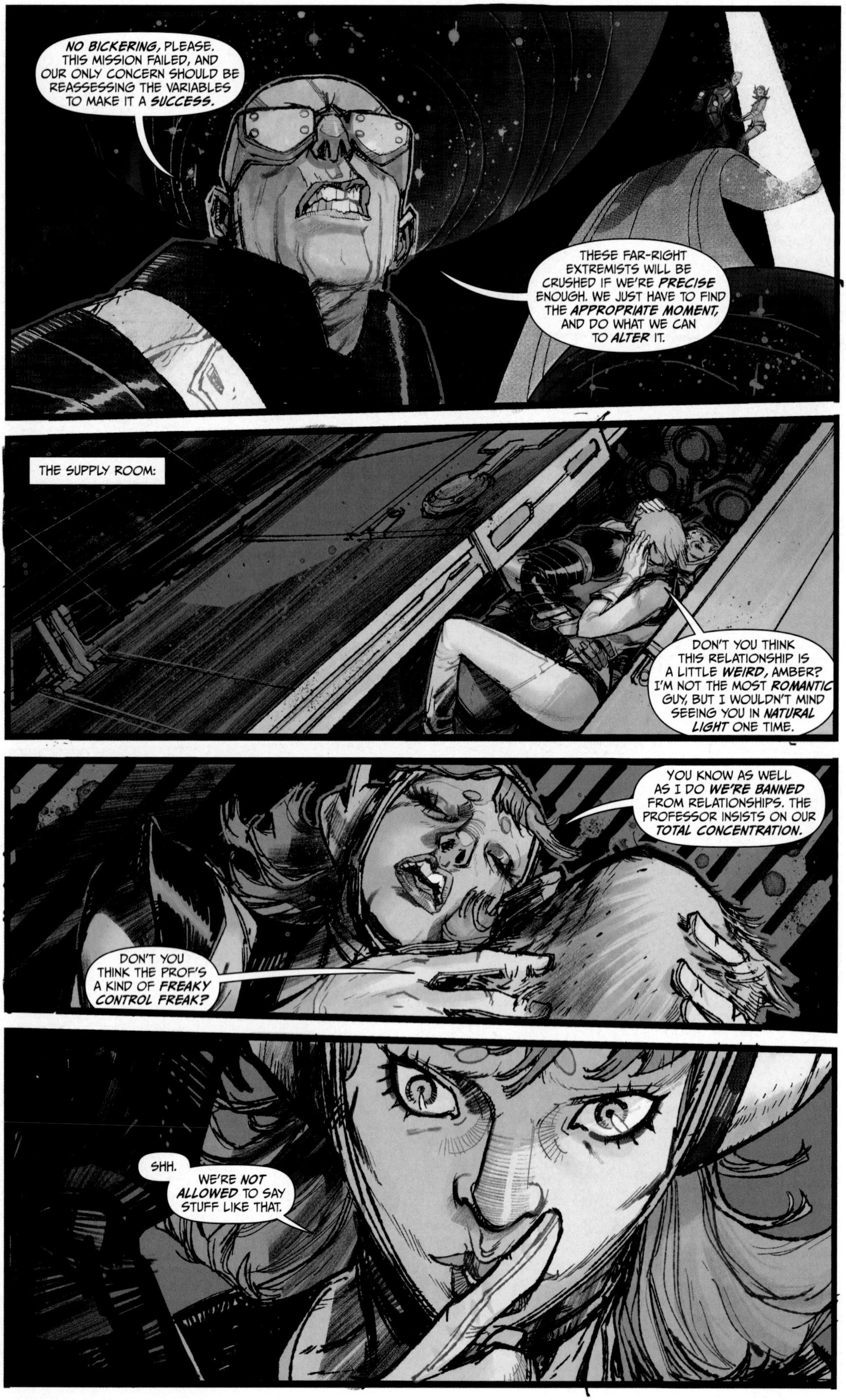
NO BICKERING, PLEASE. THIS MISSION FAILED, AND OUR ONLY CONCERN SHOULD BE REASSESSING THE VARIABLES TO MAKE IT A SUCCESS.
THESE FAR-RIGHT EXTREMISTS WILL BE CRUSHED IF WE'RE PRECISE ENOUGH. WE JUST HAVE TO FIND THE APPROPRIATE MOMENT, AND DO WHAT WE CAN TO ALTER IT.
THE SUPPLY ROOM:
DON'T YOU THINK THIS RELATIONSHIP IS A LITTLE WEIRD, AMBER? I'M NOT THE MOST ROMANTIC GUY, BUT I WOULDN'T MIND SEEING YOU IN NATURAL LIGHT ONE TIME.
YOU KNOW AS WELL AS I DO WE'RE BANNED FROM RELATIONSHIPS. THE PROFESSOR INSISTS ON OUR TOTAL CONCENTRATION.
DON'T YOU THINK THE PROF'S A KIND OF FREAKY CONTROL FREAK?
SHH.
WE'RE NOT ALLOWED TO SAY STUFF LIKE THAT.

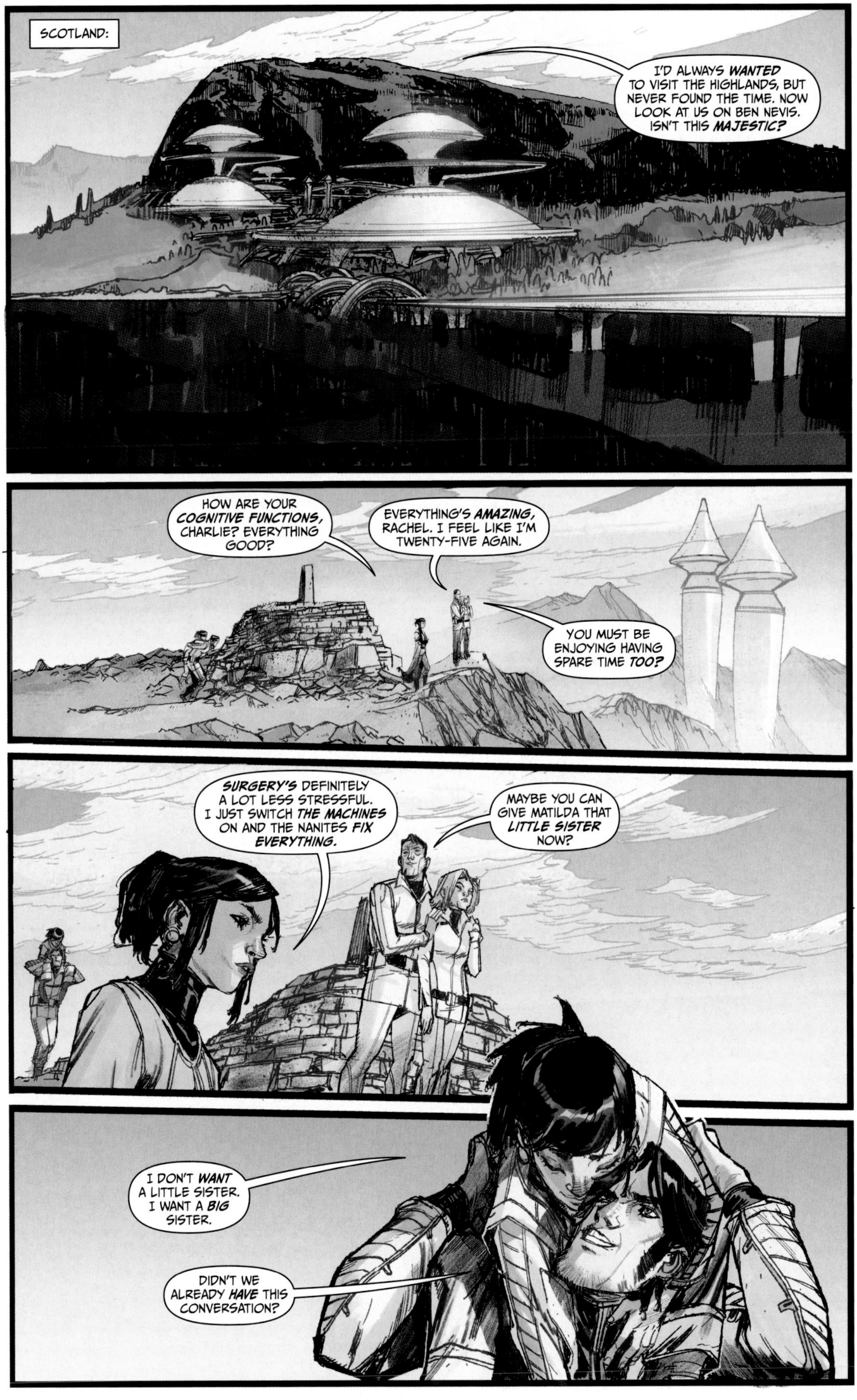
SCOTLAND:
I'D ALWAYS WANTED TO VISIT THE HIGHLANDS, BUT NEVER FOUND THE TIME. NOW LOOK AT US ON BEN NEVIS. ISN'T THIS MAJESTIC?
HOW ARE YOUR COGNITIVE FUNCTIONS, CHARLIE? EVERYTHING GOOD?
EVERYTHING'S AMAZING, RACHEL. I FEEL LIKE I'M TWENTY-FIVE AGAIN.
YOU MUST BE ENJOYING HAVING SPARE TIME TOO?
SURGERY'S DEFINITELY A LOT LESS STRESSFUL. I JUST SWITCH THE MACHINES ON AND THE NANITES FIX EVERYTHING.
MAYBE YOU CAN GIVE MATILDA THAT LITTLE SISTER NOW?
I DON'T WANT A LITTLE SISTER. I WANT A BIG SISTER.
DIDN'T WE ALREADY HAVE THIS CONVERSATION?

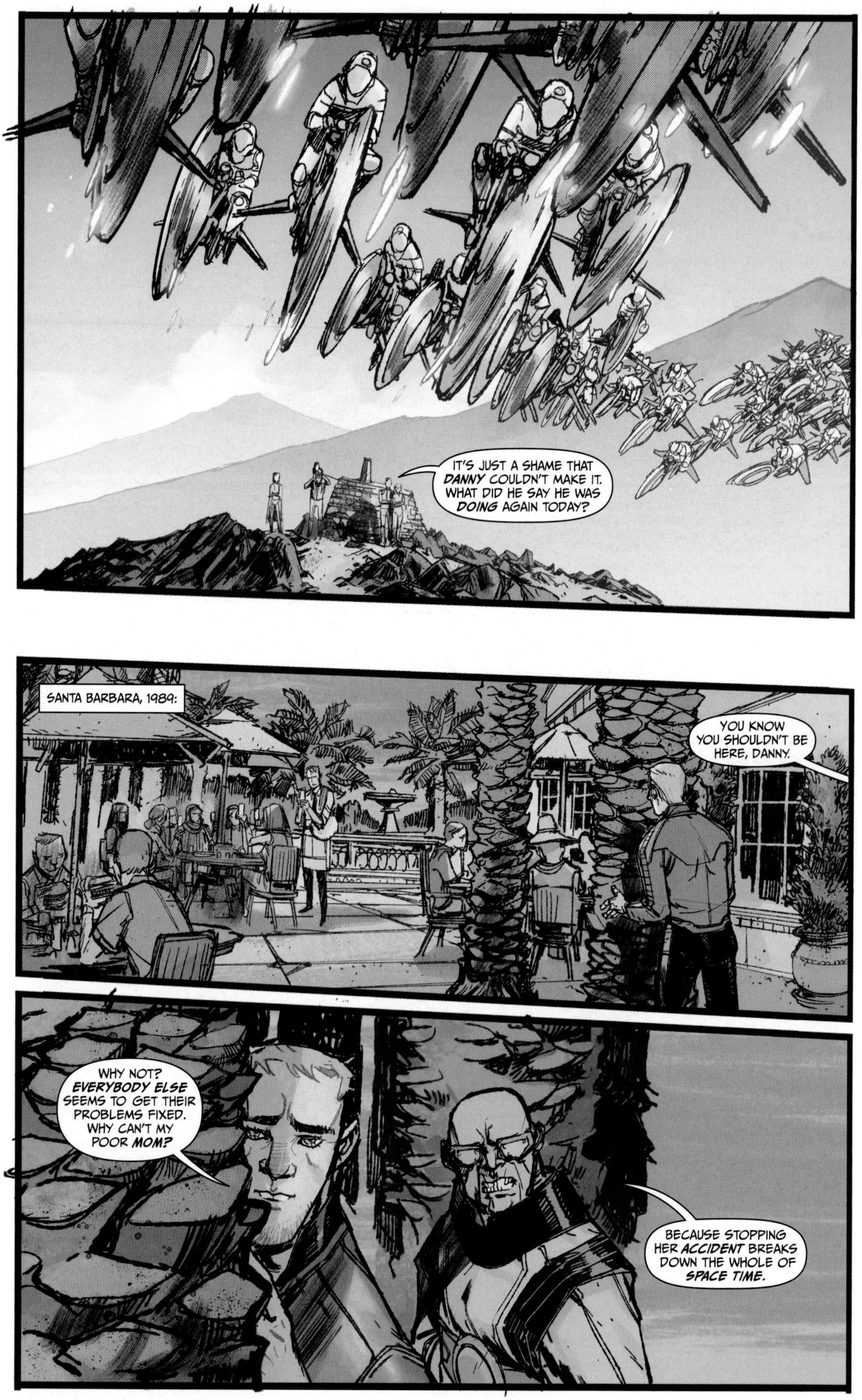
IT'S JUST A SHAME THAT DANNY COULDN'T MAKE IT. WHAT DID HE SAY HE WAS DOING AGAIN TODAY?
SANTA BARBARA, 1989:
YOU KNOW YOU SHOULDN'T BE HERE, DANNY.
WHY NOT? EVERYBODY ELSE SEEMS TO GET THEIR PROBLEMS FIXED. WHY CAN'T MY POOR MOM?
BECAUSE STOPPING HER ACCIDENT BREAKS DOWN THE WHOLE OF SPACE TIME.

NO ADOPTION BY YOUR GRANDPARENTS. NO *MIT*. NO MEETING CORBIN QUINN, OR BUILDING THE TIME MACHINE THAT SENDS YOU BACK HERE IN THE *FIRST PLACE*.

EVEN *TALKING* TO HER WOULD BE ENOUGH. JUST LETTING HER KNOW THAT EVERYTHING TURNED OUT *GREAT*.

"IT *BREAKS MY HEART* TO THINK SHE DIED KNOWING NOTHING. NO IDEA WHAT HER MOM AND DAD *DID* FOR ME..."

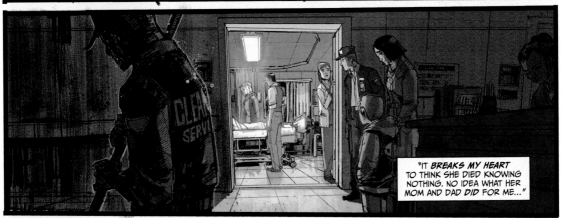

HE'S GOING TO BE *SOMETHING SPECIAL*, KATHY. YOUR LITTLE *DANNY* WILL CHANGE THE WORLD, AND YOUR MOTHER AND I WILL ALWAYS *BE THERE* FOR HIM.

I KNOW.

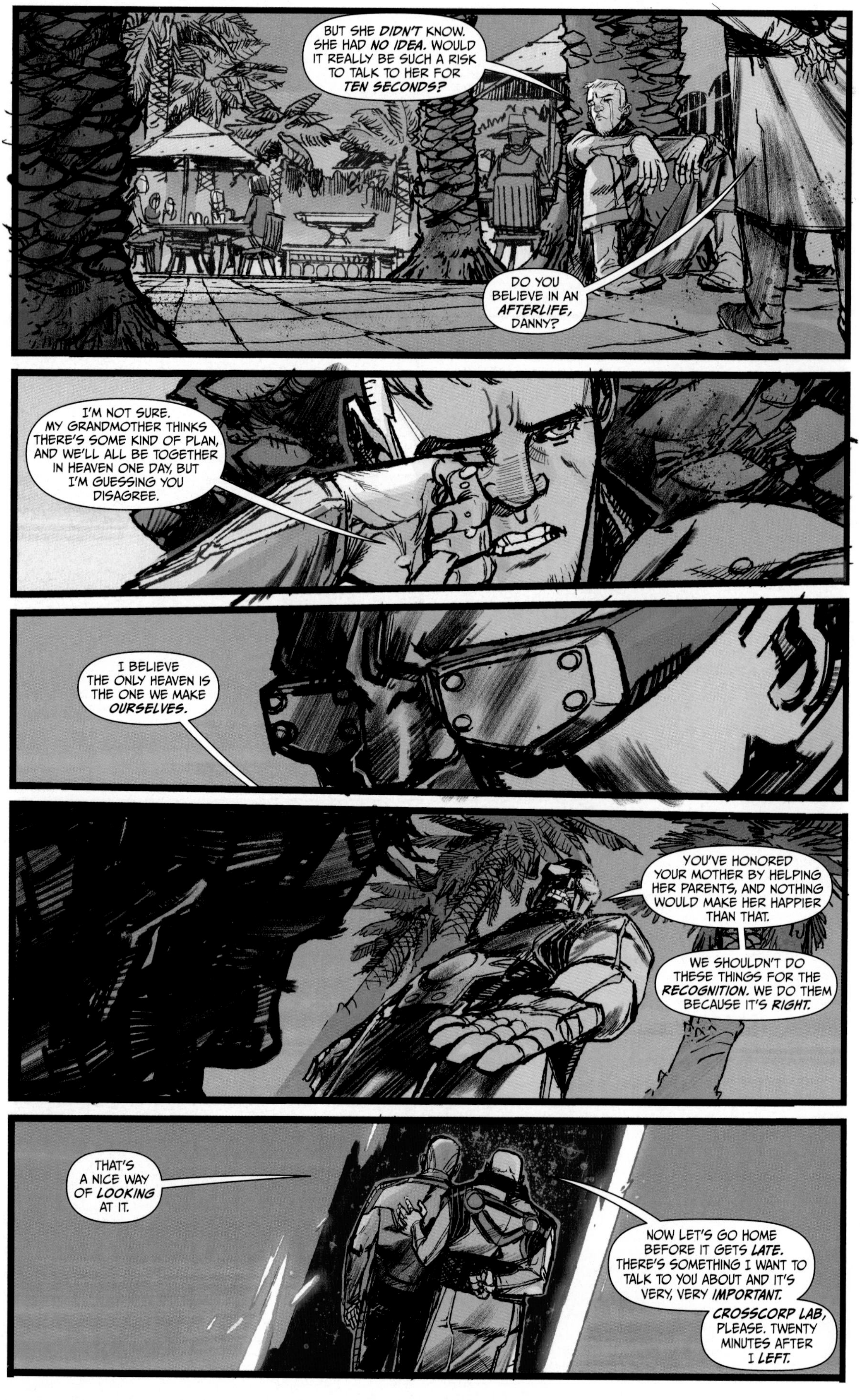

BUT SHE DIDN'T KNOW. SHE HAD NO IDEA. WOULD IT REALLY BE SUCH A RISK TO TALK TO HER FOR TEN SECONDS?
DO YOU BELIEVE IN AN AFTERLIFE, DANNY?
I'M NOT SURE. MY GRANDMOTHER THINKS THERE'S SOME KIND OF PLAN, AND WE'LL ALL BE TOGETHER IN HEAVEN ONE DAY, BUT I'M GUESSING YOU DISAGREE.
I BELIEVE THE ONLY HEAVEN IS THE ONE WE MAKE OURSELVES.
YOU'VE HONORED YOUR MOTHER BY HELPING HER PARENTS, AND NOTHING WOULD MAKE HER HAPPIER THAN THAT.
WE SHOULDN'T DO THESE THINGS FOR THE RECOGNITION. WE DO THEM BECAUSE IT'S RIGHT.
THAT'S A NICE WAY OF LOOKING AT IT.
NOW LET'S GO HOME BEFORE IT GETS LATE. THERE'S SOMETHING I WANT TO TALK TO YOU ABOUT AND IT'S VERY, VERY IMPORTANT.
CROSSCORP LAB, PLEASE. TWENTY MINUTES AFTER I LEFT.

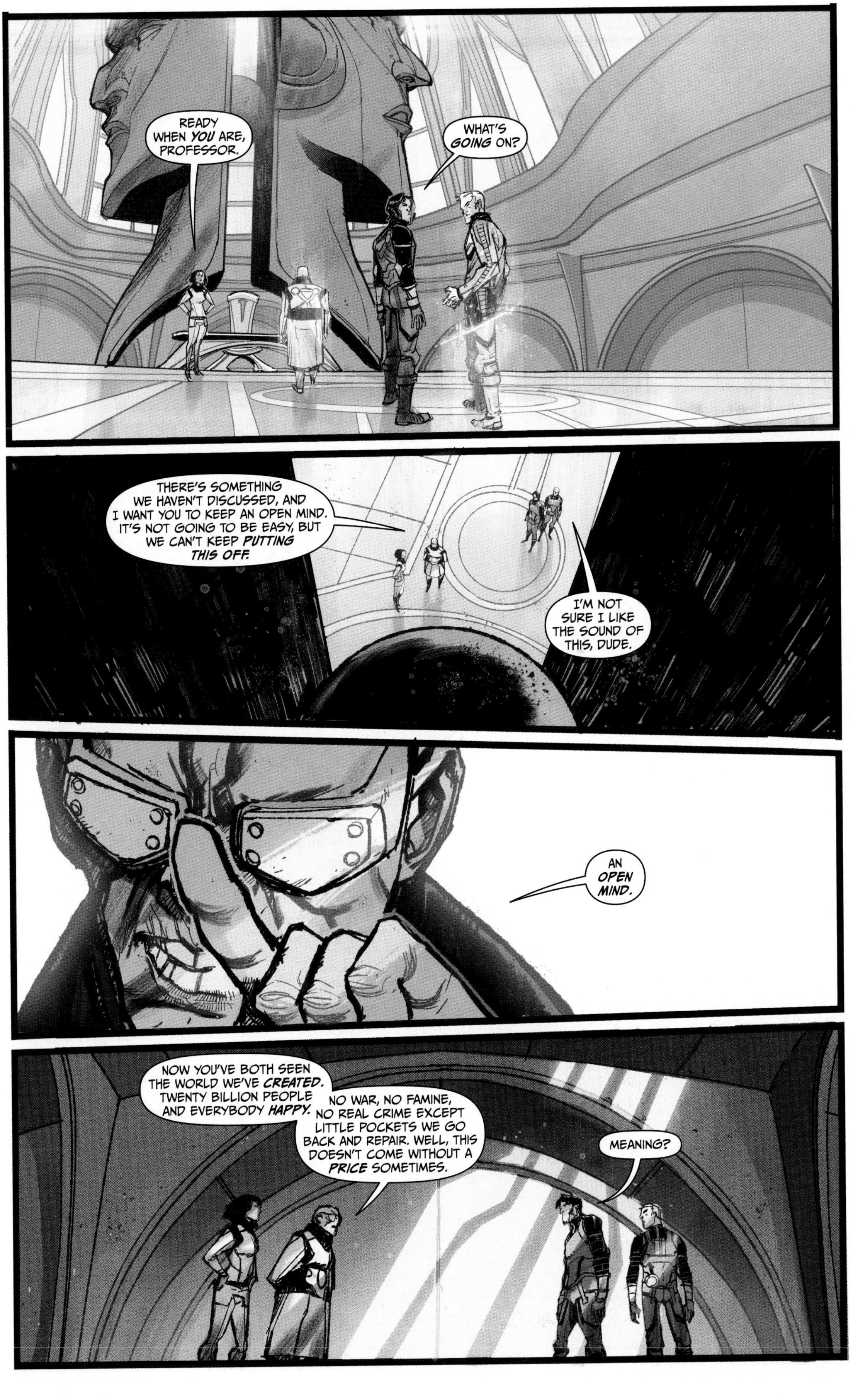
READY WHEN YOU ARE, PROFESSOR.
WHAT'S GOING ON?
THERE'S SOMETHING WE HAVEN'T DISCUSSED, AND I WANT YOU TO KEEP AN OPEN MIND. IT'S NOT GOING TO BE EASY, BUT WE CAN'T KEEP PUTTING THIS OFF.
I'M NOT SURE I LIKE THE SOUND OF THIS, DUDE.
AN OPEN MIND.
NOW YOU'VE BOTH SEEN THE WORLD WE'VE CREATED. TWENTY BILLION PEOPLE AND EVERYBODY HAPPY.
NO WAR, NO FAMINE, NO REAL CRIME EXCEPT LITTLE POCKETS WE GO BACK AND REPAIR. WELL, THIS DOESN'T COME WITHOUT A PRICE SOMETIMES.
MEANING?

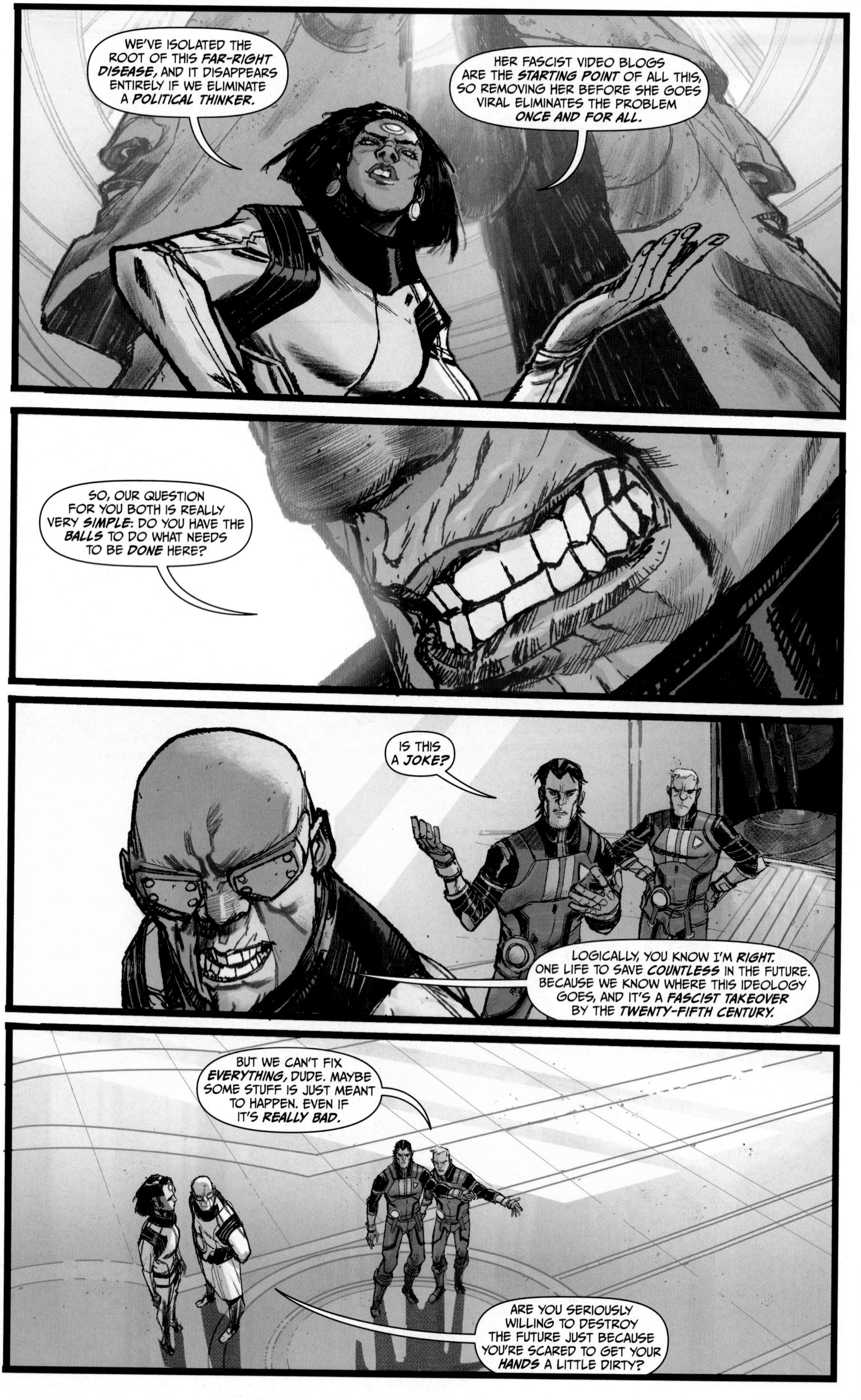
WE'VE ISOLATED THE ROOT OF THIS FAR-RIGHT DISEASE, AND IT DISAPPEARS ENTIRELY IF WE ELIMINATE A POLITICAL THINKER.
HER FASCIST VIDEO BLOGS ARE THE STARTING POINT OF ALL THIS, SO REMOVING HER BEFORE SHE GOES VIRAL ELIMINATES THE PROBLEM ONCE AND FOR ALL.
SO, OUR QUESTION FOR YOU BOTH IS REALLY VERY SIMPLE: DO YOU HAVE THE BALLS TO DO WHAT NEEDS TO BE DONE HERE?
IS THIS A JOKE?
LOGICALLY, YOU KNOW I'M RIGHT. ONE LIFE TO SAVE COUNTLESS IN THE FUTURE. BECAUSE WE KNOW WHERE THIS IDEOLOGY GOES, AND IT'S A FASCIST TAKEOVER BY THE TWENTY-FIFTH CENTURY.
BUT WE CAN'T FIX EVERYTHING, DUDE. MAYBE SOME STUFF IS JUST MEANT TO HAPPEN. EVEN IF IT'S REALLY BAD.
ARE YOU SERIOUSLY WILLING TO DESTROY THE FUTURE JUST BECAUSE YOU'RE SCARED TO GET YOUR HANDS A LITTLE DIRTY?

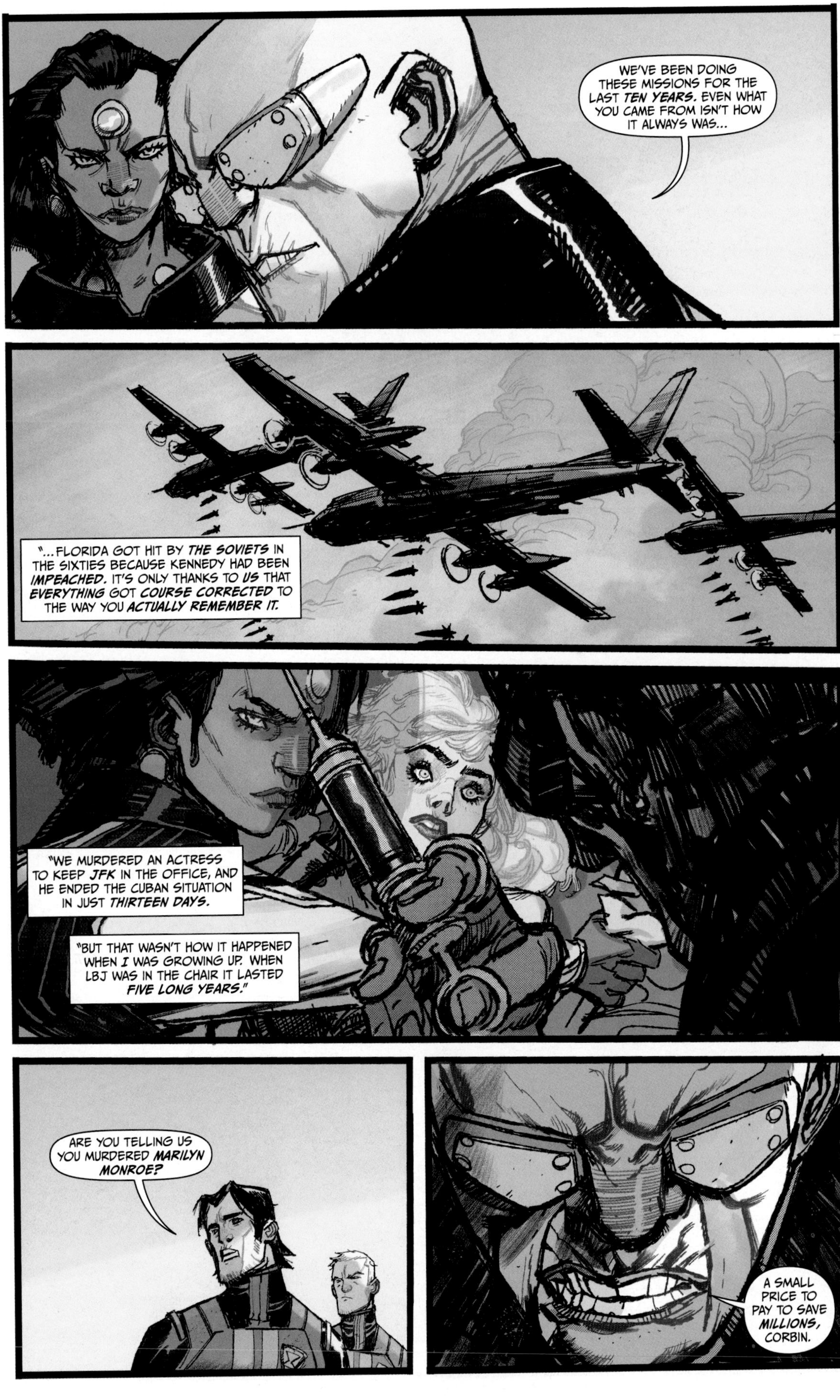
WE'VE BEEN DOING THESE MISSIONS FOR THE LAST TEN YEARS. EVEN WHAT YOU CAME FROM ISN'T HOW IT ALWAYS WAS...
"...FLORIDA GOT HIT BY THE SOVIETS IN THE SIXTIES BECAUSE KENNEDY HAD BEEN IMPEACHED. IT'S ONLY THANKS TO US THAT EVERYTHING GOT COURSE CORRECTED TO THE WAY YOU ACTUALLY REMEMBER IT.
"WE MURDERED AN ACTRESS TO KEEP JFK IN THE OFFICE, AND HE ENDED THE CUBAN SITUATION IN JUST THIRTEEN DAYS.
"BUT THAT WASN'T HOW IT HAPPENED WHEN I WAS GROWING UP. WHEN LBJ WAS IN THE CHAIR IT LASTED FIVE LONG YEARS."
ARE YOU TELLING US YOU MURDERED MARILYN MONROE?
A SMALL PRICE TO PAY TO SAVE MILLIONS, CORBIN.

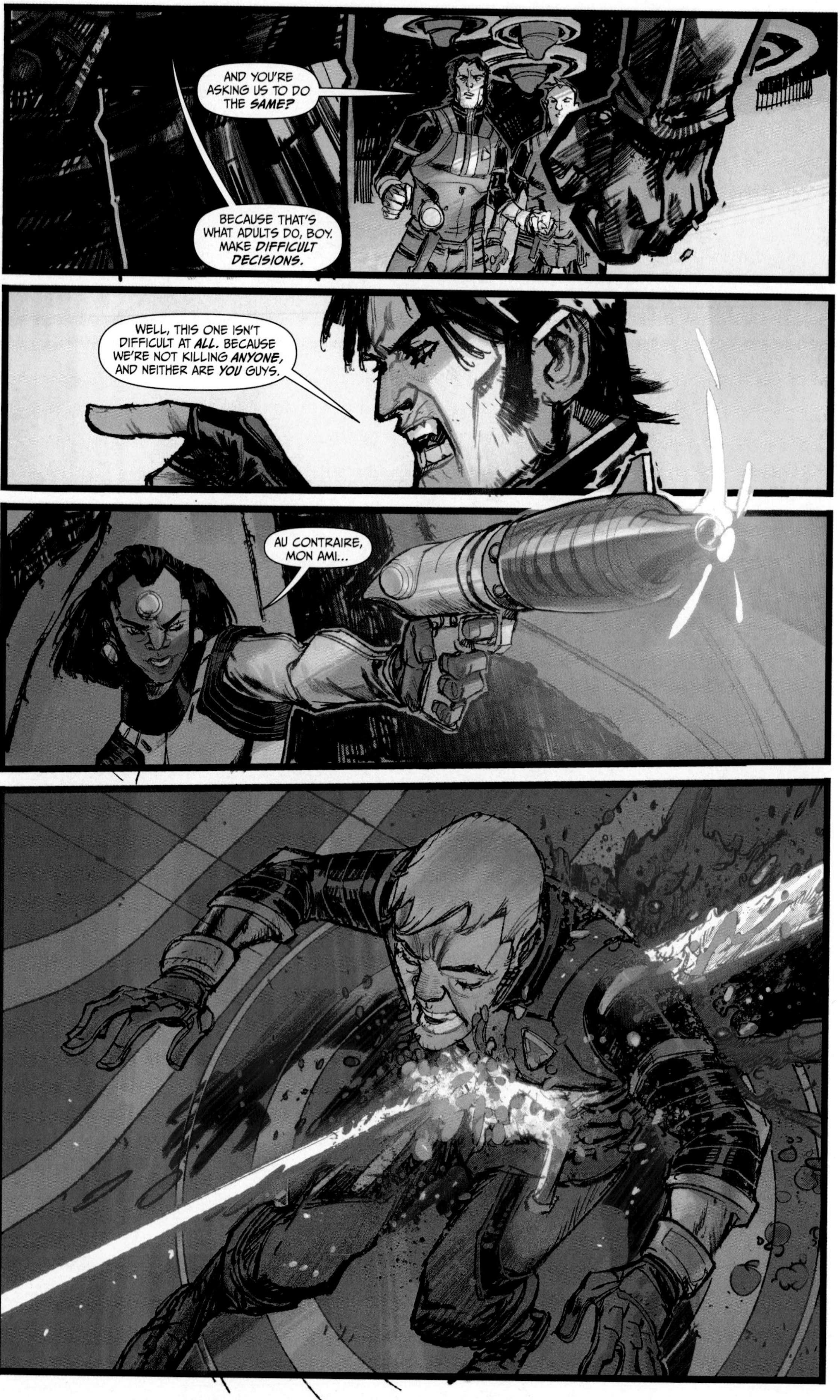
AND YOU'RE ASKING US TO DO THE SAME?
BECAUSE THAT'S WHAT ADULTS DO, BOY. MAKE DIFFICULT DECISIONS.
WELL, THIS ONE ISN'T DIFFICULT AT ALL. BECAUSE WE'RE NOT KILLING ANYONE, AND NEITHER ARE YOU GUYS.
AU CONTRAIRE, MON AMI...

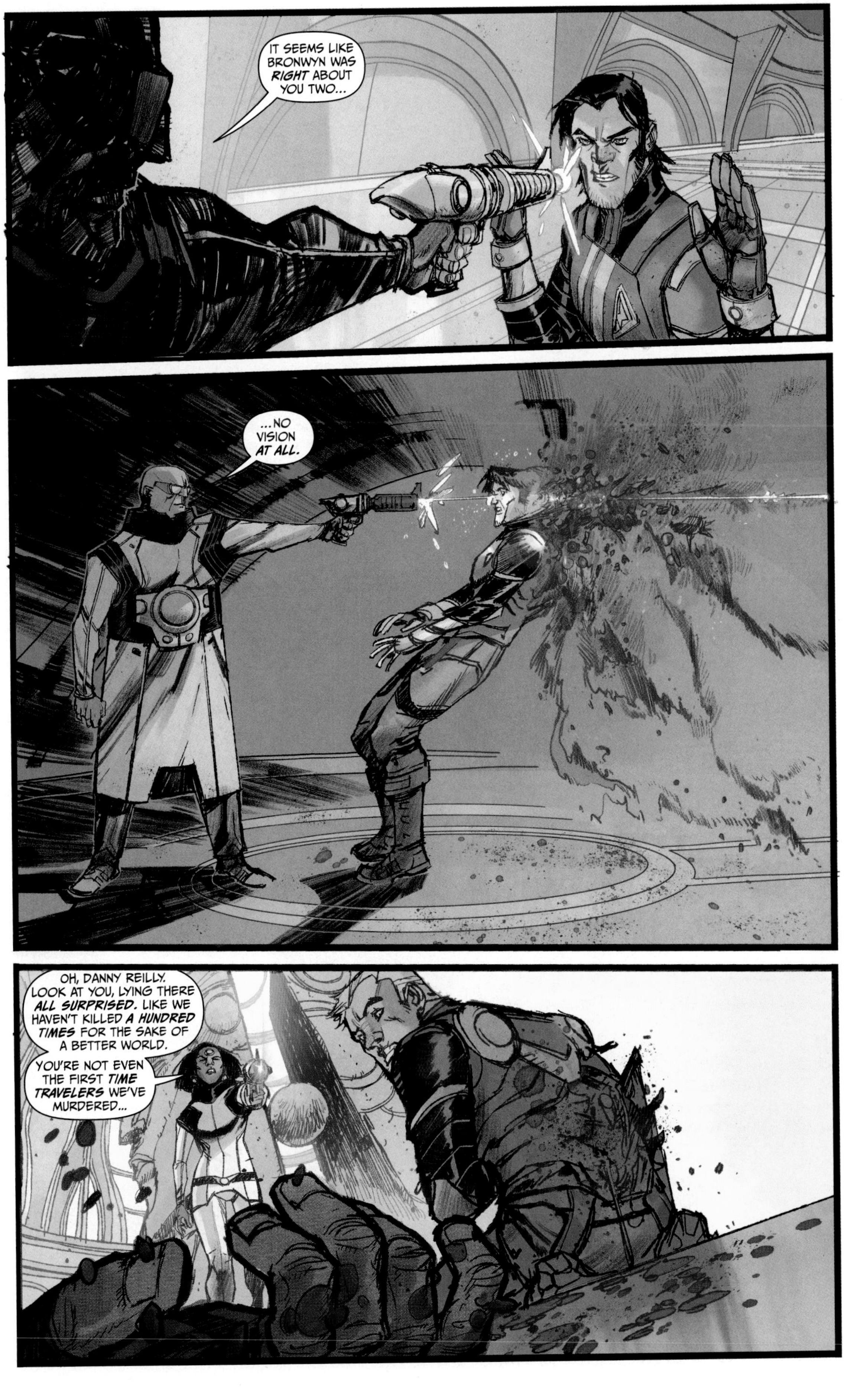
IT SEEMS LIKE BRONWYN WAS RIGHT ABOUT YOU TWO...
...NO VISION AT ALL.
OH, DANNY REILLY. LOOK AT YOU, LYING THERE ALL SURPRISED. LIKE WE HAVEN'T KILLED A HUNDRED TIMES FOR THE SAKE OF A BETTER WORLD.
YOU'RE NOT EVEN THE FIRST TIME TRAVELERS WE'VE MURDERED...

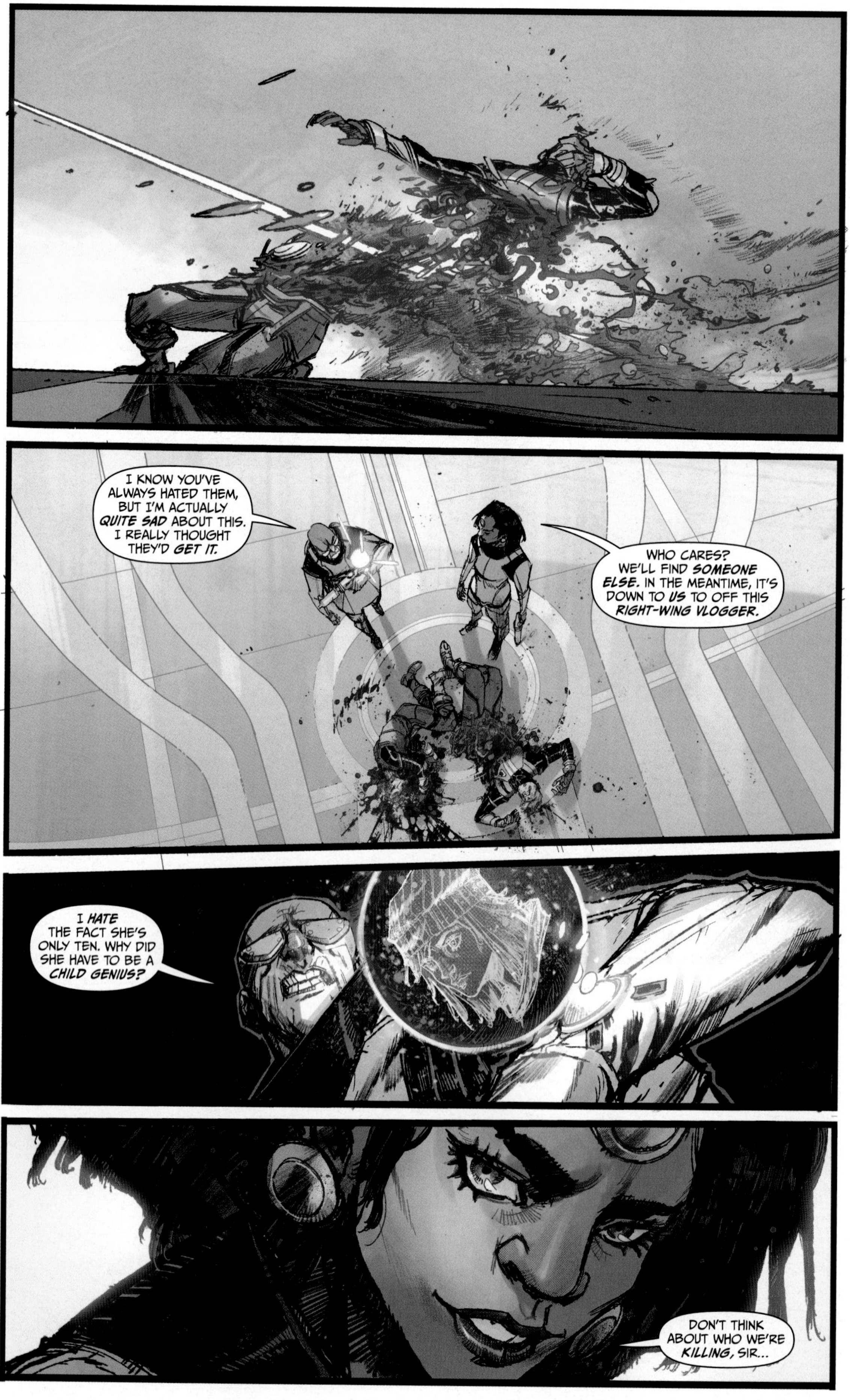
I KNOW YOU'VE ALWAYS HATED THEM, BUT I'M ACTUALLY QUITE SAD ABOUT THIS. I REALLY THOUGHT THEY'D GET IT.
WHO CARES? WE'LL FIND SOMEONE ELSE. IN THE MEANTIME, IT'S DOWN TO US TO OFF THIS RIGHT-WING VLOGGER.
I HATE THE FACT SHE'S ONLY TEN. WHY DID SHE HAVE TO BE A CHILD GENIUS?
DON'T THINK ABOUT WHO WE'RE KILLING, SIR...

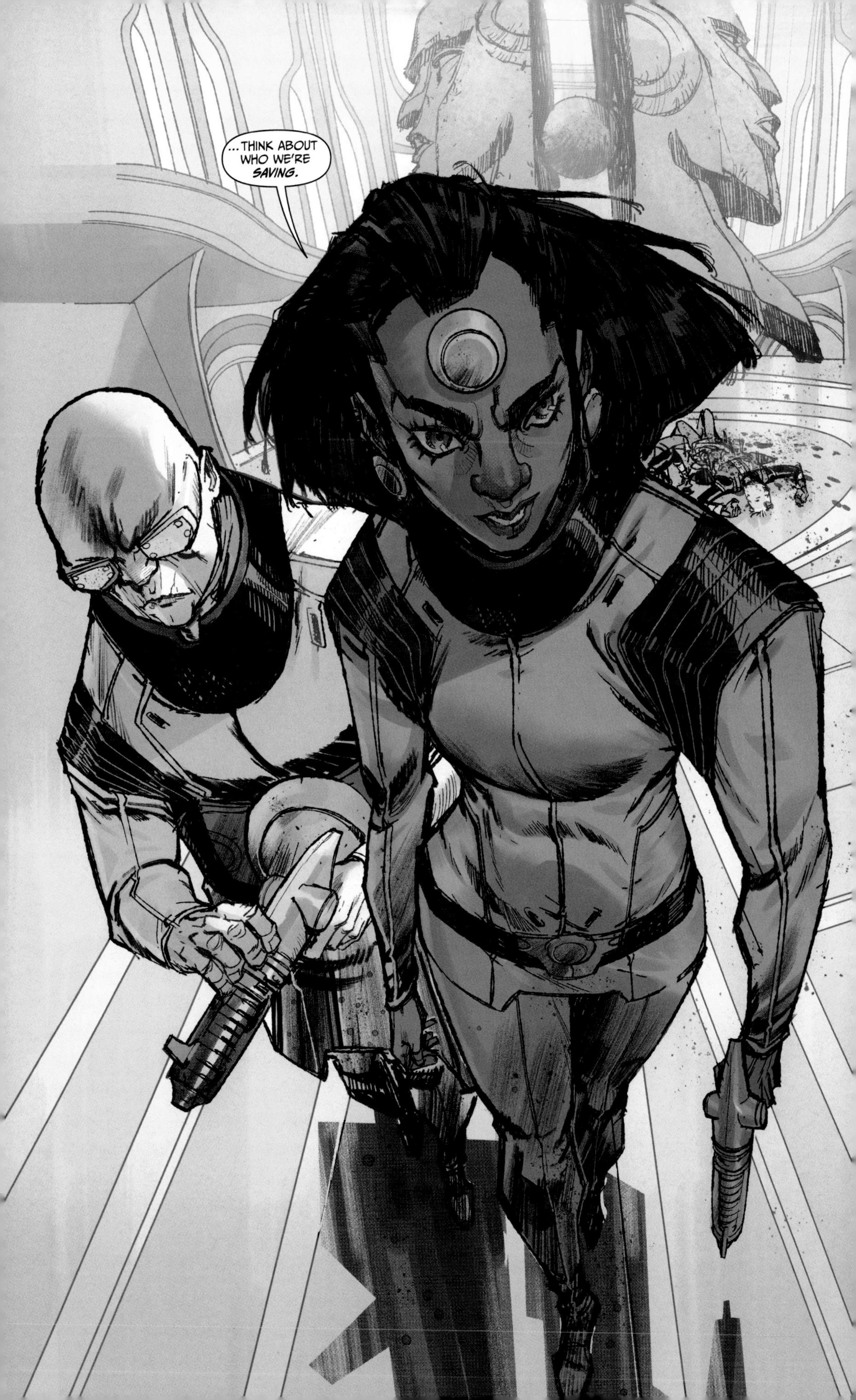
...THINK ABOUT WHO WE'RE *SAVING.*

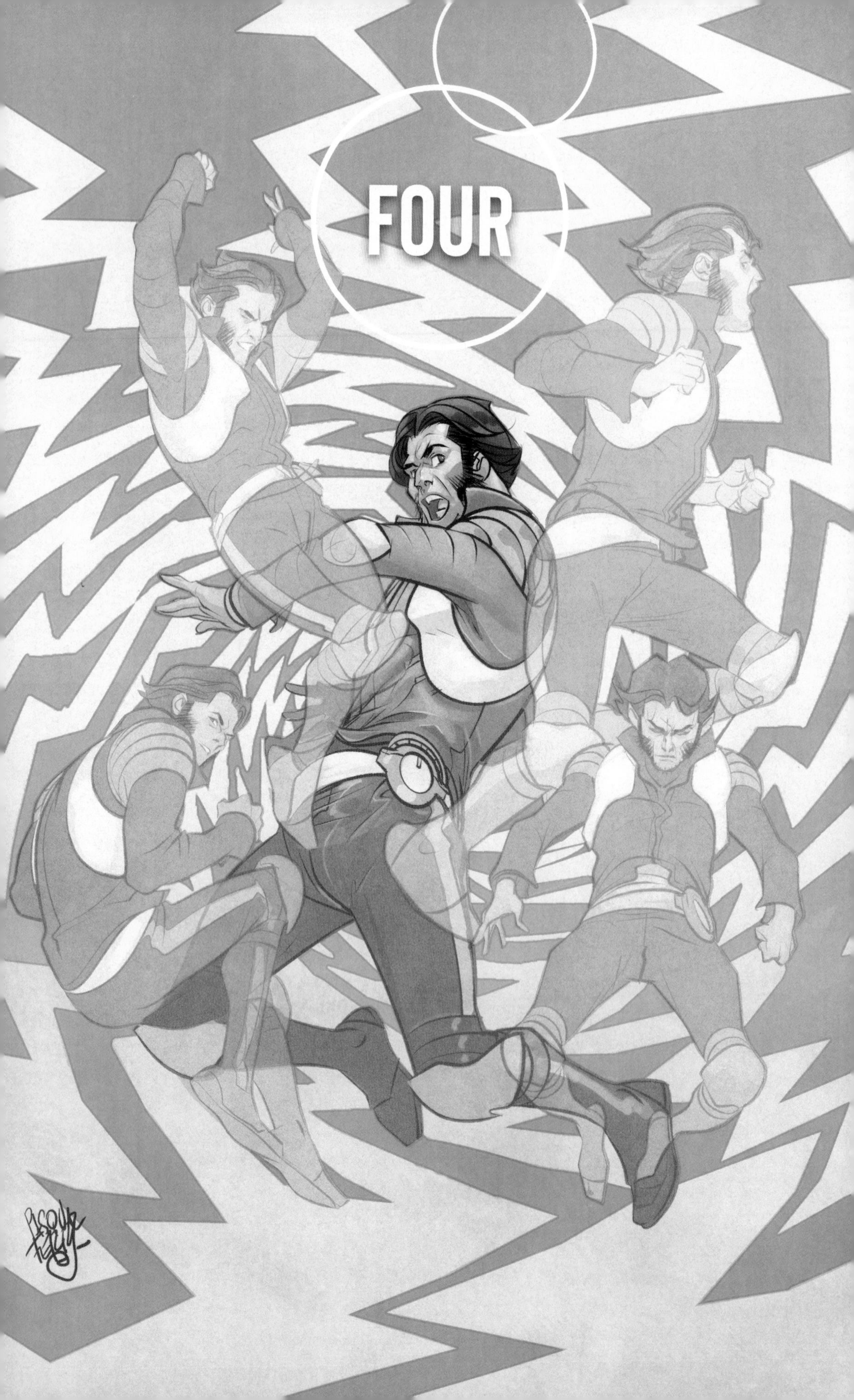
FOUR

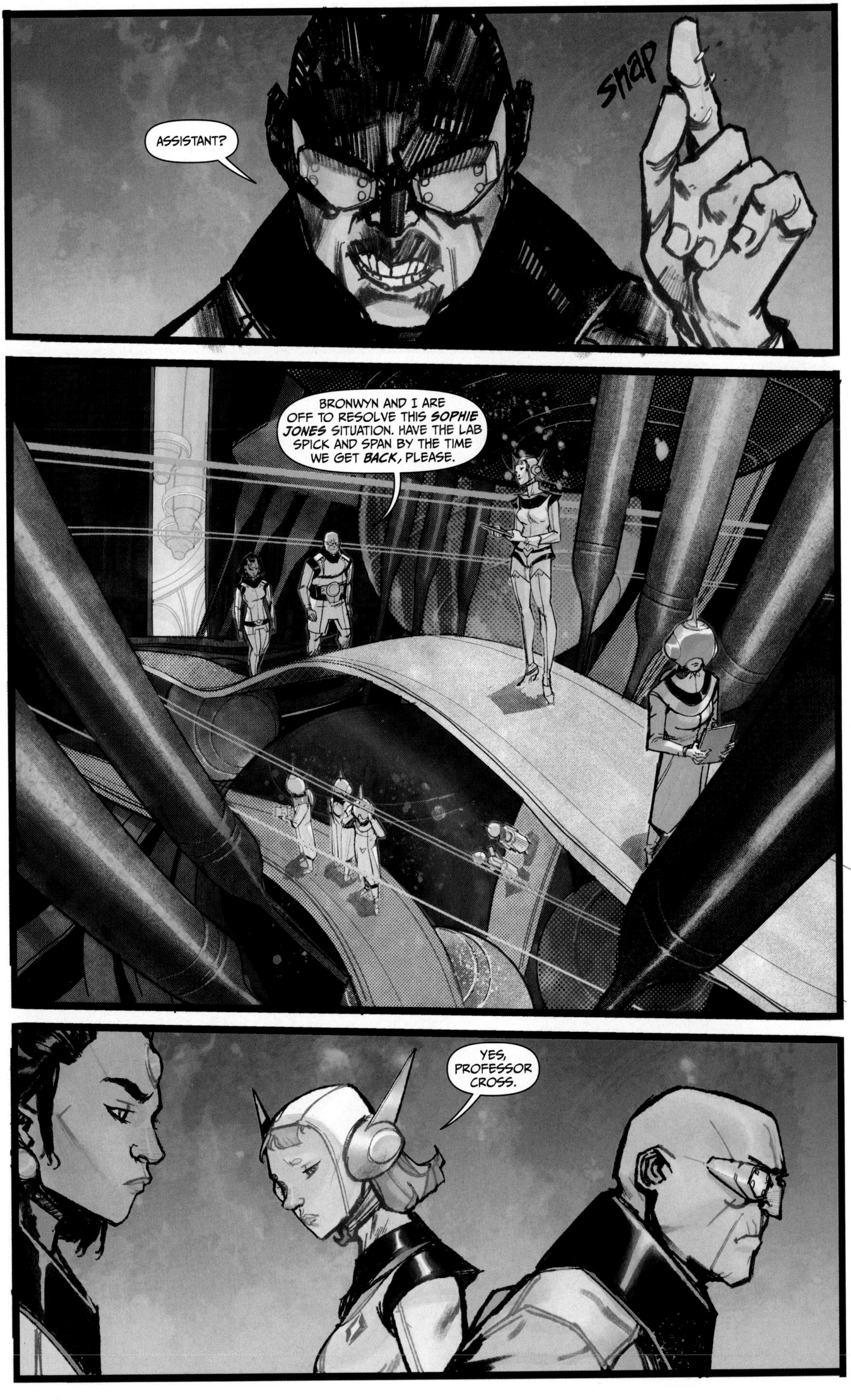
SNAP
ASSISTANT?
BRONWYN AND I ARE OFF TO RESOLVE THIS SOPHIE JONES SITUATION. HAVE THE LAB SPICK AND SPAN BY THE TIME WE GET BACK, PLEASE.
YES, PROFESSOR CROSS.

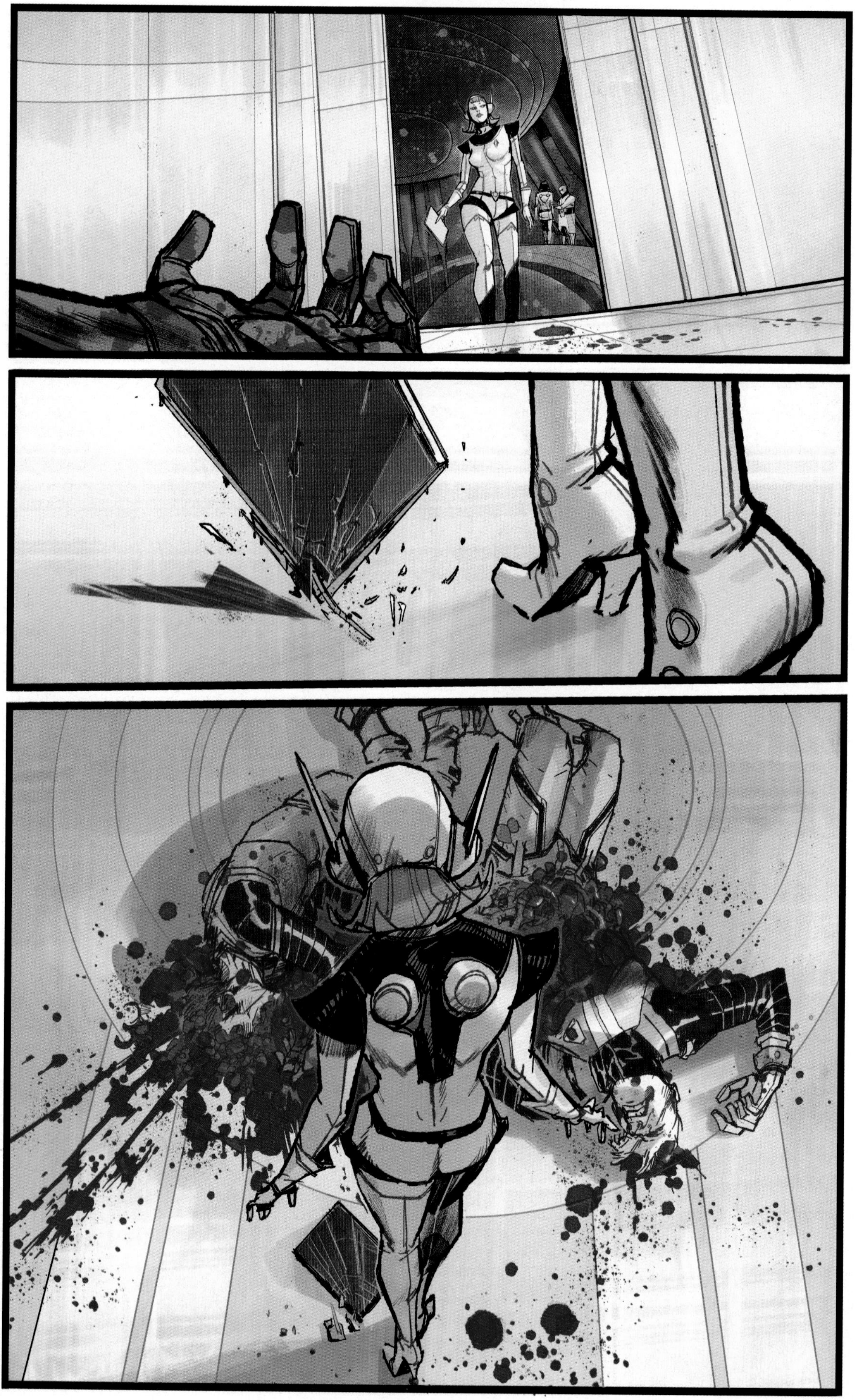

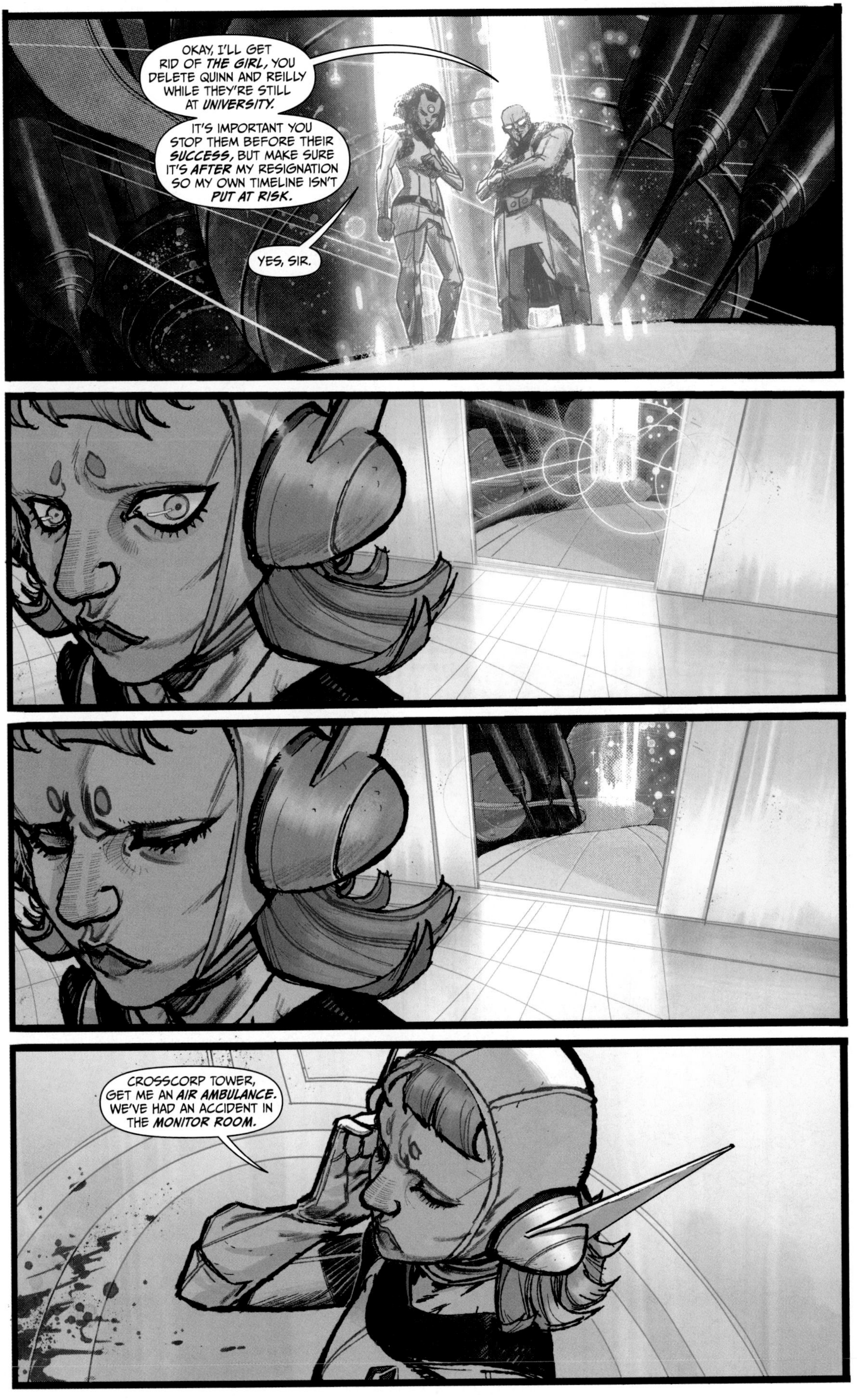
OKAY, I'LL GET RID OF THE GIRL, YOU DELETE QUINN AND REILLY WHILE THEY'RE STILL AT UNIVERSITY.
IT'S IMPORTANT YOU STOP THEM BEFORE THEIR SUCCESS, BUT MAKE SURE IT'S AFTER MY RESIGNATION SO MY OWN TIMELINE ISN'T PUT AT RISK.
YES, SIR.
CROSSCORP TOWER, GET ME AN AIR AMBULANCE. WE'VE HAD AN ACCIDENT IN THE MONITOR ROOM.

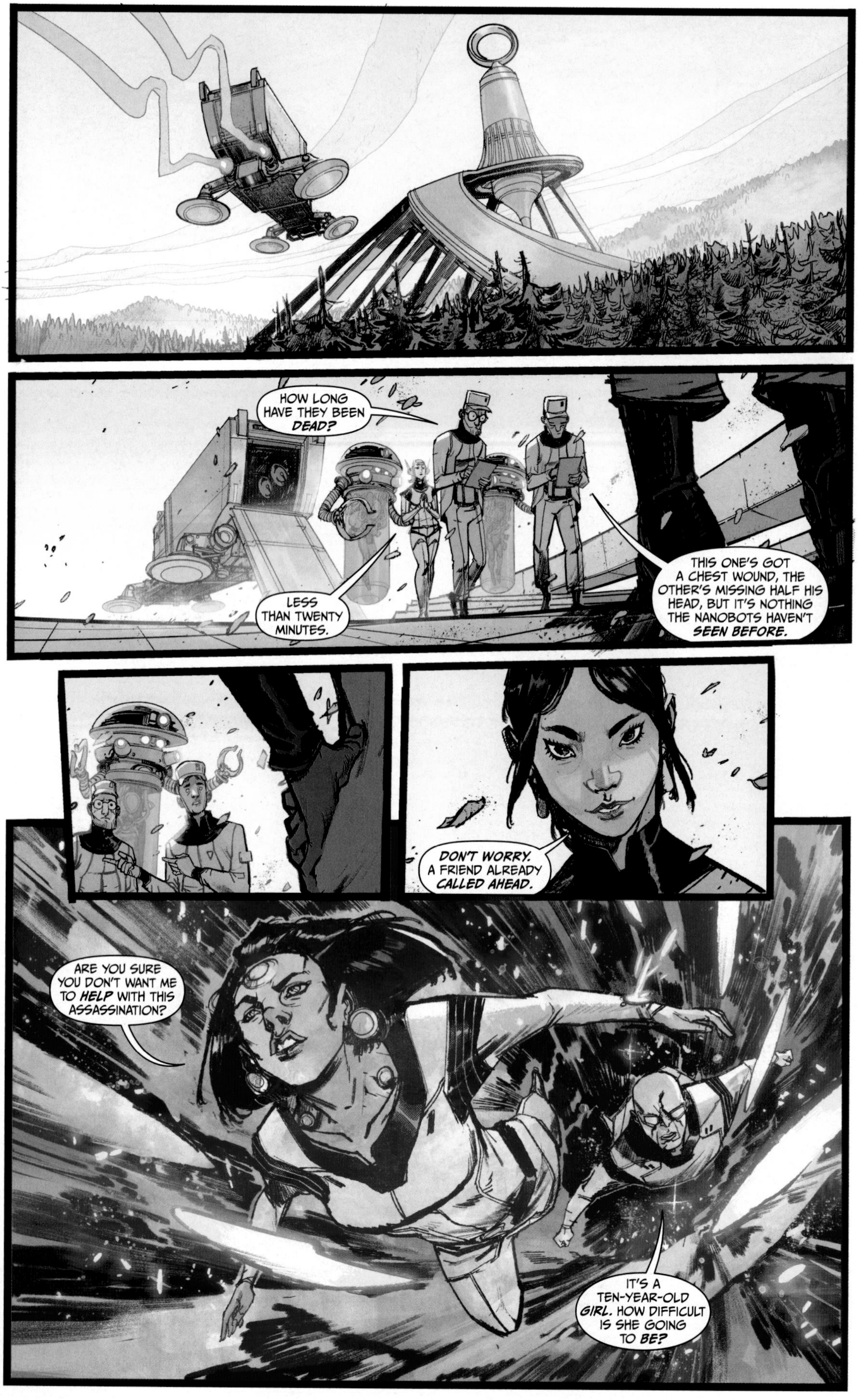
HOW LONG HAVE THEY BEEN DEAD?
LESS THAN TWENTY MINUTES.
THIS ONE'S GOT A CHEST WOUND, THE OTHER'S MISSING HALF HIS HEAD, BUT IT'S NOTHING THE NANOBOTS HAVEN'T SEEN BEFORE.
DON'T WORRY. A FRIEND ALREADY CALLED AHEAD.
ARE YOU SURE YOU DON'T WANT ME TO HELP WITH THIS ASSASSINATION?
IT'S A TEN-YEAR-OLD GIRL. HOW DIFFICULT IS SHE GOING TO BE?

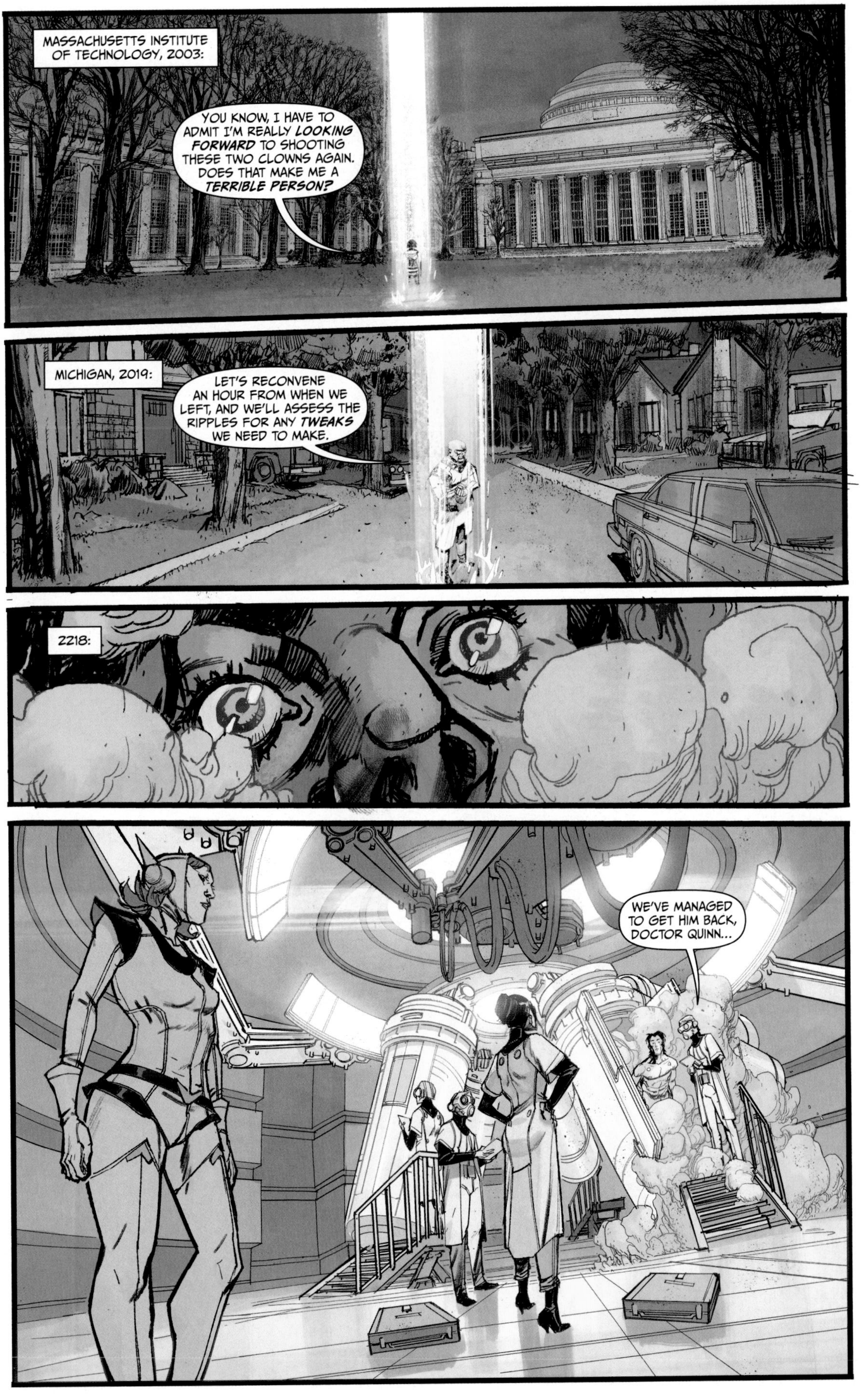
MASSACHUSETTS INSTITUTE OF TECHNOLOGY, 2003:
YOU KNOW, I HAVE TO ADMIT I'M REALLY LOOKING FORWARD TO SHOOTING THESE TWO CLOWNS AGAIN. DOES THAT MAKE ME A TERRIBLE PERSON?
MICHIGAN, 2019:
LET'S RECONVENE AN HOUR FROM WHEN WE LEFT, AND WE'LL ASSESS THE RIPPLES FOR ANY TWEAKS WE NEED TO MAKE.
2218:
WE'VE MANAGED TO GET HIM BACK, DOCTOR QUINN...

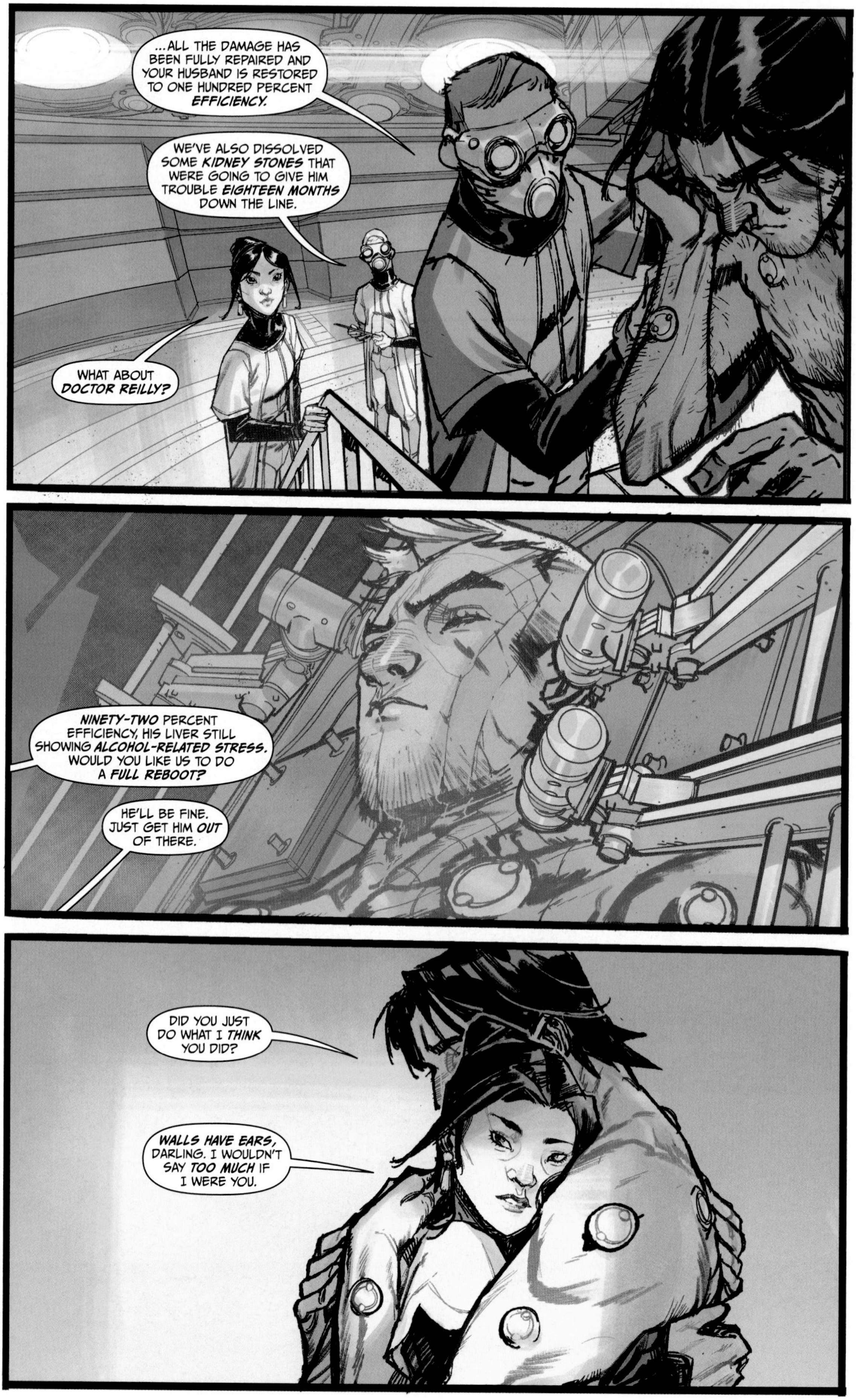

...ALL THE DAMAGE HAS BEEN FULLY REPAIRED AND YOUR HUSBAND IS RESTORED TO ONE HUNDRED PERCENT *EFFICIENCY.*
WE'VE ALSO DISSOLVED SOME *KIDNEY STONES* THAT WERE GOING TO GIVE HIM TROUBLE *EIGHTEEN MONTHS* DOWN THE LINE.
WHAT ABOUT *DOCTOR REILLY?*
NINETY-TWO PERCENT EFFICIENCY, HIS LIVER STILL SHOWING *ALCOHOL-RELATED STRESS.* WOULD YOU LIKE US TO DO A *FULL REBOOT?*
HE'LL BE FINE. JUST GET HIM *OUT* OF THERE.
DID YOU JUST DO WHAT I *THINK* YOU DID?
WALLS HAVE EARS, DARLING. I WOULDN'T SAY *TOO MUCH* IF I WERE YOU.

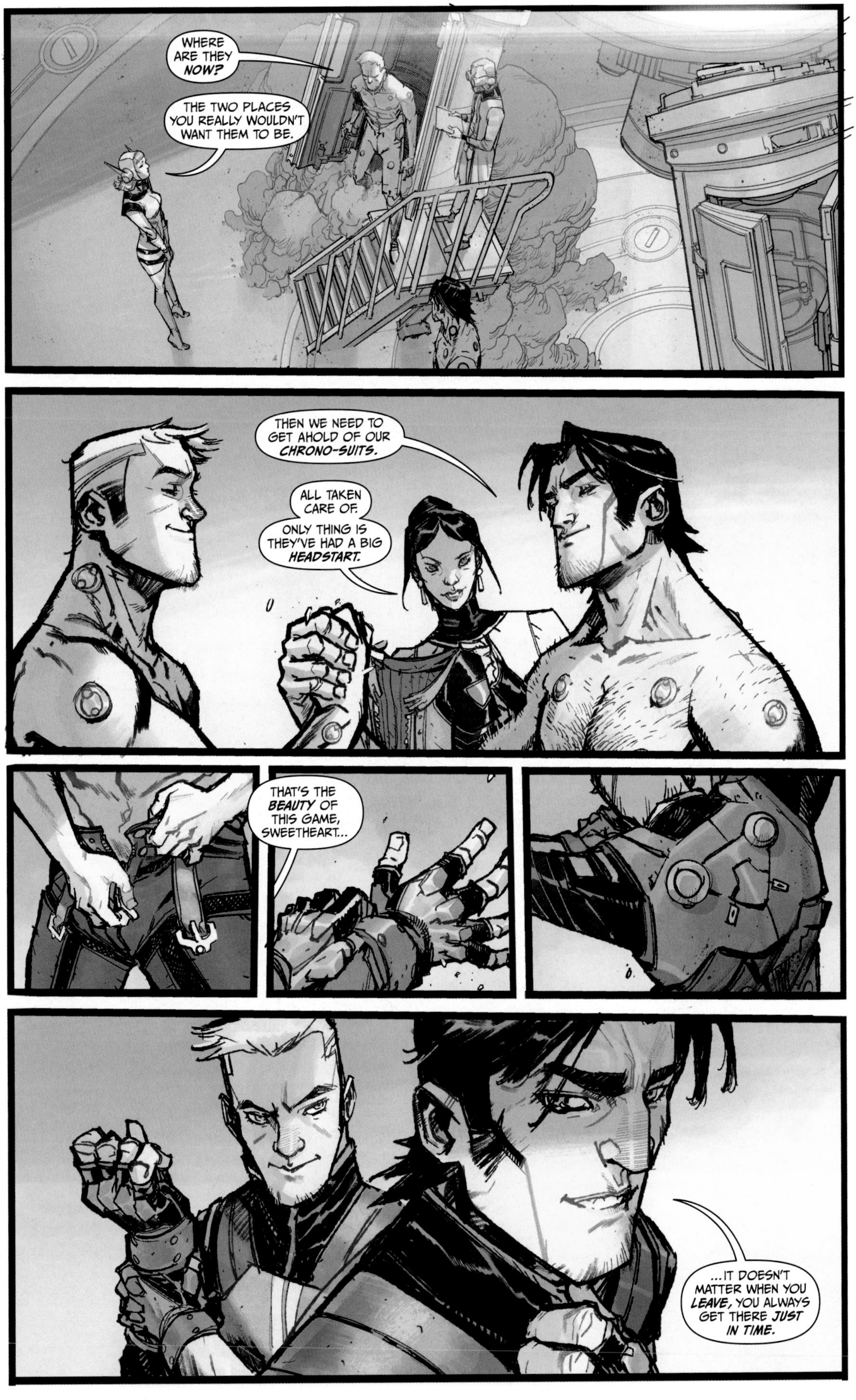
WHERE ARE THEY NOW?
THE TWO PLACES YOU REALLY WOULDN'T WANT THEM TO BE.
THEN WE NEED TO GET AHOLD OF OUR CHRONO-SUITS.
ALL TAKEN CARE OF.
ONLY THING IS THEY'VE HAD A BIG HEADSTART.
THAT'S THE BEAUTY OF THIS GAME, SWEETHEART...
...IT DOESN'T MATTER WHEN YOU LEAVE, YOU ALWAYS GET THERE JUST IN TIME.

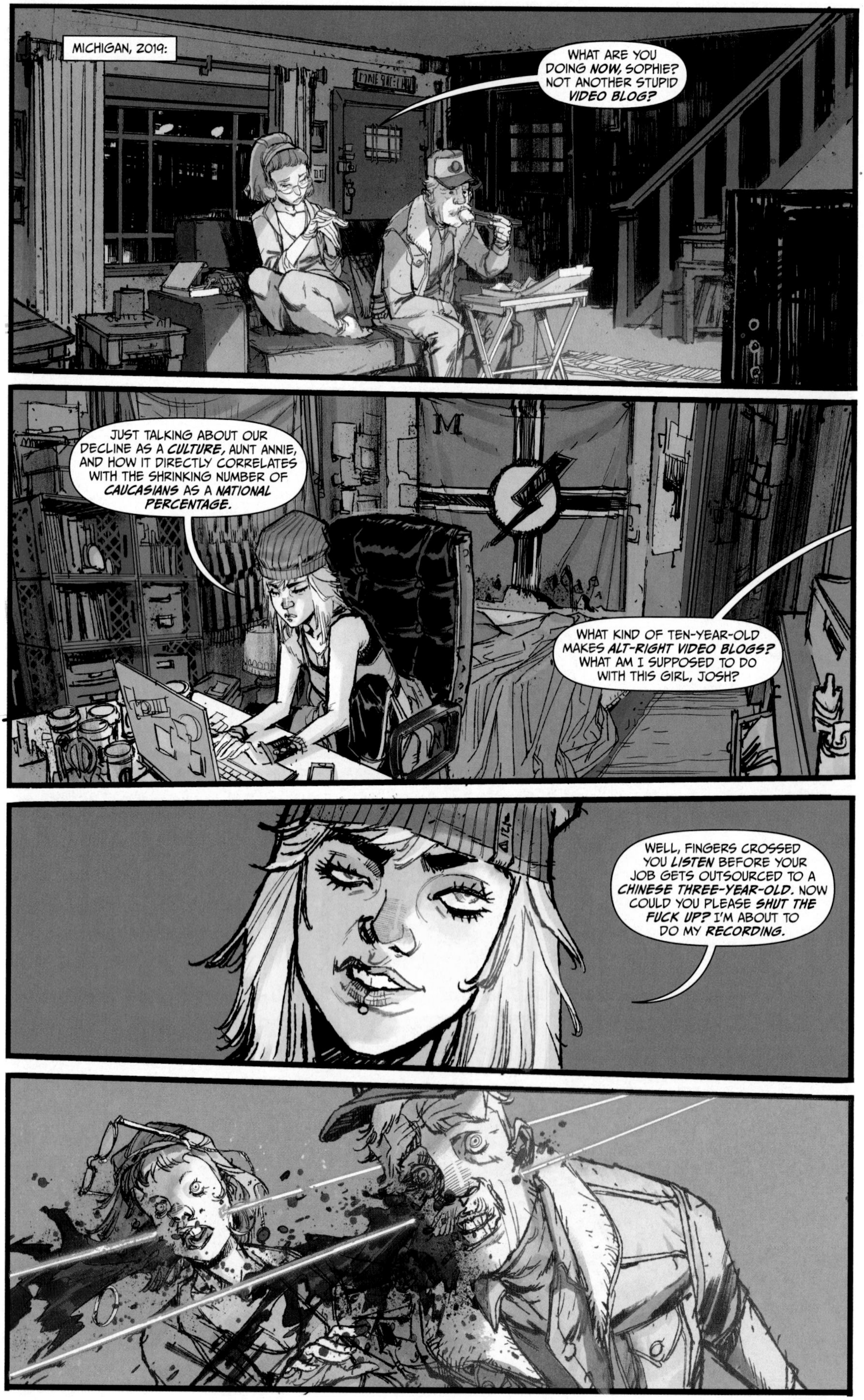
MICHIGAN, 2019:
WHAT ARE YOU DOING NOW, SOPHIE? NOT ANOTHER STUPID VIDEO BLOG?
JUST TALKING ABOUT OUR DECLINE AS A CULTURE, AUNT ANNIE, AND HOW IT DIRECTLY CORRELATES WITH THE SHRINKING NUMBER OF CAUCASIANS AS A NATIONAL PERCENTAGE.
WHAT KIND OF TEN-YEAR-OLD MAKES ALT-RIGHT VIDEO BLOGS? WHAT AM I SUPPOSED TO DO WITH THIS GIRL, JOSH?
WELL, FINGERS CROSSED YOU LISTEN BEFORE YOUR JOB GETS OUTSOURCED TO A CHINESE THREE-YEAR-OLD. NOW COULD YOU PLEASE SHUT THE FUCK UP? I'M ABOUT TO DO MY RECORDING.

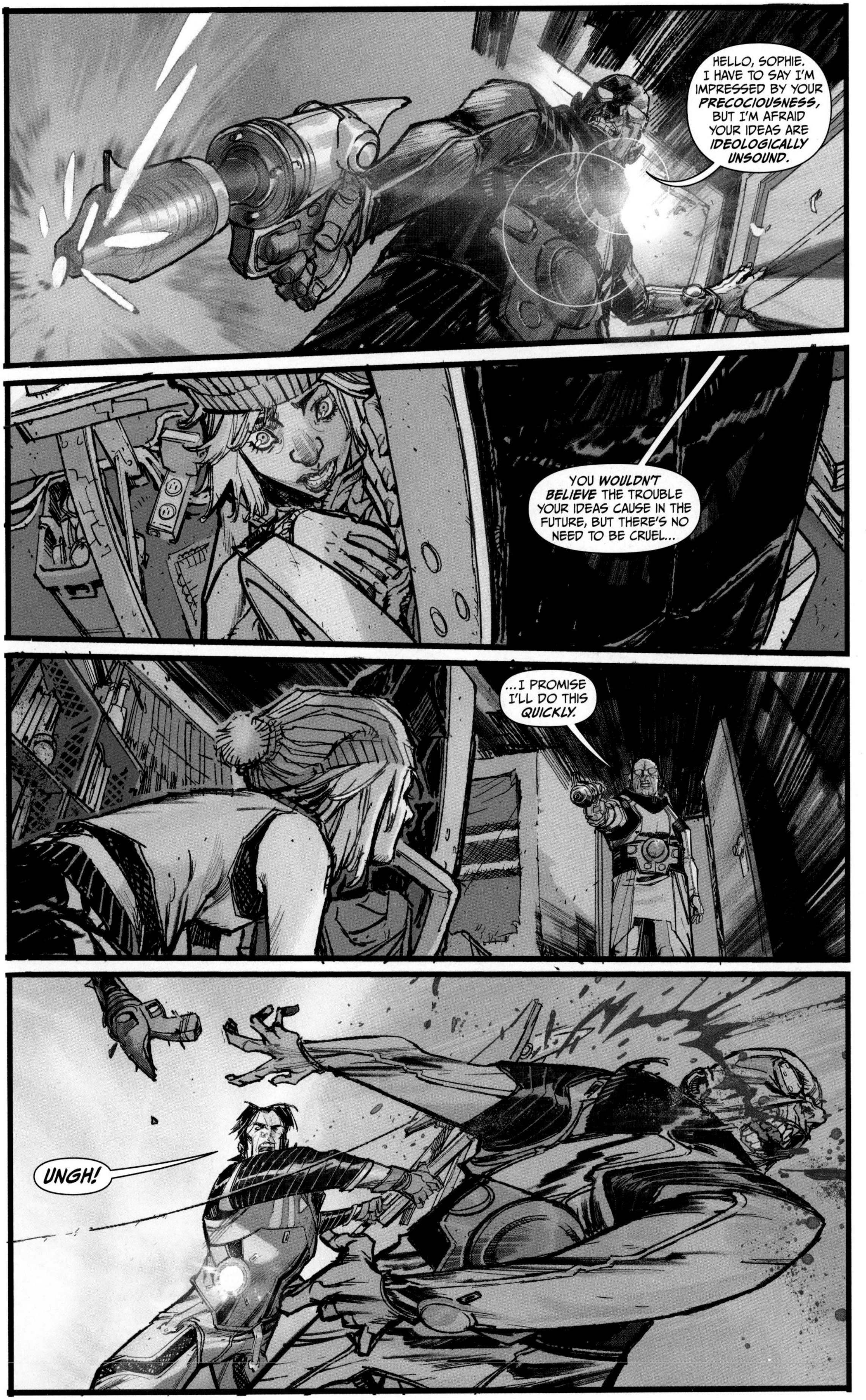
HELLO, SOPHIE. I HAVE TO SAY I'M IMPRESSED BY YOUR PRECOCIOUSNESS, BUT I'M AFRAID YOUR IDEAS ARE IDEOLOGICALLY UNSOUND.
YOU WOULDN'T BELIEVE THE TROUBLE YOUR IDEAS CAUSE IN THE FUTURE, BUT THERE'S NO NEED TO BE CRUEL...
...I PROMISE I'LL DO THIS QUICKLY.
UNGH!

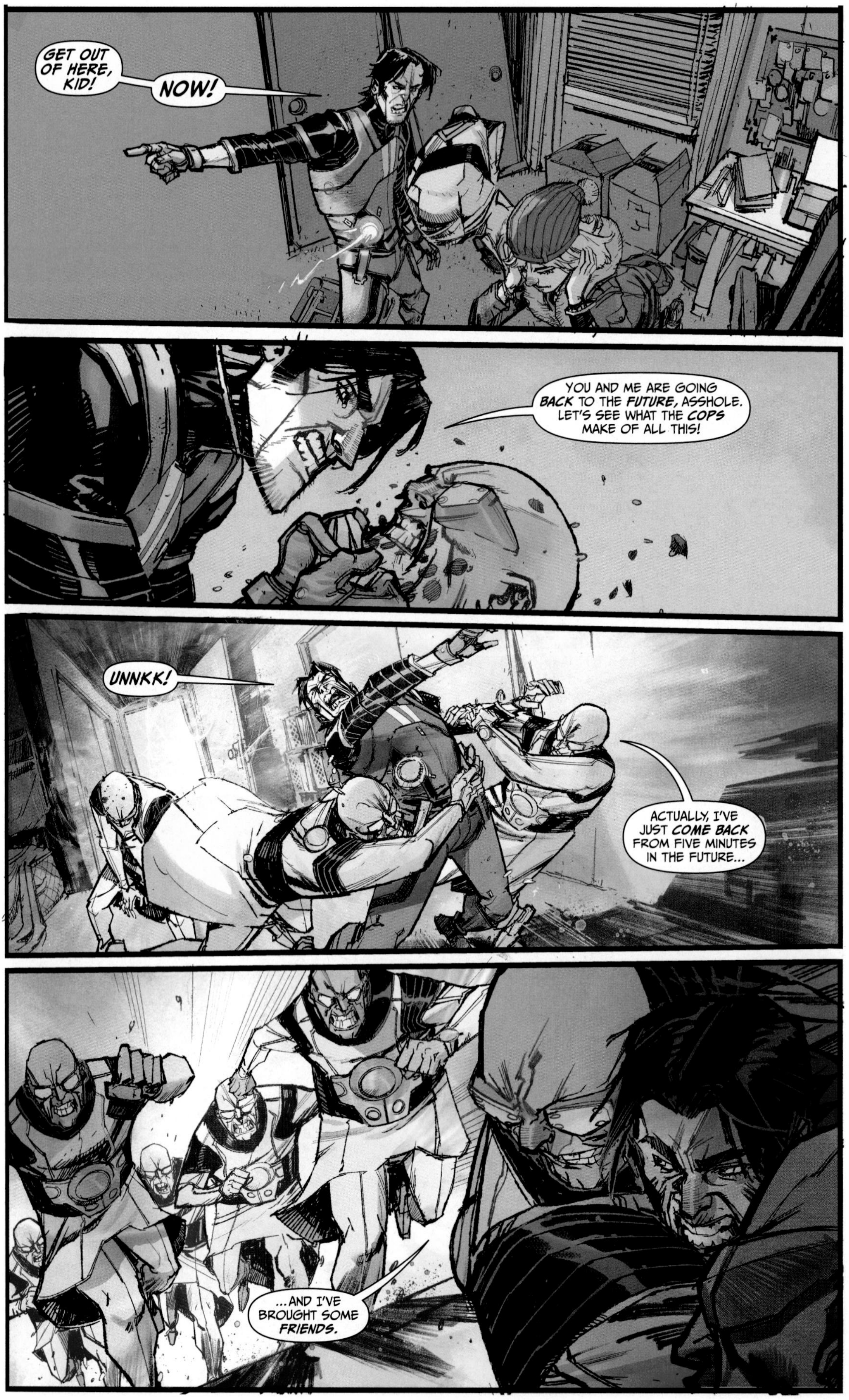
GET OUT OF HERE, KID!
NOW!
YOU AND ME ARE GOING BACK TO THE FUTURE, ASSHOLE. LET'S SEE WHAT THE COPS MAKE OF ALL THIS!
UNNKK!
ACTUALLY, I'VE JUST COME BACK FROM FIVE MINUTES IN THE FUTURE...
...AND I'VE BROUGHT SOME FRIENDS.

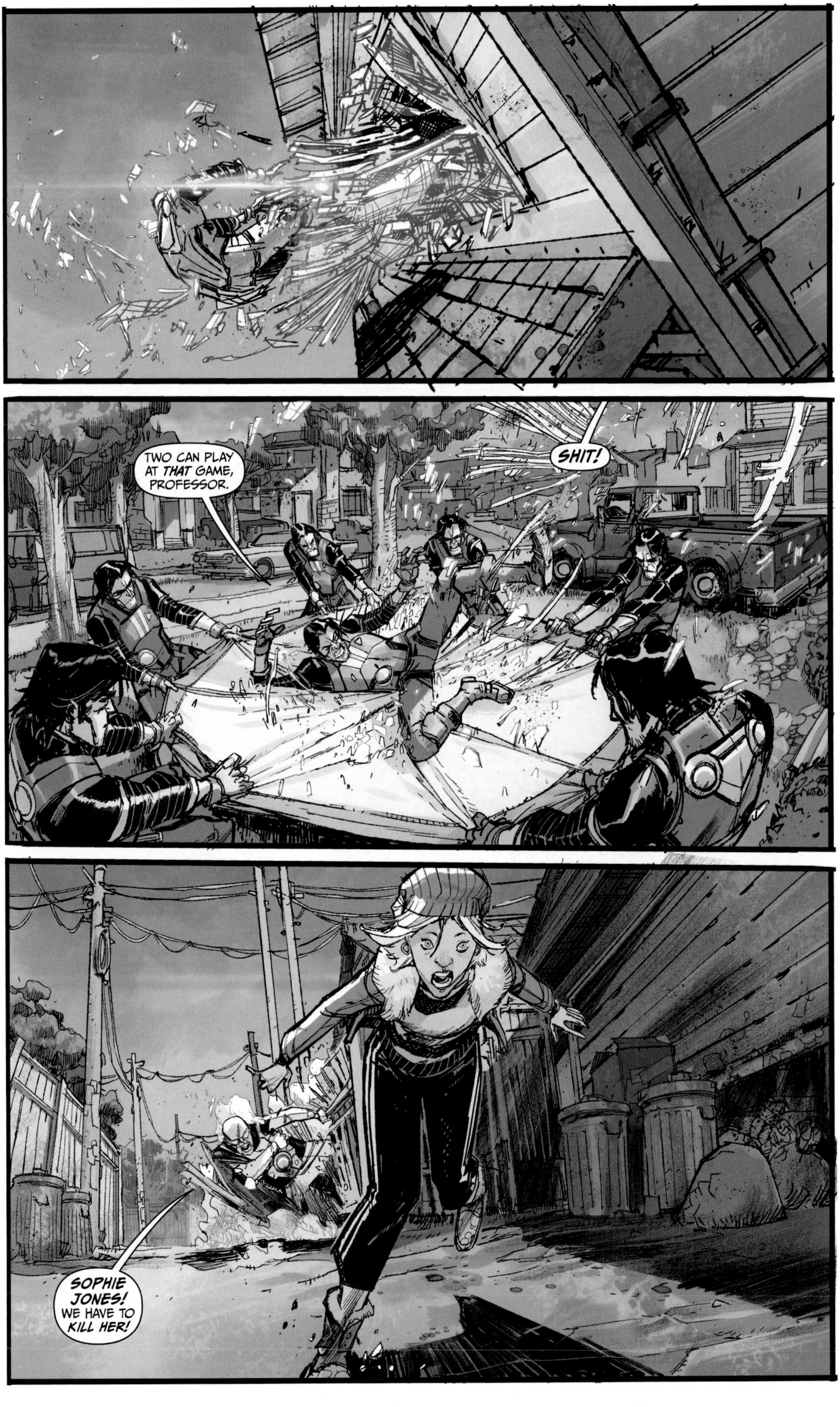
TWO CAN PLAY AT THAT GAME, PROFESSOR.
SHIT!
SOPHIE JONES! WE HAVE TO KILL HER!

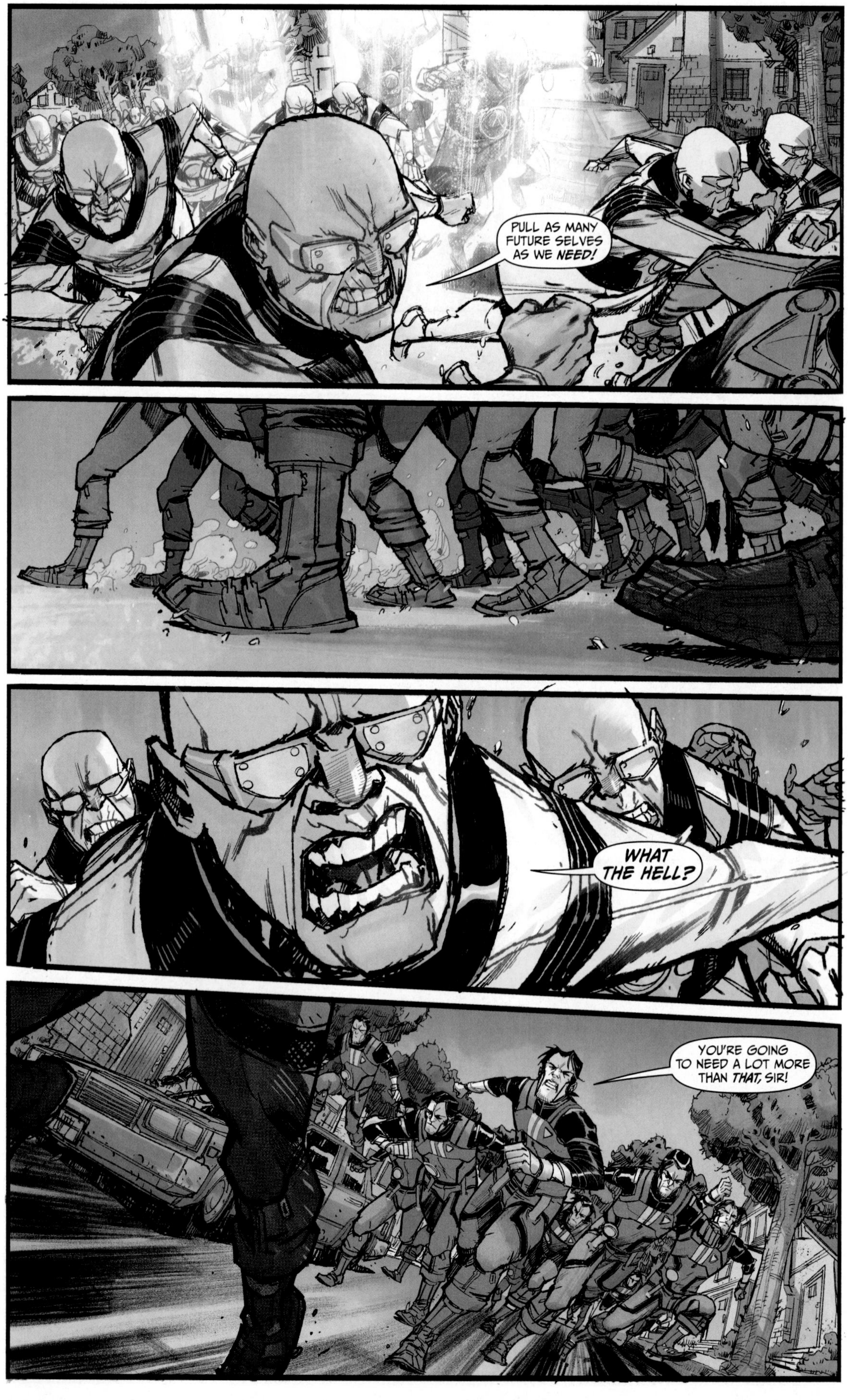
PULL AS MANY FUTURE SELVES AS WE NEED!
WHAT THE HELL?
YOU'RE GOING TO NEED A LOT MORE THAN THAT, SIR!

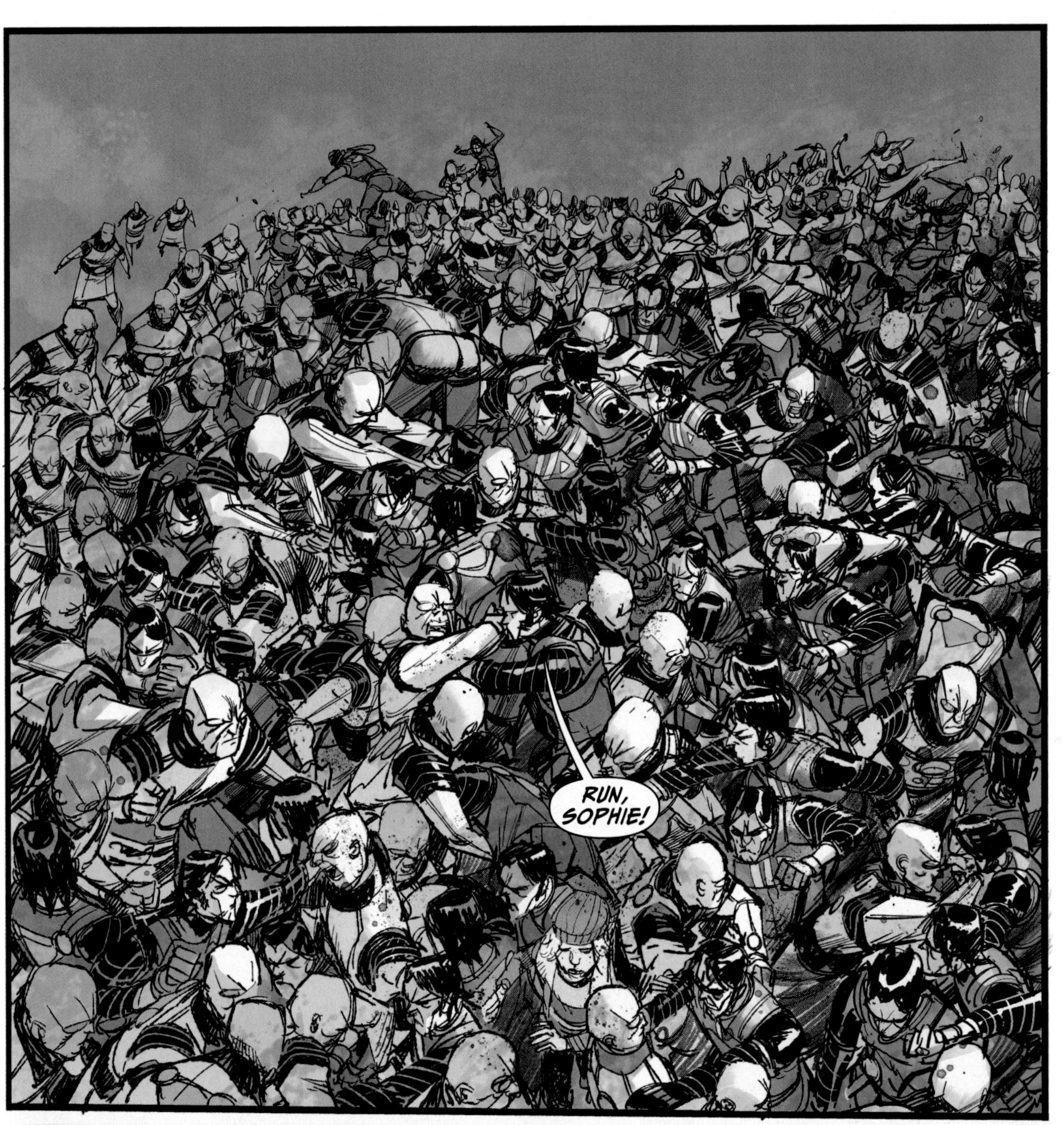
RUN, SOPHIE!

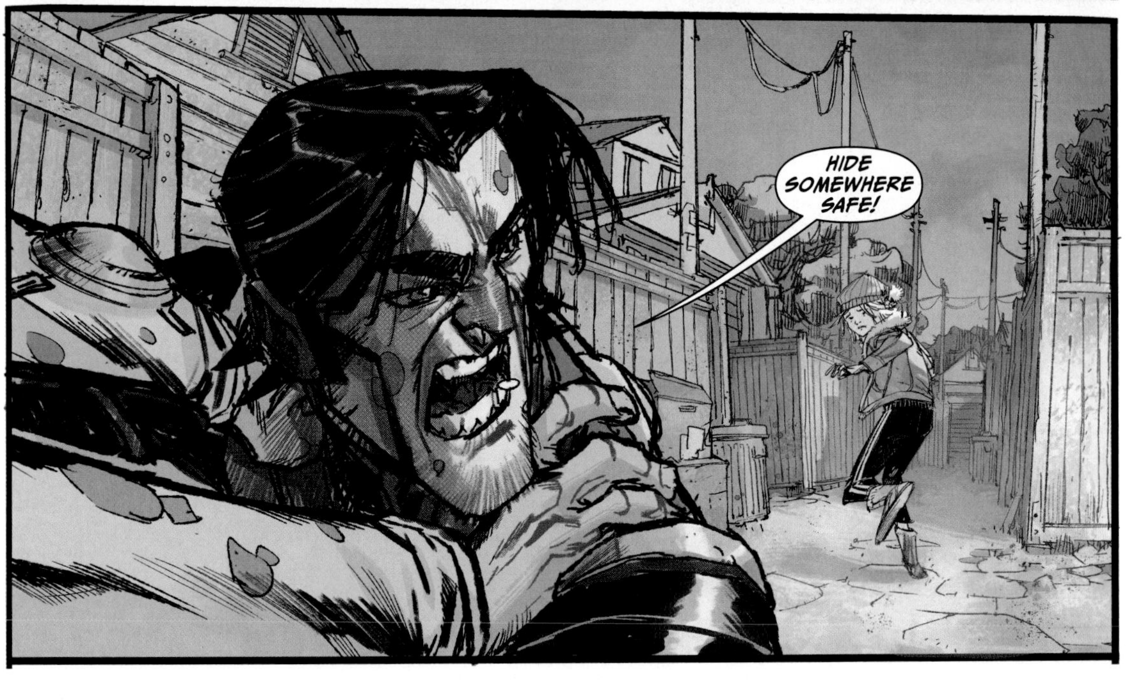
HIDE SOMEWHERE SAFE!

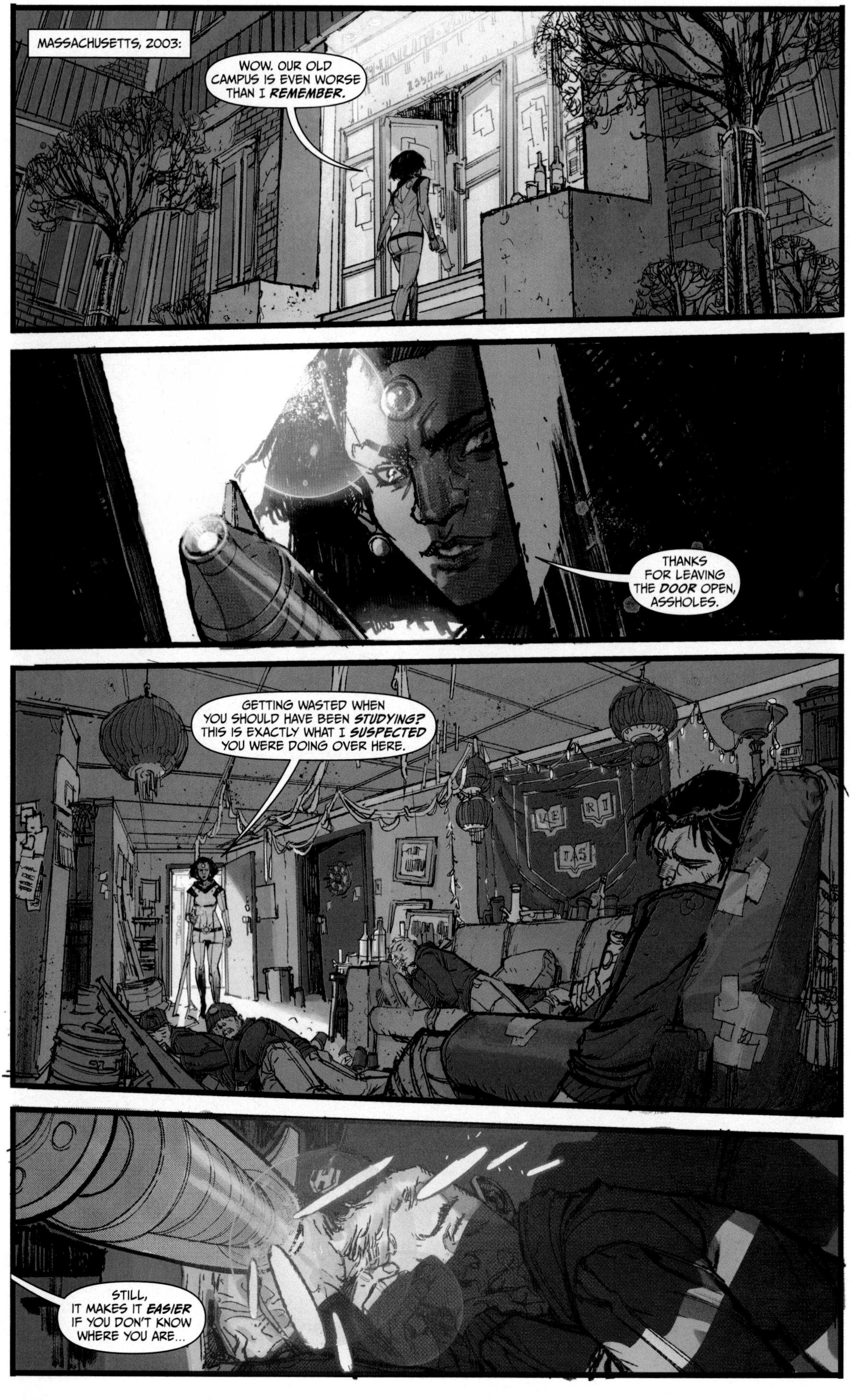
MASSACHUSETTS, 2003:
WOW. OUR OLD CAMPUS IS EVEN WORSE THAN I *REMEMBER.*
THANKS FOR LEAVING THE *DOOR* OPEN, ASSHOLES.
GETTING WASTED WHEN YOU SHOULD HAVE BEEN *STUDYING?* THIS IS EXACTLY WHAT I *SUSPECTED* YOU WERE DOING OVER HERE.
STILL, IT MAKES IT *EASIER* IF YOU DON'T KNOW WHERE YOU ARE...

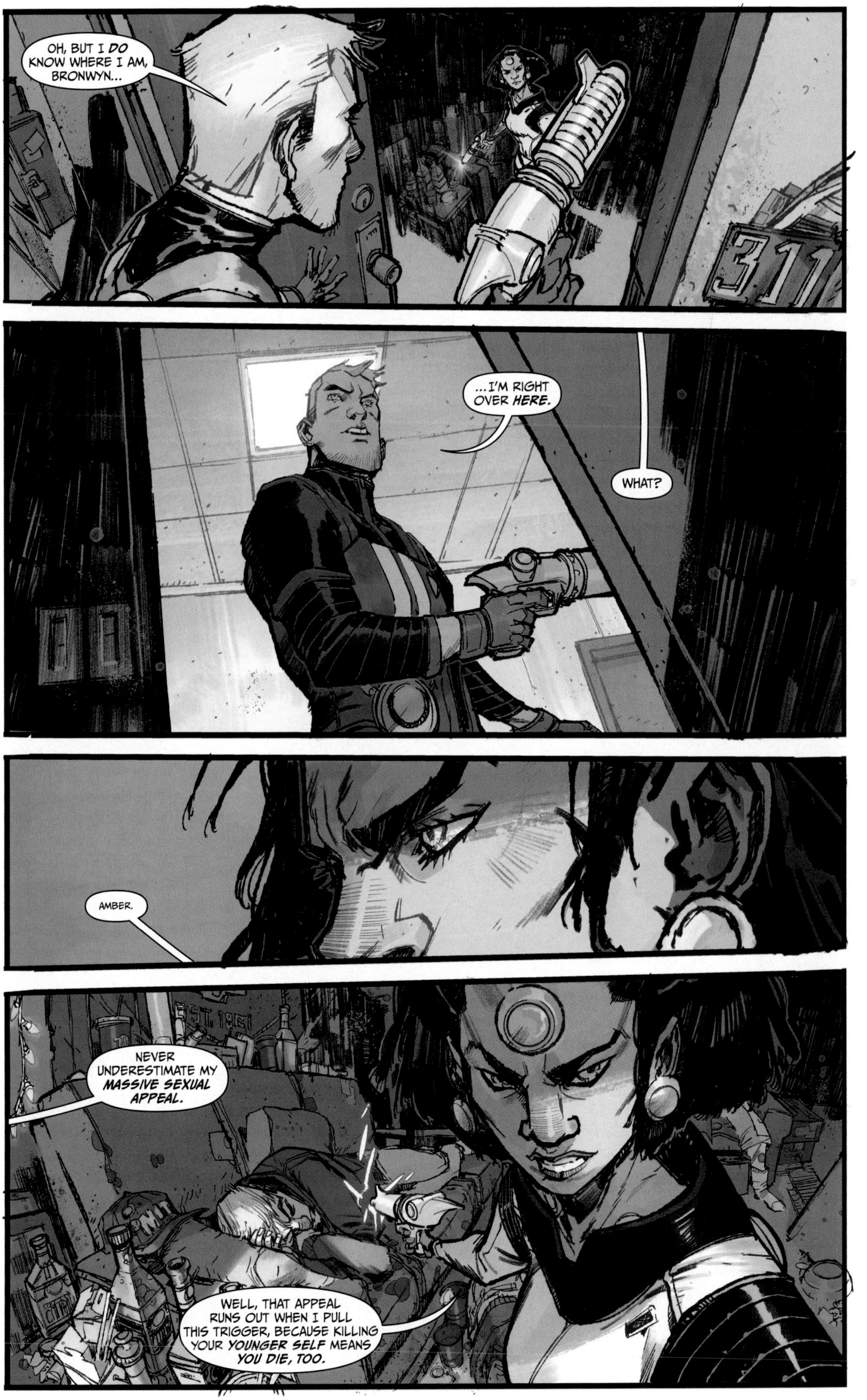
OH, BUT I DO KNOW WHERE I AM, BRONWYN...
...I'M RIGHT OVER HERE.
WHAT?
AMBER.
NEVER UNDERESTIMATE MY MASSIVE SEXUAL APPEAL.
WELL, THAT APPEAL RUNS OUT WHEN I PULL THIS TRIGGER, BECAUSE KILLING YOUR YOUNGER SELF MEANS YOU DIE, TOO.

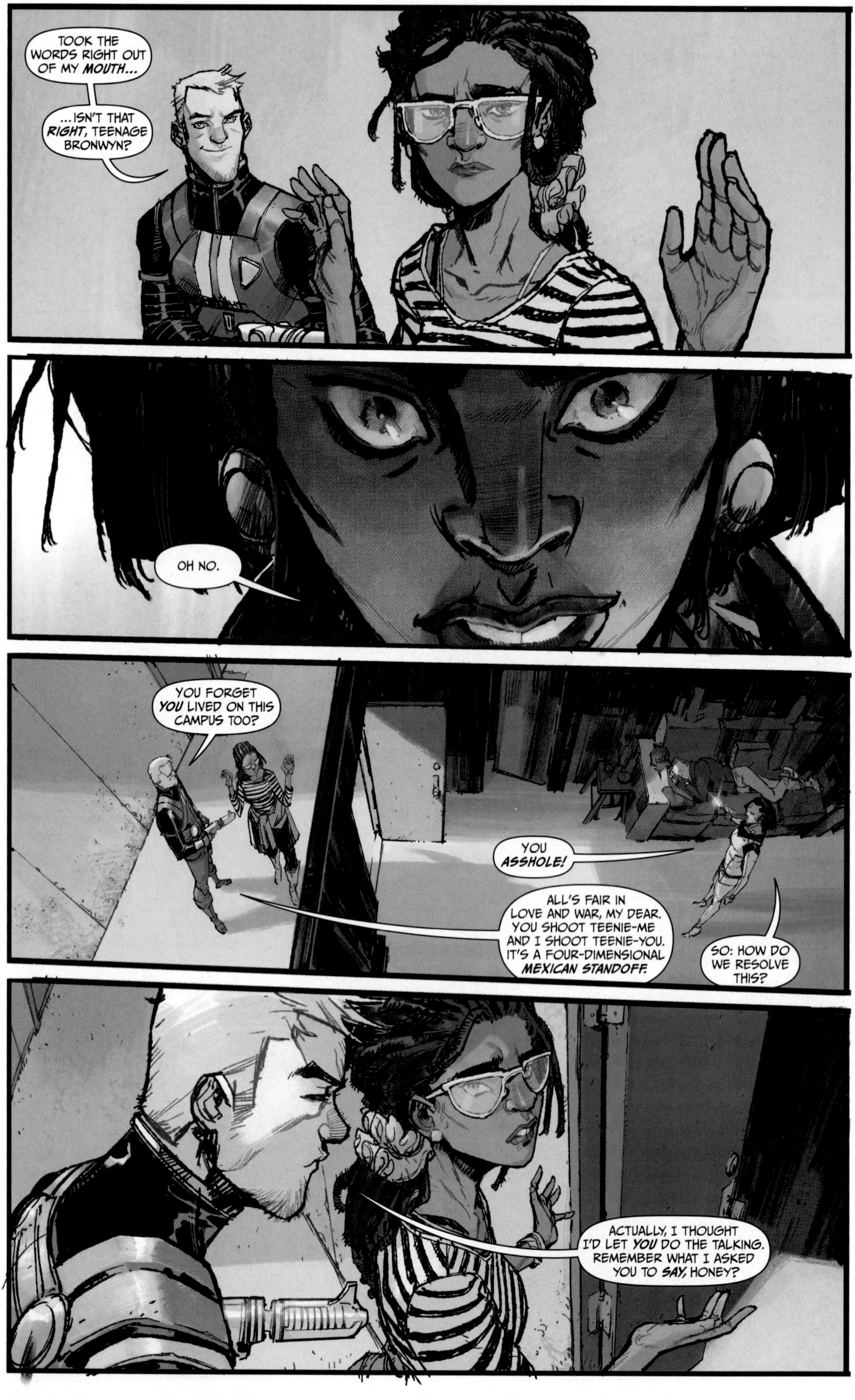
TOOK THE WORDS RIGHT OUT OF MY MOUTH...
...ISN'T THAT RIGHT, TEENAGE BRONWYN?
OH NO.
YOU FORGET YOU LIVED ON THIS CAMPUS TOO?
YOU ASSHOLE!
ALL'S FAIR IN LOVE AND WAR, MY DEAR. YOU SHOOT TEENIE-ME AND I SHOOT TEENIE-YOU. IT'S A FOUR-DIMENSIONAL MEXICAN STANDOFF.
SO: HOW DO WE RESOLVE THIS?
ACTUALLY, I THOUGHT I'D LET YOU DO THE TALKING. REMEMBER WHAT I ASKED YOU TO SAY, HONEY?

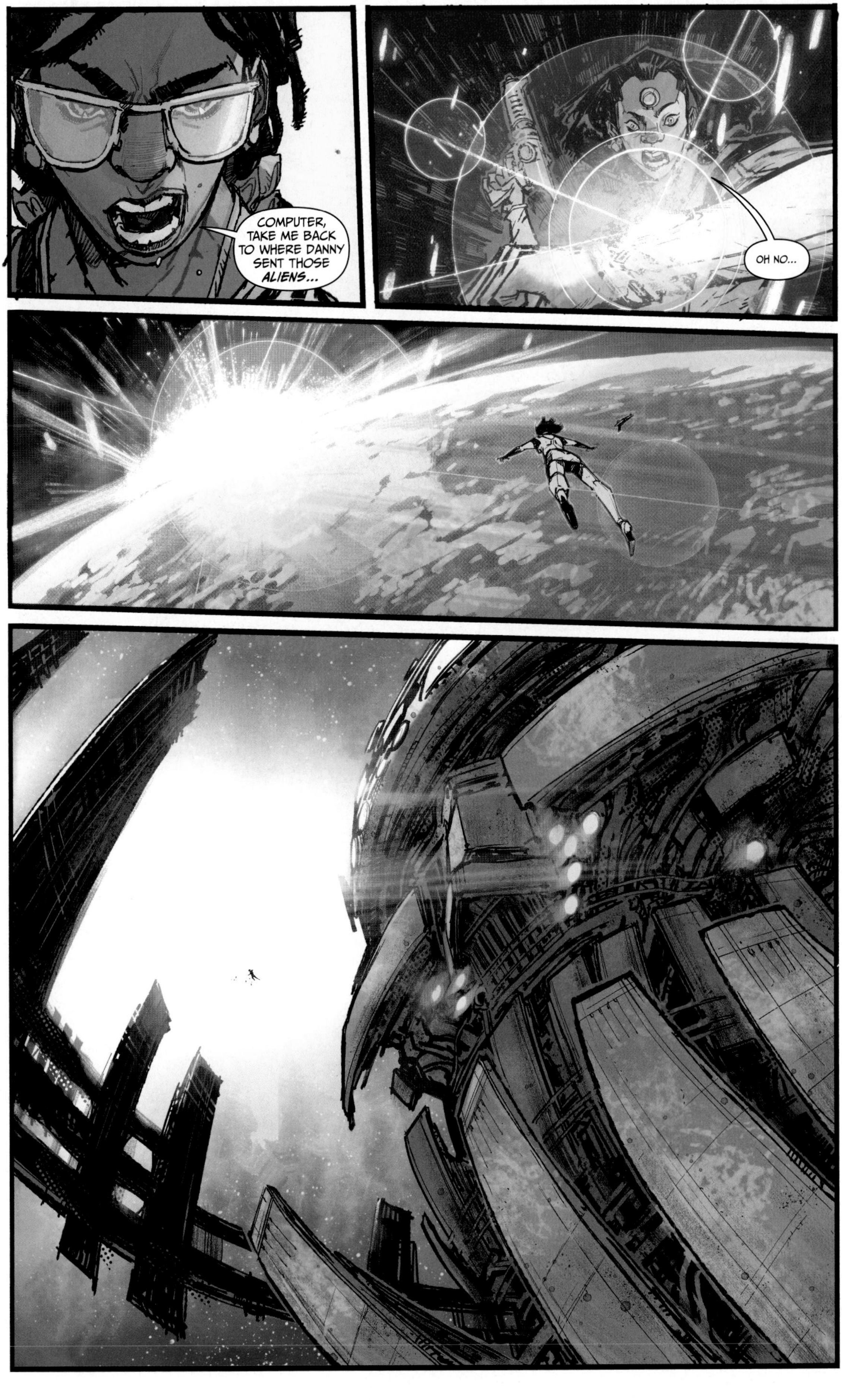
COMPUTER, TAKE ME BACK TO WHERE DANNY SENT THOSE *ALIENS...*
OH NO...

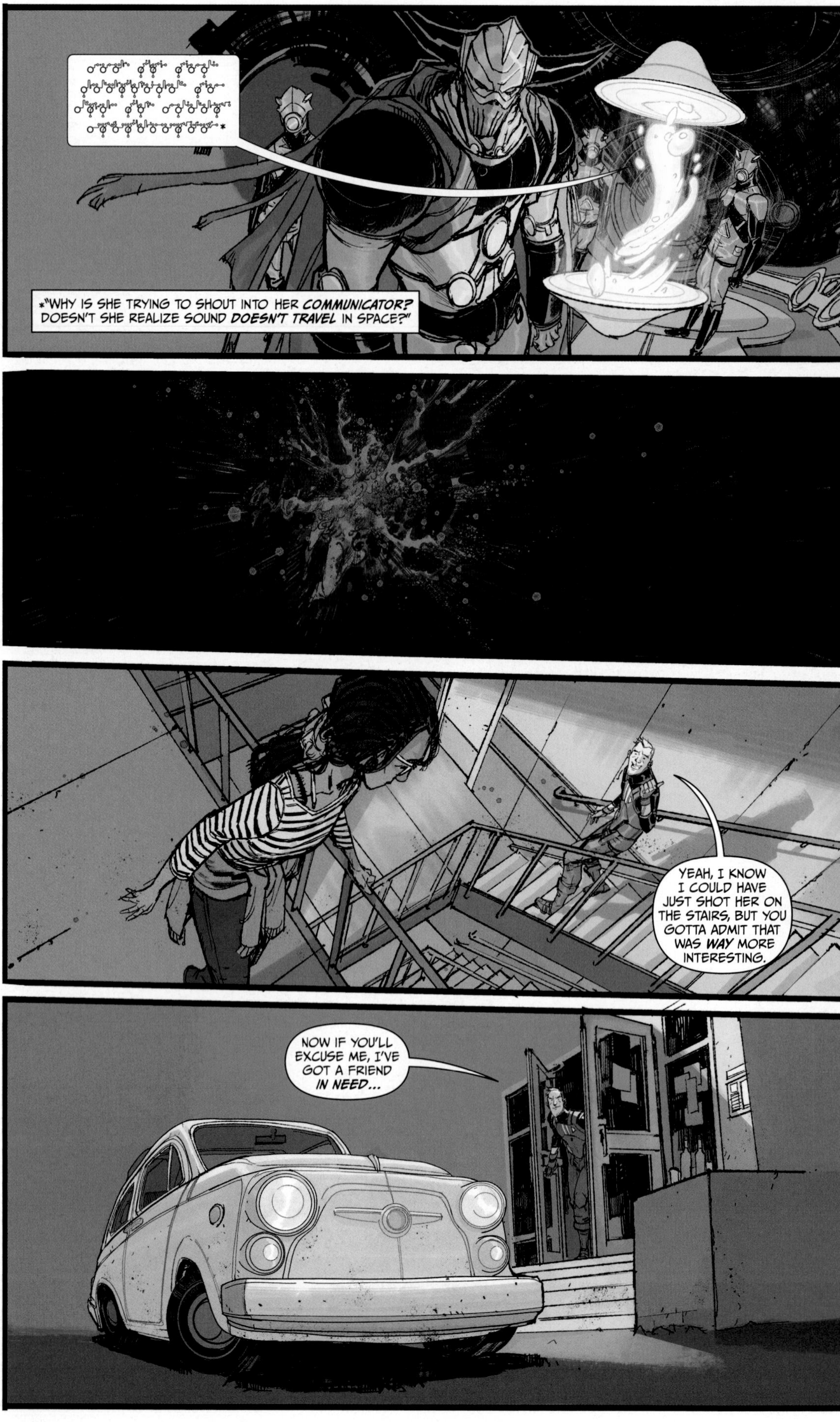
*"WHY IS SHE TRYING TO SHOUT INTO HER COMMUNICATOR? DOESN'T SHE REALIZE SOUND DOESN'T TRAVEL IN SPACE?"
YEAH, I KNOW I COULD HAVE JUST SHOT HER ON THE STAIRS, BUT YOU GOTTA ADMIT THAT WAS WAY MORE INTERESTING.
NOW IF YOU'LL EXCUSE ME, I'VE GOT A FRIEND IN NEED...

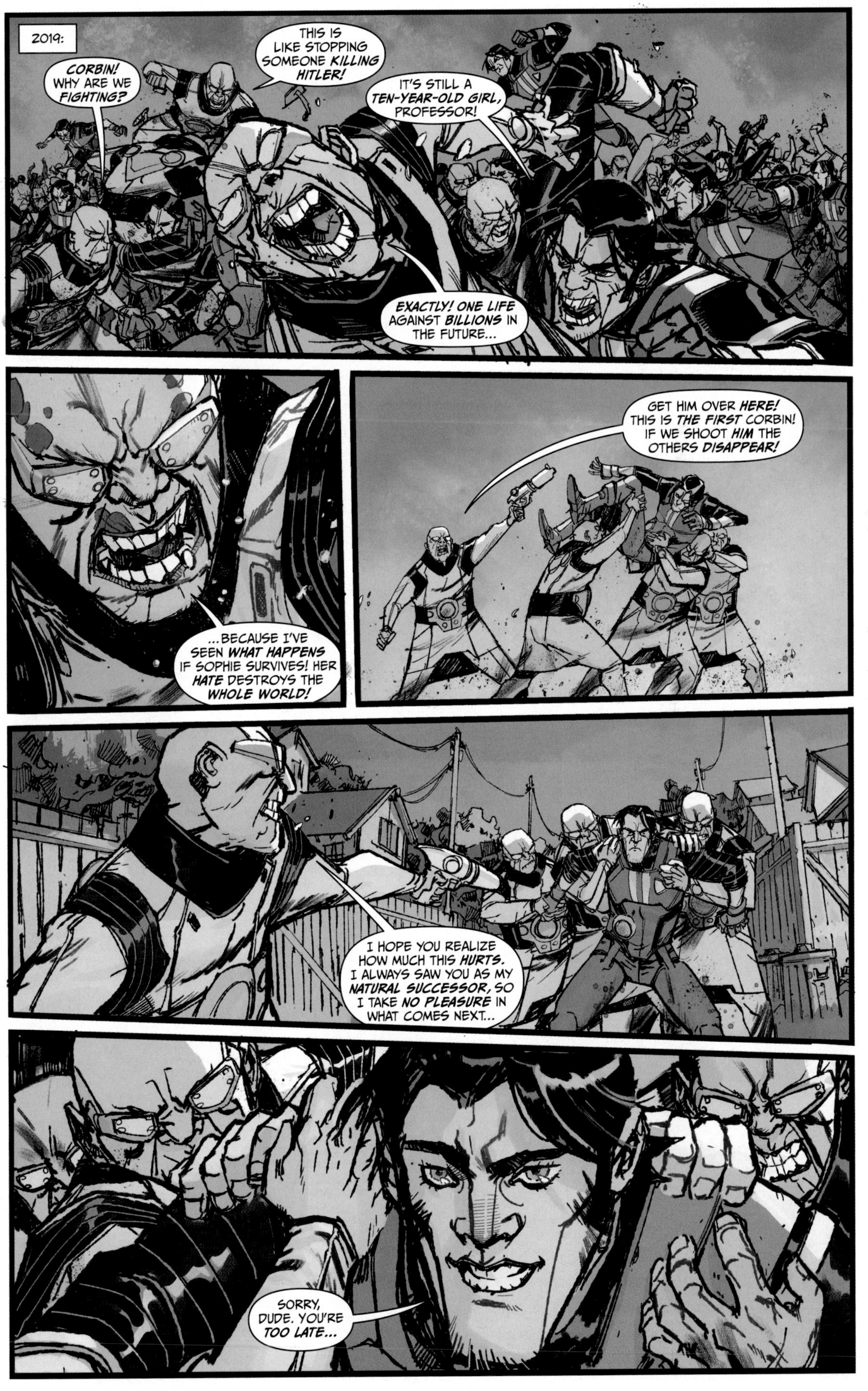

2019:
CORBIN! WHY ARE WE FIGHTING?
THIS IS LIKE STOPPING SOMEONE KILLING HITLER!
IT'S STILL A TEN-YEAR-OLD GIRL, PROFESSOR!
EXACTLY! ONE LIFE AGAINST BILLIONS IN THE FUTURE...
...BECAUSE I'VE SEEN WHAT HAPPENS IF SOPHIE SURVIVES! HER HATE DESTROYS THE WHOLE WORLD!
GET HIM OVER HERE! THIS IS THE FIRST CORBIN! IF WE SHOOT HIM THE OTHERS DISAPPEAR!
I HOPE YOU REALIZE HOW MUCH THIS HURTS. I ALWAYS SAW YOU AS MY NATURAL SUCCESSOR, SO I TAKE NO PLEASURE IN WHAT COMES NEXT...
SORRY, DUDE. YOU'RE TOO LATE...

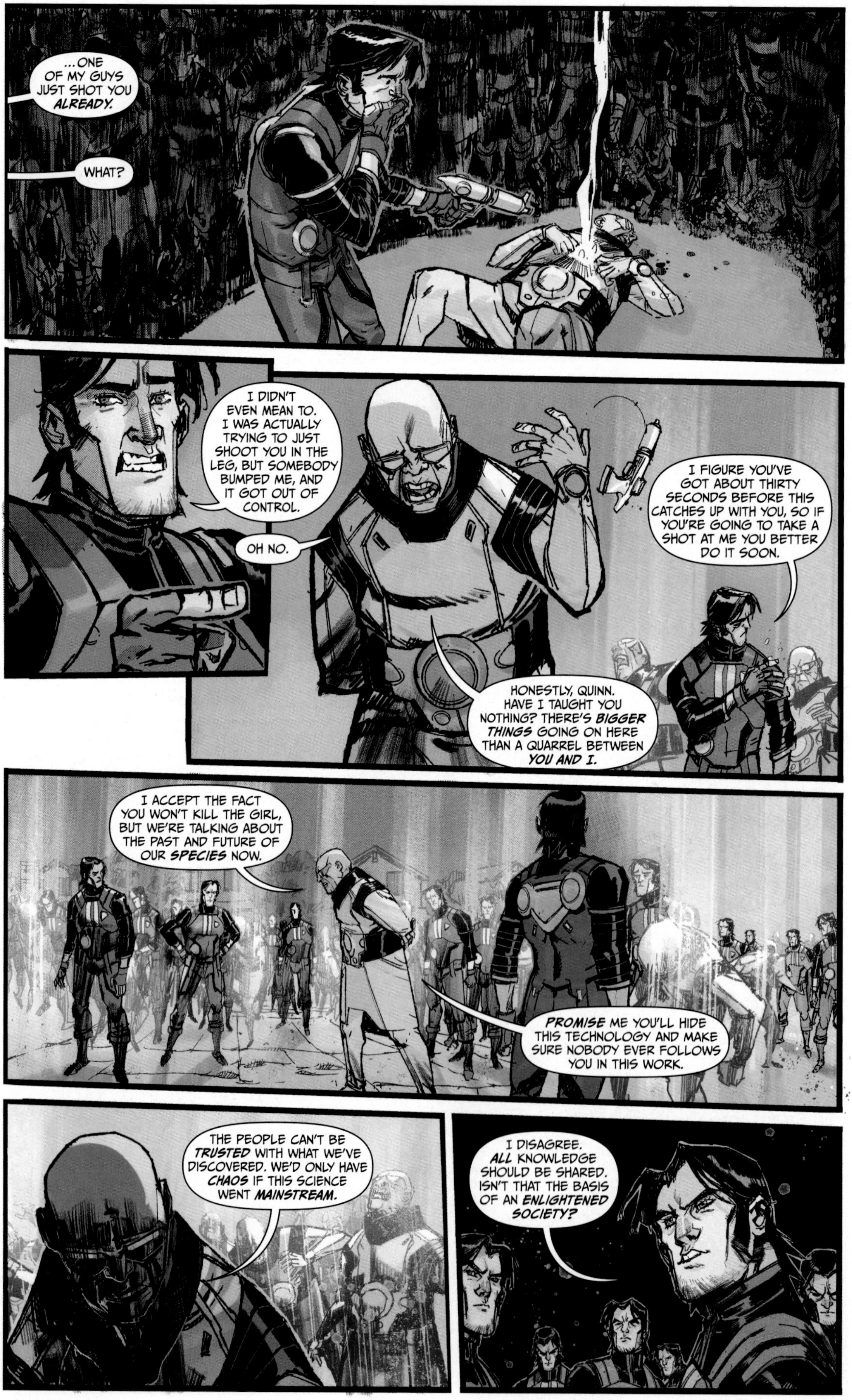
...ONE OF MY GUYS JUST SHOT YOU *ALREADY.*
WHAT?
I DIDN'T EVEN MEAN TO. I WAS ACTUALLY TRYING TO JUST SHOOT YOU IN THE LEG, BUT SOMEBODY BUMPED ME, AND IT GOT OUT OF CONTROL.
OH NO.
I FIGURE YOU'VE GOT ABOUT THIRTY SECONDS BEFORE THIS CATCHES UP WITH YOU, SO IF YOU'RE GOING TO TAKE A SHOT AT ME YOU BETTER DO IT SOON.
HONESTLY, QUINN. HAVE I TAUGHT YOU NOTHING? THERE'S *BIGGER THINGS* GOING ON HERE THAN A QUARREL BETWEEN *YOU AND I.*
I ACCEPT THE FACT YOU WON'T KILL THE GIRL, BUT WE'RE TALKING ABOUT THE PAST AND FUTURE OF OUR *SPECIES* NOW.
PROMISE ME YOU'LL HIDE THIS TECHNOLOGY AND MAKE SURE NOBODY EVER FOLLOWS YOU IN THIS WORK.
THE PEOPLE CAN'T BE *TRUSTED* WITH WHAT WE'VE DISCOVERED. WE'D ONLY HAVE *CHAOS* IF THIS SCIENCE WENT *MAINSTREAM.*
I DISAGREE. *ALL* KNOWLEDGE SHOULD BE SHARED. ISN'T THAT THE BASIS OF AN *ENLIGHTENED SOCIETY?*

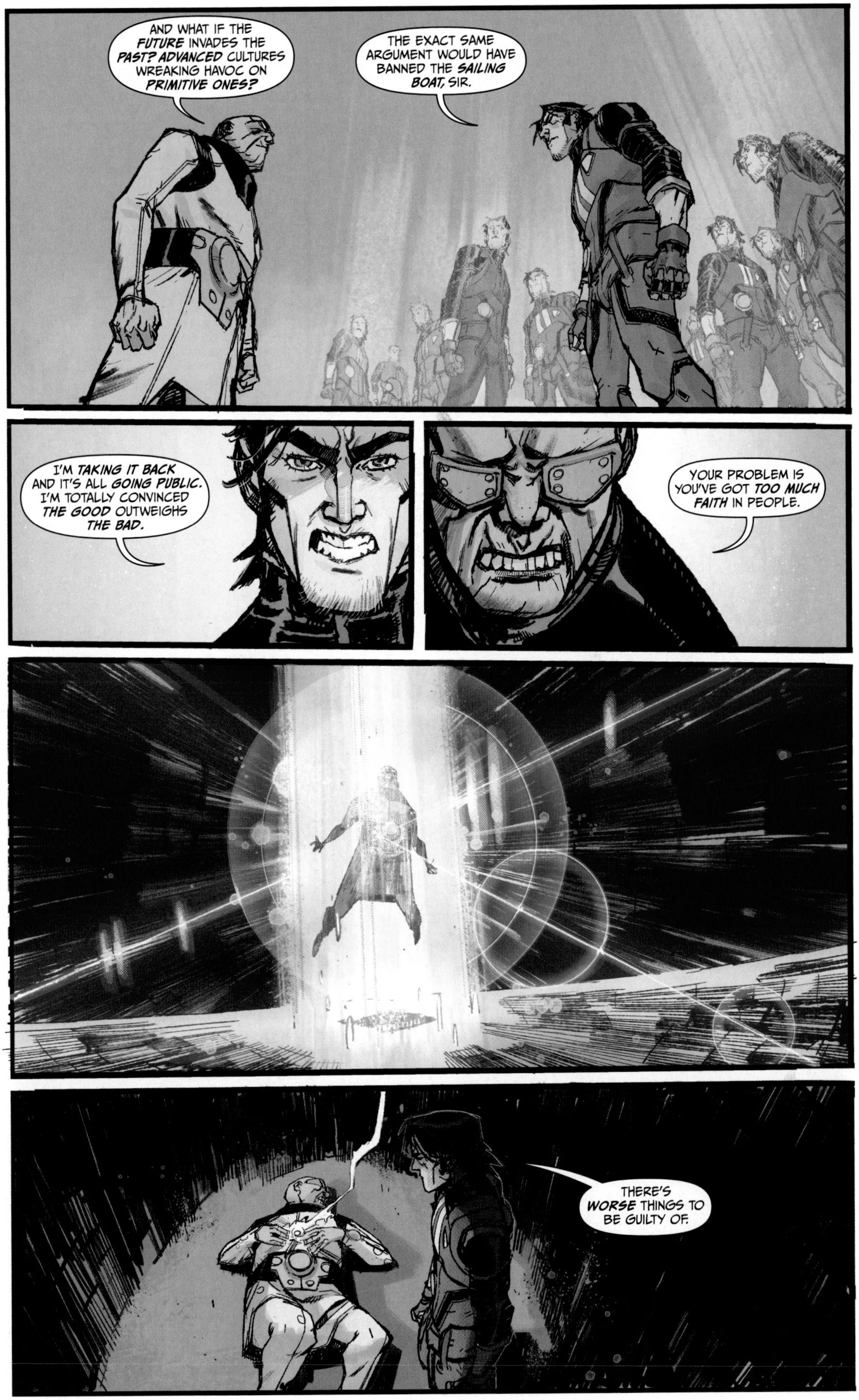
AND WHAT IF THE FUTURE INVADES THE PAST? ADVANCED CULTURES WREAKING HAVOC ON PRIMITIVE ONES?
THE EXACT SAME ARGUMENT WOULD HAVE BANNED THE SAILING BOAT, SIR.
I'M TAKING IT BACK AND IT'S ALL GOING PUBLIC. I'M TOTALLY CONVINCED THE GOOD OUTWEIGHS THE BAD.
YOUR PROBLEM IS YOU'VE GOT TOO MUCH FAITH IN PEOPLE.
THERE'S WORSE THINGS TO BE GUILTY OF.

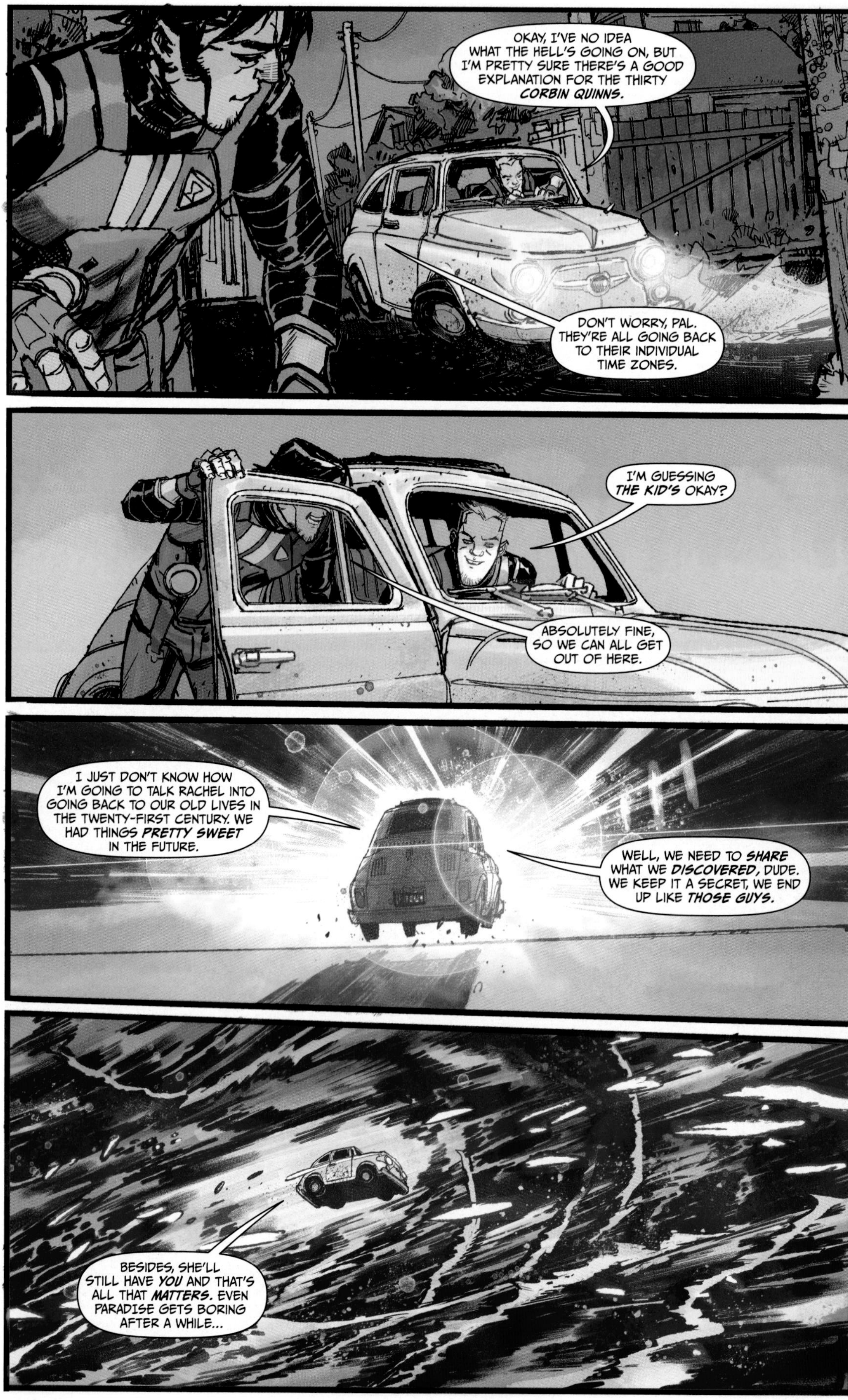
OKAY, I'VE NO IDEA WHAT THE HELL'S GOING ON, BUT I'M PRETTY SURE THERE'S A GOOD EXPLANATION FOR THE THIRTY CORBIN QUINNS.
DON'T WORRY, PAL. THEY'RE ALL GOING BACK TO THEIR INDIVIDUAL TIME ZONES.
I'M GUESSING THE KID'S OKAY?
ABSOLUTELY FINE, SO WE CAN ALL GET OUT OF HERE.
I JUST DON'T KNOW HOW I'M GOING TO TALK RACHEL INTO GOING BACK TO OUR OLD LIVES IN THE TWENTY-FIRST CENTURY. WE HAD THINGS PRETTY SWEET IN THE FUTURE.
WELL, WE NEED TO SHARE WHAT WE DISCOVERED, DUDE. WE KEEP IT A SECRET, WE END UP LIKE THOSE GUYS.
BESIDES, SHE'LL STILL HAVE YOU AND THAT'S ALL THAT MATTERS. EVEN PARADISE GETS BORING AFTER A WHILE...

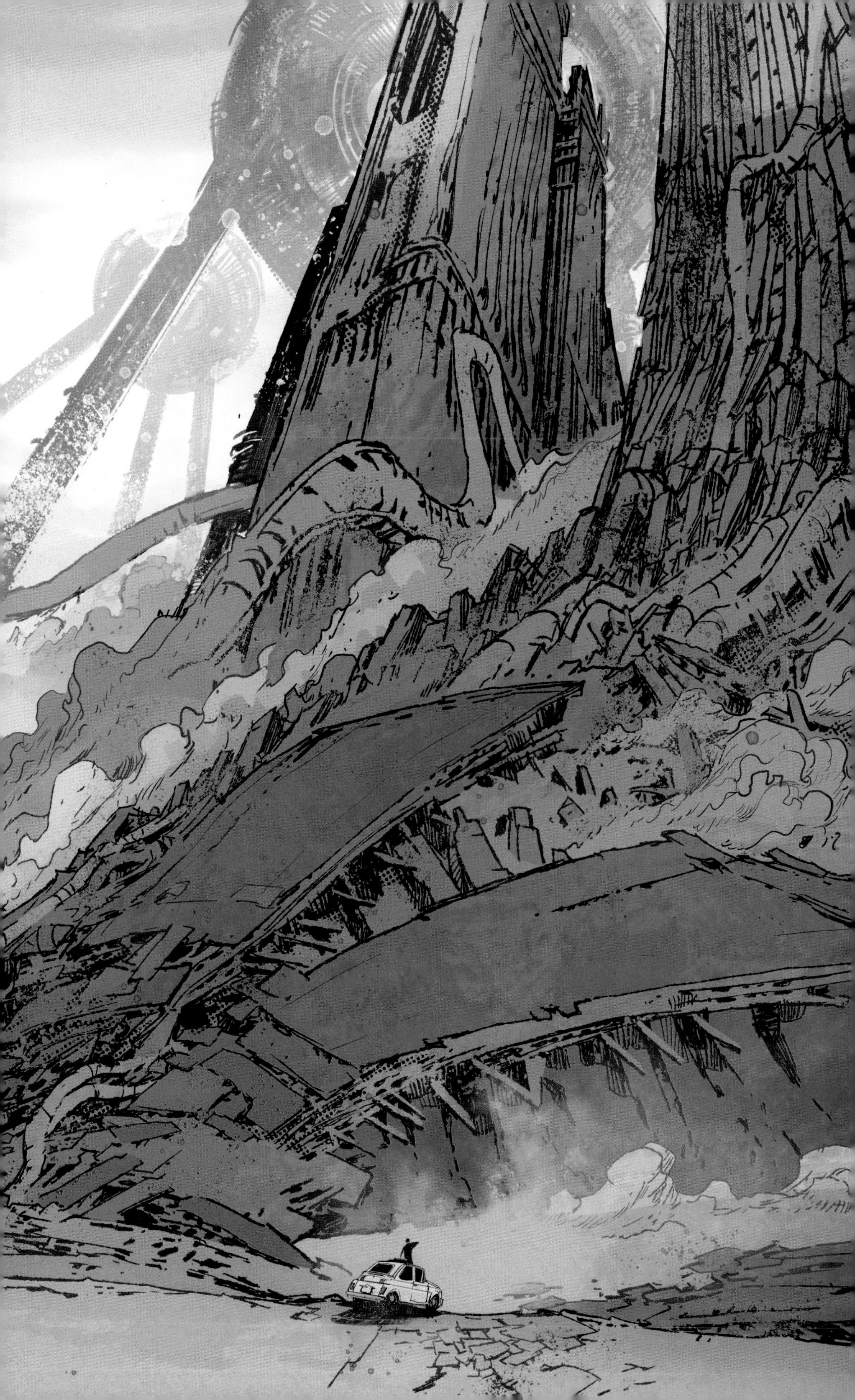

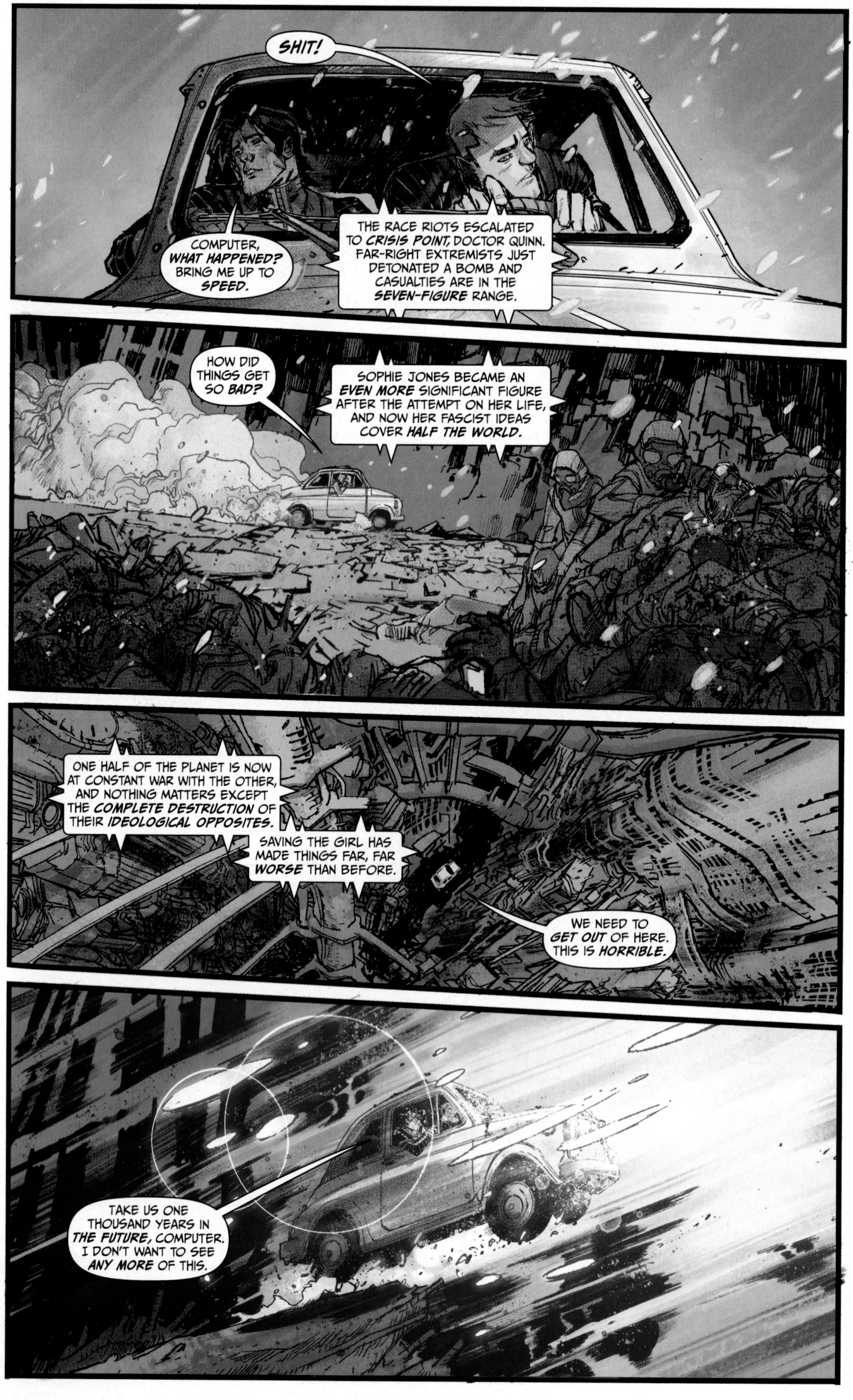
SHIT!
COMPUTER, WHAT HAPPENED? BRING ME UP TO SPEED.
THE RACE RIOTS ESCALATED TO CRISIS POINT, DOCTOR QUINN. FAR-RIGHT EXTREMISTS JUST DETONATED A BOMB AND CASUALTIES ARE IN THE SEVEN-FIGURE RANGE.
HOW DID THINGS GET SO BAD?
SOPHIE JONES BECAME AN EVEN MORE SIGNIFICANT FIGURE AFTER THE ATTEMPT ON HER LIFE, AND NOW HER FASCIST IDEAS COVER HALF THE WORLD.
ONE HALF OF THE PLANET IS NOW AT CONSTANT WAR WITH THE OTHER, AND NOTHING MATTERS EXCEPT THE COMPLETE DESTRUCTION OF THEIR IDEOLOGICAL OPPOSITES.
SAVING THE GIRL HAS MADE THINGS FAR, FAR WORSE THAN BEFORE.
WE NEED TO GET OUT OF HERE. THIS IS HORRIBLE.
TAKE US ONE THOUSAND YEARS IN THE FUTURE, COMPUTER. I DON'T WANT TO SEE ANY MORE OF THIS.

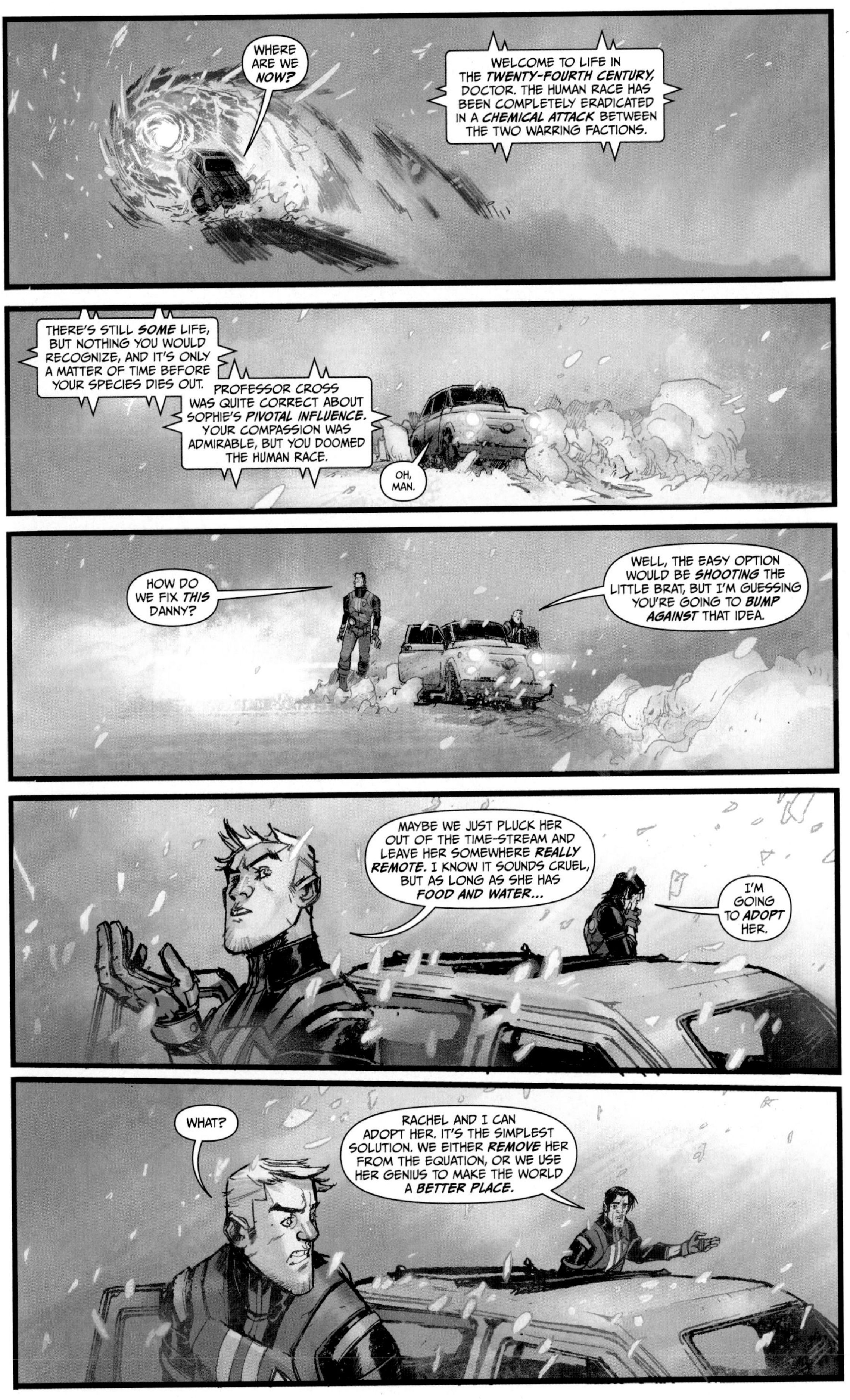
WHERE ARE WE NOW?
WELCOME TO LIFE IN THE TWENTY-FOURTH CENTURY, DOCTOR. THE HUMAN RACE HAS BEEN COMPLETELY ERADICATED IN A CHEMICAL ATTACK BETWEEN THE TWO WARRING FACTIONS.
THERE'S STILL SOME LIFE, BUT NOTHING YOU WOULD RECOGNIZE, AND IT'S ONLY A MATTER OF TIME BEFORE YOUR SPECIES DIES OUT.
PROFESSOR CROSS WAS QUITE CORRECT ABOUT SOPHIE'S PIVOTAL INFLUENCE. YOUR COMPASSION WAS ADMIRABLE, BUT YOU DOOMED THE HUMAN RACE.
OH, MAN.
HOW DO WE FIX THIS DANNY?
WELL, THE EASY OPTION WOULD BE SHOOTING THE LITTLE BRAT, BUT I'M GUESSING YOU'RE GOING TO BUMP AGAINST THAT IDEA.
MAYBE WE JUST PLUCK HER OUT OF THE TIME-STREAM AND LEAVE HER SOMEWHERE REALLY REMOTE. I KNOW IT SOUNDS CRUEL, BUT AS LONG AS SHE HAS FOOD AND WATER...
I'M GOING TO ADOPT HER.
WHAT?
RACHEL AND I CAN ADOPT HER. IT'S THE SIMPLEST SOLUTION. WE EITHER REMOVE HER FROM THE EQUATION, OR WE USE HER GENIUS TO MAKE THE WORLD A BETTER PLACE.

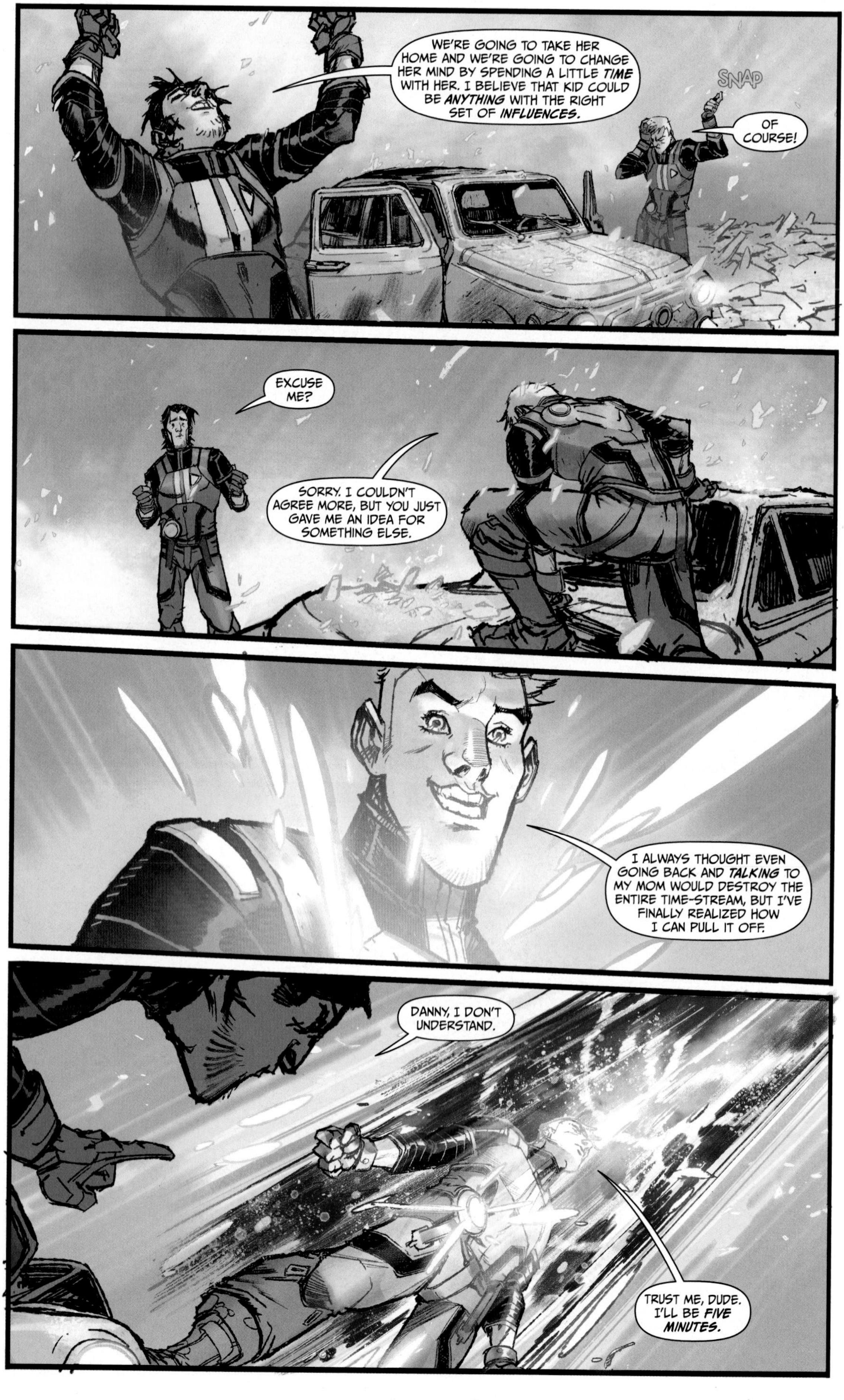
WE'RE GOING TO TAKE HER HOME AND WE'RE GOING TO CHANGE HER MIND BY SPENDING A LITTLE *TIME* WITH HER. I BELIEVE THAT KID COULD BE *ANYTHING* WITH THE RIGHT SET OF *INFLUENCES.*
SNAP
OF COURSE!
EXCUSE ME?
SORRY. I COULDN'T AGREE MORE, BUT YOU JUST GAVE ME AN IDEA FOR SOMETHING ELSE.
I ALWAYS THOUGHT EVEN GOING BACK AND *TALKING* TO MY MOM WOULD DESTROY THE ENTIRE TIME-STREAM, BUT I'VE FINALLY REALIZED HOW I CAN PULL IT OFF.
DANNY, I DON'T UNDERSTAND.
TRUST ME, DUDE. I'LL BE *FIVE MINUTES.*

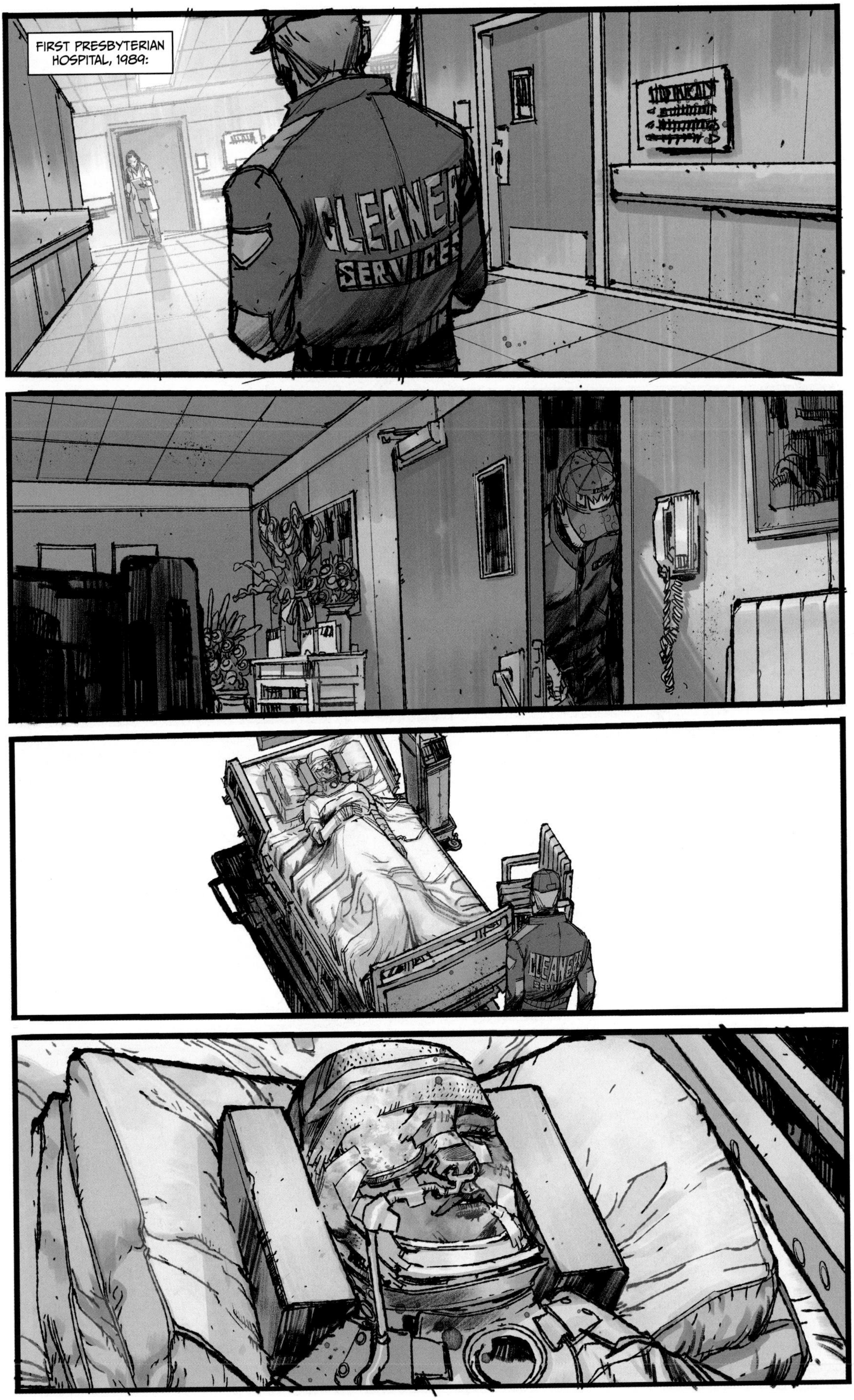
FIRST PRESBYTERIAN HOSPITAL, 1989:
CLEANER SERVICES
CLEANER

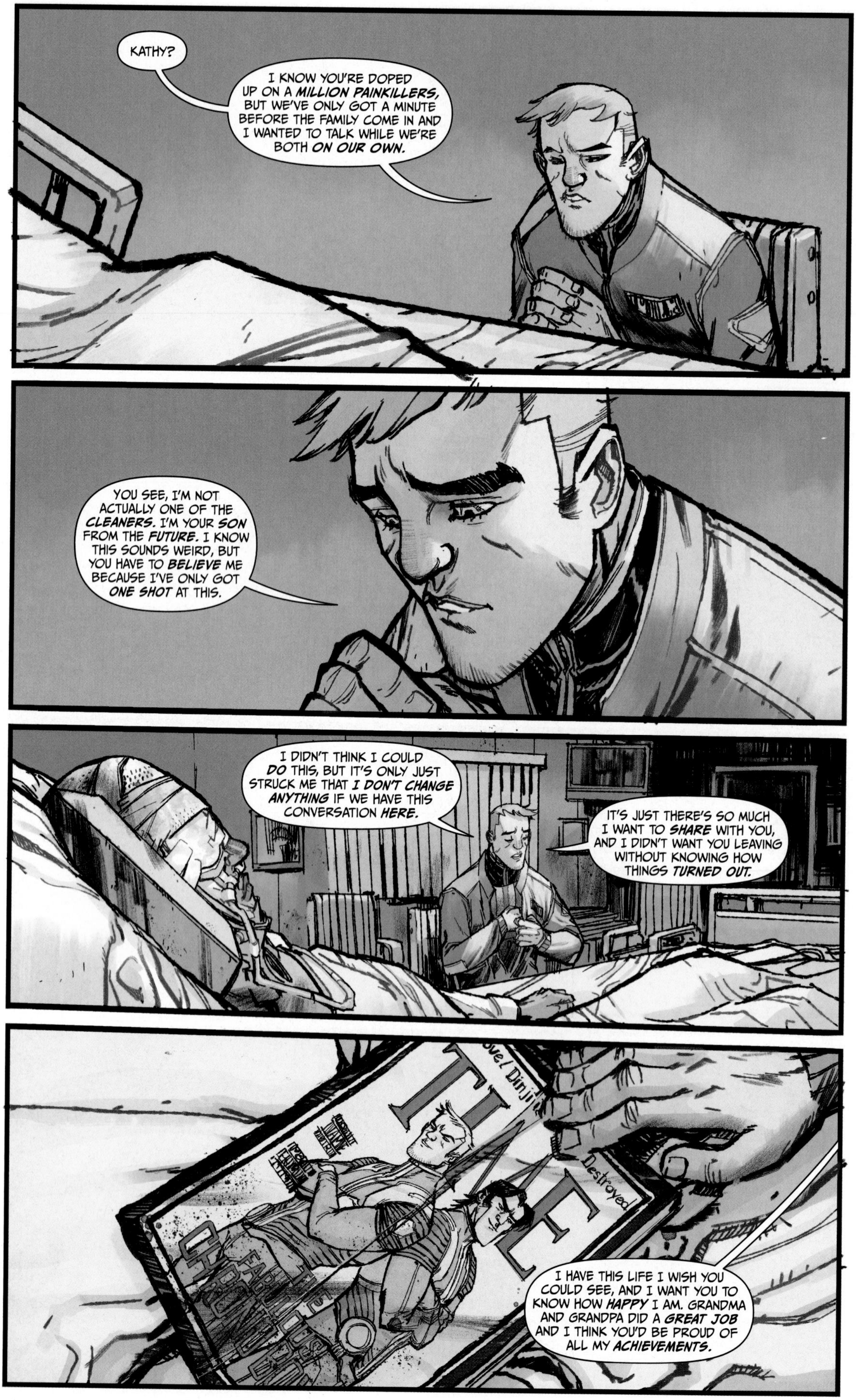
KATHY?
I KNOW YOU'RE DOPED UP ON A **MILLION PAINKILLERS,** BUT WE'VE ONLY GOT A MINUTE BEFORE THE FAMILY COME IN AND I WANTED TO TALK WHILE WE'RE BOTH **ON OUR OWN.**
YOU SEE, I'M NOT ACTUALLY ONE OF THE **CLEANERS.** I'M YOUR **SON** FROM THE **FUTURE.** I KNOW THIS SOUNDS WEIRD, BUT YOU HAVE TO **BELIEVE** ME BECAUSE I'VE ONLY GOT **ONE SHOT** AT THIS.
I DIDN'T THINK I COULD **DO** THIS, BUT IT'S ONLY JUST STRUCK ME THAT **I DON'T CHANGE ANYTHING** IF WE HAVE THIS CONVERSATION **HERE.**
IT'S JUST THERE'S SO MUCH I WANT TO **SHARE** WITH YOU, AND I DIDN'T WANT YOU LEAVING WITHOUT KNOWING HOW THINGS **TURNED OUT.**
Destroyed
I HAVE THIS LIFE I WISH YOU COULD SEE, AND I WANT YOU TO KNOW HOW **HAPPY** I AM. GRANDMA AND GRANDPA DID A **GREAT JOB** AND I THINK YOU'D BE PROUD OF ALL MY **ACHIEVEMENTS.**

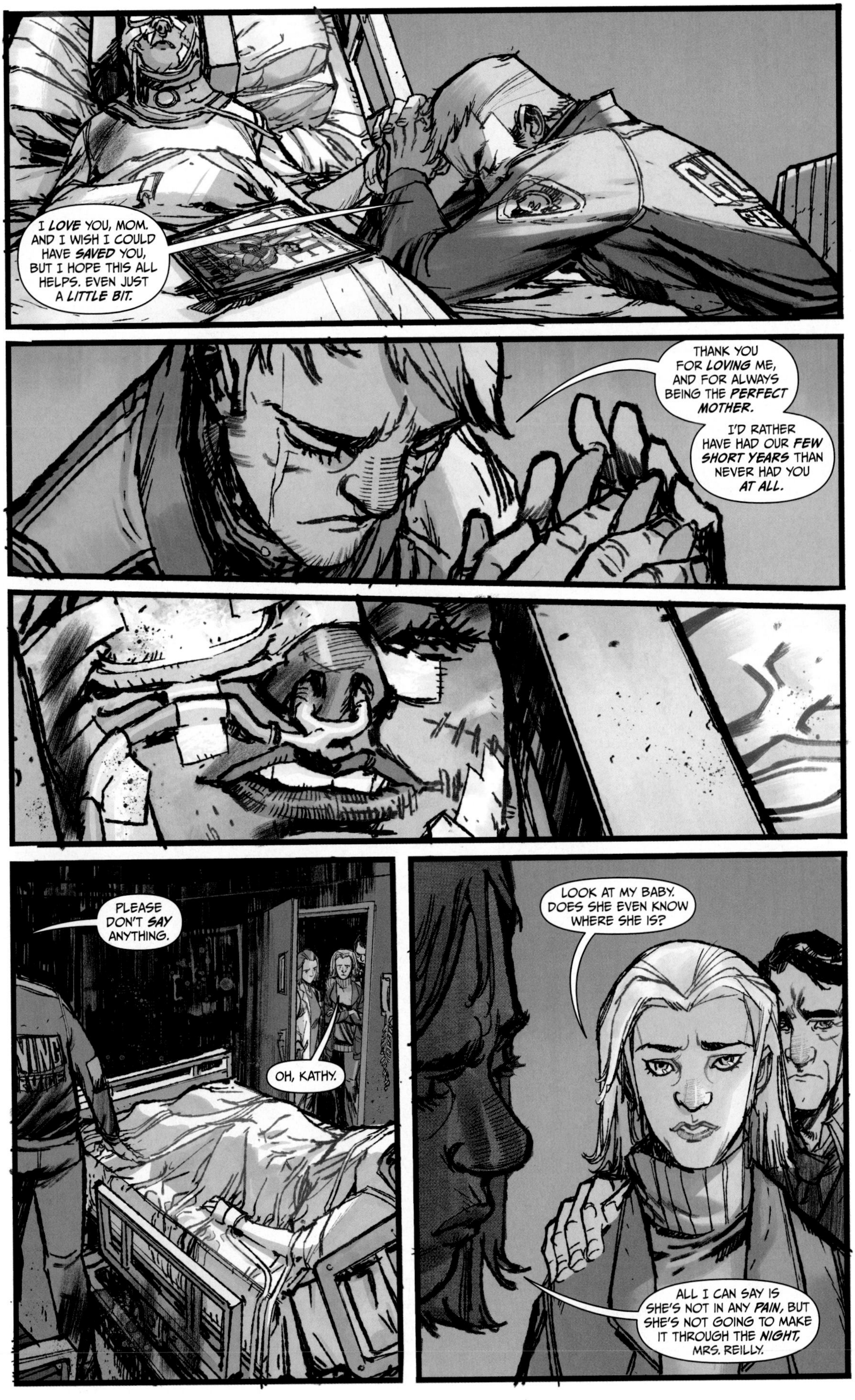
I LOVE YOU, MOM. AND I WISH I COULD HAVE SAVED YOU, BUT I HOPE THIS ALL HELPS. EVEN JUST A LITTLE BIT.
THANK YOU FOR LOVING ME, AND FOR ALWAYS BEING THE PERFECT MOTHER.
I'D RATHER HAVE HAD OUR FEW SHORT YEARS THAN NEVER HAD YOU AT ALL.
PLEASE DON'T SAY ANYTHING.
OH, KATHY.
LOOK AT MY BABY. DOES SHE EVEN KNOW WHERE SHE IS?
ALL I CAN SAY IS SHE'S NOT IN ANY PAIN, BUT SHE'S NOT GOING TO MAKE IT THROUGH THE NIGHT, MRS. REILLY.

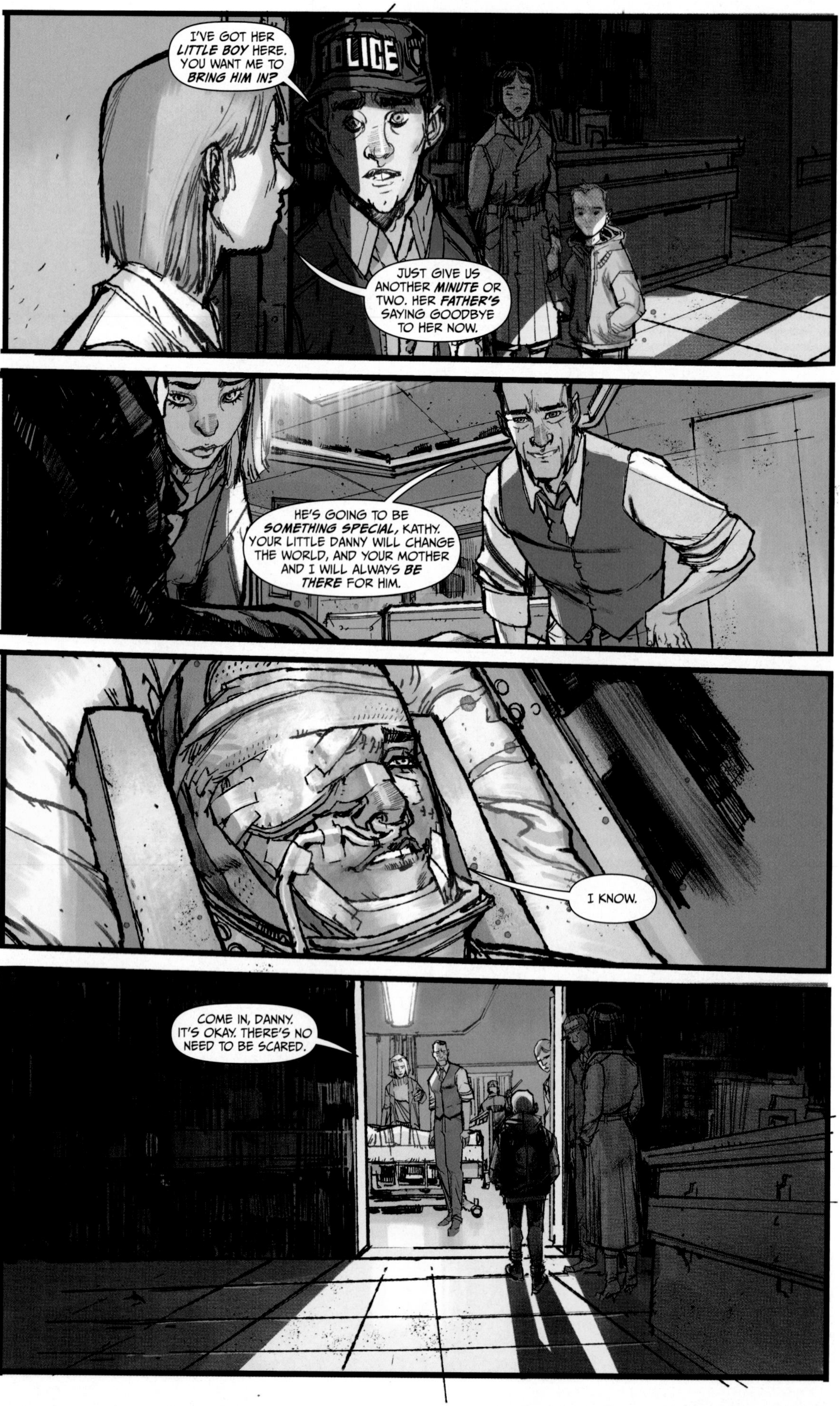
LICE
I'VE GOT HER *LITTLE BOY* HERE. YOU WANT ME TO *BRING HIM IN?*
JUST GIVE US ANOTHER *MINUTE* OR TWO. HER *FATHER'S* SAYING GOODBYE TO HER NOW.
HE'S GOING TO BE *SOMETHING SPECIAL,* KATHY. YOUR LITTLE DANNY WILL CHANGE THE WORLD, AND YOUR MOTHER AND I WILL ALWAYS *BE THERE* FOR HIM.
I KNOW.
COME IN, DANNY. IT'S OKAY. THERE'S NO NEED TO BE SCARED.

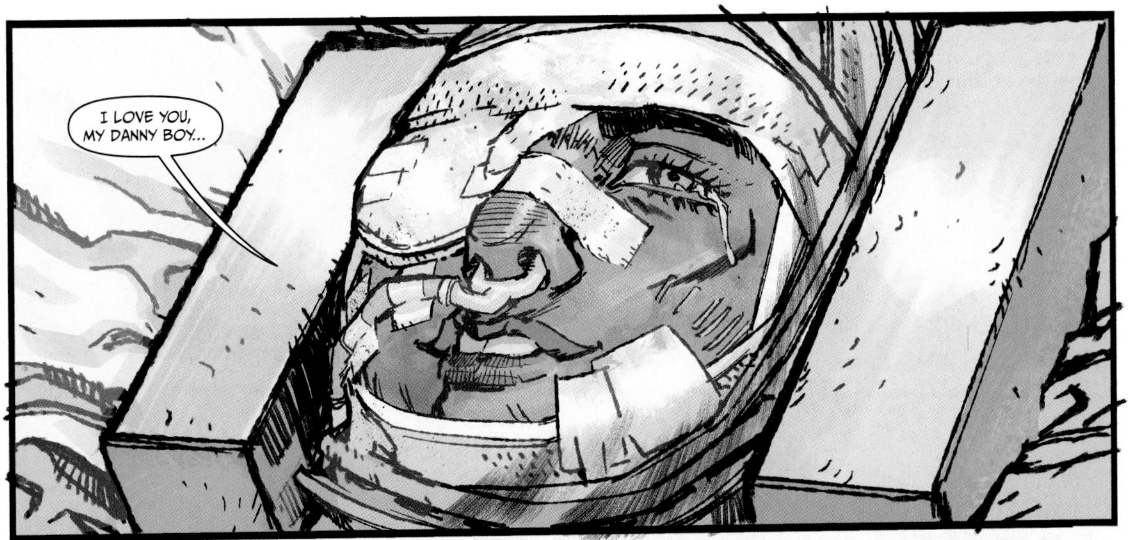
I LOVE YOU, MY DANNY BOY...

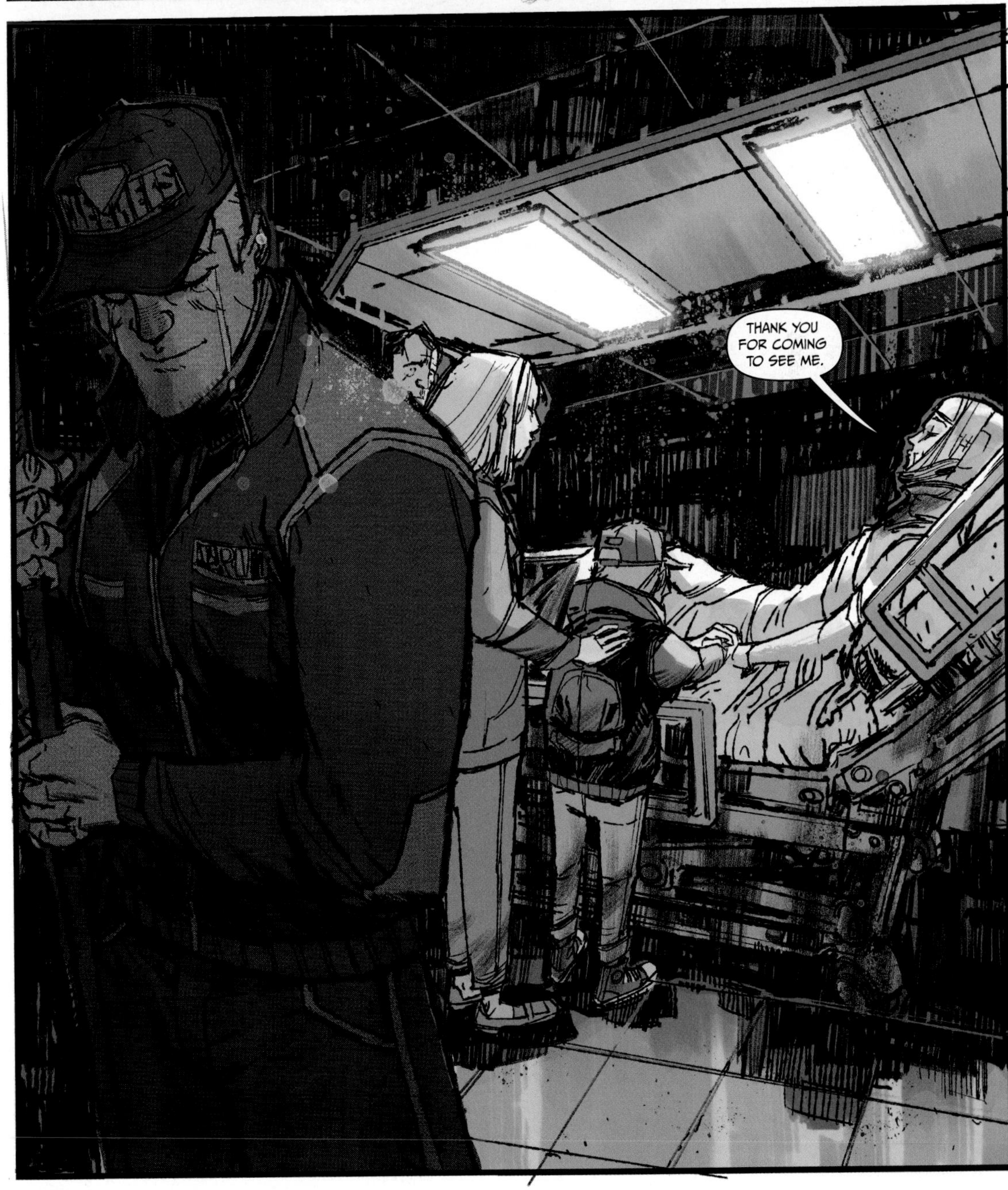
THANK YOU FOR COMING TO SEE ME.

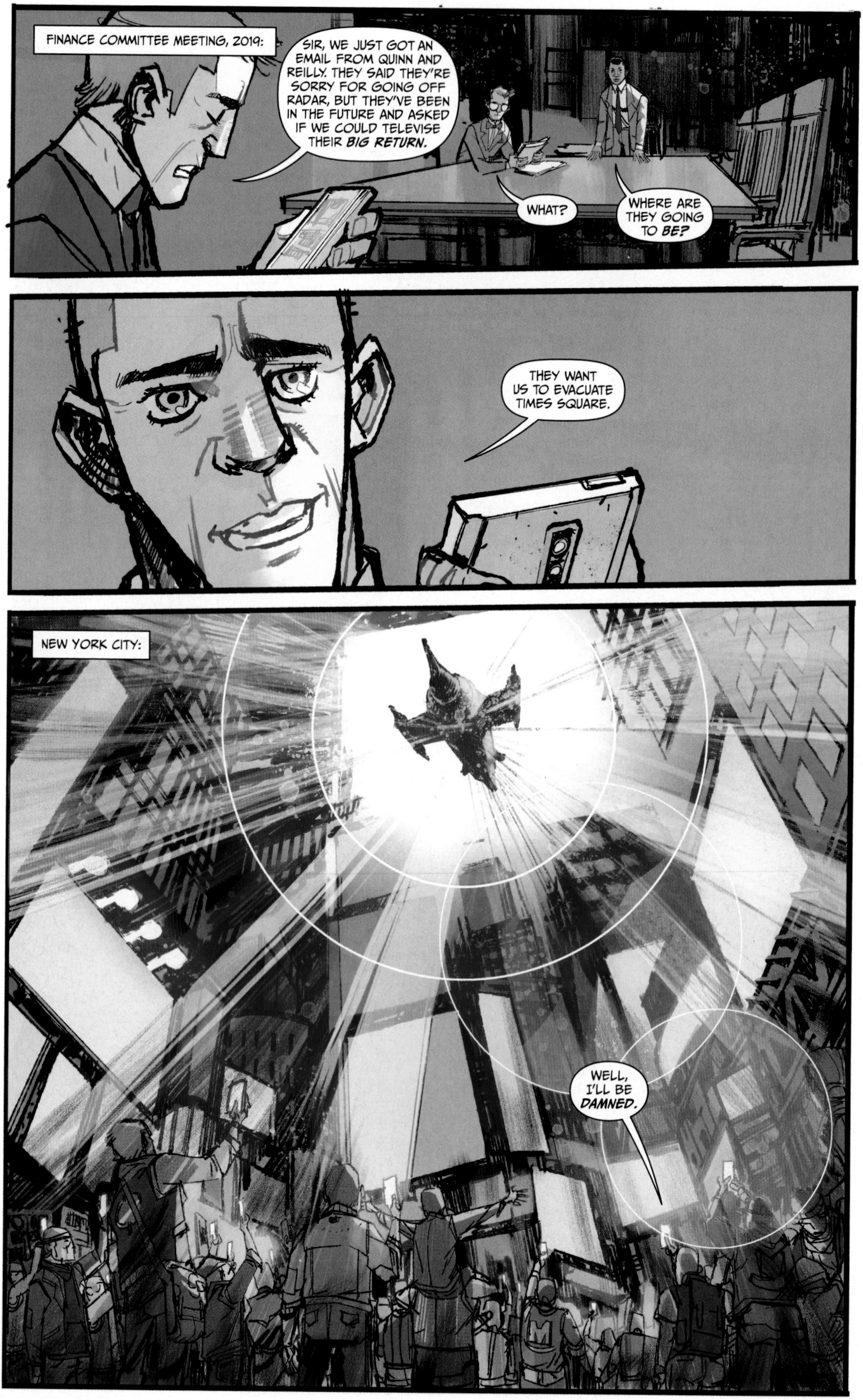
FINANCE COMMITTEE MEETING, 2019:
SIR, WE JUST GOT AN EMAIL FROM QUINN AND REILLY. THEY SAID THEY'RE SORRY FOR GOING OFF RADAR, BUT THEY'VE BEEN IN THE FUTURE AND ASKED IF WE COULD TELEVISE THEIR BIG RETURN.
WHAT?
WHERE ARE THEY GOING TO BE?
THEY WANT US TO EVACUATE TIMES SQUARE.
NEW YORK CITY:
WELL, I'LL BE DAMNED.

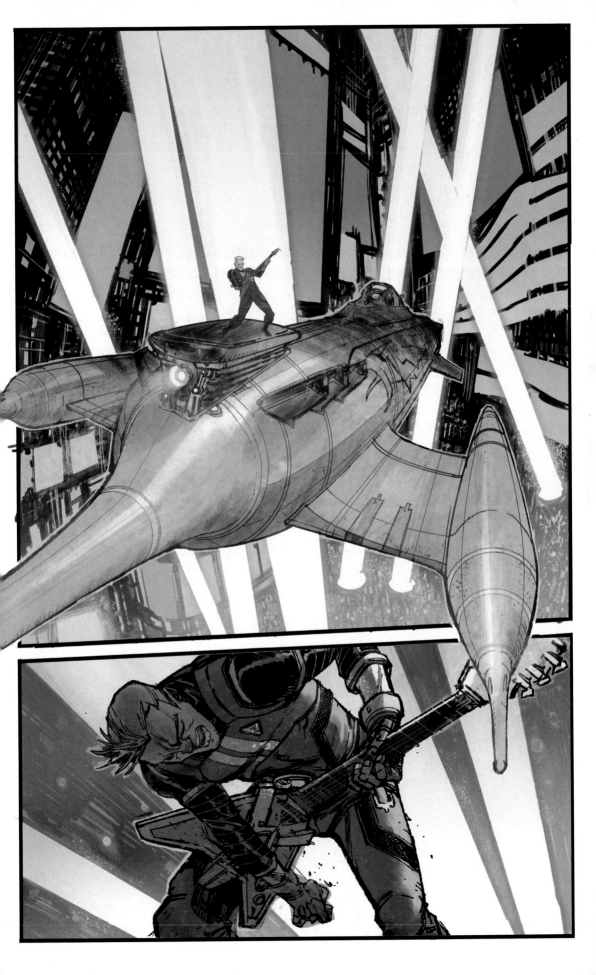

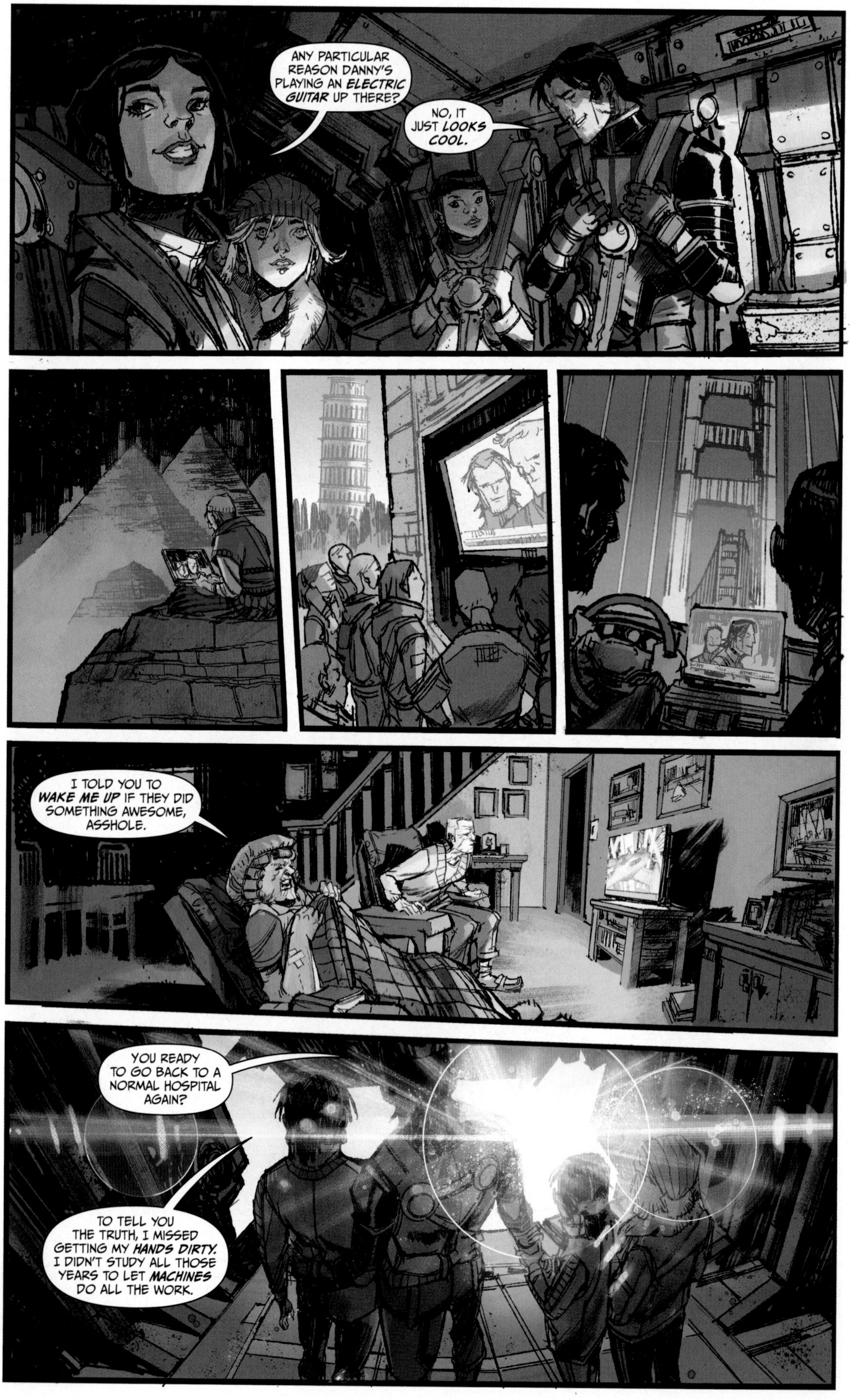
ANY PARTICULAR REASON DANNY'S PLAYING AN ELECTRIC GUITAR UP THERE?
NO, IT JUST LOOKS COOL.
I TOLD YOU TO WAKE ME UP IF THEY DID SOMETHING AWESOME, ASSHOLE.
YOU READY TO GO BACK TO A NORMAL HOSPITAL AGAIN?
TO TELL YOU THE TRUTH, I MISSED GETTING MY HANDS DIRTY. I DIDN'T STUDY ALL THOSE YEARS TO LET MACHINES DO ALL THE WORK.

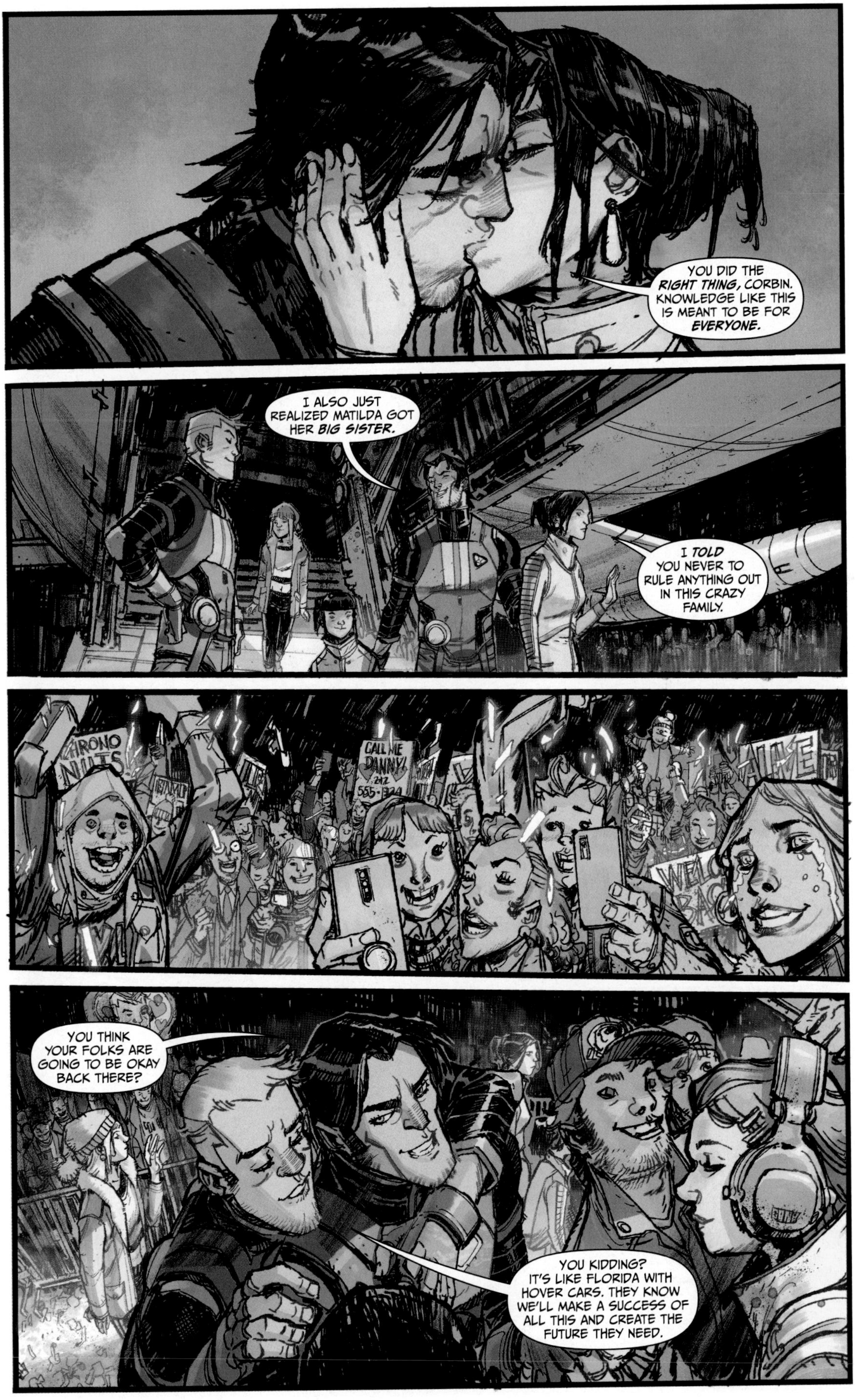
YOU DID THE RIGHT THING, CORBIN. KNOWLEDGE LIKE THIS IS MEANT TO BE FOR EVERYONE.
I ALSO JUST REALIZED MATILDA GOT HER BIG SISTER.
I TOLD YOU NEVER TO RULE ANYTHING OUT IN THIS CRAZY FAMILY.
CHRONO NUTS
CALL ME DANNY!
YOU THINK YOUR FOLKS ARE GOING TO BE OKAY BACK THERE?
YOU KIDDING? IT'S LIKE FLORIDA WITH HOVER CARS. THEY KNOW WE'LL MAKE A SUCCESS OF ALL THIS AND CREATE THE FUTURE THEY NEED.

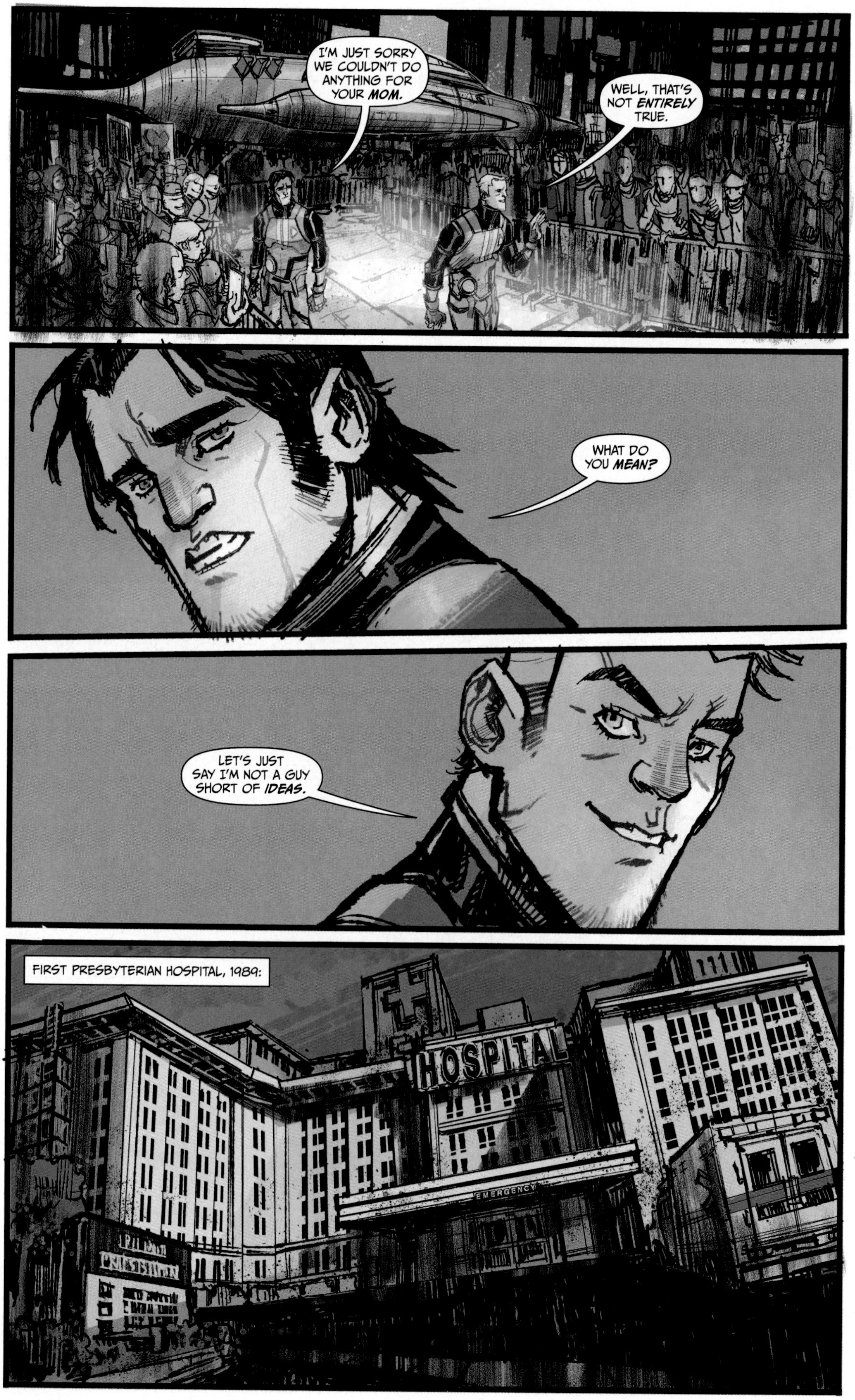
I'M JUST SORRY WE COULDN'T DO ANYTHING FOR YOUR MOM.
WELL, THAT'S NOT ENTIRELY TRUE.
WHAT DO YOU MEAN?
LET'S JUST SAY I'M NOT A GUY SHORT OF IDEAS.
FIRST PRESBYTERIAN HOSPITAL, 1989:
HOSPITAL
EMERGENCY

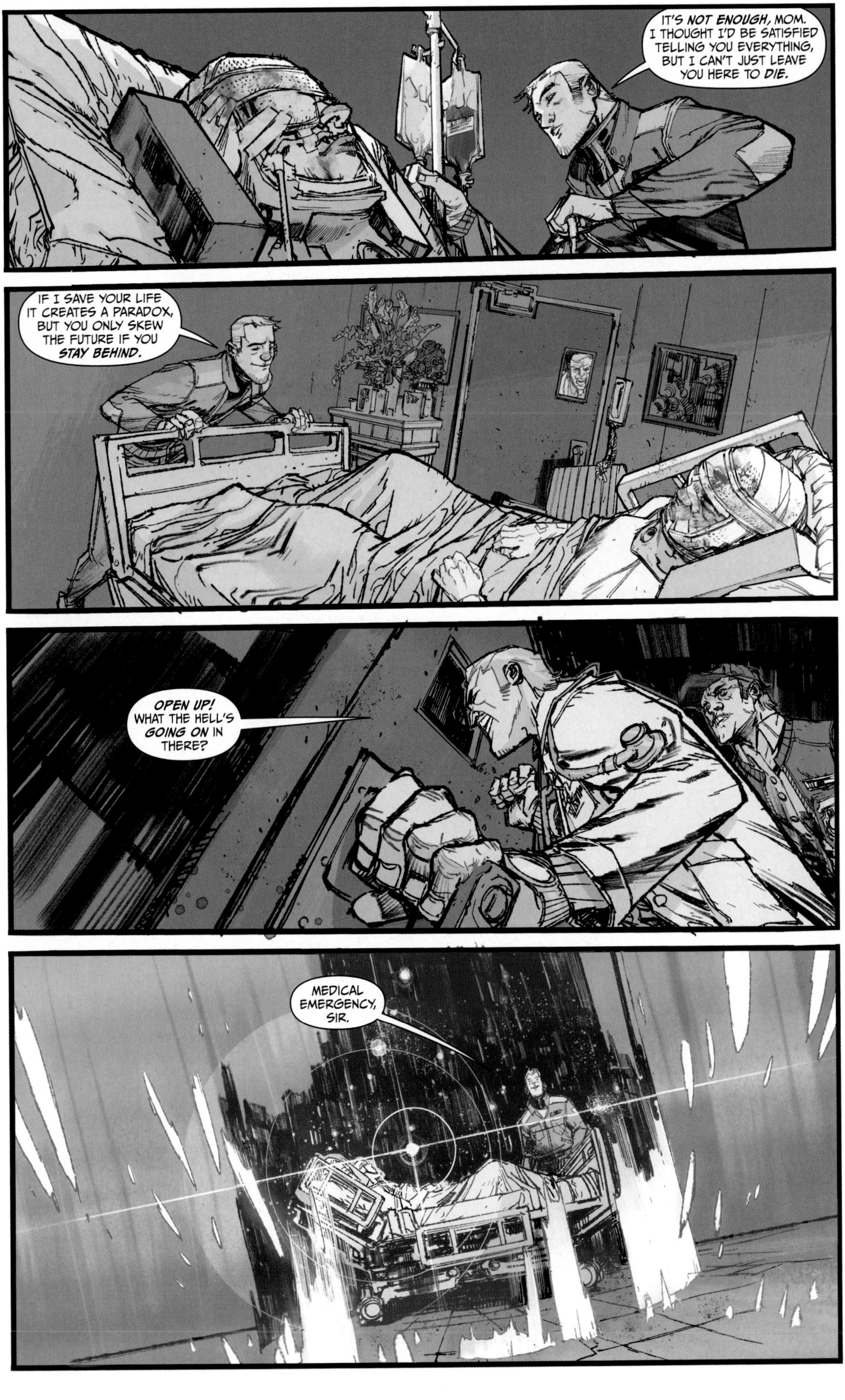
IT'S NOT ENOUGH, MOM. I THOUGHT I'D BE SATISFIED TELLING YOU EVERYTHING, BUT I CAN'T JUST LEAVE YOU HERE TO DIE.
IF I SAVE YOUR LIFE IT CREATES A PARADOX, BUT YOU ONLY SKEW THE FUTURE IF YOU STAY BEHIND.
OPEN UP! WHAT THE HELL'S GOING ON IN THERE?
MEDICAL EMERGENCY, SIR.

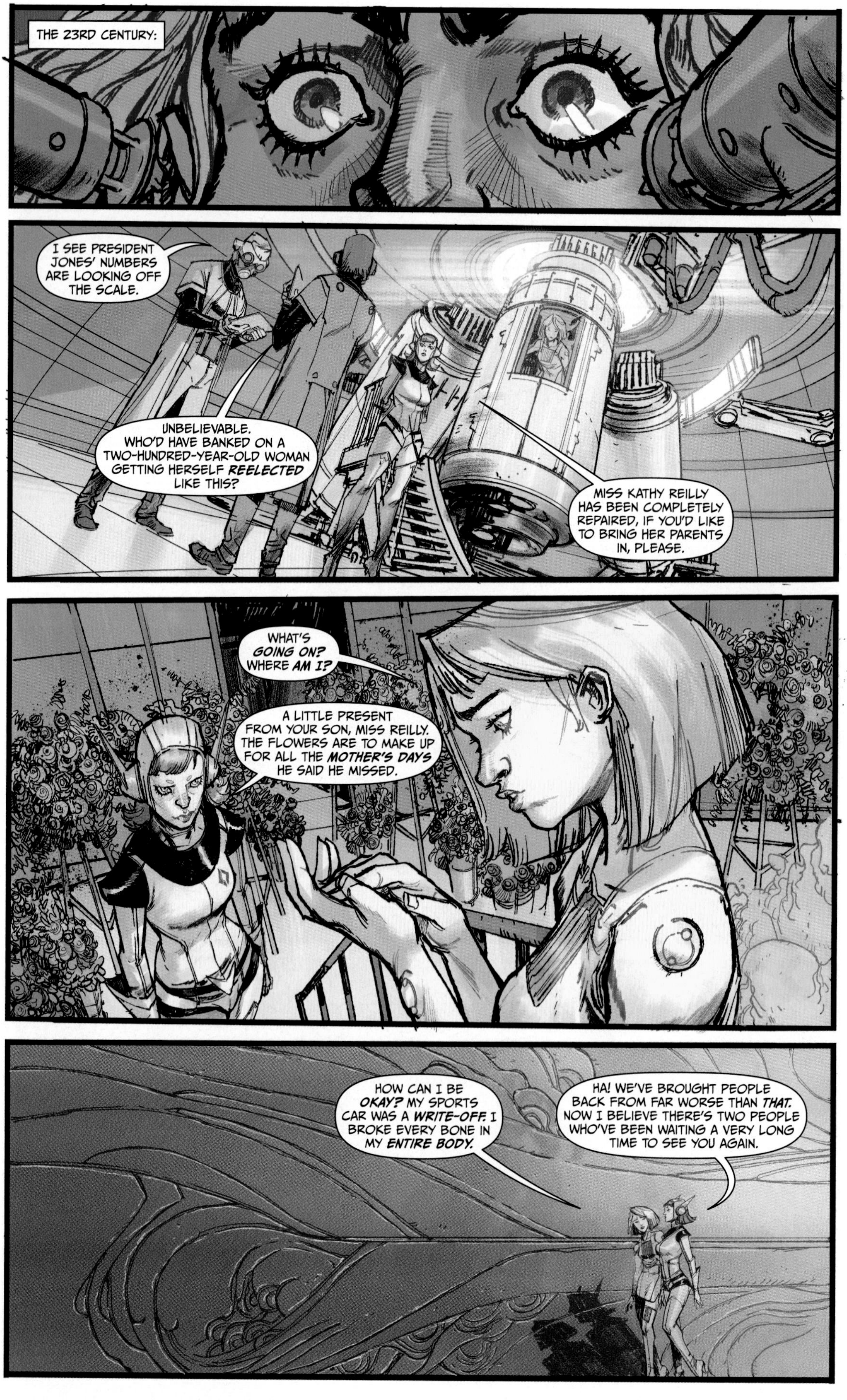
THE 23RD CENTURY:
I SEE PRESIDENT JONES' NUMBERS ARE LOOKING OFF THE SCALE.
UNBELIEVABLE. WHO'D HAVE BANKED ON A TWO-HUNDRED-YEAR-OLD WOMAN GETTING HERSELF REELECTED LIKE THIS?
MISS KATHY REILLY HAS BEEN COMPLETELY REPAIRED, IF YOU'D LIKE TO BRING HER PARENTS IN, PLEASE.
WHAT'S GOING ON? WHERE AM I?
A LITTLE PRESENT FROM YOUR SON, MISS REILLY. THE FLOWERS ARE TO MAKE UP FOR ALL THE MOTHER'S DAYS HE SAID HE MISSED.
HOW CAN I BE OKAY? MY SPORTS CAR WAS A WRITE-OFF. I BROKE EVERY BONE IN MY ENTIRE BODY.
HA! WE'VE BROUGHT PEOPLE BACK FROM FAR WORSE THAN THAT. NOW I BELIEVE THERE'S TWO PEOPLE WHO'VE BEEN WAITING A VERY LONG TIME TO SEE YOU AGAIN.

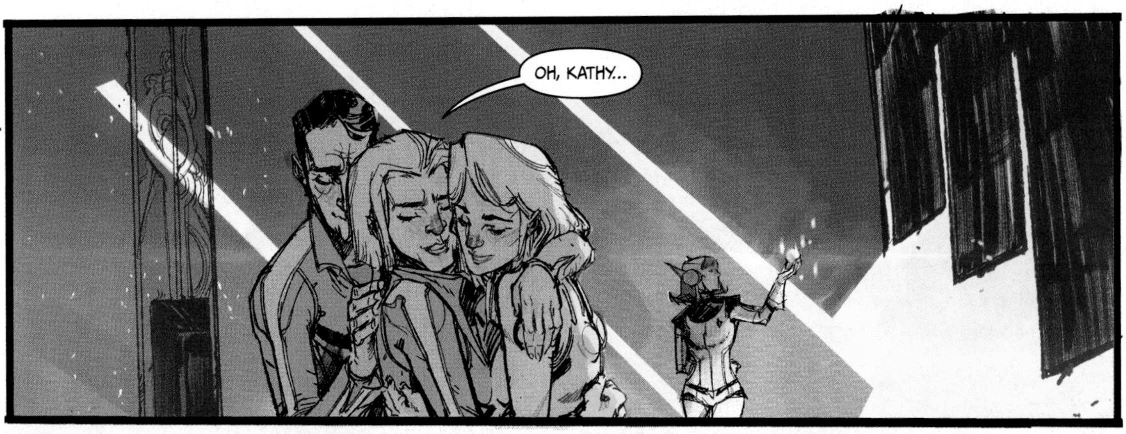
OH, KATHY...

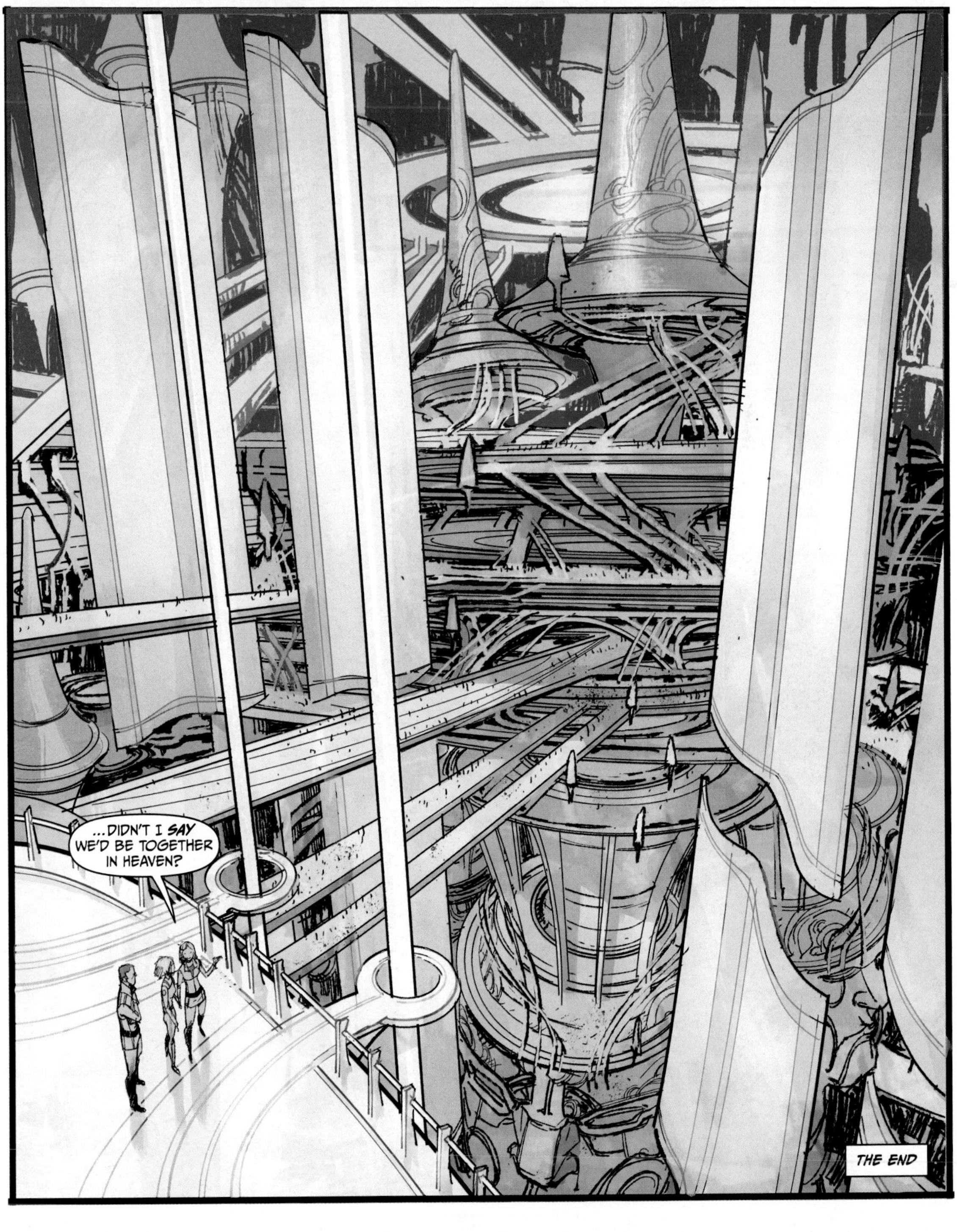
...DIDN'T I SAY WE'D BE TOGETHER IN HEAVEN?
THE END

Mark Millar

is a New York Times bestselling author, Hollywood producer, and now president of his own division at Netflix.

His DC Comics work includes the seminal *Superman: Red Son*. At Marvel Comics, he created *The Ultimates*, which was selected by Time Magazine as the comic book of the decade, and described by screenwriter Zak Penn as his major inspiration for *The Avengers* movie.

Millar also created *Wolverine: Old Man Logan* and *Civil War*. Civil War was the basis of the *Captain America: Civil War* movie, and *Old Man Logan* was the inspiration for Fox's *Logan*. Mark has been an executive producer on all adaptations of his books, and worked as a creative consultant to Fox Studios on their Marvel slate of movies.

Millar's creator-owned books *Kick-Ass*, *Wanted*, and *Kingsman: The Secret Service* have all been adapted into hugely successful Hollywood franchises.

When he sold his publishing company to Netflix in 2017, Millar also signed on to exclusively create comics, TV series, and movies for the streaming service. Adaptations of *Jupiter's Legacy, The Magic Order, Reborn, Sharkey the Bounty Hunter, American Jesus, Empress*, and *Super Crooks* are among those currently being made, and *Jupiter's Legacy* will be the first to be streamed.

His much-anticipated autobiography, *Shut Up And Let's Talk About Me*, will be published next year.

Eric Canete

is an illustrator and concept artist working in the entertainment industry.

He's worked as a cover and interior artist for Marvel and DC Comics, and as co-creator and artist for *Run Love Kill* published by Image Comics.

Some of his past animation projects include *Aeon Flux* for MTV, *The Batman* and *All-Star Superman* for Warner Bros, and *TRON Uprising* for Disney.

He currently serves as a concept artist for video games and film.

Giovanna Niro

has been a comic book colorist since 2006. Over the years, she has worked for Italian, American, and French publishing companies: Panini Comics, IDW Publishing, Image and Futuropolis.

In 2013 she started a collaboration with Sergio Bonelli Editore on the series: *Orphans, Mister No, Dampyr* and *Dylan Dog*. One of her most recent works is the limited series *The Crow*, for IDW Publishing and BD Publishing (2018).

Peter Doherty

began working in comics in 1990, providing painted artwork for the John Wagner-written *Young Death: Boyhood of a Super-Fiend*, published in the first year of the *Judge Dredd Megazine*. For the next few years he painted art for a number of Judge Dredd stories. Over the intervening years he's worked for most of the major comics publishers, and has also branched out into illustration, TV, and movie work.

Over the last decade he's worked on projects both as the sole artist, and as a coloring/lettering/design collaborator with other artists, including Geof Darrow on his *Shaolin Cowboy* project, and most recently Frank Quitely and Duncan Fegredo, on the Mark Millar projects *Jupiter's Legacy* and *MPH*, respectively.

Peter has worked on *Sharkey The Bounty Hunter*, *The Magic Order* and *Chrononauts* for Netflix's Mark Millar division.

Officine Bolzoni

has always read and collected comics. Then he discovered graphic design, lettering, and typography, and he understood how he could make these passions live together.

He has dressed and lettered several hundred comic books, but has not yet grown tired. He lives and works in Milan and his real name is *Lorenzo*.

@officine.lettering

Rachael Fulton

is a writer, journalist, and comic book editor from Scotland. She worked for four years as editor for Mark Millar at Millarworld, and later at Netflix's Mark Millar division.

Within that time, she was series editor on *Empress*, *Jupiter's Legacy*, *Reborn*, *Kick-Ass: The New Girl*, *Hit-Girl*, *Kingsman: The Red Diamond*, *The Magic Order*, *Prodigy*, *Sharkey The Bounty Hunter*, *Space Bandits*, *Chrononauts 2*, *American Jesus 2*, as well as other reprints.

She lives in rural Scotland with her family and cats. She tweets from @Rachael_Fulton

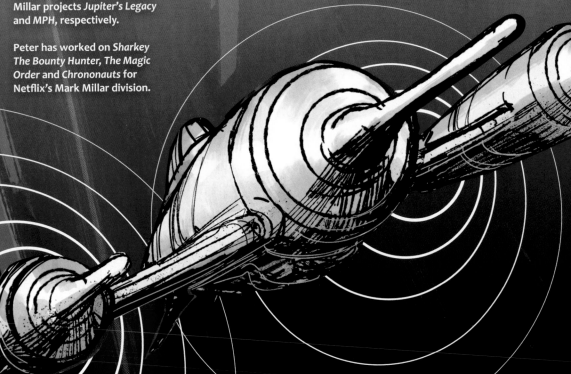

VARIANT COVER GALLERY

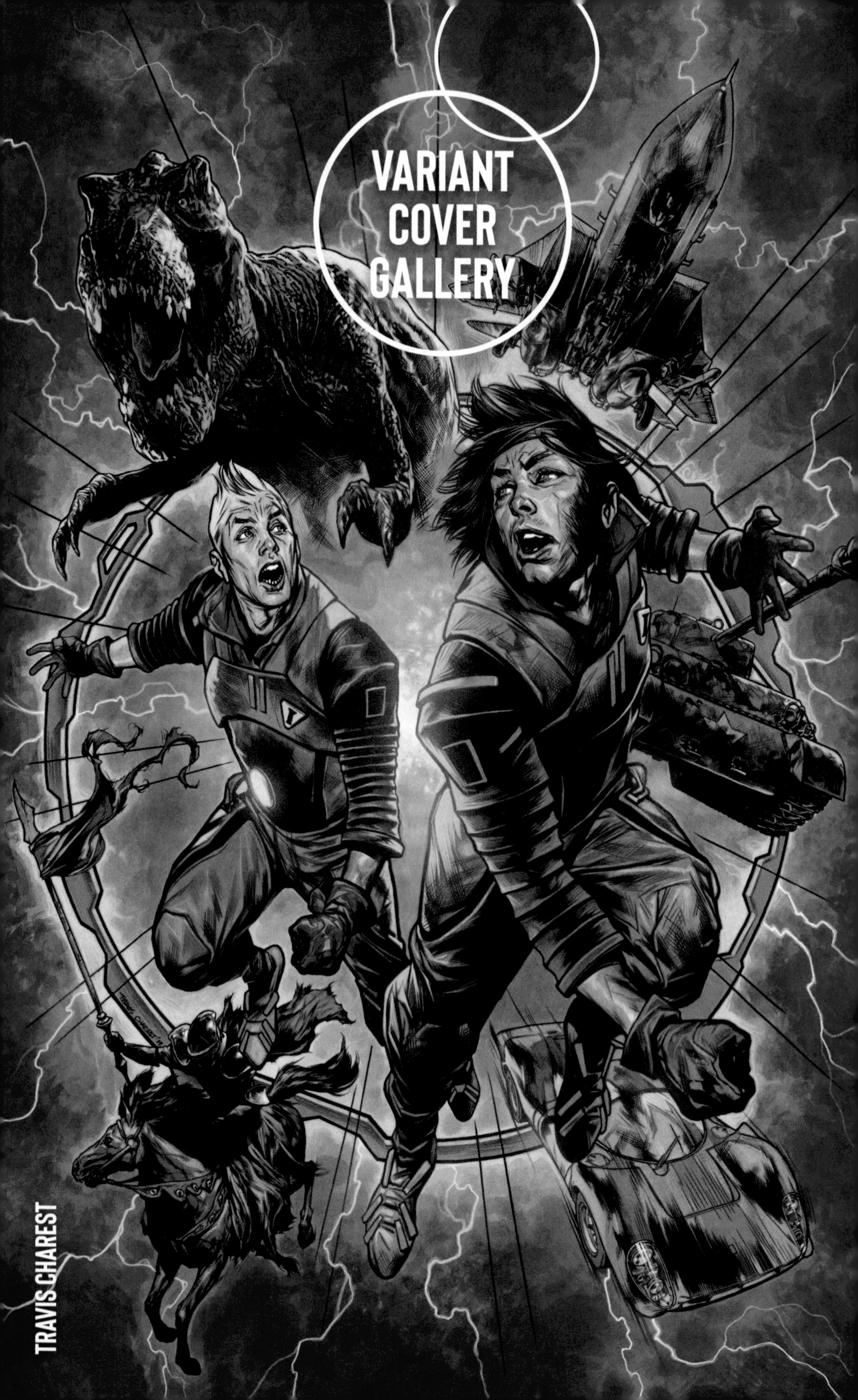

TRAVIS CHAREST

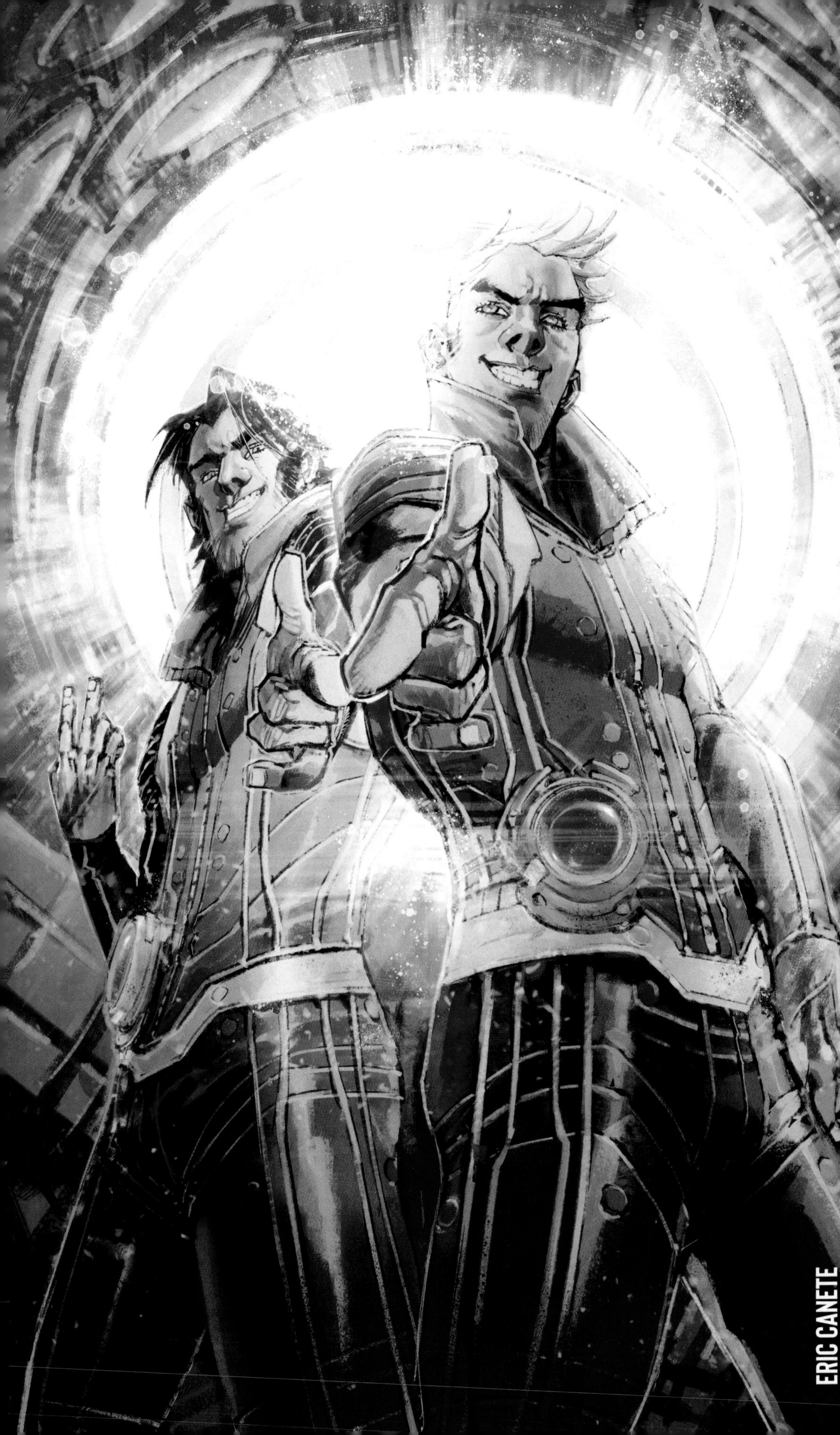
ERIC CANETE

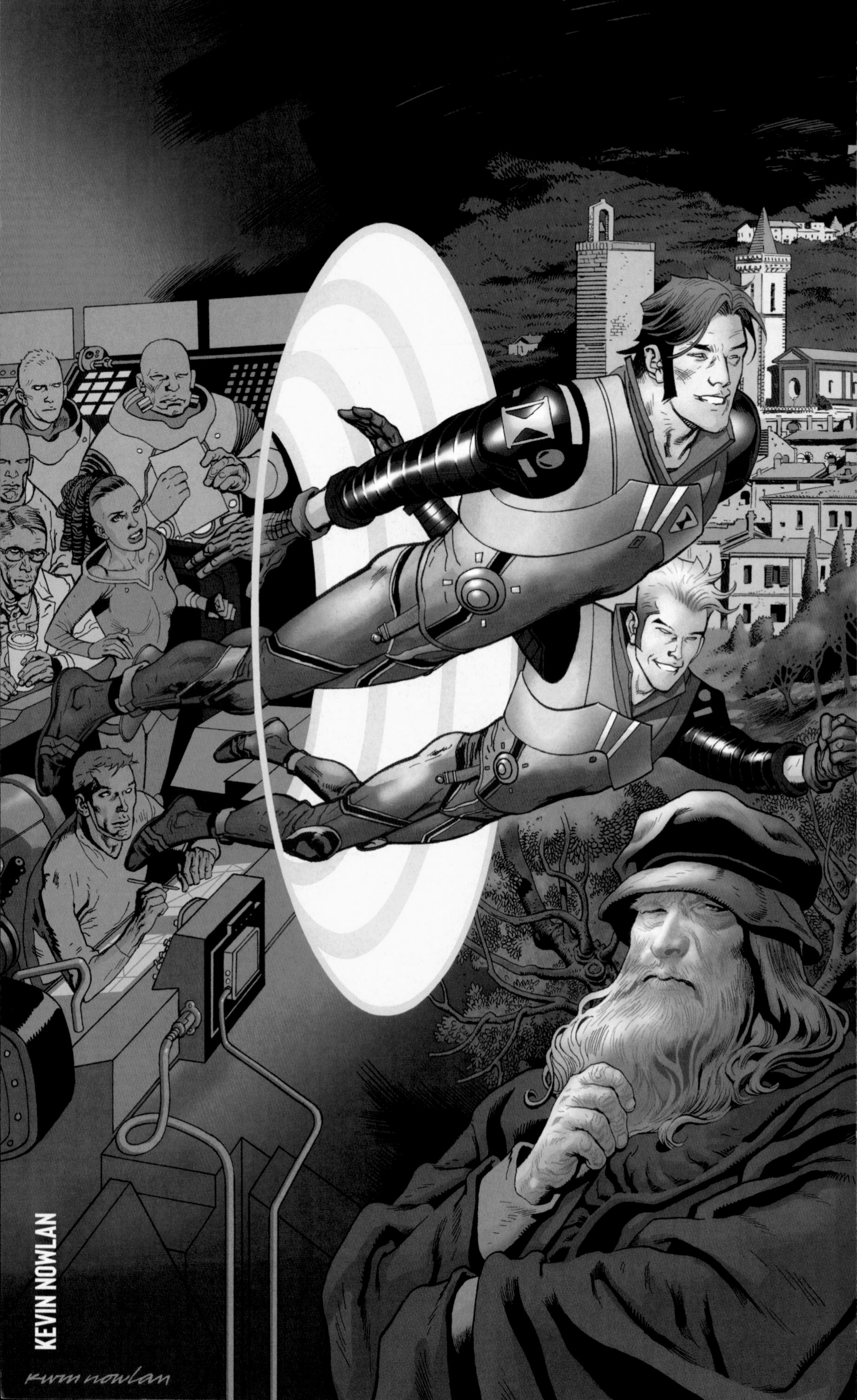
KEVIN NOWLAN
kevin nowlan

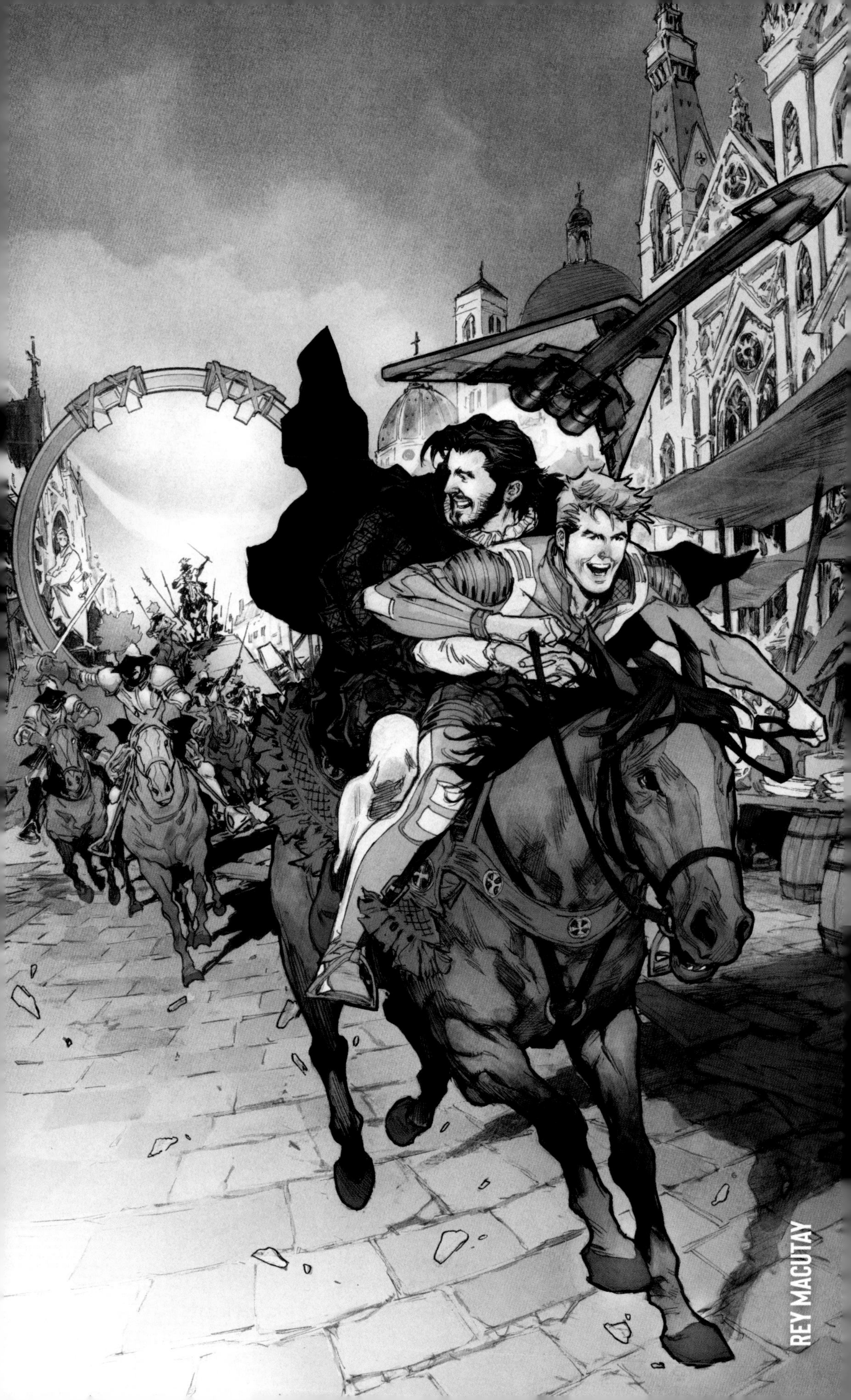
REY MACUTAY

NET

FROM THE MIND OF

Huck
MARK MILLAR
RAFAEL ALBUQUERQUE
DAVE McCAIG

ART BY RAFAEL ALBUQUERQUE

THE MAGIC ORDER
MARK MILLAR
OLIVIER COIPEL
BOOK ONE

ART BY OLIVIER COIPEL

MARK MILLAR · GORAN PARLOV
STARLIGHT
THE RETURN OF DUKE McQUEEN

ART BY GORAN PARLOV

MARK MILLAR
WILFREDO TORRES · DAVIDE GIANFELICE
JUPITER'S CIRCLE
BOOK ONE

ART BY WILFREDO TORRES

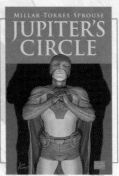

MILLAR · TORRES · SPROUSE
JUPITER'S CIRCLE

ART BY WILFREDO TORRES & CHRIS SPROUSE

MARK MILLAR · FRANK QUITELY
JUPITER'S LEGACY
BOOK ONE

ART BY FRANK QUITELY

MARK MILLAR · FRANK QUITELY
JUPITER'S LEGACY
BOOK TWO

ART BY FRANK QUITELY

REBORN
BOOK ONE
MARK MILLAR GREG CAPULLO

ART BY GREG CAPULLO

Prodigy.
Mark Millar
Rafael Albuquerque
THE EVIL EARTH

ART BY RAFAEL ALBUQUERQUE

MARK MILLAR & LEINIL YU
SUPERIOR
FROM THE WRITER OF KICK-ASS

ART BY LEINIL YU

MARK MILLAR

AMERICAN JESUS
BOOK ONE : CHOSEN
MARK MILLAR ✦ PETER GROSS
FOREWORD BY SIMON PEGG

ART BY PETER GROSS

MARK MILLAR • MATTEO SCALERA
SPACE BANDITS

ART BY MATTEO SCALERA

MARK MILLAR • SIMONE BIANCHI
SHARKEY
THE BOUNTY HUNTER

ART BY SIMONE BIANCHI

EMPRESS
BOOK ONE
MARK MILLAR STUART IMMONEN
with WADE VON GRAWBADGER & IVE SVORCINA

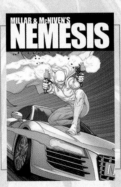

ART BY STUART IMMONEN

MARK MILLAR LEINIL YU
SUPER CROOKS
THE HEIST

ART BY LEINIL YU

MILLAR & McNIVEN'S
NEMESIS

ART BY STEVE MCNIVEN

WANTED
MARK MILLAR • JG JONES • PAUL MOUNTS

ART BY JG JONES & PAUL MOUNTS

MILLAR MURPHY
CHRONONAUTS

ART BY SEAN MURPHY

MILLAR • CANETE
CHRONONAUTS
FUTURESHOCK

ART BY ERIC CANETE

MARK MILLAR DUNCAN FEGREDO
MPH

ART BY DUNCAN FEGREDO

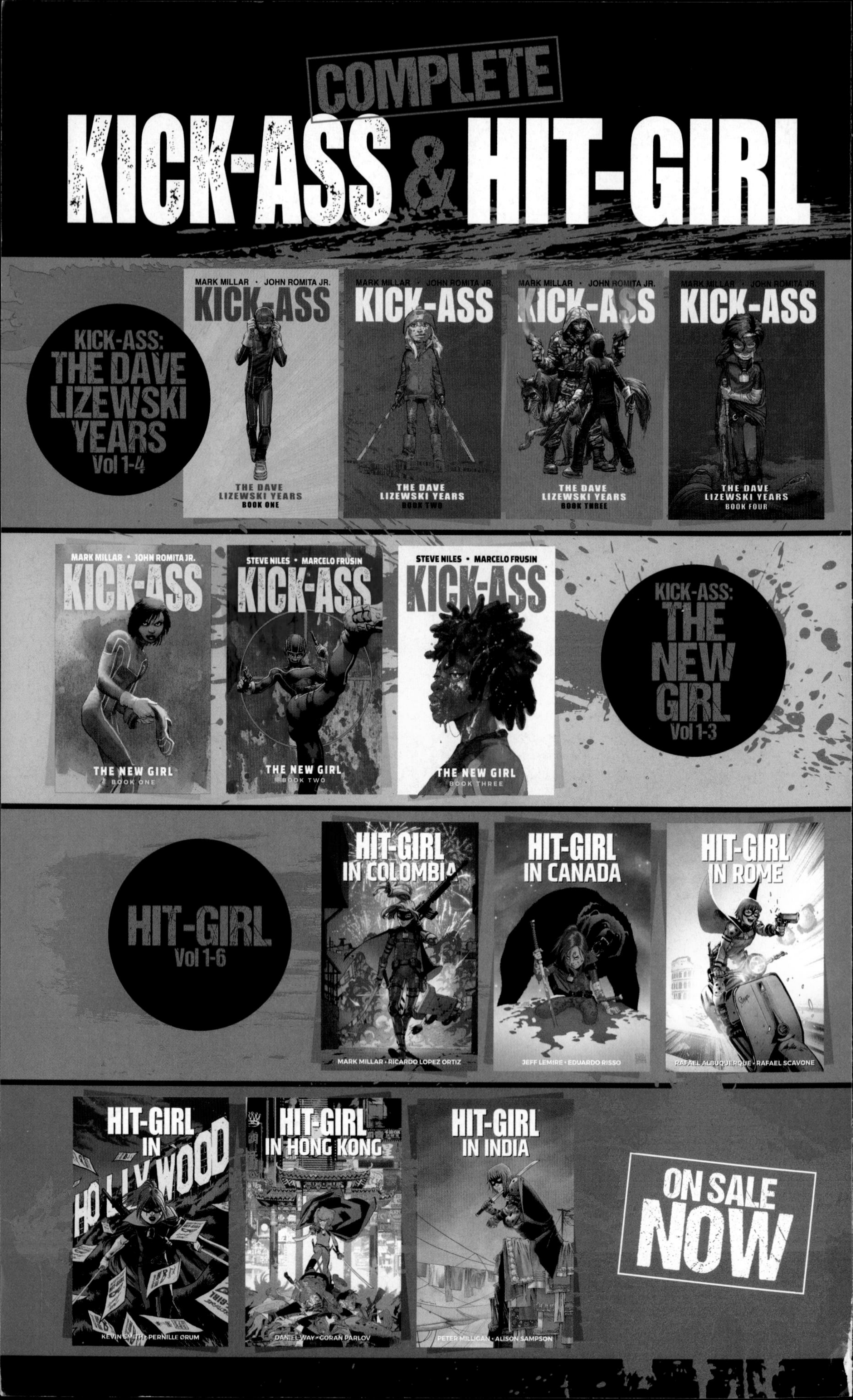
COMPLETE
KICK-ASS & HIT-GIRL
KICK-ASS: THE DAVE LIZEWSKI YEARS Vol 1-4
MARK MILLAR • JOHN ROMITA JR.
KICK-ASS
THE DAVE LIZEWSKI YEARS BOOK ONE
MARK MILLAR • JOHN ROMITA JR.
KICK-ASS
THE DAVE LIZEWSKI YEARS BOOK TWO
MARK MILLAR • JOHN ROMITA JR.
KICK-ASS
THE DAVE LIZEWSKI YEARS BOOK THREE
MARK MILLAR • JOHN ROMITA JR.
KICK-ASS
THE DAVE LIZEWSKI YEARS BOOK FOUR
MARK MILLAR • JOHN ROMITA JR.
KICK-ASS
THE NEW GIRL BOOK ONE
STEVE NILES • MARCELO FRUSIN
KICK-ASS
THE NEW GIRL BOOK TWO
STEVE NILES • MARCELO FRUSIN
KICK-ASS
THE NEW GIRL BOOK THREE
KICK-ASS: THE NEW GIRL Vol 1-3
HIT-GIRL Vol 1-6
HIT-GIRL IN COLOMBIA
MARK MILLAR • RICARDO LOPEZ ORTIZ
HIT-GIRL IN CANADA
JEFF LEMIRE • EDUARDO RISSO
HIT-GIRL IN ROME
RAFAEL ALBUQUERQUE • RAFAEL SCAVONE
HIT-GIRL IN HOLLYWOOD
KEVIN SMITH • PERNILLE ØRUM
HIT-GIRL IN HONG KONG
DANIEL WAY • GORAN PARLOV
HIT-GIRL IN INDIA
PETER MILLIGAN • ALISON SAMPSON
ON SALE NOW